THE
WARRIOR QUEEN

ALSO BY EMILY R. KING

Nhi—

THE
WARRIOR
QUEEN

The Hundredth Queen Series
Book Four

EMILY R. KING

SKYSCAPE

SKYSCAPE

Text copyright © by 2018 Emily R. King

Published by Skyscape, New York

www.apub.com

Amazon, the Amazon logo, and Skyscape are trademarks of Amazon.com, Inc., or its affiliates.

ISBN-13: 9781503903371
ISBN-10: 1503903370

Cover design by Zlatina Zareva

Printed in the United States of America

For Mom and Dad.
Your faith and obedience inspire my own.

AUTHOR'S NOTE

The religion of the Tarachand Empire, the Parijana faith, is a fictional variation derived from Sumerian deities. However, the Parijana faith and the Tarachand Empire and other empires do not directly represent any specific historical time period, creed, or union. Any other religious or governmental similarities are coincidental and do not depict actual people or events.

PROLOGUE

Thirteen Years Ago . . .

The rani rushed into the nursery. Dim lamplight revealed baskets of blocks and toys. All the nursemaids had gone to rest, and the single child under their care was put to bed. The rani hurried down a corridor and paused at the ajar door. Inside, the draperies were drawn over towering windows. A single lamp burned low on the bedside table beside the painted portrait of her and her husband. She had looked so happy then.

She pushed inside. Her sari sailed above the floor, the rug muffling her steps. Her son was tucked into bed, blankets up to his tiny chin. His gaze fastened onto hers, and he brightened.

"Mother, you came."

"I'm sorry I wasn't here sooner. I had duties." The rani hid a smudge of blood on her blouse. Her wrists ached from the beating she had delivered minutes ago. She loathed her responsibilities, but the lesser ranked ranis must learn to obey. "Shall I tell you a story?"

"My favorite?"

"Of course." The tale was her favorite as well.

She knelt at her son's bedside and stroked his head. The mural over his headboard depicted a world beneath theirs, a warrior, and a god. The rani began her recitation of the child's tale they knew by heart.

"Inanna was a cherished young woman, beloved by everyone in her village. Some said she had the loyalty of an elephant and the bravery of a tiger. Men tried to woo her, but Inanna ignored them. She was waiting for one man—the same soul she had loved in all of her lifetimes, right from the beginning when Anu plucked the stars from the heavens and named them mortals."

"What was the man's name?" asked the boy.

"We don't know, but it's said that the moment they saw each other, the ground shook and the skies sang. The whole world rejoiced that Inanna and her beloved had reunited."

"Was it the same for you and Father?"

"Just so, dear one."

Had the boy been older, he would have detected sorrow in her whisper. He clutched his covers, anticipating the progression of the tale.

"The night before their wedding, a chameleon demon took the form of Inanna and entered her beloved's bedchamber. The demon's likeness to her tricked the man. Trusting the demon was Inanna, he went off with her into the night." The boy pulled the blanket up to his nose. "The next morning, Inanna donned her wedding robes and set off to marry her love. She waited at the altar all day, but he never came. Jilted, she locked herself away and could not find the strength to change from her bridal attire."

The boy yawned, his eyelids sinking.

"Many nights later, Inanna woke to find her intended at her bedside. He could not step out of the dark, nor could she light a lamp without him fading into nothing. He had traveled by shadow to tell her he was trapped in the Void."

"I wouldn't like it there." The boy stretched out another yawn. "I like it here, with you."

"I like you here with me too," replied his mother.

The boy might have recognized her sadness had he been more awake, but drowsiness weighed him down.

His mother continued in an ever-softening voice. "Inanna spent night after night with her intended. They both tried to be content, but Inanna could not leave him in the under realm for eternity, so she sought a way to descend below to find him . . ."

Exhaustion overcame the boy. His mother watched him doze while he dreamed of slaying demons and rescuing princesses.

Had the boy known this would be the last time his mother would tell him the tale, he would have paid better attention and tried harder to stay awake.

Had he been warned that this would be his last night in the palace, he would have kissed his mother good night.

Had he known his father would prevent his mother from bidding him good-bye the next morning, he would have said he loved her one more time.

But the boy slept, unaware of the pain dawn would bring.

1

KALINDA

Darkness holds secrets few see or seek. But when one spends as much time as I do studying the shadows, they reveal unique textures that brush over the skin. The cozy fleece of the evening hour, the velvet kiss of full midnight, and the chilly silk of early morning. I have found some solace in the patterns of the night. Little else is a comfort.

Sitting at my table before my charcoal and parchment paper, I train my senses to feel and listen. Hushed winds rustle the palm fronds outside the open balcony. Under the eye of the winter moon, shadows eclipse the astral powers. We are long into the evening, so far that morning will soon place a new dawn across the heavens, peeling back the night and revealing the face of day. My tired eyes strain through the layers of shadows for movement.

He will come.

A yawn escapes me. I reach up to rub my eyes, and the blunt end of my right arm stops me. Will I ever remember?

My prosthesis is on the bedside table; I do not wear it when I am alone. Quite often my hand still feels *there*. Its spirit tricks me into thinking I have all ten fingers. The demon Kur's venom that I took into my body to harness as a weapon destroyed my hand. Teaching my left hand to draw as well as my right has taken practice, but increasingly I am satisfied with my sketches.

A smattering of finished drawings litters the table. Using my charcoal stick, I add more shading to my latest subject. The Sisterhood temple, under construction in the city, will soon house the sisters and wards from Samiya. My childhood home is gone, as is my dearest friend. Jaya was murdered by Rajah Tarek in an act of pure malice, and the temple I grew up in was demolished in an accidental fire. Though Jaya's death still haunts me, the rebuilding of the temple gives me hope that all which succumbs to death may be reborn again.

I set aside the charcoal stick and rise, stretching to stay alert. A figure stirs in the darkness near the hearth.

"Kali."

I blow out the lamp and lunge at Deven. I thought I had lost him after Kur dragged him down into the under realm. His revival was a mercy, even if he is confined to the Void during daylight hours. He follows my soul-fire home through the roadways of shadows at night and has done so for three moons.

"You took so long." He has been coming later and later.

"I'm glad I made it." Deven presses his lips to the side of my head. His thick beard sweeps against my hair. "You smell of jasmine at midnight."

He just *smells*. The muskiness of the Void has masked his sandalwood scent.

Deven tilts my chin, and his lips take mine. His touch sparks an instant reaction. My hand rakes through his hair, and his fingers knead my hips. We stand in one place until our kisses seek out more contact.

We walk, our bodies locked together at several pressure points, to my bed. He leans me back onto the covers, his weight sturdy. Small silk pillows crowd around us. Deven lobs them off one by one. Once we have more room, his lips explore. My fingertips trace the curves of his back and clutch him close.

His cheek drops against mine, and he slides his fingers through my hair, the silk sheets wrapping about our legs. His deep, calm voice resonates in my ear. "Someday you need to explain to me why you have so many pillows."

I chuckle more than I normally would. Nights when he has a sense of humor are seldom. These moments have been our temporary haven. I loathe disrupting his rare peace, but dawn looms. I smooth down his beard. "Would you like me to fetch your brother?"

"Not tonight."

He has not asked for his family in many days. I assume he does not want them to see him this way. He is thinner and sallower than even yesterday. "Are you hungry?"

"Yes." He nuzzles the tender spot beneath my chin. I dare not shut my eyes or I will lose my ability to think.

I fetch the tray on the bedside table. He wipes his hands clean on the napery and eats the aromatic rice. He does not have access to food or water in the under realm. I have tried to send rations and a lantern, but they disappear once he leaves. Nor can I enter the labyrinth of shadows with him.

"How are you?" he asks.

Deven does not need to hear about my mundane days. "I'm well. Ashwin and I are still searching every book in the city. We'll find something soon." None of us know whether our research will lead to a solution, yet I have faith. "We'll find a way to release you."

"You cannot be certain." Deven sets the unfinished plate aside. He must fill up, but his appetite has been decreasing. "We have to accept our fate."

At my lowest moments, I have almost succumbed to the same despondency. All day long I pray for the gods to free Deven. His inner light is dimming, like the reflection of the moon compared to the glory of the sun. I sit on his lap and pull his wooden arms around me. "Fate is ours to decide."

"You cannot feel what I feel." His tormented gaze climbs to mine. "My coming here is a risk. Someone has been following me."

"Who?"

"I don't know. I haven't seen anyone, but I've felt them."

I rest my forehead against his. "Ashwin and I are getting closer. We'll get you out of there. Promise me you'll keep coming." I could not bear for him to disappear.

"For you," Deven says, his muscles relaxing around me.

Outside, the heavens have lightened. Sunrise will soon reach the golden domes of the palace and sleepy Vanhi. Deven clings to me, dreading the same burden of time. I tuck into him and shut my eyes so hard they ache.

Please, Anu. Let him stay.

Deven's solid form dissolves around me. I open my eyes, and all that remains is his warmth, fading on the sheets.

⁓◦○◦⁓

Someone touches my shoulder. My face is buried in a pillow, but I sense Brac. A Burner's soul-fire radiates strongest, and only he dares to enter my chamber without knocking.

"Deven's gone." My bleak voice nearly pushes me to tears.

The mattress shifts. I look up at Brac seated beside me. His coppery hair sweeps across brows knit over honey-colored eyes. "We'll find him."

"I should go after him. I should have gone down there moons ago."

"Then you'd also be trapped in the Void, and I'd have to free you both."

He need not clarify why that is a terrible idea. We had this discussion yesterday, and the day before that, and the day before that . . . The issue is not getting into the Void but getting Deven out.

"How is he?" Brac asks.

"Weaker." Few of our friends and family know Deven is alive. We have left his name carved on the door of my mother's tomb for simplicity's sake. Explaining his imprisonment is too complicated. On occasion, he asks to visit with his brother and mother. They dined with him often during the first weeks of his visits, but he has become less sociable. The hour after he leaves is my loneliest. Most mornings I question if he was really here.

Brac hunches over his knees and scrubs at the coppery stubble on his chin. "I've thought about going after him too. Until we work out how without risking ourselves, we must stay here."

Deven learned the complicated route through the roadways of shadow to my chamber after several attempts. Even if he could find me elsewhere, now is not the time to leave. The Tarachand Empire is regaining strength, but we are like an old man overcoming a grave illness. I edge up to Brac and finish the rice left on the food tray.

"Ashwin needs us too," I say.

"He'll be safer once he's rajah."

"That's just a title."

"Titles hold power, *Burner Rani*."

Our citizens have taken to calling me "Burner Rani." It is not intended as a compliment. My tournament championship and short-term marriage to Rajah Tarek as his kindred mean nothing. I am a bhuta, same as the rebels and warlord who occupied the palace to stop the extermination of our kind.

Tarek's legacy of hate runs deep, so when the demon Udug impersonated him, our people were quick to believe the rajah was back from the dead to defeat the rebels. We unmasked Udug as a fraud, but he released the demon Kur from the Void. With the help of our bhuta allies—the Paljorian airship fleet and Lestarian Navy—we vanquished them and stopped the evernight from conquering the mortal realm.

None of our good deeds matter to the people. They care not that Ashwin banished the last of the rebels. They only care that he suspended his father's execution order against bhutas and appointed Brac as his bhuta emissary and selected Virtue Guards, including me. To protest our proximity to the throne, countless soldiers have defected from the imperial army. I knew integrating bhutas into society would take time, but after all we have done to preserve the empire, the citizenry's stubbornness rankles.

Brac claps his knees in preparation to stand. "You're expected at the amphitheater this morning."

"But I was up all night," I groan.

"Those little scamps nearly burned off my eyelashes again." Brac pats my back in a conciliatory manner. "It's your turn."

Natesa knocks and bustles in. "One of you needs to go to the dining hall. Your trainees set fire to the table linens during breakfast!"

"The prince expects me for a meeting." Brac throws me a smirk and strides out.

"I'll go," I say.

"Not looking like that you won't," Natesa counters.

I brush rice crumbs from my lips as she digs through my dressing cabinet. Natesa and I were raised together in Samiya. We became friends after Tarek claimed us, she as a courtesan and me as a rani, and we competed in my rank tournament. Her jade sari and short blouse complement her curves. I have become shapelier since my younger years, when she teased me for my thinness. Our mutual friend and healer, Indah, insisted I eat heartily to keep my soul-fire well stocked, which in turn healed the aftereffects of Kur's fiery venom and increased my weight.

While she is turned around, I put on my prosthesis, winding the leather strap around my shoulder. The wooden fingers have no joints but are the same size and shape as my functioning left hand.

Natesa holds up a black training sari. "This one will show off your full hips." She drapes the sari across my bed. "Get changed before your trainees burn down the palace. Yatin will take one of them over his knee if they don't start behaving."

My trainees are the last two Burner children in the Tarachand Empire. Yatin would never lay a hand on them, let alone any child, but another guard might. "I'll speak with the girls. Any news of your wedding plans?"

"Yatin and I agreed the ceremony can wait until we're less busy." Natesa has been working to open her inn, and Yatin accepted a promotion to captain of the guard. "The inn is ready for me to move in to."

I repress my surprise. "I didn't realize you were leaving the palace so soon."

"I didn't want to . . . ," Natesa leads off, twisting her lotus engagement ring.

Everyone does this now, calculates their speech and anticipates my reaction. They presume I will crumble under a single unplanned word.

"Didn't want to what?" I press.

"I didn't want to boast."

Her careful treatment of me pricks. Still, I keep my tone airy. "Telling your friend good news isn't boasting. When the time comes, you'll be the most beautiful bride in the empire."

Natesa glances in the vanity mirror glass. "You should see Princess Gemi's bridal sari. Asha outdid herself on the bodice. I may ask her to embroider mine."

"Princess Gemi is lovely, but she isn't you." I replay my words and quickly cover my mouth. "Please don't repeat that to the viraji."

The formal term of endearment crowds my throat. I disliked the title when it was mine. It feels odd conferring it upon another.

"Repeat what?" Natesa answers, eyes twinkling. She picks up a comb and brushes my hair. "Don't worry, Kali. Everyone knows you're glad for them."

"I am," I say firmly.

Though Ashwin proposed marriage to me, I care for him as my cousin and friend. I support his decision to take the Southern Isles' princess as his first wife. Gemi has a unique zest for life and a free spirit. The empire is in dire need of a leader with her forward-thinking views.

A crash outside draws Natesa to the balcony. She clucks her tongue and motions me to join her. Servants douse a grass fire in the garden below. A pair of girls flee into the trees.

"You didn't make it to the dining hall in time," says Natesa.

I rub at a mounting headache. "I had no idea two girls could be so much trouble."

Servants extinguish the fire and resume their work. Past the palace wall, Vanhi has woken. Men crowd the roads with their burros and carts, headed to the marketplace that is shaded by a mosaic of lean-tos. Women hang laundry on the lines strung between the huts and milk goats. Children play in the side-winding river while their older siblings collect water in baskets. Life is on the move, ready for a new day. I could fall into bed until noon.

I scoop up my clothes and duck behind the dressing screen. Natesa prepleated the sari, but I fumble with the pins.

"Kalinda?" Her voice comes at me tentatively. "Would you like help?"

"No."

A former rani who lost two fingers during her rank tournament taught me how to carry out everyday activities such as dressing and dining. By necessity, my left hand has become dominant and does well with the assistance of my prosthesis.

While pulling my sari over my shoulder, I drop a pin. *Gods almighty.* Natesa hovers nearby, waiting for me to give in.

I select another pin and try again.

2

KALINDA

My trainees—Basma, age nine, and her seven-year-old sister, Giza—gaze up at me with their hands clasped in front of their bellies. Dirt dusts their sandaled feet and legs. Historically, the Vanhi amphitheater housed rank duels between sister warriors. Basma and Giza are sisters but are far from skilled fighters.

"Who threw the heatwave at Master Tinley?" I ask.

Basma's stare does not waver from mine. "It was me."

Giza lowers her chin. A sign of agreement? Or is she letting her older sister take the blame for her mistake?

Except for the finger length of height Basma has on Giza, the sisters are identical, with rounded faces and tiny underbites that become more pronounced when they hold back tears.

Tinley grumbles from across the arena, the tail end of her long silver braid singed. Indah, acting Aquifier instructor, soaked her down with water from the practice barrels. Neither woman needed much persuasion to stay in Vanhi and train our bhuta children, though right about now Tinley must be rethinking her decision. Indah and Pons, her partner, are content raising their baby girl here, and Tinley will seize any excuse not to go home to her parents and four younger sisters in Paljor.

Though I have tried to figure out why, she has not provided any hints to her self-banishment.

Across the arena, Tinley returns to instructing the five Galer trainees, teaching them how to manipulate the sky and wind to their advantage. The archery target Basma missed remains untouched and will remain so for now.

"Practice looking for your inner star," I tell my students. "Don't open your eyes until you find the brightest one."

While the girls look inward for the manifestation of the fire powers, I stride to Tinley's section. Her apprentices push a massive granite block across the arena with their winds.

"I smell like charred yak meat," she grumbles.

"More like roasted lamb," Indah says.

Her five Aquifiers rest in the shade for a break. High above us, the benches that encircle the roofless amphitheater are empty. Even higher, on the rafters, the gongs glint in the late-morning sunshine and the Tarachandian red-and-black pennants lie slack without a breeze. We divided the oval arena into four equal parts. The bhuta children ages five to sixteen train in their respective sector.

A little over a moon ago, Brac petitioned Prince Ashwin on behalf of our bhuta youth. Accidents with their powers were occurring all over the empire. The half-god children with elemental abilities passed down through their parents' bloodlines no longer lived in fear of execution but had no masters to train them. After one mishap led to a six-year-old Aquifier drowning in her village bathhouse, Brac gathered the bhuta children, mostly orphans, and converted the arena into a training ground. Princess Gemi, a Trembler, has agreed to instruct our four Tremblers once she arrives. In the meantime, Indah oversees them.

The Aquifier lifts her wavy hair and fans the back of her neck. She has slimmed down since birthing her baby, while her proportions have fluctuated. What stayed of her pregnancy weight redistributed to her curves.

"I thought winters in the desert were cooler," she says. Perspiration shimmers across her golden-brown skin.

"This *is* cooler," I reply. I watch my apprentices search inside themselves for their soul-fire. Neither seems able to find it.

"Are you going to leave them like that all day?" Indah asks.

"I would," replies Tinley. She twirls a gust at a Galer boy who quit pushing the granite block. He scrambles to rejoin the others. Their massive rock reaches the arena wall, and she yells, "Next time finish faster!"

The children slump against the ground, panting.

"You should reward their progress," Indah says.

Tinley examines her talonlike nails. "Compliments breed laziness. They must always be on guard."

"Always be ready" is our training motto. My teaching style is less aggressive than Tinley's. Brac taught me about my Burner abilities, and I had formal weapons training at the Sisterhood temple—all wards do. Jaya put in the longest hours with me. She was firm yet heartening during our sparring sessions.

I return to my students.

"Giza, stand against the wall. Basma, face me." They both scurry to follow my orders. I set the archery target before Basma. "How many stars can you find?" She shuts her eyes again and counts. When she reaches twenty-two, I cut her off. "Let's say thirty. When you come fully into your powers, you'll raze and consolidate them into one inner star. Until then, you mustn't let them overpower you. Without looking, hold out your hands."

As my student obeys, Ashwin and Brac appear in the imperial box at the north end of the arena. My pulse trips into a sprint.

The prince looks just like his father.

That box is where Tarek supervised my rank tournament. I am still too susceptible to the memory that engulfs me.

Gooseflesh raises up and down my body. The Claiming chamber is cold. A blindfold conceals my sight from the benefactor looming behind the thin veil. I hear him step out and feel the heaviness of his gaze exploring my nakedness.

Patient, plodding footfalls come closer. I want to run, scream, cry. My chin stays high, my fingers curled. Hot, sour breaths drift across my cheek . . . neck . . . chest.

Fingers thread through my hair. The water-goddess's symbol of obedience, a wave stained in henna down my spine, burns like blasphemy.

"This one."

The echo of Tarek's voice shatters my memory. I press my prosthesis over my charging heart. Ashwin abolished the Claiming, the rite that gave benefactors the power to take orphaned temple wards as servants, courtesans, or wives. We are in the early stages of establishing alternative futures for those girls, and ourselves, but the past is hard to release.

Ashwin's arrival—not Tarek, Tarek is *dead*—stirs whispers from the trainees. The prince mentioned he might stop by to observe their improvement.

Maybe he discovered how to free Deven.

I know better than to let my hopes climb too high. Still, my breath is bated. I try to catch Ashwin's attention. He watches the trainees. The Aquifiers shoot water from barrels like jumping minnows, and the Galers take turns suspending a rectangular carpet in midair. All of this is possible due to Brac, yes, but also Ashwin. He took in the bhutas and housed them at the palace. With the sisters and temple wards also lodging there until their new temple is habitable, his home is a constant mess of people.

Basma leaves her eyes closed. I talk loudly so she is not distracted by the others training. "When I say so, release the lights."

"All of them . . . ?"

"Don't be afraid. They're born of your soul-fire."

Basma fiddles her fingers. These girls must stop cowering to their own abilities.

"Grab those stars and push out their heat," I say. "Like this."

I throw a heatwave, and Basma's eyes pop open. My shoulder recoils from the blast. I lock my elbow and regain control. My powers are half as strong as they were. Funneling them into one hand is a skill I have yet to master, if it is even possible.

Basma tries for herself. Streams of mandarin flames jet from her palms and scorch the target. Frightened, she swings upward. Her heatwave arcs high across the amphitheater and strikes a pennant. The red cloth dyed with the empire's black scorpion symbol catches fire.

Basma covers her mouth in shock. Giza hurries over and hugs her sister. My annoyance at the girl's carelessness dwindles and longing fills me. Will I ever stop missing Jaya?

"I'm sorry, Master Kalinda," Basma says.

I grab both girls and hunch down to their level. "Don't be afraid of who you are. You'll learn to control your powers eventually. The gods gave you these abilities. They believe in you. Trust that."

The center doors to the arena clang open, and a large group of men prowl in. The men, wearing all black and headscarves across the lower half of their faces, disperse around us. Their swords are sheathed. Tinley and Indah guard their students, and I reach for one of my twin daggers. My mother's blades are like a guardian spirit I carry with me always.

An intruder steps forward, presenting himself. His headscarf covers all but his gaze. Though he no longer wears a uniform or carries the military-issued khanda sword, I recognize him as the first officer to defect from the army. The former commander has not been silent in his desertion. He has been speaking out all across the city against the prince's acceptance of bhutas.

"Go over there," I say to my trainees. The girls dash to the children gathered behind Tinley and Indah.

"Commander Lokesh," Ashwin calls from the imperial box. "You weren't invited."

The commander grips the gauntlets of his sheathed twin pata swords. The handguards cover his fists. "We saw the fire and came to see that everything was under control."

"As you can see, all is well," Ashwin calls from on high.

"I think not," Commander Lokesh replies. His men still spread out, lurking closer. "Who will protect the people from these children? Your Majesty's guards are becoming scarce." He declares this with smug gratification. "My men and I are offering our services to those in need of more security in these uncertain times."

Captain Yatin and more guards march into the arena, near the imperial box. Ashwin is safe with Brac, but the mercenaries' proximity to the children sets me on edge. I sheathe my dagger and push soul-fire into my fingers.

"You need to leave," I say. Tinley summons a wind to further coerce them. While her breeze tugs at the commander's scarf, his cool gaze remains on Ashwin. I send off sparks, and Lokesh passes his attention to me.

"Burner Rani," he says in farewell.

He signals to his men and they file out. After the last goes, Tinley reels a gust and slams the door shut. Yatin and his men exit to track their departure. Indah and a student sends geysers at the burning pennant and put out the fire. I let my powers ebb.

"Something isn't right about the commander," Tinley says, reining in her winds. She drifts into herself, lost in thought. "His voice sounded . . . odd."

"I didn't pay attention," I say. "I was too busy watching his gauntlet swords."

Tinley harrumphs, unimpressed by his blades, and stalks to her trainees. The far doors swing open, and the prince enters the arena, his ambassador close behind him.

"That was a warning," Brac says. "Every day Lokesh takes in more soldiers. His mercenaries may soon outnumber the palace guards. You must divide them, Your Majesty."

"On what grounds?" Ashwin inquires. "The commander has done nothing unlawful. Lokesh has the right to vocalize his views. I cannot silence everyone who disagrees with me."

"Lokesh wants us to fear him," I say, gesturing at the huddled children.

Ashwin lowers his head. "Welcoming bhutas into the empire is a substantial change. The people will learn to trust each other. The more they interact, the less they will fear. For the time being, we'll suspend training."

"Canceling training is what he wants," argues Brac.

"Would you have the children continue as though Lokesh hadn't come here?" Ashwin challenges. He knows we would not. "We'll assess the matter day by day."

Basma and Giza sprint to Brac and leap. He catches them and swings them around. "Come play with us!" they plead.

Brac carts them off to join a game that Indah started. Ashwin's gaze lingers after them, dark circles under his eyes. He was up late reading again.

"Find anything new in your library?" I ask.

He shakes his head, and I deflate. The only record we have of a mortal traveling into and out of the Void is the tale of *Inanna's Descent*. Ashwin recalls some but not all of the story. We have been searching the library for the written version with no luck. Even if we find the text, the gate to the under realm lies at the bottom of a frozen alpine lake. Deven's mother, Mathura, has traveled to the Southern Isles with Brac's father, Chitt, to question the Lestarian elders about the existence of another gate. We have yet to receive word from them.

"Would you like to ride back to the palace with me?" Ashwin asks. "I'm stopping by the temple building site."

Out of respect for his viraji, I have avoided spending time alone with him. Nonetheless, he is still my cousin. "I'd like that. Brac can stay with the girls."

The trio are far into the game. The trainees take turns blasting their powers at a coin on the ground. Whoever makes it jump the highest wins.

Captain Yatin waits atop his horse outside the main door. His snug uniform shows off his bulky arms and barrel chest. He shaved his long beard, a mandate for officers. Natesa often complains about missing his hairy chin. I think his boyish face softens his daunting build.

"Lokesh is gone," Yatin reports. "I lost him in the market."

Ashwin assists me onto his horse and climbs on behind me. Our bodies are snug, nothing more. The attraction that was once between us has been dispelled.

We set off uphill through the flow of people. Yatin and the other guards ride close to dissuade anyone from approaching. Most hurry in the other direction when they see me. Two wash girls do not recognize me until they are in front of us. They both utter "Burner Rani" in dismay and run off.

I pretend their abhorrence does not bother me so Ashwin will not get upset. Truthfully, a piece of me misses my imperial title. Relinquishing the esteemed rank of kindred has left me off-centered. I have sought stability by serving my trainees and teaching the temple wards, but I am like a sunbird without a perch.

We ride into the temple courtyard. Celestial glories are etched into the stone exterior, patterns of the sun and phases of the moon. In the short period since we broke ground, the artistry has been remarkable. After much convincing, Priestess Mita commissioned Tremblers to perform the carpentry, shortening overall construction by half the time.

The floor plan is patterned after Samiya, except for the added windows and classroom where the Claiming chamber would have been. No more does the Sisterhood rely upon the generosity of benefactors.

As fate would have it, the brethren of the Parijana faith are very frugal. They have enough in their coffers to support every division of the Brotherhood and Sisterhood for decades to come.

Ashwin enters the archway and admires the multicolored walls. At our behest, the master architect sought inspiration from our diverse empire. Every landscape is portrayed, from the desert to the mountains to the southern seashore. Ashwin buffs a dusty tile with his sleeve and peers up at a shell chandelier, a replicated design from the Southern Isles.

"The builders should conclude their work in a few weeks," he remarks.

Priestess Mita will oversee the dedication, then the sisters and wards will move from the palace and live here. I continue onward, leaving that lonely thought behind.

Inside the chapel, painters toil on the murals. Their rendition of Ekur, the gods' mountain temple, is otherworldly. Lush flowering gardens, pillars that hold up the sky, crystal waters bursting with rainbow fish, pristine walkways . . .

"I've wished to speak to you alone for a while," Ashwin says from my side.

"We've been preoccupied."

"We both know it's more than that." He tugs nervously at his jacket sleeves. "You've been distant."

"Any closer and your viraji will be displeased." I nudge him in jest. His solemnity is immovable.

"I worry about you, Kalinda."

"You needn't." I ponder the mural of the land-goddess Ki flanked by sister warriors. Women of all ages carry blades engraved with the five godly virtues. My attention drifts to the shadowed corner of the room. I once thought I belonged with the daughters of Ki. Now I am not so certain.

"Where do you go?" Ashwin asks.

"Hmm?" I say, refocusing on him.

"You haven't been the same since the evernight came, and I'm not referring to your hand. You're hardly here. I want to find Deven as much as you do—"

"You couldn't possibly." A weight strains against my rib cage. Ashwin is not driven by this urgent throbbing. "I'm glad we had this time together, Ashwin. I need to return to the palace. My art course starts soon."

"I'll stay awhile longer," he says. Our gazes travel across the chapel and reconnect. "Will you move here when it's finished?"

"The temple is no longer my home."

"You will always have a home at the palace." Ashwin holds still in expectation, waiting for me to agree.

I cannot. The Turquoise Palace is home to my worst and best memories. Jaya died and I wed Tarek there. It is also where I witnessed the revival of the sister warriors and Deven and I fell in love. Under Ashwin's reign, Vanhi will become a home for bhutas and non-bhutas alike. This is the future I envisioned for him, but is it mine? Is happiness tied to a place or person, or can it thrive anywhere?

"Thank you," I say with a note of finality. "We'll speak soon."

I leave Ashwin and go outside.

"I'll ride back to the palace now," I tell Yatin. My conversation with Natesa from this morning resurfaces in my mind. "Yatin, if I may, why have you and Natesa postponed your wedding?"

He fiddles with a button on his jacket. "We want all our friends to be in attendance."

He means Deven. Yatin and Natesa are waiting for something that may never come. Gods, it hurts to admit that. I muster cheerfulness in my reply. "Tell the prince not to work you so hard."

"I'll think on it," Yatin answers.

He would never gripe to the prince. Natesa, on the other hand . . .

22

I mount a guard's horse and amble uphill toward the palace. Its immaculate ivory exterior reflects the midday sun, and its golden domes burnish a glorious gleam. No doubt it is spectacular, but my heart's wish is for rolling pastures and grazing sheep. A humble hut filled with books. The Alpana Mountains outside our door while I sketch in the den and Deven mills about the kitchen.

The hot desert wind pulls my attention back to the city. As I cross a road, I pass by a mother and her children. She tugs them away and flees in a rush. A painful tightness grabs at my throat. I remember a time when these roads were lined with people waving and cheering my name. They may not have adored me, but they adored the throne I represented. I gave much of myself to prove I was worthy of that throne. Some days I think I gave too much. The demands of the empire are bottomless. I had to step down, or the burdens would have consumed me.

I never thought I would miss it this much.

3

Ashwin

My return to the palace inspires no fanfare. I pass the reins of the horse to a guard and stride up the entry steps. Repairs from the battle against the Voider are finished. Although I oversaw the restoration of the damages, the palace's expansive floors still feel foreign. "Home" is too valued a term to bestow upon a residence absent of memories.

I pause at the top of the double curved staircase. Which way is my meeting?

Two ranis see me and hasten over.

"Prince Ashwin," says Parisa. Or is she Eshana? I cannot recall. They are both stunning ranis. Lords, a man could forget his own name. "Eshana and I were discussing how generous you are to house all the sisters, wards, and trainees."

"You're too kind," purrs Eshana.

My neck grows hot. "I see no need for them to stay elsewhere."

"How magnanimous of you." Parisa dips her chin as if we are coconspirators and grips my bicep. "Eshana and I were wondering if you've decided whether you will retain your father's former ranis in your court?"

I flex my arm muscles. "I'm still thinking on it."

"We can help you decide," Parisa says, her lips stretching. "You should visit us at the Tigress Pavilion soon."

"Your father loved my foot rubs," adds Eshana.

Disgust worms into my belly. I try to forget they were Tarek's wives; it helps me to think of them as more than ranis. "I'll take your offer under consideration."

They each kiss me on a cheek and sashay off. As the wetness evaporates off my skin, my guilt sets in. They have been through many trials: their Claiming, rank tournaments, marriage to Tarek, imprisonment by the warlord, and full-on war. They deserve every happiness for their loyalty to the empire, but they need not know I am betrothed to Princess Gemi.

During this tenuous transition of bhutas into society, I feel better announcing my selection for kindred right before the wedding. Once we wed, custom will constrain me from marrying another rani for two years or until we produce an heir. Tarek ignored this practice by wedding my mother and then Kalinda's mother one after the other. I will honor the waiting period to establish that I have no aspirations for a hundred wives like my father. Then I will be expected to marry the former ranis or release them from their rank and dismiss them from the palace.

I do not wish to do either.

"Your Majesty?" Pons asks.

I revolve toward the Galer. Soft-spoken and quiet in his approach, Pons serves as my steward when needed. A familiar, welcome sight. His hair is long at the back and shaved on the top of his head. He wears a sleeveless tunic and short, baggy pants. A blowgun hangs at his waist, the short bamboo pole sticking out of his leather belt.

"Ah, I was just . . . Where's my next meeting?"

"It will be at the third terrace on the fourth floor in an hour."

"Which is . . . ?" I ponder the corridors. Pons has been here as long as I have, yet he has memorized the layout. I am . . . progressing.

"Would you like me to escort you?" he asks.

"I'll find it on my own."

Pons does not follow me. He does not need to. The large-statured warrior can track my movements with his Galer hearing.

I climb several stairways to the rooftop. Upon my entrance to the aviary, doves ruffle their wings. I slip inside and maneuver through the nesting birds to the window. From the floor, I take up a small box and pull out parchment paper, a quill, and an ink bottle. The flat top of the chest doubles as my desk.

Dipping the sheared end of the quill in the ink, I set the tip to the parchment.

> *Inanna was a cherished young woman, beloved by every-one in her village. Some said she had the loyalty of an elephant and the bravery of a tiger. Men tried to woo her, but Inanna ignored them. She was waiting for one man—the same man she had loved in every lifetime.*

I transcribe the tale from my recollection, citing how Inanna's beloved was taken to the Void and later rematerialized at night, at which point my memory empties. The adaption I first told Kalinda moons ago was exaggerated for her benefit. Inanna braved the Void to liberate her beloved, but how did she survive?

My mind is blank as the parchment. I drop the quill and rise. I need to move.

Gripping the upper eave, I boost myself out the window and onto the pitched roof. My toes hang over the drop-off.

Vanhi, known to those who love it as the City of Gems, unfolds before me. Parts of the city are still in ruins. Whole districts are blocked off, their residents shut out. Tents were set up by the outer wall that borders the Bhavya Desert for temporary housing until the districts are rebuilt. What would my ancestors think of this disarray? The rajahs that came before me tamed the desert and built this oasis. My first major act as ruler undid all their hard work.

Few people know that I released the demon Udug from the Void to prevent a wicked sultan from doing the same. Udug impersonated my father and led our army in a battle against the warlord. They prevailed against the rebels, though the cost was great. The repairs have rapidly depleted our reserves.

But not for long.

In one week, I will wed Princess Gemi. In most regards, she is a stranger. I gained respect for her and her people as we fought together against Udug. I have since studied the Southern Isles' history and their inclusion of bhutas. The empire needs the materials and monetary resources I negotiated for in our alliance. I also need guidance on how to progress to peace.

For a time, I envisioned another marital union for myself. Kalinda was the obvious selection as my kindred, but her heart led her elsewhere. The hurt of her refusal clung on for a time but has since disintegrated. Kali sacrificed much to return me to my palace and throne. I see how our people look at her. Those who saw her fight for their freedoms respect her more, undeterred by her bhuta heritage. Many more do not appreciate her labors and view her only as a Burner. Their incoming kindred, who had no associations with the rebels, will more easily garner their esteem. Gaining my own affection for my first wife is not a priority. Rajahs do not have the same romantic independence as others. Our hearts must belong to our empires.

"Your Majesty?" Pons asks from the lower roof. I drop into the aviary. The Galer enters, rousing the doves. He does not remark about where I am. During our first days together, I made him promise not to tell anyone about my rooftop escapades. "Your meeting begins soon."

"I'm coming." I replace the ink and quill in the box and then pick up the parchment with the unfinished story.

"Would you like me to send that correspondence, sir?"

"This? No. This is nothing." I crush the parchment into a ball. The bottom of the wooden box is littered with crumpled papers. I toss my latest attempt in with the others and close the lid.

4

KALINDA

Wind and rain beat against my back and lash at my hair. I stand on the lakeshore, icebergs bobbing across the shattered surface.

"Kali!" Deven calls from within the hurling water, near the center of the lake. He dips under a crashing wave and up again.

I run up to my shins into the freezing waters. Ice bites into my skin. Rain distorts my vision. He disappears behind a wave. I search frantically. He reappears, swimming against currents and crosswinds.

Our gazes connect across the perilous divide, both rife with terror. The storm whips up massive crosscurrents. A maelstrom spins Deven around its outer radius.

He cannot break free.

I dive in and swim out. My right hand is whole again. I cannot stop to think about how that is possible. I funnel all my strength into reaching him. He twirls closer to the whirlpool.

We reach for each other. Our fingertips touch—

A current slices between us.

Deven careens into the vortex and goes under. I scrutinize the choppy waves. When he does not resurface, I inhale and dive.

Shadows writhe below, hooks grasping and dragging him. I swim farther and catch his fingers. The hooks pull harder, wrenching him from my clasp. The darkness arrests him and he sinks from view. I swim into the directionless pit.

"Come to me." The distinctly female voice vibrates through my skull. "Come to me or your beloved is mine." Something ugly in her voice twists "beloved."

The same hooks that stole Deven reach for me. Icy spikes impale my thighs. Not hooks—claws. I try to scream. My mouth fills with water that tastes of lead. The phantom cackles. I grasp for something solid, but the claws submerge me deeper into the pit.

Someone jostles my shoulder. I jerk awake.

"Sorry to disturb you," says Indah. "You've both been asleep awhile."

Her daughter, Jala, naps in my arms. I came to their chamber for a visit, as I do most days after I teach my art course, and sat down to rock the baby to sleep. "I must have dozed off."

"You were mumbling."

My legs ache. I can still recall that eerie cackle.

"I was dreaming." I say no more, unwilling to give credence to my nightmare by reliving its horrors, and peer down at the bundled infant.

"Jala sleeps soundly with you," Indah notes, her tone pleased.

She has hinted more than once that Jala and I were connected in a past life. More than once I have wondered if Jala's little body holds my best friend's reincarnated soul. Delusional as it may be, I like the notion that Jaya has returned from the Beyond. I appreciate that speculation more than when Rajah Tarek declared I was the reincarnated soul of the fire-god's hundredth rani. Even though I yearn for more respect from my people, mercifully, his grand assertion did not stick.

I kiss Jala's downy head and pass her to Indah. The baby wakes, her face scrunching in protest. Her grouses work up to mewling cries. The noise tugs away the final tendrils of my nightmare, save only Deven's fear when he slipped away. Nothing can clear that from my memory.

"Are you not meeting Deven tonight?" Indah asks.

My gaze zips out the open balcony at the dusky sky. "What time is it?"

"Just past sunset." Indah's response follows me to the door. "That's why I woke you. I thought you'd want to see him."

"I do." I thank her and dash down the corridor to my chamber. Natesa reclines on my bed and snacks on a mango from Deven's food tray.

"There you are," she says. "How was your day?"

Deven is not here yet, so I sit with her and steal a piece of fruit too. "Well enough. My art pupils are learning how to sketch people. They're fascinated by the fire-god Enlil. He's all they want to draw."

"They're young women infatuated with perfection."

"I was once taken with Anu," I admit. "But I'd never seen a real man. These girls have seen plenty."

"Anu and Enlil aren't men—they're gods. It's difficult not to be enraptured." Natesa stretches her toes near a stack of books at the foot of the bed. "These came from the Hiraani Temple for you. Priestess Mita couldn't find you so I brought them."

I forgot I sent a correspondence to the distant Sisterhood temple asking for their texts about the Void. "Thank you. I'll start them tonight. Aren't you supposed to be at your inn?"

Natesa swings her legs over the side of the bed. "Yatin and I decided that can wait. I'll hardly see him if I'm living in the city and he's here."

She rises to go. I should be pleased she is staying, but the feeling of wrongness from earlier returns stronger.

"Natesa, I don't want you and Yatin to put your life on hold for anyone."

"We aren't."

"First you delayed your wedding and now—"

"You aren't the only one who feels helpless, Kali. Deven is Yatin's best friend. *My* friend. We all want him home. It's hard for life to go on while we know he's down there." Natesa's frustration matches my own. She glances at the pile of books. "Most of us don't read as fast as you and Ashwin, but we're helping where we can."

They are doing plenty. Yatin is running the palace during our drought of guards, and Natesa aids me more than my servant, Asha, does.

"I don't thank you enough," I reply.

"You could do better." She tucks her tongue in her cheek and tilts her head. She is such a pest. "Good night, Kali. Tell Deven we miss him."

"I promise."

After she goes, I finish the fruit and lug the stack of texts to the table, starting with the one on top. *Lost Souls: The Realm Below.* Deven is not a lost soul, but the sisters thought this book was pertinent, so I settle into my chair.

On the first page I read a poem, "Ode to the Evernight."

> *Seven gates to ascend, one must pay*
> *A token dear and precious.*
> *Crest all below and do not delay:*
> *The Desert of Anguish, the Valley of Mirrors*
> *A broken heart and spirited tears*
> *A River of Ordeal, a Road of Bone*
> *The city of death, and Kur's home.*
> *Beware of Irkalla, Queen of Thorns.*
> *Reveal her fangs and you are never born.*

A barb of fear clenches my neck. I cannot fathom how Deven spends every day in that awful place. Turning the page, I read on.

According to the text, the under realm is divided by seven gates, each one manned by a guardian. In between the gates lie domains, some listed in the poem. One detail I recall from Ashwin's recounting of *Inanna's Descent* is that Inanna paid each guardian with a piece of her wedding adornment.

One by one, the guardians will request a token in exchange for entrance through their gates and passage through their domains.

At last some truth. This confirms a portion of Ashwin's recounting. I read in earnest, devouring page after page as I wait for Deven to arrive.

Some time later, when midnight marches into the early hours, a chapter heading nearly flies off the page: "Mortal Wanderers."

> *Woe unto the mortal who finds himself imprisoned in the Void. Man was created to turn toward the light, seeking, aspiring, ascending. But no ember lies in the belly of the evernight to warm or enrich the soul of man. He is doomed to wander, driven farther into the Void, while his soul-fire dims from eternal brightness. Once his inner star fades, he will be empty and forfeit his capacity for rebirth. A death eternal, body and soul.*

"A death eternal," I breathe.

Shaken, I glance up from the page. Dawn spreads its golden wings across the horizon. Did I miss Deven? Though distracted by my research, I would not have overlooked his arrival. I hurry out, bringing the text with me.

My footfalls liven the hushed palace corridors. I arrive at the main palace and throw open double doors. The prince's chambers are vacant. Nor is he in his dusty library, though the oil lamp is warm.

Next I check the atrium where he takes his meals. No one is there. I backtrack to the wives' wing in the hope that a rani has seen him.

I push through silk curtains billowing in the doorway into the Tigress Pavilion. The daylit training courtyard is not in use. All the weapons racks are stocked: khandas, daggers, haladies, talwars, shields, spears, and, at the far end—an urumi. None of the current wives possess the skill to wield the weapon made of flexible, whiplike blades. Only Kindred Lakia mastered it.

Off the main courtyard, servants set out breakfast. Ranis, sisters of the Parijana faith, temple wards, and courtesans kneel on floor cushions around the packed tables. My servant, Asha, dines between Eshana and Parisa. My friends motion me over.

"Kali!" Eshana calls. "Join us."

Women bow as I pass. Many of them still consider me their kindred. I have quit correcting them. Priestess Mita ignores me, her usual reaction to my presence. We have not spoken since I stepped down from my throne. She intends her silence as punishment. Her lack of nagging has been paradise.

Eshana tugs me to kneel between her and Parisa. I set the book in my lap, and Asha dishes me a plate of honey-drizzled fried bread. Her facial scars came from Tarek's mistreatment, but she fits in with the tournament-scarred sister warriors.

"You look tired," Parisa says, playing with my limp, unwashed hair. "I have a sleeping agent Healer Baka gave me. Take a little, and you'll be gone from the world for hours."

"I'm fine." Except I do need to bathe. Next to my friends, I am an unpolished gem amid rubies. I tear into my bread and chew the doughy sweetness. "Have you seen Ashwin?"

"Him? Here?" Parisa scoffs. "We're beginning to think he'll never choose a kindred and we'll be stuck in this in-between life forever."

"Give him time," I say. "He's trying to make the best decision for the empire."

Parisa rubs the back of her hand where her rank mark has long since faded. I advised Ashwin to tell them about his betrothal, but he wants to wait until Gemi arrives. It will not be long now, so I let it be.

"Kali, we heard some news," Eshana says, her tone overly conspicuous. "Shyla told Parisa, who told me, that you went riding in the city with the prince yesterday. Have you changed your mind about marrying him?"

The table of women goes quiet. I finish chewing and articulate my response. "No. Ashwin and I are friends."

Eshana bats her eyelashes in confusion. "You'll wed again, won't you, Kali?"

Asha observes our exchange without commenting. She must suspect Deven may not be entirely gone. When she is not training with Healer Baka in the infirmary, she assists me. She has tidied my chamber and left heaping trays of food too often not to have poked around for answers. I have none to give, and what explanations I do have are worrisome.

"I should go," I say, taking my fried bread with me. My friends put up a fuss, but I pull from their grasps.

"Give her time," Eshana whispers loudly to the others. "She's still mourning General Naik. Eventually she'll move on."

I speed off, blinking back tears. They know nothing. Their biggest concern is winning over Ashwin. They sit in their silk and jewels, surrounded by mountains of food, oblivious to true heartache.

Deven didn't come last night. Why didn't he—?

I bump into Shyla at the door. She shuffles back.

"Kali, are you crying?"

Tears sting my nose. They want out badly. I consider telling her everything, but when words are not spoken, they create a divide that cannot be crossed without causing hurt. "Have you seen Deven?"

"Deven?"

I stare at her in horror. "I meant Prince Ashwin."

Shyla's frown deepens. I can only imagine what she will say to Parisa and Eshana about our encounter.

"I just left the prince," Shyla says. "I'll take you."

5

Ashwin

I sit cross-legged on a rug among wooden blocks and build a tower for Shyla's daughter. My sister Rehan knocks down the structure with her chubby fists.

"You little tyrant," I chide affectionately and re-erect the tower.

The toy structure is four blocks high when the baby swats it down again. At almost a year old, Rehan is the youngest of Tarek's children. The palace nursery houses all fifty-two of my siblings. I was so overwhelmed when we met I left, intending never to return, but Rehan's brown eyes plagued me. She has our father's eyes. We both resemble Tarek, me more than her. My friends and family looked past his face to see me, so I did the same for my sister. I no longer see him in her at all.

Rehan rocks on her bottom, her sturdy legs spread apart. I restack the blocks, wishing the city was this easy to repair.

From the corner of my eye, I see Kalinda enter the nursery. Her trousers and blouse are wrinkled, her hair tangled. Her gaze slices through me, one part relief, two parts urgent.

Rehan gnaws on a block, my tower forgotten. Kalinda sits in the nursemaids' reading chair near a stack of children's books and rests a larger one in her lap.

"Shyla told me you were here," she says. "I've been looking for you."

"I come here every morning." I add lower walls to the block tower.

"To do what?"

"Sometimes I read to the children. Other times we play games." I continue to construct a miniature palace. "Visiting them helps this place feel like home."

Rehan knocks down the tower again and claps at her conquest. She does not view me as her ruler. I am simply her brother.

"Deven didn't come last night," says Kalinda.

"At all?" I ask, looking up from the blocks. She jerks her head side to side. "Could you have missed him?"

"I didn't fall asleep," Kalinda retorts firmly. Rehan grabs my leg, anxious about her vehemence. The nursemaid across the chamber sends us cautionary glances. Kalinda explains, "I couldn't have missed him. I was up all night reading."

"Find anything interesting?" I ask, my tone buoyant to put Rehan at ease.

"Something terrible." Kalinda palms the book in her lap. "This says mortal wanderers are doomed never to return to our realm. Deven will remain trapped below and lose his ability to die and be reborn. He'll suffer an eternal death."

I grimace. Severance from the gods is a penance beyond imagination for anyone, but especially for a man of faith like Deven. For a short period, he trained with the Brotherhood and almost joined them, eventually enrolling in the army instead.

"Is what the text says true?" Kalinda says, her pitch shrill.

"I haven't read anything to refute it," I reply. Rehan takes interest in the blocks again, decimating the palace.

Kalinda drops her chin, her fingers digging into her knee.

"I'm sorry, Kali."

Her head snaps up. "*Are* you?"

"Yes." I cannot place her animosity. "We've done everything we can."

"We are *not* done," she replies, pink flooding her cheeks. "We need to search harder for the tale of *Inanna's Descent*, tell more people, bring on more readers."

Her panic overshadows my concern for Deven. "This is consuming you."

"Agh!" she cries. My sister's eyes broaden at Kalinda. "Did you really forget the tale? Did you even try to save him?"

"You know I did." I do not remind her of the long nights I spent researching in my library. Deven's predicament goes beyond proving my diligence. I have not wanted to risk upsetting Kalinda more, but I finished searching the texts in my library the night after last. We are out of resources. "The gods may have a plan we cannot yet see."

Kalinda recoils, her expression wounded. "You told me we'd search until we found him."

"We *have* searched, but if the origins of the tale are oral, tracking it down may be impossible." I run my hands through my hair to ease my fidgeting. "How you're living, straddling our world and the ever-night . . . No mortal should sustain that. Maybe Deven didn't come so you'll let him go."

"I'm his only way home!" Kalinda says, jumping to her feet. Her sudden movement knocks over the chair, which hits the mound of children's books. They tumble to the floor in a landslide.

Rehan startles and sucks in a lungful of air. As she howls, Kalinda's chin trembles. I lift the baby to calm her. Her weeping rises to high-pitched wails.

"Please don't cry," I say, an appeal for them both.

"I'm sorry I upset her." Kalinda bites her inner cheek and kneels to restack the books. "I'll fix it."

"It's all right," I say. "Just leave them."

She organizes the mess while Rehan wails. I bounce the baby, at a loss for how to console either one.

The old nursemaid crosses to us. Sunsee, the nursery leader, takes Rehan and pats her back. Kalinda rights the tipped chair and drops into it, resting her face in her hands. Her nose hits her wooden prosthesis. She groans and buries her watery eyes in the crook of her elbow.

My suggestion that we may not free Deven was not meant to be callous. The longer this goes on, the more I worry I could lose Deven *and* Kalinda. She is thinking only of his well-being. Someone must think of hers.

Nursemaid Sunsee quiets my sister. "Might I suggest you read to her, Your Majesty?" she says, passing the baby back. "You could tell her your favorite story when you were little."

"My favorite story?" I ask.

"Kindred Lakia recited it at bedtime."

I comb my recollections, coming across nothing of the sort.

Kalinda shoves at her wet nose, damp from repressing tears. "I'd like to hear this story."

"Come along," says Sunsee. We follow her into a shuttered chamber in the nursery. She opens the draperies, revealing furniture and wooden toys. "Forgive the dust. This is reserved for the heir. It's been unoccupied for some time."

This was my room before I moved to the Brotherhood temple for the brethren to raise me. I explore the chamber and wait for fragments of my memories to return.

Kalinda wanders the perimeter. We reconnect at the bed. A haunting mural covers the wall behind the headboard. The painting depicts a subversive world awash with grays. A path of switchbacks divided by narrow gates meanders into the underground. As I track the path downward, I count seven gateways.

Kalinda approaches the mural in a daze. "Is this . . . ?"

"The tale of *Inanna's Descent*," finishes the nursemaid. She takes my squirming sister from me, setting her down to crawl. "This was Kindred Lakia's favorite story. Some of the nursemaids would listen at the door while she told the prince."

"Was there a book she read from?" Kalinda asks.

"No," Sunsee replies, "she recited the tale by heart."

I study the mural closer. "I have no recollection of this."

"You were four years old, Your Majesty."

Perhaps so, but Sunsee's nostalgia implies I *should* remember.

"Why this story?" Kalinda asks.

"Lakia was fascinated by Inanna." Sunsee points to a tiny outline of a woman at the top. Paths wind between her and the city at the bottom. A shining figure stands with the woman.

How could I forget my mother's obsession with this tale? I have been a reader for as long as I can recall. At the temple where I grew up, I was the only child under the brethren's care. Books were my best friends. Could my passion for reading have come from before the temple, from Lakia?

Kalinda indicates the glowing man with Inanna. "Who is that, Sunsee?"

The nursemaid's voice hushes. "Inanna could not navigate the under realm alone. As the tale goes, she visited the gods' mountain house temple and prayed for a divine guide to lead her. The fire-god took pity on Inanna and escorted her through the Void to her beloved."

"Ashwin," Kalinda utters breathlessly, "is this the detail you couldn't remember?"

I pry my heavy tongue from the bottom of my mouth. "Must be."

Kalinda blanches, her bloodshot eyes stricken.

Sparing Deven from an eternal death is possible, but only with guidance from a god.

6

KALINDA

Ashwin steps to my side. "I'm sorry, Kalinda. I should have remembered."

He was a child, and his later interactions with Lakia were less than favorable. Had Ashwin recalled the entire tale, the solution to freeing Deven would be the same.

I exit the nursery in a haze. A god. I must find a god.

Barring the story of Inanna and her beloved, deities have not dwelled in our realm since Anu bequeathed powers upon the First Bhutas and charged them to watch over mortals. Requesting a god to guide me through the under realm is less plausible than accomplishing the journey alone.

Upon entering my chamber, I stare at my bed. Just two nights ago, Deven and I laid there together. Now I may never see him again.

"Kalinda?" Ashwin asks.

I twist away to conceal my watery eyes. Spread out on the table are my drawings of Deven. The sight of them releases my tears.

"I'm sorry," Ashwin repeats.

What else can he say? He is sorry this is the end. Sorry I will never find Deven.

A knot of fury swells within me. This cannot be over. But how can I entice a god to return to the mortal realm?

I do not care how daft or improbable my mission may be. My promise to free Deven from the evernight holds true. Leaving him there is not an option.

I yank my satchel out from under the bed and drop it on the mattress.

"What are you doing?" Ashwin asks.

"I'm going after Deven. I'll find Ekur and beg the gods for help. Should that fail, I'll cut a hole in the icy lake and go down into the Void by myself."

Ashwin enters my side vision. "Wait another week and I'll go with you."

I doubt Gemi wants to spend their honeymoon in the under realm with me. "I've already waited too long. Deven needs me now."

Pons knocks at the open doorway. "Your Majesty, you have a meeting with Captain Yatin and Ambassador Brac."

"Not now, Pons."

"Sir, they're waiting for you—"

"I said *not now*," Ashwin repeats. Pons backs away and leaves us. The prince musses his hair distractedly. He should not have been short with Pons, but after upsetting Rehan, I am in no position to criticize. "Kalinda, you cannot leave. We're right in the middle of changing the temples and integrating bhutas. I cannot do this alone."

"You won't be alone. You have the support of your family and friends."

He tugs at his lower lip in indecision. "You'll miss my wedding."

"I apologize for that." Ashwin can lead without me and will probably be better off. My reputation is sullied by my bhuta heritage. Unlike Princess Gemi, I do not have food and materials to win over our people.

"You aren't really sorry," he says, his gaze fixed on mine. "You've been waiting for an excuse to leave."

"You think I *want* this?"

"I think you've forgotten that people here care about you. Tinley and Pons and Indah did not stay to help us rebuild Vanhi out of devotion to me. They are your friends first. And the ranis? They're your family. This is your home."

Is it? I have not felt certain that I am where I belong since Jaya and I lived in Samiya. Since stepping down from my throne, I have fought hard for the reassurance that I am where the gods desire. Giving up my rank was the right decision, but what did I step down to? My reward was supposed to be a quiet life with Deven. Instead I am here, living in the shadow of who I could have been.

Perhaps I *am* relieved to go. I used to believe everything serves a purpose. Yet, since Deven was taken, I am less certain of the gods' role in my life. No more can I wait for them to point out the path I should follow. I have to seize my own fate.

"Ashwin, I need to go."

"You're talking about traveling into *the Void*," he clarifies.

"My fear of the under realm is still less than my regret for what's happening to Deven. I don't imagine you'll understand."

Ashwin inserts himself between me and my satchel. "I understand you blame yourself for his capture." I attempt to maneuver around the prince, but he blocks me. "Getting yourself trapped down there won't help anyone."

"I'm not trying to help just anyone. I'm trying to help Deven."

Ashwin gives me a blank look. He cannot relate. His feelings for me hinged upon him thinking he needed me at his right-hand side to rule. He was not in love with me. His great love is the empire.

"Someday," I say softly, "I hope the gods bless you with a forever love."

He flinches as though I have cursed him. I reach around him for my bag.

"Will you say good-bye to the others?" he asks.

Defending my decision to more of my friends would take the better part of the day, or longer. Natesa and Brac are not easily swayed. "I'd appreciate your telling them."

"Natesa will be agitated."

"Then it will be a typical day at the palace." My humor does not cheer up Ashwin. "Will you wait up for Deven while I'm gone?" Ashwin agrees, his jaw muscles ticking. I stop myself from fixing his disheveled hair. "You were born for this, Ashwin. You're the rajah the people deserve."

He sniffs hard. "Come back soon. And be safe."

"You too."

He kisses my cheek and then goes, dragging his heels.

I slump over myself and stare at my bag. What do I even pack? I open my wardrobe closet, and there on the bottom shelf rests my old slingshot. The relic of my upbringing in the Sisterhood temple has been retired. Much has changed since I wielded it. I am so overwhelmed by the task of acquiring a god's aid that I wish I had never entered the world of men and was still sheltered in my ignorance.

That woman is gone now, and I cannot go back. I can only move forward, regardless of how difficult. The gods' temple might as well be the sun for how likely I am to reach it, but Deven found me night after night. I can search the unknown to locate this temple. Because if the Void exists, so must Ekur.

A steady flow of feet travels the palace corridors. By some mercy, I venture outside without a single hello and dash down a path shaded by eucalyptus trees. The supplies in my pack are minimal: warm clothes, water flask, hair comb, and a sketch of Deven.

At the rear of the palace, I reach the stables. The long, narrow outbuilding has several archways under domed roofs, stalls that house the imperial elephants. My nose itches from the scent of manure. In an adjacent riding arena, Parisa leads a bull elephant along the fence line. She visits the stables often to assist the trainers due to her gentle hand with the animals.

I pass behind the riding yard to a canopy crafted of poles and palm fronds. The temporary aviary shields Tinley's mahati falcon from the sun. As I anticipated, Tinley saddles her bird, Chare, in preparation to patrol the sand dunes.

"Going somewhere?" Tinley asks without turning around.

"I'd like you to fly me to the Alpanas," I reply. Tinley pivots and awaits my explanation. "I have to find the gods' temple and ask for guidance through the Void."

Many believe Ekur is hidden in the northern Alpana Mountains, yet I quickly grasp how ludicrous this sounds.

"I've patrolled those mountains often," says Tinley, tugging on her gloves. "The weather is moody and the northern wind is a trickster. Finding anything there will be a challenge."

"You would save me a lot of time," I press. On horseback, the trip takes weeks.

Tinley mounts her falcon and grabs a handful of Chare's red-orange plume. "You ask for more than a favor. This requires a miracle. Ekur cannot be found. It doesn't exist."

"Let that be my concern."

Chare rakes her talons into the ground, keen to take off. The mahati's feathers blaze brassy in the sunshine. Her rider scrutinizes me, Tinley's pale eyes cool.

"I'll take you to my father," she says. "He'll know how to help you." She tosses her silver hair over her shoulder and tilts an ear to the sky. "Pons knows we're leaving. He says someone else gets to tell Natesa."

"Ashwin will."

I climb on behind Tinley and clasp on to her waist. The falcon's satiny feathers skim against my ankles. The Galer grins, for she is happiest when navigating the revolving skies on her mahati.

Chare crouches and springs. We shoot up, an arrow bound for the sun. I peek down at the palace, locking a final image of the glinting domes into my mind, and then look forward to the desert horizon.

7

Ashwin

Pons sits with me on the roof, his feet and legs dangling over the edge. I came up here to watch Kalinda fly away. I presumed correctly that she would petition Tinley for aid. Although Kalinda accused me of ignorance, I understand why she had to go. She left for the same reason I stay. Love and duty require sacrifice.

"Kalinda left to find Deven," I say.

"So I heard." Pons peers up at the passing clouds and then sharply east. A wing flyer appears along the desert horizon.

"Who's that?" I ask.

"Your viraji."

Something indescribable flip-flops in my chest. The last time I saw Princess Gemi was the evening Kalinda suggested I wed the Southern Isles princess. By the time I proposed a union of states, Gemi had returned to Lestari. We have exchanged brief correspondences, but I have not seen her since she agreed to become my viraji.

Pons and I rise. Why has Gemi come early? She was supposed to arrive by riverboat with the datu and the Lestarian Navy a day before our wedding.

Her wing flyer swoops closer and ascends. Citizens beyond the palace gates gawk at the princess and her two Galer escorts as they land in the front courtyard.

"Your people will ask questions," Pons cautions.

That they will. My plan to keep my betrothal confidential until the eve of our wedding is over. Too many of my close friends are aware of our alliance. One accidental reference to Gemi as my "viraji" will be our undoing. I am surprised we held the secret this long.

"Send out the wedding proclamation," I reply hoarsely, "and advise Captain Yatin to be ready."

In hours, the citizens of Vanhi will know of my choice for kindred and our alliance with the Southern Isles. They should rejoice over the strengthening of our reserves and defenses, but some will undoubtedly oppose my selection.

After drying my perspiring palms on my trousers, I jump off the ledge and dash across the lower rooftop. I grab a rope that I fastened inside a window for a spot of adventure, swinging down to a lower terrace.

Two ranis squeal at my sudden arrival. I pause to collect my bearings. Several doorways stand as options. Next time I will scout out where I land.

I address the astonished ranis. "Which way to the main entry?"

"That way." One of them directs a crimson nail at a door.

I bow, racing off. The corridors lead me to the double stairway. I glance at the empty entry, then perch on the slick ledge of the banister and ride it to the bottom.

"Where have you been?" Natesa demands from behind me. "You missed your last two meetings."

"I was planning my wedding."

"That's what the second meeting was for." She props a hand on her hip. Her clothes smell of sandalwood incense. She must have come from the chapel. Each afternoon, she offers burned sacrifices to the gods on Deven's behalf. "Where's Kalinda? I haven't seen her all day."

I brandish my hands as if the answer is floating past us. "She left."

"The palace?"

"Vanhi."

Natesa's expression stones over. Several seconds weigh between us.

"She's gone to find Deven," she concludes, paling. "Gods help them."

Pons appears at the top of the stairway. Natesa remains locked in shock, but I do not trust the state of bewilderment will hold her. Gemi sweeps through the entry, sparing me from finding out.

"Princess Gemi," I say. "This is a surprise."

Her cheeks bloom a rosy hue. "I sent word ahead, Your Majesty." She remembers to bow. "The datu will arrive with the imperial navy in a few days. Their trek upstream was moving too slowly. I hope I'm not intruding."

I clutch her twitching fingers. "You aren't."

Gemi's lips tug up, her lashes lowering. She wears ebony trousers and a blouse, her trim midriff uncovered. The colorless, formfitting garb is not severe or masculine on her lean frame. Her ivory shell earrings match her collar necklace.

The same peculiar sensation stirs within me. She will be my wife, and I have no idea what her impression is of me or our betrothal.

Pons joins us on the main floor. Gemi rubs the side of his shiny, bald head. Natesa's lips quirk. Not often is the stern warrior reduced to a boyish playmate.

"Where's your daughter?" Gemi inquires of Pons. Her islander accent, dropping her *r* and *k* sounds, is less detectable than I recall, but more pronounced than Indah's or Pons's.

"Jala is napping. I'll take you to meet her later." Pons offers her his elbow. "Let me escort you to your chamber, Viraji."

Princess Gemi tips her chin at me. "We'll meet again at supper, Your Majesty."

I confine my curiosity until they are out of earshot. "Natesa, did you know the princess was arriving early?"

"She sent word yesterday." She tsks at my continued astonishment. "You'd know if you paid attention to your schedule."

I lower my voice to lessen the echo through the rotunda. "I do pay attention."

"Not close enough." Natesa adjusts my sagging collar. "I'm sending a tailor to your chambers. You need more appropriate attire."

"The clothes you prefer are restrictive." The garments are uncomfortable, unduly ostentatious, and difficult to climb in. "Did Pons say when I'll be alone in my library?"

Natesa pats my chest. "Go dress for supper, and I'll tell you."

"Tell me when this constant schedule ends or I won't move."

"Then you'll be a very hungry prince, won't you?" Natesa swivels me around and gives me a push toward the stairs. "Wear the black-and-gold tunic and turban. It's Gemi's favorite."

That outfit itches, and I can scarcely sit in the trousers. "How do you know?"

"As a woman, I sense these things."

"Can you sense a man's irritation?"

"Yes, but it's easy to ignore. I'm helping you represent your greatest self, Ashwin."

She is trying not to explode. She has bottled up her apprehension over Kalinda's journey to be released toward me little by little. I would have preferred she throw a fit.

"I'm not a child for you to order about," I mutter, marching ahead.

"A child wouldn't complain so much." She calls at my back, "Be at your atrium at nine o'clock! Don't be late or I'll send Yatin after you."

Captain Yatin may empathize with me as he regularly tolerates her badgering.

I trudge upstairs, too exasperated to argue. A ruler is ruled by his schedule. This regimented lifestyle is my birthright. There is no bargaining with fate.

The tailor measures the inseam of my leg and scribbles down the number. My trousers are too short for what is fashionable. I suppose I should care, but I envy the humble white robes the brethren wear and the loose trousers of the working men. This gaudy embroidery suited my father more than me.

Yatin enters my chamber short-winded. "Your Majesty, a crowd gathered to protest your betrothal. I sent out guards to disband the mob, and the protestors attacked a soldier."

"How is he?"

"Our healers are with him in the infirmary. He was beaten badly."

I step off the stool and away from the tailor. "Did you arrest the culprits?"

"We broke up the crowd and seized a handful of perpetrators, but most of them ran off." Yatin grumbles the last words, cross with himself and his men. "Commander Lokesh was speaking at the time of the soldier's attack. Lokesh didn't harm anyone, nor did he imply that his audience should. But, Your Majesty, he spoke out against you and your viraji. He said you will allow bhutas to rule the empire and seek revenge against us."

The people heard these lies and panicked. Lokesh must presume I will do the same.

"Bring me the commander," I say, "and send for Brac. Both of you will attend our meeting in the throne room."

"Yes, sir."

The tailor packs his spools of thread and needles in his basket. I notice a loose strand on the sleeve of my jacket and pluck at it. In seconds, the thread pulls out and the hem of my cuff unravels.

The rajah's throne is alone on the dais. Plum draperies sweep across the concealed antechamber doors behind it, framing the lonely seat. One leg of the gold-leaf chair was kicked off during the rebel occupation and later replaced. The plush scarlet cloth on the seat and high back was also improved. The warlord Hastin and his rebels tested the sharpness of their blades on the lining.

I ease onto the velvet and evaluate the empty hall. Rows of pillows in jewel tones cover the shiny marble floor. Tarek reserved the front row for his favored four. His kindred occasionally sat in a smaller throne on his right-hand side, but more often, the yellow cushion was hers to kneel on before Tarek. Lakia devoted her life to my father; he did not return her affections in equal measure. He put himself first, above all else.

I shift in my throne. It is here, in his direct shadow, that his memory is strongest.

Sit up. Look me in the eye. Do not fear anyone. You will be rajah. Your people must fear you. Force them to obey.

His urgings were rigid. Be better. Exude more strength. Tolerate less weakness. When I displeased him, he whipped me. Disobedience cost me the skin on my back.

Be vigilant, my son. We must protect our reign. Our legacy.

His legacy is one I will not repeat.

Brac strolls in the room. "Have you seen Kalinda? We need to discuss Basma and Giza's training schedule."

"You'll have to discuss arrangements with the nursemaids. Kalinda and Tinley have gone north to find a route to Deven."

His honey eyes flash. "She left you here to fend for yourself."

I press my shoulder blades against the high-backed throne. His lack of conviction in my fitness as ruler hangs between us. "Her departure alters nothing. I'm still leader of the empire."

Brac regards me with uncertainty. "I can only speak for bhutas, but it would console the people to see you proactive in your authority."

My tone roughens. "What are you saying, Ambassador?"

"You're still reacting from Tarek's rulership, the warlord's insurgence, and now the protestors."

"I inherited a war," I remind him. "My decisions are not all reactionary. I'm taking a wife on my own accord."

"A foreigner and stranger," Brac rejoins, expressing facts instead of his own judgement. He commended me on my selection of kindred when I first proposed. "Tarachandians want to trust your vision for the empire. They'll follow your example, but if you're ambivalent, they will be as well. Today's riot will become a habit."

My teeth slam together. Granting clemency to the deserting soldiers could be regarded as too lenient. I welcomed home the refugees and started reconstructing their huts and places of work. On reflection, I should have mandated that they contribute more to our city's rebirth. I reopened our borders to bhutas and ceased the slaughter of their kind, but have I demonstrated equal commitment to those who now reside alongside their former adversaries? Every decision I made has offended someone. I cannot please all my people, yet I will continue to exhort them to treat bhutas fairly. Consistency will prove I am not ambivalent about their equal place in the empire.

"Commander Lokesh will arrive any moment," I say, weary. My solitude on the dais tires me. "I would appreciate your support."

The ever-mischievous Burner grips the axes strapped to his back. "Would you like me to intimidate him?"

I trap a sigh. I wish General Naik was here to offer his advice and wrangle his brother. Deven knows conflict strategy and Brac far better than I. "Only if need be."

Commander Lokesh enters the throne room, Yatin behind him. Brac positions himself on the dais at my left-hand side. The captain did not disarm Lokesh of his pata swords. With Brac present, his weapons are a nominal threat.

Lokesh pauses in the shadows between the pools of sunshine cast from the high casements. He bows, a perfunctory bend of the waist. "Your Majesty."

"I hear you have grievances. State them here in my presence."

He still wears a headscarf, his face uncovered but shadowed. Although he stands tall, his shoulders have a brutish downward slope that makes his posture appear offset. Early signs of gray mark his trim beard and wiry mustache. His palms are covered by strips of cloth, a practice of soldiers when they train to prevent callouses.

"You're welcome to attend my speeches," he replies.

"Your followers nearly killed one of my soldiers."

No sign of remorse crosses Lokesh's expression. "My apologies to the soldier and his family. I have no authority over the rioters."

Brac scoffs. "You're like a boy who set two dogs upon a single bone and then backed away from the fight."

Lokesh snubs him, reserving his attention for me. "This dogfight is older than me, Your Majesty. That bone was thrown long before you or I entered the scene."

"But we're here now," I counter. "Delay your speeches until after my wedding."

"Or . . . ?" he asks.

I select my response carefully to avoid him misconstruing my remarks. "Consider your temporary cooperation a wedding present to my viraji and me."

"Then you do intend to wed a bhuta." Lokesh presses his lips into a slash. "My speech today was unplanned. The people gathered to protest your choice of kindred. I came to listen, and they demanded I explain the flames above the amphitheater yesterday. I told them the truth: you're letting children dabble with fire. Tarachandians are rightly outraged."

A discouraging reaction. Though given the damages from the rebel insurgency, warranted. "What would they have me do? The trainees are children."

Lokesh, again, is unmoved. "Ask the bhutas to announce themselves. They look the same as you and me. People are afraid of what they cannot see, cannot identify. Require bhutas to reveal their powers. A mark on the hand or forehead."

Brac recoils. "You want to *brand* us?"

"This protects you as well," Lokesh counters, a mocking ring to his tone. "You cannot identify bhutas either, and you destroyed all the neutralizer tonic after the war. What's to stop an Aquifier from striding up and leeching you?"

"Why not mark the full-mortals instead so we may know who *you* are?" Brac contends.

"Your Majesty," says Lokesh, flouting Brac's outburst, "this is not a radical policy. Your father's ranis donned henna rank markings to identify their standing in his court."

"They were competitors," I say, voice rising. "Bhutas have stepped forward by their own free will. They need not be made into spectacles or targets. When the people ask about their welfare, tell them the truth. They are safe, Commander."

Lokesh's enmity molds into steel. "Rajah Tarek would never make such an ignorant claim."

"Tarek wouldn't have entertained your impertinence." I leave my threat unfinished, as we can both imagine the repercussions. Tarek would have waited until Lokesh rallied a crowd and executed him publicly. I am satisfied to deliver a warning.

"The people cannot be silenced." Lokesh barely restrains his rage, his voice and fists shaking. "You'll regret welcoming bhutas into your palace."

My belly hardens. His inflection of speech and hatred for bhutas reminds me of Tarek.

"Are you threatening His Majesty?" Brac demands, summoning a ball of flame. It hovers before him, ready for him to cast.

"A premonition," Lokesh qualifies.

I incline forward. "Inviting you here was a courtesy, Commander. Suspend your speeches, or I'll blame you for every individual injured on your watch. Should anyone so much as trip and fall while they're listening to you, I'll hold you accountable."

Brac rescinds his powers and grasps the back of my throne to show his support. I glance at him to step back, but the damage is done. Lokesh's eyes glint, intensifying his sneer. Brac has confirmed his assertions. My orders will be reinforced by bhutas.

"Good day, Your Majesty." Lokesh bows and stalks out, the echo of his footfalls dangling in the rafters.

8

KALINDA

Tinley and I ride racing winds into winter's stronghold. Bracing cold has usurped the north, forcing dormancy over the land.

Chare speeds past the lower hills and up the craggy mountains. A solid wash of heavy clouds hampers my view, and then, like a monster transpiring from the deep, Wolf's Peak appears. Jaya believed Ekur is located upon this pinnacle of the Alpana Mountains, where land meets the sky-god's territory. The temple is a gate between our world and the Beyond, a go-between wherein the deities once ruled, free from the woes and infirmities of the mortal realm.

Great Anu . . . I stop my prayer. Is there any point? The gods have not answered any of my entreaties. Why answer them now?

But just in case the gods *are* listening, I send up a plea. *Protect Deven.*

My small effort at faith drains me. I hunker down into my fur cloak, and the clouds clear below us, revealing scorched land and trees. We have reached Samiya.

Piles of rubble fan out from the remains of the Sisterhood temple. Under the snowbanks, the last of the stone structure is nearly unrecognizable. My longing for Jaya has steadily lessened, like a wound puckering to a scar, but near our home again, my memories of our simple life cause me to ache. Before the Claiming, I knew little of the world of men. Jaya and the Sisterhood were everything. I felt certain they were my intended future.

Chare banks west and soars over the alpine lake. The frozen surface shimmers in the low light, deceiving the mortal eye. Beneath that sheen of ice lies the gate to the Void.

Burn marks stripe the lakeshore, remnants of our battle against Kur. Tinley circles the wreckage of two Paljorian airships, skeletons of their once graceful glory. Chare banks away from the lake. I twist around to prolong my view and tuck my prosthesis close. Our war was won, the cost mighty.

"*Cala . . . ,*" the sky whistles.

That is an odd thing for the wind to say.

We glide toward Wolf's Peak, snow dusting the steep ridges. I blink fast to stave off the wind and search for a glimpse of the gods' temple.

"*Cala . . .*"

Upon hearing the name a second time, I listen closer.

"*Cala . . .*"

The voice's anguish scratches at me—this is the sound I would label my own grief.

I scour the snowcapped peaks for the source as we climb higher into the flurries and the presumed site of Ekur disappears behind a wall of white.

The northern wind must have tricked me. Nothing lives up here. No one could survive this lonely cold.

We dip into a land of ice and snow. The entirety of the valley has been drained of color. Even the sun is insipid, diffused by the reflection of its greatness upon the ivory and charcoal landscape.

Chare glides lower over the tundra and kicks up swirls of powder. The falcon's feathers soon bear a fine coat of soft crystals. Every so often we fly over ancient arches that rise from the flatlands like empty doorways to nowhere.

"What are those?" I call over the wind.

"Gates to the Beyond." Tinley's silver hair is pinned under her fur cloak to prevent it from whipping at me. "Our ancestors erected them centuries ago. We believe the souls of our loved ones pass through them when they die."

We approach the next arch; it is so wide Chare could fly through without touching the stone. The plain yet noble gates have two protrusions on top like horns.

"What do the embellishments mean?"

Tinley shouts her reply. "They symbolize the wings of a mahati falcon. The mahatis have existed since the primeval era when Tiamat ruled. They usher souls from our world to the next."

Paljorians are not alone in answering the complex question of what becomes of our souls after death. Lestarians believe primordial sea dragons guide their spirits to rest. We have no such notions in Tarachand, but it is feasible that ancient creatures cohabitated with the gods long before Anu plucked stars from the heavens and forged them into mortals.

We fly past an archway and onto another. If only the gates to the Void were this plentiful.

On the horizon, the pinnacles of an ice-blue palace glow against the setting sun. Chare doubles our speed for Teigra. The northern city thrives despite the nearly year-round winter. Steeply pitched roofs appear in abundance. Teigra must be twice the size of Vanhi. The glittering spires of the Crystal Palace, like inverted icicles, lure us to the dazzling stronghold.

Mahatis take off from within the city and zoom toward us. They bleed into the sunset, their reddish-orange feathers painted from the sundown sky. Tinley pumps her fist into the air and whoops loudly. Chare screeches in reply and flies headlong for the flock. We soar past them, and their riders wheel around to follow.

The other mahatis line up, a wingspan apart. Falcons fly in unison in battle, but this is not an offensive maneuver. The flock escorts us over the city in a parade.

Rooftops glisten, crusted in ice. Sleighs glide down the snowy roads, their riders warmed by red lap blankets. Smoke billows from countless longhouse chimneys. On the outskirts, four single-level buildings, large as mountains, tower over the central city. They must shelter the airships. Military barracks lie within the fenced compound around the dockyard.

We fly up to the Crystal Palace, and our escorts turn around to land elsewhere. Chare swoops near the frosty spires. Ice bricks compose the outer walls, and sculptures of mahati falcons perched on the eaves watch over the inhabitants. Welcomers occupy the courtyard along with drummers thumping wooden crates topped with tanned animal hides. I pick out the tall and strapping Chief Naresh. White fur covers his shoulders, leaving his deeply tanned arms bare to the cold.

"Do they always welcome you home like this?" I ask Tinley.

"I sent a message ahead. They're excited to meet the Burner Queen."

We circle over the congregation and glide to the ground. Chare brings us to a halt and folds in her wings. My stomach gradually rises from my knees.

Tinley drops into her father's outstretched arms. Chief Naresh swings her around in a haze of polar fur.

"Welcome home, daughter."

Tinley withstands her father's public display amiably. The chief switches his generous warmth to me. I slide off into his grasp. His skin and long white hair smell of peat moss.

"Welcome to Teigra, Kalinda. Every time I see you, I'm reminded how much you resemble your mother. Yasmin was a treasure to behold." Chief Naresh knows I hang on his every word when he speaks of my parents, his old friends. He can give me what many cannot: memories of them. "Kishan's presence was unmatched. When your father strode into a hall, every person felt his authority. I would have liked to have seen them together."

"I would have as well," I reply.

"Perhaps in our next lives." Naresh directs Tinley and me into the palace.

His guards carry khandas with hilts crafted from the long, twisted horns of blackbuck antelope. Everyone wears fur but has more skin exposed to the cold than I could withstand.

We pass through a high archway into the reception hall. Carvings of the fire-god's flame symbol decorate the walls, beams, and pillars. Chief Naresh stops in front of an ice sculpture of Enlil gripping a lightning bolt spear like a staff.

"Isn't he magnificent?" the chief asks.

My face warms. The fire-god is the most arresting of the deities. He inherited his good looks from his mother, the land-goddess Ki. Enlil's true father is the demon Kur, yet he bears some resemblance to his adopted father, Anu. I have often chosen to sketch Anu instead of his son. Enlil's chiseled physique has a sensuality that unnerved me as a girl. As a woman, I am even more aware of his full lips and muscled abdomen. I glance down the long entry hall for more sculptures. This is the only one.

"Your people worship the fire-god?" I ask.

"Uri, the First Burner, was a member of our tribe," replies the chief. Brac taught me a little about the First Burner during my training but did not specify her heritage. "The fire-god Enlil favored Uri. Before the gods left the mortal realm, he foresaw that we would suffer great trials and passed on his teachings to her. The first winter after the gods left was frigid. The skies and land lamented the deities' exodus and treated us liked a scourge. Uri set a fire and kept it burning for ninety days and ninety nights. Her living flame saved our people. As winter thawed, Uri implanted the embers from the dying blaze into our ancestors' soul-fire so they would never again fear the cold. We have no Burners among us now, but we still carry the flame of Uri's lasting fire in our souls."

My gaze wanders up Enlil's sculpture. "We have stories of Enlil too. Every temple ward is required to memorize *Enlil's Hundredth Rani*."

"Oh?" queries the chief. "We've never heard that story."

"Never?" I press. "Tarek justified the rank tournaments with this tale."

"Can you recite it?" Tinley asks.

"If you'd like." I rummage around in my memory for the correct words and start down the hall. Speaking of Enlil beside his likeness is too awkward. "The fire-god took many wives and courtesans. All of them were blessed with astounding beauty, enough so that the sky-god began to covet his son's good fortune. When Enlil announced that he would wed his hundredth wife, Anu was wroth with his son's greediness and wouldn't allow Enlil more wives than him. Anu told Enlil he could have only one hundred women and he was to drown those he did not keep in the Sea of Souls.

"Enlil was distraught. He cared for all his wives and courtesans and could not pare them down to so few. In his grief, he asked his father how he should choose which of his women to retain. Anu replied by saying, 'Let them decide.'"

Tinley grimaces and her father harrumphs. *Good. They understand why I'm not enthused about this story or the god it portrays.*

"Enlil's wives would not give up their rank. They loved their husband and honored him, but the courtesans loved Enlil as well, and they did not think it was just that they should die. So the courtesans challenged Enlil's final wife and battled for her rank as the last rani. Enlil's final wife was the loveliest of them all and had a merciful heart to match, but she was also a fierce fighter. She defeated every challenger and held her position until she was the last warrior standing. She wed the fire-god and was his favored wife forevermore."

"Quite a story," says the chief. We stop before the doorway to the great hall. "It aggrieves me that Tarek twisted your beliefs to suit his selfish desires. But this story founded your people's love for sister warriors, did it not?"

"Mortals began to replicate the tournaments, so the land-goddess Ki taught women to defend themselves and embrace their sisterhood. Ki didn't want her daughters' virtues exploited."

Chief Naresh gives a wide, pearly smile. "Our tales are much alike. From hardship comes great blessings and strength." He pats my shoulder and strides into the great hall.

His unique interpretation locks my knees. My aversion for the fire-god comes from his role in the origin of rank tournaments, but Anu forced Enlil to limit his wives, and Enlil's women elected to battle for his affections. From their decision much heartache was born, as well as the Sisterhood. I cannot envision my life without my friends, my sister warriors.

Tinley waves me forward. "Kalinda, come on."

I double-time after her, circumventing long tables and benches, all formed of ice and secured to the floor. Chandeliers hang low from the ceiling, and a giant hearth dominates one wall. Piles of peat moss are heaped in the corner, fuel for the fireside. Its warmth raises the temperature so my exhales no longer stain the air silver.

"Tinley, why do the walls and floors not melt?" I ask, eyeing the cathedral ceiling.

"Northern Aquifiers hauled ice by sleigh from the arctic ice cap and laid it brick by brick with their powers. The Crystal Palace will never melt or break away. This fortress has outlasted generations and will do so for centuries to come."

Ice that can withstand fire. I might need to return to see the frozen palace defy summer. What a wonder that would be.

Tinley's adamancy for staying away confuses me more. She takes pride in her home. Whatever kept her away must hurt more than not being here.

The chief directs us to the table nearest the hearth. An older woman and a younger couple await our arrival. The young man rises to embrace Tinley. She does not hug him in return.

"Welcome home," he says.

"Sister," says the woman beside him, "you missed our wedding."

"Did you receive my endowment?" Tinley asks.

"The carton of fruit?" the woman replies. "The pomegranates were overripe."

The older woman, donning a stunning red fox fur, interrupts. "Daughters, you're being impolite. Burner Queen, this is my daughter Maida and my son-in-law, Bedros, the next chief of our clan. I'm Sosi, Naresh's chieftess."

Maida takes after her mother, her complexion and hair both ebony, but the sisters have identical light eyes.

"Her name is Kalinda, Mother," says Tinley. "She relinquished her throne."

"Oh?" Sosi studies me anew. I can practically see her opinion of me waning.

Chief Naresh sweeps us along. "Shall we dine?"

I sit between him and Tinley while Sosi and the newlyweds dine across from us. Bedros's attention is so strong on Tinley that Maida nudges his side. Three girls run into the hall and pile onto the bench by Sosi. They must be the rest of Tinley's siblings.

Servants roast root vegetables and antelope meat over the hearth, then dish the mixture into bowls and bring them to us. The hearty stew and spiced wine refuel my soul-fire. I eat while Maida regales the table with details of her wedding. Bedros watches Tinley the entire time. Not once does she look up from her food.

"Burner Rani," says Sosi, "how is the integration of bhutas proceeding in Tarachand? Your prince has a great deal of work ahead."

"He does," I reply, stirring my stew and thinking of my friends at the palace. "So far it's promising."

Naresh addresses his younger girls. "That's enough grown-up talk. Why don't I recount your favorite story about Kalinda?"

The girls bounce up and down.

"Favorite story?" I ask. "You have more than one?"

"You're a popular subject at supper." He winks at me and dives right into the story. "Watching from above on the airship, I saw a young woman atop a dragon of fire, lobbing heatwaves at Kur. The First-Ever Dragon was terror incarnate." Naresh deepens his voice to frighten the children. "He had blue-black scales and talons large as a man. His demon commanders were hideous and had powers much like bhutas."

Naresh goes on in detail about Kur's attack. I half listen, more interested in my second helping of stew than remembering that battle.

His captivating narrative pulls me back.

"When the stars and moon had faded, and all seemed lost to the evernight, the Burner Rani turned Kur's venom against him and burned his snout and eye." The children gape at me. "Kalinda sacrificed her hand and saved us all."

My chewing slows. Naresh's retelling of the war is missing the most important part. Had I saved everyone, I would not be here in need of his help.

Maida jumps into the break in conversation. "Tinley, you should see the sleigh Bedros built me. It's large enough for a whole family."

Tinley's chin jerks up. "Are you with child?"

"Not yet." Maida clutches her belly and beams. Bedros glugs down half a glass of wine. "We want a son."

"With your temper and Bedros's indecisiveness?" Tinley asks.

"No," Maida protests. "With his big eyes and my powers." She centers her attention on me. "I inherited my mother's northern Aquifer abilities. We can manipulate ice and snow, unlike those half-Aquifiers from the south."

"Tinley and I have an Aquifier friend from the Southern Isles," I reply, sounding appropriately offended. "She's healed me many times."

"I'm certain southern Aquifiers are good for something," Maida counters, "but I couldn't bear having my powers be so limited."

"You better hope you're never in need of a good healer," Tinley mutters.

Bedros downs the last of his wine and dismisses himself from the table. Maida's hold on her chalice tenses. Frost creeps out from her grasp and shrouds the cup.

I lean into the chief's side. "Might we have a word?"

"Please." His eyes sparkle. "Let's escape."

Sosi fills the silence between her daughters with chatter about the weather. Naresh and I sneak off to the reception hall. I left my fur cloak behind, so he covers my shoulders with his vest, and we stroll down the corridor. The center of the icy floors is textured for traction, the outer areas gleaming pale blue.

"My daughter told me why you've come," Naresh says. "You're not the first to seek absolution from the woes of mortality by finding the paradise of the gods."

"I don't seek Ekur for myself."

"Tinley alerted me to General Naik's predicament. He asked you to do this for him?"

I pause, taken aback. "No."

"I thought not. Deven is a godly man. He knows you have more to lose in the under realm than your life. Why have you come, Kalinda? Besides finding the general, why do you seek Ekur?"

We walk in silence, Naresh waiting expectantly. A confession slips off my tongue.

"I cursed the gods. The night Deven was taken, I blamed them. As soon as I learned he was alive, I pled for forgiveness, but what if I don't get it?"

Naresh halts me. "Perhaps this is the fate the gods want for you and Deven."

"Or maybe seeking them out is what they want."

The chief absorbs my vehemence with a quiet "hmm," and we continue down the corridor.

"Mortals looking for Ekur are often fleeing a pain so vast and burdensome they believe only a god can liberate them." Naresh's voice extends between us, both temperate and persistent. "What relief do you seek?"

My deepest worry slips out. "What if they won't help me free Deven? What if they allowed Kur to take him to punish me for not wanting my throne?"

Staying on as Ashwin's kindred when I love Deven would have been wrong. But what if Anu thinks I defied him for choosing Deven over my throne? Nothing I do may be enough. I could give my all to liberate Deven, and the gods may still leave him in the under realm.

Or could our fates be tied? I cannot say how much of our lives is predestined, or what, if any, is within our control. I do know that whether I live in Samiya or the Turquoise Palace or the hills of the Alpanas, peace comes through following the gods' path for me. Finding Deven may be my godly purpose or it may *give* me purpose. My task is the same. I cannot leave him to suffer an eternal death, even if it risks my own standing with the gods.

"You attribute your circumstances too much to the gods and not enough to chance," says Naresh. "I was there as well. Kur took Deven on a whim. The gods did not plan that."

"Maybe you're right, but I still need a god to rescue him."

The chief's mouth tugs downward. "I see why my daughter favors your friendship. You're both stubborn as yaks."

I accept his comparison of me to Tinley as praise. "Can you direct me to Ekur?"

"Regrettably, I cannot, but I know who may. Our stories are passed on orally from one generation to the next. It is a gift to learn and teach them. Our matron, my mother, was training Tinley to memorize them, but my daughter set aside her orator duties to take to the skies."

"Is that why Tinley stays away?"

Chief Naresh halts before an open casement. Tiny fractures of ice glitter in the night sky. "Tinley's betrothed was killed in a tragic accident. He was to become the next chief and she his chieftess. Sosi and I raised him with our children. His death was a devastation to us all."

I have no words. Moons ago, when Tinley and I first met, I learned she had lost her intended through Indah. Tinley has never mentioned him. I assumed she was somewhat relieved to dodge an arranged marriage.

"The matron is ill and needs her rest," says Naresh. He does not include details of his mother's ailment, but his protectiveness suggests he worries about her recovery. "Tinley will take you to her tomorrow." He swivels toward his daughter at the end of the hall. She has my fur. We join her and I return the chief's vest. "Please show Kalinda to her chamber," he says.

Tinley shoves my cloak at me, and I scurry after her.

"Your mother and sister are . . . conversational."

"They're exhausting."

I scrounge up an optimistic reply. "Bedros is pleased you're home."

"Yes," Tinley says, "he is."

She enters a chamber on the main floor. A cozy fire blazes in the hearth, a bear rug laid out before it. More furs are piled on the bed. The furniture is constructed of ice, and the window and bedposts are etched with snowflakes, each unique and delicate.

I set down my satchel. "Thank you for bringing me here. I know how hard it is to survive loved ones. Our memories are strongest in the places we were happiest."

"Stop," Tinley says, low and direct. Her surliness is a poor, false front for her pain. I should have seen her grief before, recognized it and given it a name.

Before I can apologize or offer sympathy, she swivels and stalks out.

I drop onto the bed, too tired to dwell on her prickliness. The mountain of fur protects me from the hard, cold ice. I loosen the strap around my wrist and release my prosthesis. Turning toward the hearth, I watch serpents dance in the flames.

Hello, my friend.

I extend my hand, and several flames disentangle from the nature-fire. The burning tendrils zip across the room and twirl above me. The fiery offshoots combine into a dragon no bigger than a lynx kitten.

Siva, as I named her, lands on top of me. I stroke her head, and she curls up on my stomach, crackling contentedly. On occasion, I summon Siva to keep me company while I wait for Deven. Her warmth soaks inside me, tinder for my soul-fire. I pet her long, thin back and pray I am on the eve of my own contentment.

9

ASHWIN

I am seven minutes late to supper. Captain Yatin and Pons sit in the lamplight beneath the pagoda, already into the wine. My effort to educate Natesa about my independence is squandered. She and the other women are not present.

"Where's everyone else?" I ask.

"Natesa likes to make an entrance," Yatin replies. He drinks from his chalice, his jacket unbuttoned. I cannot recall when I last saw him relaxing. Typically he is at the main gate directing the guards. "Two of my men are following Commander Lokesh as discussed. They'll report back when they uncover his employer."

Spying on Lokesh was my recommendation. Mercenaries are merely front men for another person's agenda. "How is our guard head count?"

"We can cover the day and evening watches," Yatin replies, sipping more wine.

His lack of specificity troubles me. Those under my command tread carefully in their reports, a practice retained from Tarek's reign. My father was intolerant of unsatisfactory news. "Captain, I would appreciate your evaluation on our drought of guards."

"Yatin gave his full report this morning," Pons replies. "You missed the meeting."

He refers to the appointment he reminded me of while I was with Kalinda. "I apologize for my absence and for my terseness with you, Pons. Captain, please repeat the foremost items."

Yatin clears his throat. "Another eight men have left to serve Commander Lokesh for higher wages. His operation must be funded by his employer."

A wealthy sponsor, no doubt. Structural repairs have depleted our coffers. Tarek was fair in his payment of his personal guard, perhaps his only reasonable decision as rajah, but I have already elevated wages to entice guards to stay. I cannot afford to increase them again.

"You could offer a short-term signing bonus for new guards," Pons suggests.

I do not like incentivizing my own men to serve me. Still, I must slow the depletion of our defenses. "Instruct the treasurer to find the coin to pay for the bonuses."

I drink down my water, then adjust the waist of my trousers pinching my sides.

Our female diners arrive, and all of us rise to greet them. Natesa regards my matching tunic and turban approvingly and then goes to Yatin. Indah joins Pons, leaving Gemi in the doorway.

She has traded her trousers for a crimson sari fringed with beadwork. A black comb pins up half her hair and the rest tumbles down her back. She still wears her shell earrings and necklace. Beneath the hem of her skirt, her feet are dyed with henna markings of the moon phases, the style in the Southern Isles, and her toenails are painted pink.

More noticeably, someone drew a henna line down her nose, a signal to all that she is intended to wed.

Brac enters next and in three big steps reaches Gemi. "Welcome, Princess. Wonderful to see you again."

The princess bobs into a curtsy. "Ambassador, Mathura and Chitt send their well wishes. They'll arrive later with my father."

"My mother does love a wedding."

"Don't we all?" Gemi's gaze flits to me. "Ashwin, you look handsome."

As Natesa goes around the table, she bumps me with her hip to further establish her dominance as my fashion delegate.

"Everyone sit," Indah says. "It isn't often Pons and I have an evening without Jala."

We kneel around the low, circular table under the pagoda. Indah refills the water and wine chalices, sending perfectly measured streams from pitchers and bottles. Servants bring a hookah on a tray. Brac picks up the pipe and draws in a puff of smoke.

He speaks as he exhales. "I didn't know I would be the only person without a companion, or I would have found one for the evening."

"Do you have someone in mind?" Natesa's arch tone implies she has thoughts on the matter.

"One or two ladies of court. They're on hold for the prince." Brac sets the hookah mouthpiece against his lower lip. "They're waiting for him to determine their fates."

I wince at his phrasing. "They can remain in the palace during the two-year interim after the wedding. I won't ask them to leave."

Servants set dishes of food before us. Yatin finishes his chalice of wine and yawns. Natesa leans against his side, also fatigued.

"What will happen after two years?" Brac inquires. "Will you retain them in your court or require that they resign?"

"Whatever is determined, I will not alter their way of life." This is the ranis' home, the place many of them bore and raised their children. I would never force them out.

Gemi adjusts the side pleats of her sari, disengaged from the conversation. Her arrival is the ideal pivot point.

"Princess Gemi, tell us more about you." The second I speak, I recognize my error. Out of everyone at the table, only Yatin and Natesa do not know her well. And myself, of course. Brac spent time with Gemi on his last visit to the isles, and Pons and Indah lived in Lestari at the palace with her for several years.

"I'm an instructor at an all-girls seminary," she says. "I studied higher learning under several prestigious sages. Now I teach language and reading."

"What are your favorite literary categories?" I ask, then quickly add, "I also like to read."

Natesa laughs stridently. "The prince would read constantly if he could."

Everyone around the table mutters in agreement. I am not offended or ashamed. A fascination with books is not a vice but a hobby.

"Reading is the gateway to learning," Gemi says, receptive to our shared interest. "My favorite categories to teach are animals and plants. The girls are eager to learn."

"Those are fascinating subjects to convey to children," I say.

Gemi casually runs her finger around the rim of her chalice. "I like to watch them discover new things. It gives them a deeper appreciation for our world."

Brac releases another puff of hookah smoke. "Ashwin, you should show the princess the library."

"Didn't you see it during your last visit?" I ask her.

"The door was pointed out on my initial tour," Gemi replies, "but I was not let in."

I give undue attention to the smoke curling upward. "I, ah, will have to correct that."

Gemi regards me closer. She may sense my offer is disingenuous. Everyone stays out of my library. It is the only place I am guaranteed solitude, and I want to keep it that way.

"Did you see more of the palace today?" I ask. The grounds were under construction and repair the last time Gemi visited. I worked long hours to ensure they were restored before her arrival.

"I did. Pons tried to complete our tour, but we only made it halfway."

"The princess spent too long in the gardens," Pons explains.

"You have lavender," Gemi says excitedly, "and birds we don't have in Lestari."

"You have no lavender in the Southern Isles?" Natesa asks.

"Our soil is too wet. Did you know if you run your hand over the flower stems they mark your skin with their scent?" She smells her hand and offers it to Natesa for a sniff.

I am too far across the table to smell. She seems disappointed that I do not get up, so I say, "I'll remember to try that next time I'm near lavender."

Indah and Pons's nursemaid appears at the courtyard door, bouncing a crying Jala. Indah goes to calm her child, but the infant is inconsolable. She returns and whispers to Pons. I overhear Kalinda's name, nothing more.

"We should put Jala down for bed," says Indah.

Pons bows. "Please excuse us, Your Majesties." The couple sets off. Before Jala's cries have faded, Natesa touches Yatin's cheek.

"We'll go too," she says. "This one needs to rest."

"We can stay, Little Lotus," Yatin replies before repressing another yawn.

"Go ahead, Captain." Although supper is unraveling, I will not deny them a respite.

"We'll have a welcome gathering for the viraji tomorrow," Natesa says. "The ranis are excited to meet you, Princess."

Her emphasis on "excited" alters the connotation. *Are* the ranis glad about the princess? Gemi misses Natesa's borderline wryness and thanks her. Natesa pulls on Yatin and they set off.

Silence fills the gazebo. Brac's long stare pushes me to say something. When I cannot think of anything worthwhile to discuss, he speaks to Gemi about his visit to Lestari. I am not jealous of their connection but do envy their easiness.

I twist my untouched wine chalice and munch on fried black mustard seeds. Kalinda's absence has left a hole inside me. I will wait for Deven tonight, though I am concerned my friends have both left Vanhi for good.

"What do you think, Ashwin?" Gemi asks. I meet her amused gaze. She knows I have not been listening. "What are your thoughts on bhutas displaying henna markings for identification?"

Lords, Brac must have told her about Lokesh's scheme. "The markings would further divide our people. What do you think?"

"I agree," Gemi says. "When is your next speech? You can contest the commander's proposal and set your people at ease."

I glance from her to Brac. "Speech?"

"His Majesty prefers to let the people learn by his example," Brac says.

His bland statement pokes at me. "I don't want to disrupt their exchange of ideas and solutions. Growth comes from higher intellects discussing the idealistic outcome of transitions."

"Higher intellects?" Brac snorts. "How is permitting mercenaries to rile up our citizens intelligent?"

My temperature rises. Brac is portraying me as a foolish idealist. The Southern Isles is a progressive nation where men and women are free to debate and discuss ideologies. Then the people may bring their concerns and philosophies to the datu for deliberation. After my short visit there last year, I was impressed by their nonviolent methods of initiating change.

"Datu Bulan believes every citizen should have a voice," says Gemi. "People should speak their minds without fear of retribution. But,

Ashwin, your people need to hear from you. They'll come together with your guidance."

A guard interrupts to whisper in Brac's ear. The Burner wipes his mouth and sets aside his napery. "Your Majesties, I'm needed elsewhere."

This must be pressing. Perhaps another issue arose with the protestors. I wait for Brac to allude to an explanation, but he takes his leave.

The servants deliver dessert, and Gemi piles a mountain of yogurt onto her plate. She dips her spoon into the creaminess and slips it in her mouth. Her eyes shut and her shoulders drop in a full sigh. Her delight is so infectious that although I prefer fried bread drizzled in honey for my final course, my own yogurt tastes sweeter than usual. She pauses to drink her wine and empties her chalice. I refill it for her.

"You haven't touched yours," she says, gesturing at my cup.

"I don't drink." Rajah Tarek carried a flask with him and regularly stank of spirits.

Gemi pushes her tongue to the side in amusement. "Pretend to be grateful when my father gives you a prized bottle of apong as your groom's gift."

"I'll try," I say on a chuckle.

She sets down her spoon and fingers her napery. "Thank you for receiving me early. You must want to know why I came."

"I have wondered."

"The letters we exchanged were polite but formal, and your marriage proposal was . . . succinct."

I bristle at her thinly restrained criticism. "Your father and I negotiated until we felt the terms were fair."

"How could I have refused?" she replies dryly.

I tug at my scratchy collar. "I could have reworded my intentions. My apologies for hurting your feelings."

"You didn't," she replies swiftly. "I was used to something else. My parents wed for love. After my mother passed away, my father hasn't remarried. Your culture has different views and customs." She twists her earring. I wonder if she realizes her accent thickens when she speaks of her home. "Your marriage proposal helped me to interpret our nuptials for what they are—a binding of unions. Our negotiations are fair, but my own needs were omitted from the dialogue."

I sharpen my attention on her. In a roundabout way, she has reopened negotiations. "What do you wish to include in our agreement?"

"I want to train with the sister warriors." Gemi stirs her finger through the last of the yogurt on her plate. "My father treated me like a fragile shell, and my people . . . The throne intimidates others. The rector at the seminary let me teach without asking for my qualifications. Even though I have the aptitude, the other teachers did not receive me well." She quits drawing in her yogurt and looks up. "People either are too polite and pretend to like you when they don't or they're harder on you than they would be on others. Proximity to power unnerves many."

"So you've come to train?" Her desire to teach and be taught intrigues me. I assumed she was content in her authority in Lestari.

Gemi sets her elbows on the table and licks the yogurt from her finger. "My training focused on my Trembler abilities. As kindred, it's important that I learn *your* ways."

No one could accuse Gemi of complacency. The first time we met she defied her father and coerced herself into a position in the war. She must have anticipated I would allow this latest request, but I am not the one she must convince.

"The ranis are tough to impress," I hedge. "They're rank tournament champions with no tolerance for weakness."

"I'll work as hard as they require."

I recognize her expression. A woman wears it when she has made up her mind. Kalinda and Natesa use it daily. However, I worry Gemi has hinged her happiness in Vanhi on gaining the sister warriors' approval. "I'll speak to the ranis about your training."

"Thank you. I knew you would understand."

Her pale-gold eyes glitter. Even her skin has an iridescence that is riveting.

I lean across the table toward her, transfixed.

Brac stalks back in. "Pardon the interruption. Ashwin, you're needed in the infirmary."

I puzzle out his summons. The only patient in the infirmary is the battered guard.

"Gemi," I say, "please excuse us. Help yourself to the rest of the yogurt." I wave and follow Brac out.

He ducks through passageways and lantern-lit corridors. We arrive at the infirmary moments later. Healer Baka waits outside.

"He just passed on," she says. "We did all we could, Your Majesty."

I sweep past her. The soldier lies propped up on his bed, his lips possessed by a disturbing colorlessness. He was young, not much older than me. "What happened?"

"He was bleeding inside his head. Indah tried to stop it, but nothing could be done."

"His family?" I ask, and Healer Baka defers to Brac.

"A comrade told us that his mother, a widow, lives across the desert." Brac's voice coarsens. "We haven't notified her of the accident yet."

The soldier's limp hand is lukewarm. His final moments of consciousness must have been horrifying. Beaten to death in the streets of his own city, by his own people. For what purpose? To protest my choice of kindred, my trust of bhutas, my dissimilarities to my father?

"Thank you for not letting him be alone," I push out.

"Anu has him now." Healer Baka covers the man's face with his blanket. "I summoned a brother to bless the body. Would you like to stay?"

My pulse slows, the thuds in my chest steady pangs. "I need to do something first. I'll return soon for the Prayer of Rest." I start out and Brac falls into step alongside me.

"Lokesh must be stopped," he says. "Send me to silence him."

I usher Brac from the infirmary faster. I will not discuss retaliation in front of the still-warm body. "And do what?" Brac may be skilled at surveillance and scorching people to dust in battle, but he is no cold-blooded killer.

"I'll leave him in the desert and let Anu have his wrath," he rumbles.

"Tarek may have employed those tactics, but I will not."

"Your father would not have let an innocent guard die without recompense." Brac's heated words barrel down the corridor into the obscure corners where my sire's memories are entrenched. "I'm not a proponent of your father's policies, but you should understand why he ruled as he did and not choose the opposite path simply because you believe it's better."

The ambassador's second admonishment of the day is two too many.

"My methods aren't up for debate." I hold strong against Brac's disapproval. He did not survive the near extermination of his people because he is irrational. With Kalinda's parting and Lokesh's threats, this has been a wearisome day for us both. "Lokesh will face recourse, but his removal now would turn him into a martyr. We must find his employer and cut off his profits. Without earnings, the mercenaries will abandon Lokesh forthwith."

"Your Majesty, call back the spies following him and send me." At my protracted stare, Brac adds, "Son of a scorpion, I won't hurt him . . . much."

I disregard his warped humor. "Find out who Lokesh is working for and why he's doing this. A man like the commander is after more than treasure."

Brac accepts the task. I set off to inform Yatin of the fallen soldier. Afterward, before I return for the Prayer of Rest, I will pen a condolence letter to the deceased's mother and break her heart.

10

DEVEN

I have become an expert at seeing in the dark. During the mortal realm's daylight hours, the sky of the under realm lightens to elephant gray. At night, those same shadows deepen to stone and ice, and the narrow roadways splinter off like stairways into the sky. Some are dead ends, while others lead travelers right back to where they started.

One path, just one, leads me to Kali's chamber.

Using a needle that I snapped off the thorn tree, I etch the ivory hilt of my janbiya dagger. The long handle of my weapon already reads: 1ST RIGHT. 6TH LEFT. RIGHT AT FORK.

I start the next instruction. 200 PACES, THEN LEFT.

The thicket I hide in crouches up to the Road of Bone. The bones, taller than any man, are laid out in a path, resembling the rib cage of a sea monster. I imagine the primeval creature was a casualty in the premortal war between the saltwater-goddess Tiamat and her son, Anu. This grisly roadway is the only thoroughfare in and out of the city in the distance. Other pathways form at night, but all lead back to the City of the Dead.

Nothing travels the road now. As far as I can see, the nocturnal wanderers that dwell here are dead. I am the only living thing. To keep it that way, I scratch the hilt harder.

Closer to the city, Kur's serpentine tail lies outside his cave. His rumbling snores resound from the towering entry. I have not seen him leave his abode since he entrapped me in the under realm. I remember the war in the mountains, trying to save Kali, and winds sweeping us into the lake. After I failed to reach her in the waves, I recall little except shocking cold, then waking in a fallow field nearby. Kur had disappeared to his lair. He must have assumed I was dead or would be soon.

I pause carving the handle. *200 paces, then . . . was it right or left?* To remind myself, I rub the inscription at the top.

PATH HOME

Going up to the mortal realm is akin to surfacing for air. This inscription on my dagger will ensure I do not forget the complicated pathway to Brac and my mother, to Natesa and Yatin, to Kali. My friends and family are my purpose for enduring, but the route to the mortal realm is becoming harder to remember. This place, this pervasive darkness, eats away at me one day at a time.

I have been stuck in the evernight without a reprieve for too long. For two nights in a row, I have tried to go home. The night before last, Kur summoned his top commanders from the city to his lair. I recognized Asag, Lilu, and Edimmu from our battle on the mountaintop and from their warped forms of bhuta powers. The paths that lead to the mortal realm are on the other end of the Road of Bone. To get there, I would have had to violate one of my survival rules: never sneak past Kur's lair at night.

Kur's minions finally returned to the city this morning. I do not trust this change in their behavior. They have never visited their ruler all at once. Though I have tried to puzzle out the purpose, I have been left with more answers than questions and a deeper urge to find a way out of here for good.

A branch creaks overhead. I glance up at a crow perching in my tree, my janbiya in my fist. The feathers on the crow's wings molt, its bony legs cracked and bleeding.

From what I have gathered, when spirits of animals or souls enter the under realm, they are less distinct in form. Within hours of dwelling in the shadows, they harden to physical beings once more. They are more corpse than flesh, as if they were put back into their rotting bodies.

The brethren teach that death is not the end. This is not what they meant.

I shrink toward the ground, my senses twitchy. The crow takes no interest in me, but fear is useful. Fear means I am still myself. When I am numb to the terrors of this place, the Void will own me.

11

KALINDA

My grumbling stomach draws me to the great hall for breakfast. Servants cook pots of spiced rice over the hearth fire. Maida sits at the long table alone, knitting.

"May I join you?" I ask.

She scans the empty table. "I don't know if there's room." Her lips turn upward.

Unexpected. She has a sense of humor.

I plunk down across from her. A server delivers me a bowl of steaming rice pudding that smells of rose water and cardamom. My first bite sends delicious warmth into my belly.

"What are you knitting?" I ask.

Maida holds up a partially completed infant's cap. "My grandmother says no woman fulfills her purpose without preparation."

She must really want a child. I have never, not once, felt such an inclination, though I expect someday that may change. Deven would be a good father.

The sentiment comes at me without forethought, and I immediately suffer retribution.

Gods, I miss him.

As predicted, Deven did not visit me last night. My estimation that he can only find his way to my bedchamber in the Turquoise Palace may be accurate.

I tap my toe while I eat and glance at the door often, hoping for Tinley. Maida's knitting needles click together. Upon another glance, I notice they are ice picks.

"Did you sleep well in my sister's room?" she asks.

"That was Tinley's bedchamber?"

"You didn't displace her. She sleeps in the aviary." Maida eyes me again. "You and my sister are friends. Tinley rarely makes friends."

"You're friends, aren't you?"

"We're sisters. That's different."

Why can they not be both? Maida and Tinley share a sense of irritability, so I keep quiet. I do not want to get caught between their tempers.

Deep laughter carries through the hall. Chief Naresh and Tinley saunter in, joking with each other, and join us at the table. Tinley's tangled hair is windswept and her eyes aglow.

"Where have you been?" Maida asks. "I've been entertaining our guest alone."

I peer sidelong at her. I did not realize my company was such a burden.

"We flew to the mountains to watch the sunrise." Tinley bumps her shoulder into Naresh. "Father thought his falcon could outrun Chare."

"Your mahati is swift for a runt." He eats from a bowl that a servant puts before him.

Maida knits faster, her ice pick needles clicking furiously. "I'd like to go flying with you, Father."

"Hmm?" He glances from Tinley to her for clarification. "Oh, Maida. We can go flying anytime." Maida balls up the knit cap and drops it into her lap. "Were you warm last night, Kalinda?"

"Very," I reply. Siva kept me toasty. After I woke, I returned her to the hearth.

"Are you finished, Kalinda?" Tinley asks. "The matron is waiting."

Maida turns interested. "You're visiting Grandmother? May I join you?"

"Not this time, little sister." Tinley rises to go.

Maida fists her knitting needles. "Don't call me little. I'm married now."

"How could I forget?" Tinley retorts. "You remind me every five minutes."

"Now, now," drawls Chief Naresh. "Maida, let your sister go without you. You've had plenty of time alone with your grandmother. Let Tinley have hers."

Sadness creeps into his tone and drags down his expression. The matron must be more unwell than he disclosed.

Maida pushes to her feet. "You're right, Father. I'll visit Grandmother this afternoon, as I've done every day since she fell ill. *I* didn't abandon my family and duties." She storms off, the ball of yarn lagging after her.

"Make peace with her," Naresh quickly tells his eldest daughter.

"Spend more time with her," Tinley shoots back, and Naresh looks sheepish. Tinley tugs my sleeve to go.

Out in the corridor, Tinley stalks ahead. I skip to catch up. "Do you and your sister compete at everything?"

"She was always jealous that I would be chieftess. I thought she'd be content once she secured the title."

Maida seems to want her father's and sister's approval, but that may be oversimplifying years of discord. Tinley and I exit the palace and trudge across the snowy grounds. A shoveled path leads down an embankment to the rear of the palace. Rows of massive buildings lie in the gully. Behind the compound, pieces of turquoise ice shimmer beneath a dusting of snow.

I pause to absorb the view. The ice reminds me of my mother's daggers. "What is that?"

"Blue Lake. We fish for alpine trout here during the summer. When the water freezes, the ice turns that brilliant hue."

We side-foot down a slick trail to the compound. Long, low flat buildings, not too dissimilar in size to the elephant stables in Vanhi, compose the aviary. Between them, yaks bed down in pens and chew on alfalfa. Tinley slides open the door to the third building, and we go in.

Steam wafts through the high, open aviary. Lamplight shines from the rafters where a variety of smaller birds nest. The mahati falcons nestle below them in moss on the ground. I search for Chare, but she must be in another building.

Tinley directs me through the massive birds. Their huge eyes, the size of plates, follow our movements. A handful of stable hands add fresh moss to the nests and exchange the old water for fresh drink. In the center of the aviary, an old woman rests on a stool and cleans the talons of a mahati with a large brush. Behind her, a hot spring bubbles and steams. Two middle-aged women sit at a workbench off to the side.

"Matron Anoush," Tinley says, "Father said you shouldn't be working."

"I'll stop working when I die." The elderly woman looks up from her task. "If it isn't my wayward granddaughter. You missed your sister's wedding."

"So I've heard."

Matron Anoush harrumphs. "Should have been you."

I swivel on Tinley. The matron did not say Tinley should have been chieftess. Was she implying she should have wed Bedros?

Tinley waves a pointy nail at me. "Grandmother, this is Kalinda, former kindred of the Tarachand Empire."

Matron Anoush tips her chin higher. "You married Rajah Tarek." I nod. She judges me closer. "You killed him."

Tinley stills. We have not discussed my part in Tarek's demise. I cannot fathom how her grandmother knows, except that she is more perceptive. As I see no reason to lie, I nod again.

Anoush puckers her wrinkled lips and returns to grooming the bird, brushing the talons clean with great strokes.

I step into her line of sight. "Naresh said you can direct me to Ekur."

"I cannot."

Tinley's gaze flickers to mine and back to her grandmother. "But you know how to get there?"

"Of a sort." Anoush's brushstrokes slow, her old, veiny hand shaking. She drops the brush and clutches her chest, as though she is pushing air inside her. Tinley rushes to her side, as do the two women at the workbench.

"Let your aides take you to lie down," Tinley says.

"Do that, and I'll never get up." Anoush clutches at her granddaughter. "I have someone for the Burner Rani to meet." The aides move back. Tinley supports her grandmother, and they shuffle to the other side of the hot springs. An ivory egg, bigger than my head, is snuggled in the moss. "The mother wouldn't keep this one in her nest. Tried to roll it into the hot springs."

"Mahatis are territorial," Tinley explains. "Chare is in another aviary. This flock would tear her apart."

"But this is their own egg," I say.

"See the crack?" Anoush points to a tiny zigzag on the shell. "The mother noticed it was damaged and saw fit to do away with the egg. She reserves her care for her other hatchlings. They all broke out of their shells this morning. This one has been trying since last night. She has to get out on her own, or she'll never have the strength to survive."

I crouch down and listen to the bird's pecking. "How do you know it's female?"

"The female eggs are yellow, and the male eggs are green. We raise the males until they learn to fly, then set them free. They're wilder than the females and more dangerous to tame. Every spring we release the females to mate. The domesticated ones return."

The pecking drums onward. I inspect the egg for breakage but see none. "You'll just leave her in there?"

Matron Anoush rubs the shell. "She has to want to live. We cannot decide that for her." She squints at me. "I cannot direct you to Ekur, but I can tell you who can."

A buzzing sensation travels across my skin.

I'm getting closer, Deven.

The matron's gaze bores into mine. "This journey will lead you into great darkness. When you finish, you won't be as you are now."

"I understand."

"You don't yet, but you will." Anoush flounders forward, shrinking into herself. Tinley helps her sit at the bank, and the matron slips her feet into the gurgling water. The aides come closer, yet give us distance. Anoush wheezes heavily. "Burner Rani, I have a tale for you. It is our most sacred story, passed on from matron to matron. I have not told even my granddaughter, but your journeys are entwined."

Anoush pulls a necklace from under the collar of her robe. A gold medallion, wide and thick as a coin, bears a strange design. "This is the emblem of the gods, the quad symbol. I have been told it marks the entrance to Ekur."

I study the emblem, a wave for the water-goddess, mountain peaks for the land-goddess, a flame for the fire-god, and a curl of wind for the sky-god. Together the crest resembles a shooting star.

"You see it, Burner Rani," Anoush remarks. "Some truths are never forgotten."

"Grandmother, what story does it tell?" Tinley says.

Anoush licks her dry lips. "Many generations ago, the gods lived among mortals. We served and obeyed their every command but were easily corrupted." She wheezes between every word. "Kur sought to enslave mortals for his own. When Anu saw we would fall, he sent mahati falcons, enemy to serpents, to fend off the demons. The mahatis stayed and we became their stewards."

Within the egg, the tapping increases. A beak punctures the shell. Anoush turns to watch the egg, and Tinley supports her. The hatchling pecks and pushes. A head pokes out, then a neck and wings. The bird wriggles from the tattered shell, squawking with her eyes closed and covered in white down.

"She's so little," I say, unable to imagine she will grow as big as the adults.

"Go on, Burner Rani," Anoush says. "Pick her up."

I scoop the mahati into my cupped hands. The hatchling beds down on my wooden palm. "One of her wings is shorter than the other."

"Her cracked shell must have caused it." Anoush clucks her tongue. "Shame."

"Grandmother," Tinley says, "what was the purpose of that story?"

Anoush runs a finger down the back of the fluffy falcon. "Mahatis ferry the souls of the deceased to the Beyond. To access the gods' holy home, the falcons pass through Ekur."

"What about the arches outside the city?" I ask.

"Our people built those for souls *returning* to our realm. A mahati can lead you to Ekur. Many have searched the mountains in vain. They went on foot when they should have gone by sky." Anoush sinks into Tinley's lap, winded.

Tinley strokes her white hair. "I'll ask the aides to take you to lie down now."

"Leave me be." Anoush removes the medallion. "For you, Burner Rani." Her whole arm quakes, so I accept the charm. "I have finished my purpose."

"What purpose, Grandmother?"

Anoush's rasps crackle into pants. "Moons ago, when I was very ill, I was visited by a god. He said the Burner Rani who dethroned the tyrant rajah would come, and after I directed her to Ekur, I could return to the Beyond. The god gave me the medallion to pass on to Kalinda, but he called her by another name."

I set down the hatchling and kneel by Anoush. "What name?"

"He called you"—she wheezes—"Cala."

I rock back. That is the name I heard while we were flying near Wolf's Peak.

"Tinley, you know all the stories now," Anoush says, patting her cheek. She coughs, each more painful sounding than the last. "Assist Kalinda. Go with her and find peace." Her head lolls against her granddaughter's middle.

"Grandmother? Grandmother?" Tinley listens, her ear over Anoush's mouth. The aides rush over. "She's breathing. We need to get her home. Someone fetch my father!"

A stable hand sprints off to find the chief. One of the aides feels Anoush's forehead.

"Why did you let her come here?" Tinley demands. "She should be in bed."

"Today started as a good day," an aide replies. "She was feeling well and insisted on meeting you and the Burner Rani. We couldn't persuade her otherwise."

Anoush does not strike me as someone who is easily swayed, yet I sympathize with Tinley's outrage. My gut has wound into tangles.

More stable hands arrive to lift the limp old woman. Tinley and the aides stay close as they carry Anoush out. I begin to follow them, but the hatchling squawks and squawks. Uncertain if the bird is safe to leave alone, I shove the medallion into my pocket and pick her up. The tiny falcon cozies into my prosthesis. I cradle her, needing her comfort more than she needs mine.

12

ASHWIN

The ranis and courtesans quiet as I enter the Tigress Pavilion. Few men are let into this den of sister warriors. As a rule, we are advised to stay out. This long-held custom originated from a general sense of propriety. Only Brac routinely defies it, but he has left to spy on Lokesh.

Eshana greets me, and Parisa follows her over. The other women—a mixture of sisters, temple wards, and former courtesans—chatter lowly, their stares on me. I swipe restless fingers through my hair. Why are they all dressed in training saris? And where are Natesa and Gemi?

"Your Majesty," Eshana gushes, "we weren't expecting you."

Parisa folds her arms across her chest. She wears her hair tied back, revealing the missing piece of her earlobe. A purple scar runs down her neck from the earlobe. Both were injuries sustained during her rank tournament.

"Is that aftershave?" Eshana asks. "Parisa, would you say it's cinnamon?"

Parisa turns up her nose. They must smell the cinnamon sweets I took from a bowl during my previous meeting. The last candy I ate is still on my breath.

Eshana drapes herself down my side. "Have you given more thought to that foot massage?"

"He doesn't want a massage from you," Parisa snaps. "He has his foreign viraji for that."

"Sssshhh . . ." Eshana pushes Parisa off to a corner. "You could be reprimanded."

"For what?" Parisa does not lower her voice. "An outsider cannot be our kindred. The rajah's first wife should be one of us."

Other women mumble in accord. Shyla appears at my side.

"Your Majesty, let's seat you." As she leads me away, she says, "Those two have been bickering nonstop. Parisa told everyone you'll wait two years to decide which of us, if any, will migrate to your court. Eshana insists you won't make us wait long."

We stop at the black-and-white-tiled fountain. Cushions are laid out opposite the weapons racks, and a sparring ring is marked on the training yard floor with chipped paint.

"Will you?" Shyla inquires. "Make us wait two years, I mean."

I have not told anyone, not even Kalinda, that I am developing a long-term solution for the women of the court. Before I present my proposal, I need to finish my research. Shyla does not want flimsy promises. She needs the truth. "Firstly, this will always be your home. I will never ask you and Rehan to leave. Secondly, I—"

Natesa and Gemi enter the pavilion, and I lose my stream of thought. Kohl lines Gemi's eyes, and her lips are dyed a daring red. Her hair is partially braided and circled around her head in a crown while the lower half flows down her back. The compromise between the ranis' customary loose locks and the courtesans' single, thick braids is striking. She fits in with a black training sari, wrapped so the skirt sweeps through her legs and tucks into the back of her waist. Our women don this fashion for ease of movement when they spar. Gemi could have accomplished the same freedom in the trousers she regularly wears, but she wore the Tarachandian traditional garb.

I take her clammy fingers in mine and guide her to the floor cushion on my right. Shyla occupies the one to my left. Everyone else kneels as well. None of the women invite my viraji's attention with a jubilant welcome.

"Everyone is so quiet," Gemi whispers to me.

"You're doing well."

Natesa stands in the center of the training pavilion. She outglows everyone in a tangerine sari with fuchsia embroidery. "Welcome to the arrival celebration for Princess Gemi of the Southern Isles. We will open with a sparring demonstration. Viraji, we will now introduce the wards of the Samiya Temple."

Pairs of girls, between ages eight and sixteen, rush into the training section. They confront their companions with bamboo staffs and lift their weapons at the ready. Natesa claps and the show commences.

The girls sidestep and swing their staffs in a choreographed dance of striking and evading. Gemi observes, fully absorbed. One by one, each skirmish brings about a victor. We applaud them, and the wards scurry off.

The bhuta trainees run into the area next. Indah, who must have been waiting with them elsewhere, instructs her charges.

"Bhutas ready!"

The children bend into their knees. Giza and Basma, the Burner sisters, cast flames above our heads. I jump, concerned that the girls might inadvertently char us, and startle Gemi. We both exchange a nervous laugh.

The Galers stream wind at the flames and arc them higher. The Aquifiers steal water from the fountain and propel streams at the fire. Steam bursts above our heads, and, in unison, the floor rumbles from the Tremblers' collective stomp.

All goes still.

Gemi begins the ovation. In Lestari, bhuta powers are displayed for entertainment, but the ranis and courtesans wear dazed expressions. I clap and some of them applaud half-heartedly.

The bhuta children dash off, and Shyla enters the sparring ring.

"Sister warriors," she says, "select your weapons."

Several ranis in the audience go to the weapons racks. Once they have picked their weapon of choice, they line up across the pavilion.

"As daughters of the land-goddess Ki," Shyla says, "we face each other in battle to prove our honor, godly virtue, and strength. The ranis of Tarachand have a rich history of defending their families and homeland. We now ask the viraji to step forward." Gemi complies at once, and Shyla squares off with her. "As first wife and kindred, you will represent us to the world. Will you defend our families and homeland?"

"I will," Gemi vows, shoulders back, chin high.

"Will you fight now?" questions Shyla.

I stiffen in protest. Natesa must have suspected this is where Gemi's introduction would lead and dressed her appropriately.

"Yes." Gemi beckons Indah. The Aquifier takes a trident from the weapons rack and gives it to the princess.

"Who will spar with the viraji?" Shyla asks the crowd.

"Me." Parisa stalks forward with a khanda. Her lithe movements are practiced and powerful. For a moment, I see Gemi's confidence flicker.

"Competitors will spar until first down," says Shyla, retreating from the ring. "Either one concedes if she breaches the circle. No powers allowed."

"I'll compete fairly," Gemi replies, holding the trident across her chest.

I assess the audience for any signs of alarm. No one appears to think this is an antagonistic welcome. Their hierarchy remains with or without the rank tournaments. My father's ruthless legacy lives on.

Gemi lunges first. Parisa evades and swings. My muscles twitch in anticipation of either one sustaining a hit. Gemi blocks with the center of her trident, and Parisa shoves her back.

"What happened to your ear?" Gemi asks.

"I avoided a khanda blow to my skull." Parisa aims her blade at my viraji while they circle each other. "Do you have any scars?"

"One on my thigh. I fell out of a tree when I was a child."

"A tree." Parisa laughs. Most of the spectators snicker as well. Gemi's complexion deepens to scarlet. "I'll give you a scar to be proud of."

Parisa hacks at Gemi, forcing her to the rim of the ring. My viraji's heel nears the line. Using both arms, she flings Parisa back. Gemi jabs the trident's triple prongs at the rani and sweeps the long end under her feet. Parisa hits the floor on her bottom, sitting upright. Gemi lowers the prongs over her neck. Scars or not, she is spry for a novice fighter.

Parisa is still in the match. She whacks Gemi's ankle with the blunt end of the sword. Gemi hobbles back, and Parisa hops up and kicks her in the knee. Gemi drops forward. Parisa goes behind her and knocks her in the head with her hilt. Gemi falls onto all fours.

I begin to stand, but Natesa motions me to stay back.

Parisa punches Gemi hard in the chin. My viraji falls into the center of the sparring ring, abdomen down. Parisa lowers the tip of her blade to the back of Gemi's head, which bleeds from an earlier strike.

"First down," Parisa says. Gemi rolls onto her back and looks up at the rani. "You'll have to try harder to become our kindred."

"Enough," I interject.

Parisa falls back. She sets her khanda on the rack and prowls out of the pavilion.

Gemi picks herself up and retrieves her trident. She approaches the line of waiting opponents. "Next," she says.

"One test will suffice," I say.

"I'll meet any challenger." She hoists her trident at the ready. "Who's next?"

None answer. They will not defy me.

Natesa slides between Gemi and the armed women. "This concludes our demonstration. We will now partake of fried breads and chilled wine in the dining terrace." She guffaws nervously.

The women rack their blades and disband.

Gemi marches over to me and steels her voice. "You undermined me. You cannot defend me or they'll always view me as an outsider."

Her rosy complexion and smoldering eyes twist my tongue. "One test of skill was sufficient. You aren't obligated to perform another."

"But I *am*," she hisses. "They must learn to trust me or I cannot lead." She stomps to Indah, her knuckles white on the trident. The Aquifier tends to her head wound.

"She's riveting," Shyla says.

Heat pushes up my neck. "Gemi wasn't raised as we were. To her, these rituals are strange."

"Yet she's shown she's capable of rising to our standards." Shyla touches my forearm. "Most of us didn't receive a happy welcome upon our arrival, but few of us had the same innocence."

I have also sensed Gemi's goodness. She has not been jaded by the brutality of the empire. Training as a sister warrior will evolve her fighting skills, but what attributes will she relinquish for that knowledge? Is she doing this for herself, her peers, or for me?

"She wants a sister warrior to train her," I say. "Will you do it? I trust you'll be kind."

Shyla blushes. "It would be my honor."

"Your Majesty?" Pons calls from the doorway. I excuse myself to meet him. "Captain Yatin asked me to notify you that protestors have rallied by the river. At least two hundred, and their numbers are expanding."

I leave the pavilion with Pons and go to an open casement that overlooks the city. People have clustered at the main riverbank. Lords, I hope Gemi does not hear of this.

"Where is the captain?" I ask.

"At the gate. Would you like me to escort you?"

"I'll find my way."

I get turned around twice. Once in a servants' passageway, staggering a kitchen server, and again in the garden. (In my defense, the gardener clipped back the rhododendron trees, which were my previous marker.)

"Your Majesty," Captain Yatin says, meeting me outside the guardhouse, "we must take you inside. The protestors are marching this way."

Chanting resounds from the city. "Return to tradition!"

The protestors round the bend in the road to the main gate. Commander Lokesh leads the parade on his horse. He slouches in the saddle, relaxed in his arrogance, as the people intone.

Yatin ushers me to the palace entry steps. The commander halts at the gate. His headscarf masks his face except for his bold stare.

Anger scalds my tongue. Who is he to come to my door and terrorize me?

I revolve from Yatin and stride to the gate. With each step, the cries of the mob mount. Commander Lokesh signals for quiet, and the protestors silence. Several of my former soldiers and guards are mixed into the crowd.

"You've disobeyed a direct order, Lokesh."

"As I'm no longer your commander, I elected to ignore it." His headscarf does little to muffle his voice, which rings clear across the expanse.

I endeavor to keep my words between us. "Call this off."

"These people have gathered on their own. I'm merely their figurehead."

I grasp the bars. "Because of your lies, they beat a soldier to death."

"I regret that you've lost another defender, but his demise could have been prevented had you listened to your people." Lokesh goes on, plainspoken and loud. "We disapprove of a bhuta foreigner as our rani and will reject her as our kindred."

Countless men stomp in accord. A cloud of dust drifts up and flows through the bars.

"You're too shortsighted." I drop my voice. My anger makes my every word crisp and clear. "Princess Gemi brings with her the assurance of fair trade, ample treasuries, and naval protection for generations to come. This union will provide us with the resources to rebuild stronger than ever. No other rajah has made a more profitable alliance."

"Then you don't wed for love," states the commander. "If you want what's best for Tarachand, then select a rani from the existing court. A rani who battled for her throne and earned our respect."

His brazenness stokes my temper. "This is my decision. Accept my choice and advise your followers to do the same."

Lokesh's attention strays behind me and his tone darkens. "Someday you won't have bhutas to hide behind. Then what will you be?"

I follow his gaze to the palace. Gemi and Indah are watching from a balcony. Yet again I appear to rely upon my bhuta allies for compliance. I push away from the bars. "That's enough, Commander. We're done here."

"Heed my warning, Prince," Lokesh says. He spits through the bars to punctuate his distaste for me and then steers his horse around and saunters off.

The crowd disbands, casting glowers in my direction. I recheck the balcony. Indah and Gemi have returned inside. How long was my viraji standing there?

Yatin enters my peripheral vision and waits for my order.

"How many men do you estimate are in Lokesh's ranks?" I ask.

"Approximately a hundred and fifty. Close to our same number of palace guards." Yatin scratches his bristly chin. "A dozen men joined after they heard about the bonus, but three more defected in the middle of the night."

Lokesh continues to fatten his support while we bleed ours. This public spectacle was for intimidation. Now that he has a taste for humiliating me, his behavior may escalate.

"Double the guards on watch. I don't care where you find the men, just do it. I want to know if Lokesh comes anywhere near the palace." I relax my taut jaw. "And ask Pons to send for Brac. We need to talk."

I march inside and nearly trip over two girls playing marbles in the entry hall. How in the gods' names did Tarek live with people constantly underfoot? I sidestep around them and head for the only place in the palace where I can be alone.

13

KALINDA

Wind rages against the village of mourners trekking up from Teigra. They have sleighs, but it is their ritual to carry the dead on foot to their resting place. *A burial procession,* Chief Naresh called it when he told me his mother had passed on. He said the matron slipped away quietly, surrounded by her family and friends.

We crest the snowy hill. Two guards lay the body wrapped in cloth on top of an altar, a slab of stone on stacked rocks. The afternoon sun, partly veiled behind a horde of clouds, gives no warmth over the winter landscape. Chief Naresh and Tinley lean together. Maida and Bedros comfort each other, and Sosi holds her younger children.

Snow flurries zip around us in unnatural sideways patterns, a manifestation of Maida's or Sosi's northern Aquifier powers. I watch from outside the group, my rabbit fur shielding me from the worst of the cold. Anoush's final words to me burrow into my mind.

He called you Cala . . .

A spiritual leader in white robes uncovers the body, preparing it for excarnation. She speaks in a language I do not recognize. Tinley warned me beforehand that they leave their deceased open to the elements to decompose and serve as carrion to scavenging animals, including wild mahati. The grisly process suits their belief that the falcons take hold of the soul during their feeding and carry the departed to the Beyond. The only part that is like ours in Tarachand is that their deceased also face upward toward the sky.

The leader stops singing and steps away from the altar. Anoush's remains collect snowflakes. Tinley buries her face in her father's cloak. He tries to embrace her, but she lets him go and speeds off downhill, her feet packing down snow.

Maida and Bedros leave next, then Sosi follows with her younger children. One after another, everyone else returns to the city until the chief and I are alone.

"My mother wanted our whole family there with her when she passed," Naresh says. "It was her last wish. She held out until Tinley came home."

Tinley must not have told her father about our conversation. "Did Anoush ever mention a godly medallion?"

"She may have. My mother's head brimmed with stories. She could spin a tale unlike any other. Her words inspired people to strive for betterment." He hunches his shoulders. "She will be missed."

Naresh kneels in the powdery snow before the altar. I fist the medallion in my pocket. Anoush believed a god held her in this life though she was ready to pass on. Would a deity be so cruel? Or was that the final story she wished to tell?

A powerful gust blows me back a pace. In the distance, the Crystal Palace captures the sparse sunshine and glints in defiance of the moody clouds. I select the spires as my beacon and set out for Teigra.

I enter the aviary and slide the door shut. Steam from the hot springs melts the snow on my clothes as I start for the middle of the longhouse. A man's voice halts me.

"Please don't leave again. Your family needs you. *I* need you."

"I cannot stay," Tinley answers.

The mahati falcon bedded down nearest me pops open an eye. I peek around him. Tinley and Bedros stand close.

"Tinley, I love you."

"You should not say that." She wields no anger but an undercurrent of disgust. "We're not children anymore. Your marriage to Maida is sanctified by the gods. As next chief, you must honor your vows."

I lean forward and peer through the mist wafting off the hot springs. My movement draws the attention of the hatchling in her nest. She cranes her head but does not spot me.

"Why didn't you come?" Bedros asks, his thumb brushing Tinley's chin. "You could have contested my betrothal."

"My sister loves you. I couldn't do that to her."

"Maida was never for me, just as my brother was never for you."

Brother? Bedros's brother was Tinley's betrothed?

"We'll go to Naresh," Bedros insists.

"He cannot undo your vows." Tinley stalks out of my line of sight.

"I waited for you," Bedros counters, disappearing after her.

My eavesdropping has gone on long enough. I back up for the door. The hatchling sees me and squawks shrilly. I shush her, but she wails on and on. I hurry over and scoop her up. She stops screeching. *Little imp.*

"I waited for you on my wedding day," Bedros rants at Tinley, both out of sight. I move backward with the falcon, and they enter my view again. "Even as I stood before your sister, I wished to Enlil you would come."

"I couldn't!" Tinley's shout rouses the mahatis. They ruffle their feathers and turn their attention to the couple. "Our fates cannot be changed. The gods care nothing for our desires. Heart's wishes are for fools."

"Then I'm a fool." He springs at Tinley to kiss her.

She pushes him off. "Leave before I tell my sister and father."

Bedros's whole body hardens. She balls her fists. He defies her for two breaths . . . then three. She persists, so he trudges off.

Tinley slumps over and kicks at a mound of moss. I cradle the hatchling and wait for an appropriate amount of time before I step out. Many moments pass. When I emerge, Tinley looks right at me.

"Bedros is a fool." She stomps to a workbench. "He's married to my sister."

"If he weren't, would you be together?"

"No." Tinley shoves supplies into a leather satchel.

I close in on her, still carrying the hatchling. "How did your betrothed die?"

"His name was Haziq." Tinley latches the bag and ties her crossbow to it. When she finishes, she has composed her frustration. "The wild falcons will arrive soon."

I gesture at their docile counterparts. "Why not take one of these?"

"These belong to us. The free ones hail the gods." She throws her bag over her shoulder. "We must go. Put the hatchling back."

I set the baby bird in her nest and she squawks loudly. "I think she's afraid. What do we do?"

"She'll adjust to your being gone soon. Our falconers will raise her until she's old enough to fly with you."

"Fly with me where?"

"Wherever you like," Tinley answers. "My grandmother wanted you to have her."

"Have her?" I sound like a dolt, repeating her replies.

"Mahatis imprint on the first person who holds them. We only touch the male hatchlings after they learn to fly. She's connected to you."

I run my finger down the hatchling's bony head. "She's *mine?*"

"She'll learn to fly in a few short weeks. In about a year, she'll grow large enough to carry a rider. What will you name her?"

Nothing comes to thought. "Must I decide now?"

"It's your bird." Tinley starts for the door. "Come along. Ignore her weeping."

The falcon is indeed shedding tears. Each one compounds my regret.

"I'll return for you," I say, though I have no idea what I will do with a full-grown mahati. "Behave for your caretakers and get along with the other falcons."

Tinley's eyebrows shoot up. "Impressive mothering."

The falcon squawks forlornly. I nearly weaken, but Tinley grabs me and keeps me on course.

"They must learn who's in charge," she says. At the exit, her clutch lessens. "She'll be well cared for, Kalinda."

Under the thickening clouds, we enter a yak pen. A driver is harnessing a pair of yaks to a sleigh. Sosi waits by him, tugging on leather mittens.

Tinley pulls up short. "Mother, Kalinda and I are leaving."

"I'm taking you to the burial site." Sosi climbs into the sleigh and picks up the reins.

Tinley curses under her breath and gets on. I ride beside my friend. Sosi spreads a red wool blanket across our laps and leads the yak team past the Crystal Palace and out of Teigra. The sleigh glides over the snow and ice with minimal joggling.

"Your sister was hurt when you didn't attend her wedding," Sosi says to her daughter.

Tinley groans. "You made that more than clear, Mother."

"Maida loves Bedros. He's wrong to have eyes for you."

"I'm sorry, I truly am, but I cannot change what happened. I can only stay away."

Maida's anger against Tinley takes a firmer shape in my mind. Paljorians are betrothed from infancy . . . which means Bedros was intended to wed Maida while he and Tinley were together.

Sosi's eyes glow in the late-afternoon light. "You cannot run forever, Tinley. It's unfair to your father and me and your sister. Maida wants you to help her lead."

Tinley sniffs in derision. "She doesn't need my help."

"If you believe that, then you've been gone too long," replies Sosi. "We all mourned Haziq. I know your heart was broken, but have you considered how the rest of us felt? We lost more than Haziq. We lost you."

Tinley stares stonily at the wintry hills. Her manifested winds mount at our back to assist the craft up the snowy rise. The yaks pull the sleigh to a stop near the burial site. Birds of prey and arctic foxes scatter from the altar. I hop down, careful not to glance at Anoush's remains.

"Thank you," I say to the chieftess.

Sosi bows her head. "Let the sky lead you, the land ground you, the fire cleanse you, and the water feed you, Burner Rani."

Tinley steps out after me. "Mother, will you look after Chare while I'm gone? She gets lonely when I'm away."

"I will." Sosi kisses her daughter's forehead. "Come home soon."

"Tell Father good-bye for me," Tinley replies. We move from the path of the sleigh, and Sosi journeys back. Tinley treads to an outcropping and waves me over. We lie down on our bellies behind two rocks. Our white furs camouflage us from above, and we have a direct view of the altar.

Night unfolds across the horizon. The muffled splatter of snowflakes rests upon us, a quiet attack that slowly collects on our cloaks. Tinley leaves her crossbow strapped to her back and tilts an ear to the wind. I prop my elbows on the ground so I can see through the gap in the rocks and monitor the stone altar and surrounding hilltop.

"What now?" I ask.

Tinley answers, her resolve ringing through. "We wait."

14

ASHWIN

The door squeaks open. I pay closer attention to my book, *The Imperial Guard: A History of Tarachand's Elite Forces*, and ignore my intruder.

Footsteps approach. They pause.

"There you are." Brac peers up at me seated atop the bookcase, his head cocked to the side. "Should you be up there? What if you fall?"

I slam the book shut. "Did you bring your report, Ambassador?"

"Come down and I'll deliver it to you."

Why must everyone have an ultimatum? I jump to the floor beside the discarded pile of my boots, tunic jacket, and belt. They came off the second I was alone in my library. "Tell me what you've learned about Lokesh."

"Not much to tell." Brac helps himself to an untouched decanter of apong. He bypasses the dusty cups and takes a swig from the bottle. After he swallows, he gives me an empty envelope addressed to Commander Lokesh. "I managed to lift this from his hut. He must be corresponding with his employer by dispatch to circumvent Pons tracking their movements."

"We still know nothing," I say, tossing the envelope aside.

Brac downs another pull from the bottle. "Captain Yatin secured the palace. After your impromptu exchange with Lokesh, the men were dissatisfied. They thought you should have spoken up on behalf of your loyalists. Yet another guard has turned in his khanda and left."

"To serve the commander?"

"Does it matter?" Brac's unruly coppery hair falls into his defiant gaze. "Yatin has our guards pulling double shifts. He thought for a time that he might have to employ the ranis to stand in. From here on out, don't engage Lokesh. Let us manage him."

I drop my book on a side table. "Any word from Kalinda?"

"None." Brac puts down the apong bottle. He needs a shave, a trip to the bathhouse, and a clean change of clothes. "We must keep our focus. I suspect Lokesh is hiding something. Something he really doesn't want us to find out. I'll keep following him. Until the datu and navy arrive, you and every member of the imperial court must not leave the palace."

My own city, my home, is unsafe for me. Lokesh's lies have cultivated fast and farther than I anticipated. I press my fists into the table. "If you think so."

"I do." Brac squeezes my shoulder. "This is a temporary reprieve. Enjoy it."

What is there to enjoy? I have the duties of rajah without the official title. This is not a reprieve from my responsibilities. This is detention for not silencing Lokesh when I had the opportunity. "Thank you for your report, Ambassador."

Brac recognizes he has been discharged and bids me good night.

I drop into a lounge cushion and resume my study about the imperial guard. The words soon blur into a misshapen jumble on the page, and the quiet library closes in around me. I rub my sore eyes and look up from the text. Down the way, in the child-studies section, one of my shelves has been disturbed. From this angle, I see a line of dust where a book once was. I rise and inspect the gap in the bookcase.

Someone was in my library.

It is difficult to determine which text is missing. Based on the section it was taken from, a couple suspected intruders come to mind. One more than the others.

I clap my book shut and reshelf it on the way out.

By some mercy, I locate the nursery on my first try. The nursemaids have put the little ones to bed and turned the lamps down low. Nursemaid Sunsee travels between the rows of beds, tucking in the squirrelly children. She soon meets me near the play area.

"Your Majesty, Rehan is asleep."

"I came to see you."

"Oh?" she asks. "What may I do for you?"

"I'm missing a book from my library. Might you or one of the other nursemaids have borrowed it?"

"I'm certain we did not, Your Majesty. We know not to go into your library." She brushes residual dust off my sleeve. "I'm glad it's getting use. For all your mother's love of stories, she wasn't much of a reader."

"You knew Lakia well." After seeing my old room in the nursery, I have tried to remember Lakia as a loving young mother who read to me nightly, but I have too many contradicting recollections.

"I'll tell you about her. Sit. Sit." Sunsee points to the reading chair. "Your mother gained a reputation for her malice. When you were little, Kindred Lakia was quieter, less certain of herself. You remind me of her. Take that as no offense, Your Majesty. Lakia held herself to a lofty standard and was intolerant when she fell short. She was not rigid, per se, but had an idea of how things should be done."

The nursemaid digs around in her pocket and pulls out sugared pieces of cinnamon. "These were her favorite." She pops one in her mouth, giving me the other. I tuck the sweet against my cheek. They are the same ones found in dishes about the palace. "After you were sent away, Lakia was never the same."

I cannot muster much sympathy. She was my mother. I was her child. "She never said good-bye. The day I left she wasn't there."

"She was devastated. She ordered us not to touch the nursery. The first year you were gone, she slept in your room more than her own bedchamber." Sunsee grabs my chin and holds me in place. "Lakia had many flaws, but she loved you."

Some part of me wants to believe this, yet I still cannot equate the rani I knew with a gentle woman who told stories and had a sweet tooth.

Sunsee gives me her last sugared treat. As she checks on the dozing children, I savor it, letting the gritty sugar dissolve to a bitter cinnamon center. Are people the same? Do we start off saccharine and eager to love, then, as life goes on, we dissolve away until all that remains is a bitter hardness?

I ruminate on this while I leave the nursery and go to the wives' wing. Before I reach Kalinda's door, an army of servants exit another room, lugging water buckets, and leave the door ajar. As I approach, I hear Gemi speaking within.

"Thank you, Natesa. The water helps me feel less homesick for the sea."

"Would you like more bath oils?" Natesa asks.

"May I? My skin has been so dry."

I peer through the crack in the doorway. Gemi bathes in a tub set in the middle of the chamber. Her body is concealed by the washbasin, only the back of her head visible. Her hair hangs outside the steaming bath, a rich curtain of brown.

My tongue goes papery. I am torn between getting closer to see her better and slinking away.

Natesa brings a pitcher to the side of the tub and begins to wet Gemi's hair for washing. On the next pour, the flow exposes my viraji's bare shoulder. Her skin truly glows when damp, a radiance I would like to see more of.

Lords, I am a scamp.

I hurry on to Kalinda's chamber. Asha, her servant and friend, left an oil lamp burning. She also set out a food tray and a full water pitcher. I sit on the bed and rub my eyes. An image of Gemi's hair draping her glistening skin fills my mind. I should have presumed she was homesick. After I left the Brotherhood temple, I longed for the familiarity of those stone walls.

A memory of my mother starts to come, foggy pieces of a hurt so strong I shut it down before it drags me into the past.

Resting against stacks of pillows, I hold the childhood pains at bay. Deven needs me alert. I clear my thoughts, centering myself upon my priorities, and monitor the night for his arrival.

15

DEVEN

The moment nightfall hits I slide out of the thicket and set into a run. In minutes, the Road of Bone will be full of wanderers. I have to cross to the other end by the sky pathways before the inhabitants of the Void wake.

Kur's tail no longer blocks the road outside his lair. As an officer, I would order my men to retreat and remain hidden, but I can almost smell Kali's jasmine-scented hair and taste the food her servant has left out for me. On the other side of this pitlike doorway is nourishment. On the other side is my love.

I sprint across the entry, alert for a golden-eyed stare. Nothing stirs within the lair. Kur could be asleep or still nursing the injuries Kalinda gave him. I waste no more strength pondering his disinterest in me. Fortune has swung in my favor. I am overdue for a little luck.

My footfalls thunder down the Road of Bone. Unlike the hard skeletons beneath my feet, my bones feel brittle. No man this unfit could serve in the imperial army. I tire sooner than the day before and the day before that. The long stretches of fasting are emptying me. I hardly feel hunger or dehydration anymore.

At the end of the roadway, a haunting melody carries from the City of the Dead. I stumble along faster. I can see the pathways zigzagging the sky like crooked spiderwebs.

The first three directions inscribed on the ivory hilt of my janbiya are memorized.

1st right. 6th left. Right at fork.

Ahead is my path, a sharp, narrow incline without rails. I start up, sticking to the middle to avoid the vertical drop-offs.

6th left. Right at the fork. 200 paces, then . . . right?

Closing my eyes, I funnel all my concentration into the next direction. *200 paces, then left. Yes. That's the path.*

Another hundred steps, and I pause. By this point, I usually sense Kali's soul-fire to guide me the rest of the way home. I blink several times and peer up the road. The shadows go on, icy against my skin.

A presence stirs behind me. I spin around, dagger out, and stop to listen. Seconds roll into minutes. The presence, whatever it was, has left. My alarm has not. By now Kali's luminosity should be visible, a beacon high above. I have executed this trek dozens of times, but never without her guiding me.

Think. What now? Where to next?

I stay still until I remember. Little in the mortal realm prepared me for the loneliness of the Void. More so, the stillness. I can endure the loss of sunshine, constant chill, and foul air. But the lack of life stirring in the grass and trees, the quiet without the insects or birds, the absence of rich-smelling dirt and spices, even the monotony of this weather without seasons, tear at me. Life is loud and shouts for attention. It makes a man feel seen. Standing here, so motionless, my breaths feel like a betrayal to my survival.

Finally, my inner voice responds. *200 paces, then left.*

Trusting my intuition, I feel my way into the nothingness, praying Kalinda's soul-fire will appear and lead me home.

16

KALINDA

Tinley blows into her cupped hands. In the descent of nightfall, gales chased off the snow clouds and the temperature plunged. My soul-fire burns high to shield me from the weather, but Tinley's teeth chatter uncontrollably. I touch her, skin to skin, and send a small pulse of soul-fire into her. The Galer's whole body unclenches, and the wind whispers her thanks in my ear.

We have sat in our hideout for hours, Tinley observing the sky while I inspect every shadow for the man I long to see.

Come on, Deven. See my soul-fire and follow it to me. I am so determined to draw him out of the Void by sheer will, I nearly miss my friend tensing.

"They're coming," she says, her voice faint as a heartbeat.

I arch my chin to see over the rocks. A trio of mahatis casts shadows over the moon. I thought domesticated falcons were fast, but these feral monsters fly like an avalanche falls. Aggressive. Unstoppable. They could outrun the northern wind.

They are upon us, circling the hilltop. The largest one, their leader, screeches so loudly my eardrums pound. His razor-sharp talons are curved into hooks. He has an intelligence in his eyes that his companions lack and a wingspan that is equal to ten sleighs end to end.

Tinley watches the behemoth. "When I say so, throw a heatwave at the smaller mahatis."

My powers swell under my skin.

The mahatis' landing trembles the ground. They crowd up to the altar and tear the flesh from the dead with their sharp beaks. I grimace at the feeding noises. Can these mahatis truly ferry Anoush to the Beyond? Must a deplorable act precede peace?

The younger falcons snap at the same limb and screech at each other. Behemoth cuffs one with his wing. I dare not move. Their behaviors differ from the tamed flock in the aviary. These wild males are vicious. One wrong move and we could be their next meal.

As their feeding comes to an end, Tinley draws her winds. Behemoth's head goes up—he spots us. The mahati throws out his wings, the feathery tips standing upright like blades, and dips his head aggressively. The smaller falcons detect our presence and bristle.

"Now!" Tinley launches to her feet.

Gods. She runs right for the monstrous mahati.

I rise and hurl a heatwave at the smaller falcons. They launch into the sky. Their leader jerks his head toward Tinley. Without warning, a wall of wind slams me forward into the rock. A second later, the gale releases me. I push up, gasping.

Snow flurries rage, thick as a blizzard. Through the fluctuating whiteout, I make out Tinley's shape. The Galer pins Behemoth to the ground. Her convex of winds holds him while warding off the mahatis screeching above.

Tinley leaps onto Behemoth's back. "Get on!"

She wants to *ride* him?

A falcon dives. I throw a heatwave at him. The wind devours most of my flames, but the bird flaps off.

"Kali, hurry!"

I dash into the whiteout and up to Behemoth. The mahati's legs are wedged beneath him. He strains to stand, his wings locked down. Tinley hauls me up behind her. I clutch her middle, and the gusts die off.

Behemoth secures his footing and launches into the sky. The impetus nearly flings us off. A momentary weightlessness tingles down the length of me. I crouch behind Tinley, arms tight around her. She lifts her chin to the moon as the mahati ascends at breakneck speed. Finally, when I fear we may slide off and fall forever, he flattens out.

Tinley pumps one arm and whoops. I wish I shared her elation. We are *so high*.

Below us, moonbeams illuminate the dips and rises of hills— correction, peaks. Behemoth races over the snowy crests of the Alpanas. Our swift pace prevents me from guessing our location along the mountain range, but Tinley has patrolled this region. She probably knows which direction we are headed.

Shrieks sound in the night. The smaller mahatis fly up and flank us. Tinley and I hunch farther over Behemoth's neck to hide from the others. I rest my head against her shoulder. The high altitude is shrinking my lungs and fuzzing my concentration. She grasps my forearm, and sunny air inflates me, returning my focus.

"What was that?" I ask.

"A lung boost. The air is too thin up here. The boost should last a couple hours."

Our flock soars at a distant summit—Wolf's Peak. From our northern approach, the mountain's slopes drop in deadly gradients. Behemoth soars toward its face. A passing rush of rock and snow fill my view. We ride gales to the top and suspend over the whole of the world, equal to only the stars. The extraordinary moment lasts a fraction of a breath. Behemoth tucks in his wings and spirals into a dive.

Tinley and I lean forward as our bottoms lift off his back. The sky and land spin into a whirl of gray and white. My grip starts to slip from Tinley's waist. On the next roll, her own grasp fails.

We plummet head over end, tumbling faster and faster. A scream expands in my throat. Tinley summons a gust and rights herself. Plunging headfirst, she rides a gale to me and grabs my cloak. I lurch at the sudden connection.

The ground is seconds away. Tinley throws out her hand. A mighty wind bursts up, flipping us onto our backs and slowing our fall.

We hit the frozen land and the sky quiets. I ache everywhere, especially my head. I rest my palm over my chest and seek the assurance of my heartbeat. Tinley pants beside me as the falcons disappear over the peak.

"Bastards," she says.

I get up and help her next. She walks to the precipice and tilts her ear to the night. By some mercy, we both retained our packs in the fall and Tinley still has her crossbow.

"They landed close by." She starts uphill. "Follow exactly in my footsteps. The ice is unstable."

I place my footsteps in her tracks. We have not gone far when Tinley switches directions, and I follow her parallel up the mountainside. After we return to our original course, I see that we circumvented a crevasse.

"You've done this before," I say.

"Haziq and I were on a routine flight over the Alpanas. His novice falcon got spooked by lightning and knocked us off. Haziq sent a warning call for help. He wanted to wait, but I suggested we find shelter from the storm. We were almost to a cave when he fell in a crevasse. It took me a day to climb down to him." Tinley's voice folds in on itself. "Bedros found us. I held Haziq between us during our flight home. I tried to bury my grief in my affections for Bedros, but no one can replace Haziq."

"I'm sorry." As trite as they may be, platitudes are all I have.

Tinley's glowing eyes match the moon. "I prayed the entire climb down. I hoped Haziq had hit his head and couldn't answer me. But I knew, *I knew*, he was already gone." She sniffles and maneuvers around another chasm. "I understand why you keep looking for Deven. If the gods had given me the same chance of seeing Haziq again, I wouldn't give up either."

She refocuses on our climb and trudges upward. My freezing limbs barely keep up, but I do not complain about the cold or steep hike.

When we've almost reached the top, Tinley drags me down and points at fresh falcon tracks in the snow. We scramble up the overhang, and their trail leads to a cave. Tinley shuffles up to the entry and listens.

My neck prickles. Though I cannot recall another time when I stood at the top of the world, I know this place.

"I don't hear anything inside," Tinley reports, her tone testy.

She cannot *hear* hear. Her powers are not working.

I throw a flame inside the cave, and the murk swallows it. Bhuta powers are rarely stifled, yet a similar dampening happened in the presence of the Voider. Perhaps the same barrier occurs around godly gates.

"This could be a good sign," I say.

"Let's find out."

Tinley pulls a torch out of her pack and drizzles the end with lamp oil. I ignite the oil with a thread of soul-fire. We follow the falcon tracks into the cave, Tinley leading with the torch while I wield my dagger. Glistening ice coats the rock faces. We leave the frosty entry and proceed deeper into the mountain. Soon our torchlight does not reach the ceiling and walls. Tinley jumps at every drip or rattle. It must be disconcerting for her advanced hearing to suddenly be gone.

The falcon tracks peter off in the gravel at our feet. Behemoth has fluttered away like a butterfly. Did he really come in here? Or did the mountain lead us astray? I try to toss a heatwave for more light. My powers are barred. Not even my skin glows.

Our cautious pace gradually leads us into warmer air. Mixed in with the humidity comes a putrid sourness.

Tinley stares into a hot, stinky breeze. "That sounds like"—a low snort comes from the same direction—"breathing."

A beast strides into our dome of illumination. The horned creature stands on his hindquarters, his torso, arms, and face that of a man, the lower half of him bovine.

A kusarikku—a bull-man. In stories of the gods, they are doorkeepers to the Beyond.

The kusarikku's hooves thud closer. His tasseled tail swings between his upright hind legs, and his flat nose spews stinky exhalations. The stench of manure overwhelms me.

"Did you see a door?" I whisper to Tinley.

"No, did you?"

The kusarikku chuckles. "Lowly mortals shall not pass through the gate."

"We're bhutas," I reply.

His right hoof paws at the gravel. "Prove yourselves and you shall pass."

This must be a trick. "We cannot. An unseen force won't let us access our powers."

"No mortal shall enter." The bull-man lowers his horns at us and charges.

Tinley and I jump apart. She trips over a dip in the ground and falls. He barrels past and circles back for her. She throws the torch across the cave. We scramble to different spots and go still. The kusarikku stomps to the torch. His yellow eyes stare out, searching for us in the darkness.

Something bumps into my back. I squeak in surprise. Tinley covers my mouth. The bull-man releases a throaty chuckle and charges again.

We roll apart, each in the opposite direction. The kusarikku redirects for Tinley. I get up and run for the torch.

Come out, Siva.

The fire flickers without any sign of her. I lower my palm over the flames. My soul-fire might be unreachable, but this nature-fire is right in front of me.

I am fire, and fire is me. A face appears in the torch's flame, heeding my beckoning. *Come out, Siva. I need you.*

A spindly flame threads off and twirls above my skin, hot but not burning. Siva takes shape into a little ball, the size of a cicada, the smallest form my fire dragon has taken. The kusarikku slams his horns into a wall. Tinley has wedged herself inside a gap in the rock face.

I hold out Siva. "Get him."

My fire dragon zips across the cave and jumps on the bull-man's head. He swats at the dancing flame, forgetting Tinley. Siva flies about and lands on his nose. The kusarikku howls and bats at her. I crook my finger, and she floats back to my open palm.

"There's your proof," I yell. "I'm a Burner. Now let us pass."

The kusarikku snarls. I raise the torch, preparing for him to charge. He lifts his horns and stalks off, each footfall echoing into the dark. Tinley squeezes out of the hole and limps to a stop. Blood drips down her thigh from a gore wound. I reach into my bag for a cloth.

"You need a bandage," I say, frowning.

Tinley waves me off. "No, it's shallow."

Siva flies above us, drawing my gaze to a design on the wall. I swing the torch near it and reveal the quad symbol, the same design on the medallion in my pocket.

This is not a wall. This is the door.

Anoush said the gods' emblem adorns the gate to Ekur. Something compels me to touch the symbol. A cracking noise fills the cave, and a fissure opens at the floor. Light slices into the cave. Tinley and I squint as the section of wall lifts.

Siva flies back into the torch, becoming one with the nature-fire. I set it aside and swing Tinley's arm over my shoulder. We venture into an immense garden. Sweet-scented flowers and leafy trees ring with birdsong. Lush foliage lacking briars tumbles around the banks of a mellow stream. Rainbow fish swim in the crystal waters. Farther ahead, a stone bridge arches over the waterway.

Tinley looks up. "What in the name of Anu . . . ?"

The sky is a vivid shade of violet. My eyes ache at the intensity of the color. The hues of this animated dreamland are sharper and more refined.

Above the sky, an arched, domed ceiling spans the entirety of the garden. Puffy clouds drift within the cage of the ceiling, defying nature's laws. Nearby, an antelope grazes in a patch of wildflowers, and across the stream a rabbit chews on grass. Behind us, the stone door to the cave slides closed.

"How did you know how to open the door?" Tinley asks, favoring her injured leg.

"I don't know." I acted on impulse.

"I suppose you don't know which way to go?"

"No. I . . . wait." Upstream, high above the treetops, a gazebo overlooks the garden. The same instinct that prompted me to touch the door urges me to go there. "This way."

My decision earns me another skeptical glance from Tinley.

"I don't hear anyone else," she says.

My soul-fire glows through my skin. Our abilities are back, but they will not make our journey to the gazebo easier. "Can you walk?"

"Do I have a choice?" Tinley hobbles as we start upstream. "I don't like this place."

"Why not? Everything here seems perfect."

"Precisely." She glares at a patch of cheerful yellow flowers. "Nothing this beautiful can be trusted."

Her cynicism may be founded. Where does the wind come from? How can a sky exist inside a mountain? Why are the colors so pure? My mind is too limited to understand these wonders, but I smell the flowers and feel the breeze. This paradise is real.

The stream leads us to a waterfall storming down a cliff into a pool. The staircase alongside the cliff must lead to the gazebo.

Tinley plunks down on a mossy log. "I'll wait here."

I crouch in front of her and lift her bloody sarong. Her gouge is deeper than she let on. I remove a tunic from my pack and tie off the wound. She winces as I tighten the binding.

"Go on, Kalinda. I've brought you as far as I can go. Whatever is up there is for you."

She may be wrong, but I cannot let my doubts overpower me. I start upward, glancing back at her several times. Each step brings me higher above the garden. A low-hanging bough eventually blocks my sight of her.

At the top, I pause to marvel at the gazebo. The edifice is octagonal and has pillars instead of walls. A gold throne rests in the middle of the polished marble platform. I climb the steps one at a time. Out of respect, I slip off my sandals and pad to the throne.

My pulse thrums. My mortality feels more pronounced here, my fragile life minuscule. I kneel and bow my head. Stillness flows inside me, a rare abiding quiet.

"Great Anu, God of Storms and Father of the Sky, I've come to speak with you. I didn't mean to blame you for Deven's capture. I'm sorry."

The whole of the garden hushes. Even the sound of the gushing waterfall drifts into the distance. I listen and listen, yet no voice answers. I try again.

"Dear Gods, I'm Kalinda Zacharias, daughter of Kishan Zacharias, former bhuta ambassador of the Southern Isles, and Kindred Yasmin, former rani of the Tarachand Empire. I humbly request your aid." My final words choke out, ragged and faint. "I—I need you."

Quiet prevails.

Time and place lose all meaning. My knees and back ache, and the vacant throne needles at me. Just as Inanna knew she could save her intended, I believe I can free Deven. I am not getting up until my prayers are answered.

I lay my cheek against the cool floor. "I know you're there. Please come."

White luminance falls over my head, increasing in power. I raise my gaze, and the luster stings my eyes. I tuck my chin to my chest. When the supernal glow fades, I look again.

Two sandaled feet are planted near my head. My vision gradually meanders up the length of him. Tan, muscled legs rooted in majesty. A sarong wrapped snugly around his trim waist. A golden, bare chest formed from sensuous dips and rises. Arms thick and mighty as rivers. A face sculpted from beauty eternal, exquisitely idyllic from plump lips to firm chin to high cheekbones. Chin-length ebony hair with a natural shine and waviness. Eyes like two living flames, a physical manifestation of everlasting soul-fire.

He embodies everything distinctly masculine about a man, yet he is too handsome, too flawless. He beams down at me, a molten smile meant to melt mortals to their knees. Fortunately I am already on the floor.

He speaks, his voice full and gentle like a summer rain. "Welcome home, dearest Cala."

17

ASHWIN

Standing outside the palace in the courtyard, I watch the main entry for movement.

"Prince Ashwin, I'm sorry," says the nursemaid. "Your mother is caught up with her duties. But it's all right, young sir. She said good-bye last night."

We said no farewells when Mama came to my chamber late, nor did she say she was sending me away. I fell asleep listening to her tell our favorite story.

The carriage and horse team wait behind us, as do the soldiers. Our guards follow Mama and me when we ride in the city. I peer up at the ivory walls, which are lemon from the sunrise, and search the balconies. Mama's coming. She must be. I'm not allowed to leave the palace grounds without her or Father.

The driver signals for us to go, and the nursemaid carries me to the open carriage door. A quiet tightness crouches inside me. When we breach the threshold, I grab the doorframe.

"Mama! Mama!"

I kick and thrash, the tension springing out of me all at once. So much is jammed inside, big tears pour down my face. Only Mama can make this better.

Did I upset her? I tried not to fall asleep during her story last night, but I was so tired.

"Mama! Mama, I'm sorry!" Maybe Father found the potted plant I tipped over while running down the corridor. "Father, please! I'll be good. I won't run in the palace!"

A soldier pries my fingers from the door. The nursemaid holds me on her lap and pins me against her. I cannot make myself be still. I squirm and yell myself hoarse. The carriage leaves the palace grounds and jostles through the city.

We near the outer wall. Whimpers bubble from my lips. I've never been this far from home, but the soldiers let me through the gate without my mama.

My first up-close view of the desert hushes me. The nursemaid dries my cheeks. I've never seen anything so full of nothing.

Our carriage bumps and jostles as we navigate into the dunes. The nursemaid lets me go to grip the bench. I hang on to the windowsill. The orange reds, burgundy browns, and palm-tree green of Vanhi drift farther away. High above the city, the golden domes of the palace remind me of honey-drizzled fried bread.

The nursemaid urges me inside. I stay in the sun. I love my home and city, but more than anything, I love that Mama lives there. Why hasn't she come?

A thumping noise pries me from the memory, yet it pangs onward, a well-established sore. Every detail of that day has stayed with me. Hanging out the window, I combed the desert horizon for hours. I thought my mother would gallop up on her horse, lift me from the carriage, and carry me home. I was sunburned for days after. Mother never apologized or explained. I grew up thinking she wanted nothing to do with me. After what Nursemaid Sunsee said, I wonder what really stood in Lakia's way. Is there a sufficient excuse? Does anything merit sending away her child without a good-bye?

Seldom do I pray. The gods do what they please, regardless of what I want or hope for. But I tire of carrying around this heaviness.

Gods, please forgive Lakia . . . and help me forgive her too.

A thud sounds nearby. Kalinda's lamp has burned out, so I push up in the bed and study the chamber. Deven lurches from the shadows and stumbles to the sitting table. He pours a cup of water and guzzles it down.

"General?"

Deven swipes his forearm across his lips. "Where—is—Kali?"

Something stirs behind him. I look for the source but detect nothing more. I stride to Deven. His beard has grown scraggly, and his garments sag off his frame. He is a fraction of the soldier I remember. "She left to find you."

"No." Deven grabs my shoulders. "Tell her not to come. Kali cannot enter the Void. She'll never get out again."

"She left for Paljor two days ago. I haven't heard from her."

Deven presses the heels of his palms into his eye sockets. "I tried to find her . . . Her soul-fire was hidden." His fingertips dig into his hairline. "Kali is gone."

"Come sit down." I help him into a chair at the table. Kalinda told me nourishment is scarce in the under realm, so I refill his cup and pass him the flatbread. He rips off half a piece and shoves it in his mouth.

"When did Kali leave?" Deven asks, chewing.

I just explained this. Perhaps he did not hear me. "Two days ago. No word from her since."

He swallows the bread and gulps more water. "Where's Brac?"

"On an errand. We've run into . . . complications with my wedding."

"What sort of complications?"

Deven is the best soldier I have, but I will not burden him. "Captain Yatin and Brac can manage it. Why have you stayed away?"

"Kur summoned his demons to his lair. Their meeting lasted days and let out just this morning. This was the soonest I could come." Deven runs a shaky hand over his lips. "Kur may be planning something. You have to get word to Kali."

"She won't listen. She's determined to find you."

"She cannot come." Deven's gaze grabs at mine. "Kur isn't the worst monster down there."

Although I cannot imagine who could be more terrible, I trust his estimation.

Deven drinks the last of the water and presses the cup to his cheek. "Tell me about the complications with your wedding. I may be able to help."

He pushes his tray away and waits. Doubting I can sidetrack him again, I slide his tray back in front of him. "I'll talk. You eat."

While I recount Commander Lokesh's public protests and the people's anger with my selection for my first viraji, he returns to his meal. Deven, of course, latches on to my immediate problem.

"You have too few guards. Station your nearest units of soldiers at the palace temporarily. Set up tents for them outside to make their presence known. This will discourage the protestors from marching on your gates again."

Armed troops on these grounds could be interpreted as a countermove. The people may credit Lokesh for influencing my choices. However, I would rather they see me depending on my army than bhutas.

"You've done well, Ashwin," Deven says, "but Lokesh is not for you to confront. Don't give him any more credence. If there's anything malignant about Lokesh's employer, Brac will find it and Yatin will organize your defenses."

"The captain has been invaluable." I add belatedly, "and the ambassador."

"Brac can be difficult, but you can rely on him." Deven scrubs at his beard, his eyes owlish. "You should promote Yatin to general. He's fit for the task. When he denies the advancement, tell him it was my idea."

"Why do you think he'd turn it down?"

"Don't take offense. He's loyal to my friendship." Deven uses the table to push himself up, every movement paining him. "I have to go."

"Stay a little longer. I'll get you some more food and drink." His departure is a bitter end to this reunion. What the Void is doing to him is unbearable.

Deven closes his eyes and draws a deep breath. He reopens them again and answers in monotone. "Find Kali and keep her safe."

The night shifts forward around him. Shadows clutch his wrists and ankles like manacles.

"Deven—" I reach out and my fingers pass through him, leaving me with a fistful of cold emptiness. I stare at the bare wall he was in front of, my insides encased in ice.

A shadow darts past the balcony. I rotate in that direction. Nothing is visible, but the sensation of not being alone nags at me. I grab the empty pitcher and creep over. My heartbeat ramps up as I near the fluttering curtain. I snatch the drapery back.

Fresh air pours in through the ajar door. The place is empty, the movement a trick of the wind.

Before my imagination can deceive me again, I leave the wives' wing and travel up one floor. I knock at a door. A moment later, Indah answers in her robe.

"Ashwin, it's the middle of the night."

"I'm sorry. May I come in?"

She lets me inside the chamber. Pons is up, pacing the floor with Jala. The baby squirms and fusses. It is too late for pleasantries, so I rush to the point.

"Deven came and told me to warn Kalinda. He thinks Kur is planning something. Has any word come from Paljor?"

"No," Indah replies. "Pons, what can you hear?"

While Pons listens to the wind, Indah takes their child and bounce-paces her around the room. Jala rarely cries, yet every time I see her lately, she is in tears.

"Is she ill?" I ask.

"She misses Kalinda. Her fussiness started right after she left." Indah bounces Jala some more and asks Pons, "So?"

"I cannot hear her."

Indah paces faster.

"What about Tinley?" I suggest.

Pons clears his throat. "She's unreachable as well."

I sit on their rumpled bed. Deven said Kalinda's soul-fire was hidden from him. I should have never let her leave. "Can we send Tinley a message that they can receive once they travel closer?"

"It isn't a matter of distance," Pons replies. Worry wears his voice down to a murmur. "Where Kalinda has gone, no message on the wind can reach. She's alive; I would know if she had passed on. It's as if she's disappeared. As if . . ."

"She's left our world," I finish.

18

KALINDA

The stranger extends his hand to help me up. I hesitate, uncertain if I should touch this being with flames for eyes. He persists, so I lay my fingers in his.

A vision blinds me.

Fire Eyes locks me against him. I hang from his broad shoulders, my hands secured around his neck. My cheek rests above his collarbone. I am tall, but my head fits neatly under his chin. He is mountainous and warm as a bonfire.

His shoulders sear into my fingertips. Within him, his soul-fire illuminates little pathways up his arms for me to trace. Tingles dance across my skin. His feverish touch soaks into me like a hot drink in my belly and brings out my inner sunshine. My own veins come alight with powers.

He presses his lips to my forehead. "My dearest Cala. How I have missed you."

My vision fades and a shudder ruptures from my core. I yank from his touch. "Who are you?"

"You know who I am, Cala," he says, his voice liquid warmth.

"My name is Kalinda."

"Of course." He steps closer. The air between us sizzles, a repeat of my vision. "Do you remember me yet?"

We have never met. Or maybe we have . . . ? The brief vision of us was extremely convincing. Gods alive, it felt so *real*. "Who are you?"

"I could revive your memory." He extends his hand again, and I retreat. *No more of that.* He puffs out his chest, appearing even bigger. "I am Enlil, Keeper of the Living Flame."

"You're a . . . a . . . *god*." I should have guessed. His good looks are unparalleled. No mere man could be this entrancing.

"Just so, and you are a bhuta. A chosen Virtue Guard of my father, Anu."

I gawk at him so long I nearly forget what he said. "Yes, I'm a Burner, but that's not why I invoked you." I pull out my portrait of Deven. "This man is trapped in the Void. Deven Naik, a faithful soul. I need your help to bring him home."

Enlil skinnies his eyes. "Who is this man to you?"

"Deven is the general of the imperial army." I point to his decorated uniform jacket. I selected the portrait for this very reason. Establishing Deven's importance to our world may persuade the fire-god to return him to us. "I would have gone after him alone, but I need a god to guide me through the Void, do I not?"

Enlil's tone chills, a contrast to his impassioned eyes. "The demon Kur and his queen cannot harm any god, or any mortal with a god, who enters their realm. To traverse the Void without a divine guide would be imprudent."

"Deven didn't do anything to justify this fate. He cannot suffer an eternal death." I maintain eye contact, afraid to blink lest Enlil disappear.

"You wish to free this man." Enlil sounds bored with me and our conversation.

"Deven doesn't belong there. Several moons ago, Kur dragged him through the gate for trying to save me." I show him the portrait again. "Will you help us as you helped Inanna save her betrothed?"

The fire-god flexes his fists. "The journey to the City of the Dead is fraught with perils."

"I would be amazed if it weren't."

"You are willing to risk yourself to save this *mortal*?" Enlil surveys my prosthesis coolly.

I boost my chin. "I risk only what he's worth."

"Love fortifies the heart," he says almost sadly. The voice of the wind crying from Wolf's Peak returns to the forefront of my mind. It was *the fire-god*? Enlil brushes his finger across my cheek. "I will assist you in exchange for a favor."

"You want something from me?" I thought gods were benevolent overseers tossing out blessings like coins to beggars.

"Compensation for my aid."

Wary of bargains, especially with a god, I stare slantwise at him. "What kind of favor?"

"We will negotiate the conditions later. If this mortal man has been in the Void as long as you say, he will not survive much longer. The evernight will gnaw him into fragments of who he was, and he will be broken, never to reassemble."

A persistent suspicion warns me to understand his terms. "When the time comes, what will you ask of me?"

"Would knowing change your need of my assistance?" Enlil asks and awaits my reply. Knowing would not amend my reasons for coming. I sought the gods for aid, and one answered. I am already in his debt. "You need not fret, Kalinda. If we fail to free the man, you will owe me nothing."

If we fail, I will have lost everything.

The heat from Enlil's touch lingers on my cheek. Whatever payment he wants could not cost me more than Deven. What else could the gods desire besides increased obedience?

I measure my response so as not to insult him. "I appreciate your willingness, but I must know your conditions first."

Enlil gazes far into my eyes, seeking something. He seems to peel back layers of me, flesh and then bone, right down to my soul. The intensity of his focus knocks something loose far down inside. My breath catches on a dig of pressure, and the sensation abates.

"On my father's name, Great Anu of the Sky, I will require nothing that you are unable to fulfill," Enlil promises.

A warmth starts at my toes and zips straight up my spine. No greater vow have I witnessed. No greater assurance have I received.

The gods answered my prayers. The fire-god came and offered to serve my will. This is everything I wanted. What could a god ask of me that would be worth risking this chance for?

"We have a bargain."

"Magnificent." Enlil extends his hand, and a spear of lightning appears in his grasp. I stop myself from backing up a step, more impressed than afraid. "I will take us to the nearest gate."

He whistles, and a chariot of fire charges toward us, arcing across the violet sky. The whole chariot, including the horses, is made of flames and sends a trail of embers in its wake.

"Is that chariot made of fire?" Tinley asks from behind us. She has climbed the stairway by herself.

I slip on my sandals and dash to her. "How is your leg?"

She no longer wears the binding around her thigh. The puncture wound has healed closed. "Don't ask me how," she says.

"Ekur is a place of rejuvenation," Enlil replies. "A haven beyond the woes and pains of the mortal realm." Grasping his spear, he resembles the sculpture in the entry hall of the Crystal Palace.

"Is that . . . ?" Tinley's voice trails away, her light eyes gaping. "I need to sit." She plunks down on the temple steps and drops her head between her knees.

Enlil casts a strange look at her. "She is distressed by my presence?"

"Tinley's a little surprised you're real," I say, which only befuddles him more. I explain. "The gods have been gone a long while."

"Mortals' memories are short." He waves his staff as he speaks in wide, grand gestures. "How speedily they forget the gods' greatness and mercy."

His indignation can wait. The blazing chariot is almost here.

"Tinley has no way to get home," I say.

Enlil whistles, and Behemoth swoops down out of nowhere. The falcon must have been perched above the clouds the whole time. The wild mahati lands by Enlil, then spreads his wings and bows to the fire-god.

"Star-Jumper will take Tinley home." Enlil strokes Behemoth . . . Star-Jumper. The falcon preens, fluffing his red-and-gold plume. "We have been friends for decades."

The fire chariot and horses land behind Enlil. The mahati ruffles his feathers and eyes a horse. Star-Jumper probably dines on real steeds for his meals.

Tinley rises and squares herself to the fire-god. "I won't leave until you tell me what's become of my grandmother."

Enlil swings around, his countenance thoughtful. "Your grandmother . . . ? Ah, Anoush. You fret for nothing. She has returned to the Beyond."

"Oh." Tinley wrestles against tears.

Enlil slowly approaches her, his expression marked with consternation. "Mortals are blinded to the Beyond so they will not mourn their temporary exclusion from paradise." His merciful tone could smooth away any care. "As a comfort, I can return your sight for a brief glimpse."

Tinley looks up at him with needy eyes. "Would you?"

Enlil sweeps his spear above his head, and a portion of the rotunda vanishes. Through the opening, another realm appears, where stars, sun, and moon shine. Beneath them, green hills roll into the horizon.

My heart trips into a run.

A tidy grass hut with a thatch roof overlooks the greenery. A garden has been planted off to the side, alive with rows of vegetables and herbs. Deven comes out from behind the hut carrying a spade.

He is not alone.

Jaya pushes open the door of the hut and steps out, balancing a laundry basket on her hip. She holds the door open, and I exit next, hefting a second basket. Our hair hangs loose, swishing across our backs as we stride down to the creek chatting.

The sight of my best friend captivates me until our forms disappear below the rise. My gaze jumps to Deven toiling in the garden. I prepare to call to him, but Tinley speaks over me.

"Grandmother," she whispers. I rip my attention away from Deven. Tinley's tears flow, her expression full of wonderment. "Can you see her, Kali? She looks so young and happy."

I stare back at my picturesque scene. "I see—"

Tinley covers her gasp. "Haziq is there. He's waving to me." She clenches my hand hard. "He said he'll find me in my next life."

"But how?" I stammer. We are both viewing the same opening in the heavens, yet Anoush and Haziq are nowhere.

Enlil sweeps his spear over his head, and the glimpse into the Beyond ends. Deven and our hut in the lower Alpanas vanish.

Rawness boils up inside me. I reel on the fire-god. "I don't understand."

"The Beyond is a mirror of your heart's wish." His voice gentles to velvet. "What did you see, Kalinda?"

My deepest wish is vanishing a little every day. It is too fragile to speak of. "What's *your* Beyond like?"

Enlil's brow creases. "Incomplete."

My annoyance dissolves. I should not be short with him, but my heart's wish is a thin comfort without Jaya and Deven at my side.

"It is time for Tinley to depart." Enlil strides to the falcon and pets its beak.

Tinley presses closer to me. "Kali, are you certain trusting him is a good idea? He looks at you strangely."

Everything about this is odd, but Enlil is a god. I have worshiped him since my childhood. For Deven's sake, I have to accept his aid.

"I'll be all right. Will you?"

"I think so. My grandmother was right. Fate led us here to find the answers we seek." Tinley pulls me close. "Find Deven, Kali. Find him and bring him home. Your friends and family will be waiting."

I squeeze her harder than I normally would. She swiftly kisses my cheek, a rare show of affection, and strides to the falcon. Enlil boosts her onto its back. She waves farewell, and the mahati leaps into the sky. Star-Jumper flies into the clouds, and they vanish beyond the floating rotunda.

Enlil greets his horses and beckons me over. They remind me of Siva. One of them jerks at his bridle, also crafted from fire. I shrink from the enormous beast.

"Chaser recognizes you," Enlil says.

From where? I would recall meeting a stallion of fire. Chaser butts his head against my extended hand. As with Siva, Chaser's flames do not harm me. I pat his back and step onto the chariot after Enlil. He is so big I cannot avoid our sides touching.

"Most mortals are afraid of my chariot," the fire-god notes.

"I'm not."

"Then I hope you enjoy this." He snaps the reins, and the horses take off.

Our ascent is more gradual than a mahati falcon's. We rise into the violet sky through delicate clouds and closer to the unreachable dome. The higher we climb, the faster the horses gallop. I could fall out the back of the chariot, but Enlil stands behind me and blocks the opening. His protective stance spurs a thought.

We've ridden this way before.

Nausea simmers in my belly. I was someone else before this life. Many someones. One of the former versions of myself must have been close to the fire-god. Close enough to meet his horses. And if I am correct, she was of importance.

Our chariot speeds toward an expanding hole. We pass through it, exiting the splendor of Ekur, and fly over a desolate land of moody grays. Enlil lands beside a circular stone in the ground. We leave the chariot and approach the slab. Glyphs of an ancient script are etched all over it.

"What do they say?" I ask.

"It is a warning to intruders. This is the main portal to the under realm."

Enlil hunts for something on the marker and then drives the end of his spear into a small indent along the rim. Brilliancy bursts across the stone, flowing out in a steady ripple, and the slab disappears. I peer over the edge.

A sludgy darkness percolates in the pit, not velvety or satiny like the shadows in the mortal realm but alive and squirming. The inky nest wafts of rotting sinew. Gooseflesh puckers my skin. The chilly evernight pours over the lip of the hole and swipes at my feet. I sidestep from contact, my joints rattling.

Enlil hoists his spear and straps on a satchel I did not notice he had. He may have summoned it from nothing. Gods can do that, I think.

"Kalinda, you have your powers, but are you otherwise armed?"

I reveal the turquoise hilts of the daggers at my hip. Since I am down to one hand, he must think I need another defense. "They were my mother's."

"Yasmin's."

"You know her?"

"We are acquainted." Enlil disregards my astonishment and edges up to the portal. The writhing sludge retreats from him and simmers. "You will possess your Burner powers in the under realm, but they will not replenish. Do not rely on them unless you are in dire need."

Standing at the doorway to the Void, all hope and love in my life feel far removed. "The gods cannot reach us where we are going, can they?"

"Anu and Ki have no authority in the under realm." Enlil takes my hand. "I will not let any harm come to you, Kalinda."

And I will defend him.

The whisper comes from far down inside me. Before I can pinpoint its origin, Enlil puts his toes over the pit.

"We could lose each other in the pathways of shadow, so we must jump as one."

His warmth shields me from the cold emanating from the portal. I lock my knees to quiet my trembling and gaze into his burning eyes. The same strange voice inside me expels a dreamy exhale. I feel around for the source of it and discover a barrier, like a sealed hatch. Something dwells down past my inner sight. I dare not investigate further or I may let it out.

Enlil threads his fingers in mine, and we leap.

Seething winds accost my ears as the evernight charges in around us. Enlil's lightning spear casts illumination at our surroundings. The portal opens to endless paths and upside-down stairways. We plummet past them, unobstructed by the meandering trails. Black scorched ground appears below.

"Bend your knees!"

I do as Enlil orders, and we land in a pile of sludge. The sticky muck absorbs our fall. Enlil lifts his staff overhead, illuminating our location. We fell into a tar pit. The gritty wetness rubs abrasions over my bare arms and legs where my trousers rode up. I squirm to get out only to sink deeper.

"Be still." Enlil dives his hands into the tar and heaves me out of the sludge. At eye level, his gaze shines like piercing stars.

He slogs through the tar.

"How are you not stuck?"

"Nothing may kill me here. When you and I are close, the elements of the under realm cannot harm you as well."

The tar gurgles. A bubble pops near my feet, and cold air flashes out, stinking of moldy chickpeas. Each inhale crowds my nose and throat, the very air strangling me. At the embankment, Enlil sets me down. We dropped into a massive cavern riddled with pits. Spiky rocks protrude down from the cave ceiling and up from the floor. In the places they nearly meet, the points look like fangs in an unwelcoming grin.

I wipe at the tar on my clothes and the sores where the substance chafed my skin. We have barely arrived and already Enlil has rendered me incompetent.

"Thank you," I push out between set teeth. Enlil chuckles and melts the patches of tar off his legs. "What?" I ask.

"Your pride amuses me."

"This isn't pride. I simply prefer to take care of myself."

"But you are unconfident in your ability to do so." He lowers to one knee and cleans the tar off my skin. The stickiness melts and drips into puddles. "In another life, you were the greatest warrior of your generation."

My heart thuds against the trapdoor. "I was?"

"I could remind you. Should you desire, I will retract the veil over your memories."

I am tempted to see myself as he does, but that is not why I summoned him. "Who I was isn't relevant to who I am now."

He finishes and stands, his expression downcast. "The future is relevant to the present."

"But you want to show me the past."

"The past reminds us where we were so we may understand where we must go." Enlil considers my glower and crosses the cavern. Rid of the sticky tar, I keep up at his side. "When you are ready, I will show you. You will be pleased. Your memories are yours, but they also include people you love."

He stops before a network of tunnels. No signs are posted to specify where they lead or how long they go on for. His spear casts a glow down the beginning of the paths, his corporal light wreathing us. Enlil peers down each one and then signals at the second to last.

"This is the route to the first gate."

A gate? Of course. According to *Inanna's Descent*, we must pass through seven gates before we reach the City of the Dead. I presumed they were figurative symbols. I had not considered they were literal distance markers. "How do you know this tunnel is the right one?"

"The stench." Enlil wrinkles his nose. "The reek of pain is most putrid down there."

I cannot smell anything over the drying tar on my cloak. We enter the tunnel of the fire-god's choosing and rely on his effulgence to carve a path into the dim.

19

Ashwin

Breakfast is always quiet in my atrium. I dine alone and watch the door.

After leaving Pons and Indah's chamber last night, I wasted no time issuing a relocation order to the troops stationed at the city wall. At dawn, a unit marched through Vanhi and up to the palace. Yatin is currently supervising the settlement of their camp.

Even knowing the palace residents were safe, I could not sleep. Every time I shut my eyes, I was with Deven in the middle of the desert. Kalinda and my mother were trapped in quicksand. No matter how hard we pulled and dug, we could not free them.

The cook made my favorite fried bread with extra honey. I pay more attention to the doorway than my plate. At last my chamber servant enters.

"I found it." He sets a small jar before me.

"Are you certain this is the one?"

"Healer Baka assured me it's lavender."

I spin the lid off and sniff the cream. Clean lavender with a hint of rose hip. I tuck the small jar into my jacket pocket as a messenger brings in a letter. In the message, Priestess Mita requests my attendance at the Sisterhood temple. The builders have come upon a complication that requires my input. Brac asked me to stay in the palace, but I will not postpone the completion of the temple.

I grab a handful of cinnamon sweets off a dish on the table and thank the servants. "If you need me, I'll be in the wives' wing."

The path there is direct and unencumbered. At the entrance, Eshana rushes out and speeds off without a word.

"Good morning, Eshana," I call after her.

She spins around. "Your Majesty! Have you seen Parisa? She was gone from our chamber when I woke, and she missed breakfast."

"I haven't."

"She may be at the elephant stables." Eshana glances about the vacant doorway and drops her voice to a scratchy whisper. "Her father was an elephant handler. He died when Parisa was young, and she was sent to the Hiraani Temple where we met. Did you know we were claimed together?"

I was unaware. She goes on without my reply.

"Our rank tournaments were consecutive. The cut on Parisa's head was more severe than she lets on. The blade nearly shattered her skull. She's struggling with your choice for kindred, but I hope her apprehensions don't influence your decision for who you retain in your court." Eshana plucks a stray thread from my jacket sleeve and leaves her hand there. "Whatever you decide, I'll go with Parisa. We came to the palace together, and if we must, we'll leave together."

I cannot speak intelligently about Parisa's state of mind, though I do appreciate Eshana's perspective. "I'll take your thoughts into consideration. One question: Were you or anyone from your court in the library yesterday?"

"*Me?*" She sounds scandalized. "Skies, no. We all know not to go in your library."

"Thank you, and thank you for informing me about Parisa. You're a considerate friend."

Eshana reddens from ear to ear, then waves good-bye.

I pass into the wives' wing. Down the same corridor, a group of sisters gathers at an arched casement to view a crowd at the front gate. The protestors have returned.

I fist the lavender lotion in my pocket. Visiting Gemi will have to wait. I hustle outside to the guardhouse. The angry mob throws stones into the grounds and at the guards on the ramparts. Yatin leads me into the garden, out of view of the gate.

"Captain Yatin, what's going on?"

"The people are alarmed, sir. Commander Lokesh told them you rallied the soldiers to guard your viraji and left our people defenseless. They blocked every access in and out of the palace grounds."

"Lokesh lied." Or did he? I summoned the soldiers to guard us from his growing rebellion, but never at the expense of our people's safety. "The city has sufficient protection. Is Lokesh out there now? I'll speak with him."

"He'll twist your words to reinforce his lies. Sir, you're best off returning inside and letting us manage him."

Everyone's recommendation is for me to ignore Lokesh. No one thinks hiding behind my army is gutless. "As you say, but you need the proper authority to represent me. The army needs a leader. Serve as my general, Yatin. You're doing the work; you're entitled to the prestige."

"I'm honored," Yatin rumbles in his mild baritone, "but I cannot accept. The army deserves its true general."

"This was Deven's idea."

Yatin's eyes expand. "How is he?"

"He's holding on." I regret minimizing Deven's pain, but reminding Yatin that his friend is in grave danger will do no good. "Will you lead in his stead?"

Yatin dips his head. "I will serve as you command."

A soldier runs down the path and draws up short. "Your Majesty, pardon the interruption. Captain Yatin is needed at the guardhouse."

"*General* Yatin will be right with you," I reply.

The soldier aims an amazed look at Yatin, bows, and dashes off. Yatin rubs fingers over his bushy eyebrows, pressing them down. He must be overwhelmed, and, for the foreseeable future, overworked.

"When this is over, I'll send you and Natesa on a honeymoon wherever you wish."

Yatin chuckles. "You're concerned Natesa will be mad that my advancement may occupy more of my time."

"Regardless, you deserve a break." I did not expect to share these feelings, but they must be said. "Having lost some of my men, I'm even more grateful for those who stay."

Yatin grabs me in a hug, lifting me off the ground. He sets me back down and his face reddens, comprehending his casual handling of his ruler. I smile to lessen his embarrassment. He pulls at his chin sheepishly until shouts compel him to return to his post.

Alone in the garden, I notice a lavender bush along the path. I run my hand over the blossoms and sniff. It has a sharp smell that is both medicinal and floral. Oddly pleased that Gemi's experiment worked, I refocus on my next task. Choosing a lemon tree with ideal boughs, I climb halfway up. Above me, a family of monkeys swing to an adjacent tree and chatter to one another. I settle on a limb and watch the happenings below. The leafy branches shield me from the soldiers setting up camp and afford me a view of the gate.

Yatin and the soldiers clear a path in the crowd for a string of military wagons to pass through. The foolish protestors chant, "Return to tradition." What is it they miss most? The tyranny? Bloodshed? Total disregard for their happiness?

"What are you doing?" a voice calls from below.

Gemi stands beneath the tree, gazing up at me.

This is not how I wanted to see her today. I hope she loses interest and continues on her way, but she lifts herself onto a low-hanging branch and climbs. My branch quakes as she straddles the bough in her trousers, her bare feet dangling.

"Why are you hiding?" she asks.

"I'm not. I like to climb."

She tugs at my tunic sleeve. "You need more comfortable recreational attire."

"Natesa snuck into my chamber and removed all my favorite clothing," I say. My viraji laughs, the merry sound like the jingle of a dancer's wrist bells. "What are you doing in the gardens?" I ask her.

"I was studying the monkeys. We don't have their kind in Lestari."

I have given no thought to the types of monkeys in Tarachand versus those in the Southern Isles. Monkeys are widely considered pests. "Learn anything of interest?"

"They sleep, travel, and hunt together. The mothers carry their young on their backs for what I think is the first year or so of their life, and when the guards are not paying attention, they snitch their food." We chuckle together, and she asks, "Why are you up here?"

"I was investigating a route out of the grounds. I need to visit the Sisterhood temple in the city, but the gates are blocked."

Gemi watches the throng beyond the wall. "They don't want me as their kindred." I shake my head in objection. "Don't patronize me, Ashwin. I heard what Lokesh said. They want you to wed one of your father's ranis."

"The people are acclimating to new ways. They'll learn to accept you."

Gemi readjusts on the tree branch and our fingers meet. I pull away from her touch.

"The ranis aren't warming to me," she says. "Shyla and the temple wards like me, as do the Trembler trainees, but the others barely tolerate my presence. My training with Shyla is progressing slowly. We can only use the sparring ring when no one else is around or the ranis become testy. I'm fairly confident Parisa would like to slit my throat with her pretty red nails." Gemi's pale-gold eyes meet mine. "I like them, Ashwin. They're faithful, brave, clever women." She sounds dissatisfied with herself by comparison.

"They may be seasoned competitors, but you've been a ruler over a peaceful nation since birth. These women know how to survive—you can teach them how to live."

Gemi smiles, the reward I wanted. "You make a good speech. You should voice your opinions more often."

"My parents discouraged original thought. I was to think of the empire first and them second. After they were pleased, I could think of myself. They were never pleased."

"My father kept my world small and secluded on the island." Gemi leans into my side and stares at the far-off sand dunes. I let her brace against me, her shiny hair brushing against my shoulder. "Leaving Lestari to fight in the war challenged us both. I speak my mind more, and he listens better. You can speak up, Ashwin. Your thoughts hold value, and your people will listen."

Watching her from the corner of my eye, I see her intense focus does not waver from the desert. "What do you see?"

"Pardon? Oh, nothing." Her accent thickens. "Sometimes when I stare at the dunes, I can almost trick my mind into seeing the sea."

I search the horizon for the promise of waves, yet find ceaseless concourses of sand. Gemi scratches at her elbow. Patches of her dry skin have turned to inflamed abrasions.

"This is for you." I pass her the lotion jar that I had stowed in my pocket.

Gemi unscrews the top and sniffs the contents. "Lavender!" She rubs the lotion into her elbows and sniffs her skin. "Thank you. That was very thoughtful."

Loud shouting sounds from the gate. The supply wagons enter the grounds, and the protestors return to the bars, chanting and casting rocks.

"A trip to the temple will be impossible today," I say.

Gemi twists one of her shell earrings and narrows her eyes in contemplation. "What if I can get us out?"

"Do you own a magic carpet?"

"Something better," she promises.

I eye the crowd. Not two days ago, they beat a man to death. "I'm not sure we should leave. Someone could recognize you."

"Hardly anyone knows what I look like."

Perhaps, but Tarachandian women do not have pale-gold eyes and dewy skin.

Yatin posts a dozen more men outside the main gate to enforce a barrier between it and the protestors. The people stop throwing stones but remain, undaunted by the threat of arrest.

What right do they have to imprison us? No matter what Yatin and Brac say, hiding is cowardly. Though Rajah Tarek may have been a tyrant, no one dared hold him captive in his own palace. I am beginning to comprehend how he convinced himself that his ruthlessness was just.

Gemi climbs down the tree, pausing partway. "Are you coming?"

20

KALINDA

Our tunnel goes on without end. Enlil charges ahead, undaunted by the obscurity we crest or the shadows chasing our backs. I hurry to match his long strides.

We are trapped between closed-in walls and a continuously low ceiling that barely misses Enlil's head. The only change is the downward slope of the ground, a gradual, almost indiscernible gradient that leads us deeper into the under realm.

Though Enlil's true father is the demon Kur and his powers carry his father's venom, and thus do my own Burner abilities, I could never be at home in this dreadful place. Does Enlil's fearlessness come from his comfort here or his security in his godliness?

I deliberate on this as my legs ache in exhaustion. Enlil shows no signs of tiring. Maybe I can distract him and he will ease up to a less punishing pace.

"When did you learn Kur is your father?"

"He is *not* my father. Kur would try to convince us that we are his children, born of fire and venom, and therefore we belong to him. But I have sworn my allegiance to the God of Storms, and your very soul-fire originates from his glory. Kur has no claim on us."

Enlil walks faster. I groan and skip to avoid falling behind.

At first, when the end of the tunnel appears, my mind convinces me that I am seeing more of the fire-god's glimmer, but a new dimness fills the opening. Forgetting my exhaustion, I rush along. Enlil stops before the end of the tunnel. The opening is partially blocked by a low stone wall.

"Do not speak," he says. "Rabisus are spirit feeders and tricksters. They will twist your words and trap you in a bad bargain." The fire-god ambles up to the gate and says louder, "We have come for safe passage across the first obstruction."

A shadow the size of a grown wolf slinks out from behind the low rock wall. The rabisu's empty eye sockets repel me. I shift closer to Enlil's side.

"Payment," the rabisu garbles out, a voice of ash.

Enlil takes a mango from his bag. The rabisu snatches it from the fire-god. "A skiff waits at the shoreline. Cross the Sea of Desolation and follow the coast north. Go ashore at the cliffs."

The creature exposes scraggly teeth and tears into the flesh of the fruit. A narrow section in the wall vanishes. A gate. Enlil drags me through. When I look back, the wall and its guardian are gone, as is the tunnel that led us here. In their place is a barren field.

"Quickly now," Enlil urges.

"A mango?"

"Rabisus like sweets. They especially crave children. It is said a child's innocence sweetens the flavor of his soul." My insides contract, reminding me I have not eaten in some time. Enlil tosses me another mango. "Eat up. Retain your strength."

"How did you know I'm hungry?"

"I am a god."

I huff at myself. What other response did I expect?

He chuckles, a rolling rumble. "I cannot read your thoughts, Kalinda. I discerned you were hungry by fact. Mortals need sustenance."

"Gods don't eat or drink?"

"Only when it suits us. The fruit I gave you is enhanced with all the nutrients and rest you need for a day. Finish it and your strength will be replenished."

I nibble a bite. The mango tastes sweet, a tad sour, and very juicy. I devour it on our walk to the seaboard and am indeed refreshed. "What else do you have in your satchel?"

"The satchel is but a prop. I am Enlil, Keeper of the Living Flame." He holds out his hand, and a tiny, intense glow, like a direct ray of sunshine, manifests over his palm. The flame forms into a little white bird. "I create life and nourishment from my living fire." He closes his fist around the bird, and it vanishes.

"Why don't you summon your horses and chariot? We could fly right over the sea." Or to the City of the Dead and bypass the gates and guardians.

"We must follow the guidelines of the rabisus and not cheat the rules of the under realm, or we will be expulsed."

He does not explain what our expulsion would involve. I trust it would be unpleasant.

Ever so steadily, like a sunrise, the sky changes from bitter midnight to glum gray. A strange, directionless wind combats our every step to the coastline. The Sea of Desolation fulfills its lonely name. A dreary expanse of water stretches beneath a stormy sky. Thunder grumbles overhead from a lightningless storm.

A two-passenger skiff is wedged into the rocky shore. Pieces of ivory, like shells, are mixed in with the rocks. My mouth turns sour. They are shards of bones.

Enlil and I haul the skiff and oars against the wind down to the lapping sea. Each wave grasps at the pebbles and slinks away. Unlike a sea in the mortal realm, this one has no briny scent. The smell of iron carries off the waves, diffused by the strident winds.

"Climb in and do not let the sea touch you."

I get in the skiff, and Enlil pushes the bow into the waters. The murky liquid is thicker than water and clots in spots. High winds howl, their tenor eerily mortal, and break the surface into choppy ridges. The skiff undulates against the pulling tide.

"Can we not walk?" I ask.

"We must cross the sea to reach the mortal man."

"You mean Deven."

Enlil ignores my correction and wades into the sea. Once the skiff floats, he jumps in across from me, the two of us knee to knee. The water staining his legs is crimson.

"Is that *blood*?"

He wipes off his shins with his hands and picks up the oars. "A millennium ago, the spirits of the fallen attempted to escape the Void. The demon Kur's high queen, Irkalla, would not part with a single soul. Thus, she crafted the seven obstructions with their adjoining gates and formed the rabisus from a drop of her venom to serve as their guardians. The fallen souls still tried to run, so Irkalla set a plague upon the under realm and cursed the sea, turning the water to blood." A large bone floats past the skiff. My stomach pitches on the mango I ate. "The lowest trenches of the Sea of Souls in the mortal world empty into the Sea of Desolation. Do not fall in or you will be lost between the realms."

I scoot into the center of the bench. Enlil rows us farther into the swells, the grim waves extending to the horizon.

"How do you know which way to go?"

"In the under realm, the correct direction will be the most treacherous."

He maintains his rhythmic labor, paddling into the upsurges. Red droplets splash against the hull. I must think of something beyond the gore holding us afloat. One of Enlil's earlier comments circles back to me.

"When you said my loved ones are in my memories, who did you mean?"

He hesitates on the next stroke and then compensates with more vigor. "It is easier to show you."

Something bangs against the trapdoor far down inside me. Whatever is locked away desires the acceptance of Enlil's offer. "Never mind. I was only curious."

"Mortals are inquisitive by nature. I can select a memory with Jaya."

All my senses hang upon his words. "You know about her?"

"The gods know every soul, now and through all generations." Enlil rests an oar in his lap and lifts his hand. I cannot shift away without tipping the skiff. He presses his thumb to my temple. "Shut your eyes."

To see Jaya again, I forget his bossiness and do as he says.

My soul-fire shines behind my eyelids, a star in my private sky. A blinding glare overtakes my inner vision, and my mind spins into a vortex of noises and sounds.

All goes quiet.

I reopen my eyes and the skiff is gone. Enlil sits beside me, grasping my knee. Both of us wear the finest silks and softest leather sandals. We lounge on satin pillows beneath an opulent canopy. People fill the hall before us, dancing and dining at tables brimming with dishes of food. Women wait in a line before me. They approach our dais one at a time and lay precious tokens of adoration at my feet. Perfumes, veils, lotions, spices, finely crafted weapons . . .

In the shiny blade of a khanda, I view my reflection. The woman I see wears a gold-and-crimson sari—bridal attire. Our features, hair, and physique are identical, save that she has her right hand. Swirling henna trails up her arms.

I am the woman in the bridal sari with matrimonial markings. I feel her heartbeat. Taste the wine on her lips. Smell her jasmine perfume. Detect the heavy rubies around her neck.

How . . . ? I review the banquet hall for answers. Several dancers twist their wrists and shimmy their ankles, rattling their anklets and bracelets to the drumming. Servants refill wine chalices amid the tables where attendees kneel. One of the servants stands out.

"Jaya," I gasp.

Her shorter frame has a powerful stance, her body a proportional measure of muscle. I adored sketching her; she is not flashy like a peacock but lovely as a dove. I leave the dais, and Enlil grabs my wrist.

"This is a memory, Kalinda. You cannot change what was."

"I don't care." I wrench from him and weave through the tables to my friend. Next to her, I nearly burst from gladness. "Jaya?"

She refills a patron's dish and continues down the long table.

"I'm so sorry." Tears wobble my voice. "I've missed you."

Jaya turns around, and her stare goes through me. I try for contact, but my tap passes through her. I return to the dais in a daze, pained by her blunt disregard. Enlil comes to my side.

"She's . . . she's forgotten me," I say.

He guides me back to my floor cushion. "She is a servant in your parents' household. You are her master, and she knows her place."

Her place is with me. I kneel behind the pile of gifts and look out over the grand dining hall. "You said this is my parents' household?"

Enlil points to a couple greeting guests in the center of the room. The woman's silky hair shines under the lamplight, and the man wears a trim beard and mustache. They are dressed impeccably in fine silks and leather. Their elbows are linked in a casual manner. Though I have never seen them in the flesh, they look just as Chief Naresh described.

"Mother! Father!" I shout.

They are close enough to hear me, but neither responds.

"You cannot speak to them," Enlil says. "This is a memory. It cannot be altered."

I rise to go to my parents, but he blocks my path. "Why did you bring me here? This is torment!"

Enlil encircles me in his arms. "That will suffice for now. Wake, Kalinda."

"Don't make me lose them again. Let me stay." I writhe against him, but his hold is unbreakable. He shushes me and presses his lips to my temple. The banquet hall starts to fade. "Please don't take them from me. Please."

A flash blinds me, and a vortex sweeps me off-center. I spin, all strength from my limbs draining out.

I wake in the bottom of the skiff. Enlil stands in the knee-deep water and pushes it to shore. Cries embed in my breastbone. I scramble out and brace against the side of the boat, waiting out my unsteady legs. Enlil tries to support me. I wave him back and toughen my voice as much as I dare.

"That memory wasn't mine. Unless you can show me something that will help me find Deven, leave my past alone."

"This Void will root out the less appealing parts of your soul's progression," Enlil answers sympathetically. "You are better off to remember your past lives through me."

Far inside my center, a pounding sensation ricochets through my chest cavity. I cast him a direct glare. "I don't need you interfering with my head."

Enlil draws up to his full height, his toned abdomen tucked in. "As you desire."

I set off ahead of him toward the cliffs. The pounding inside me quiets to raps.

"The second gate is ahead," Enlil says, his footfalls behind mine. "Beyond it lies the Valley of Mirrors."

"Sounds less ominous than the Sea of Desolation."

"A misconception. The obstructions become more hazardous the nearer we are to the city." He takes a mango from his bag. "Be wary. The rabisu has scented you."

The path in the cliffs closes after us. Another wall appears ahead, taller than the last. A rabisu the size of a brown bear waits to receive us. He smells the air and licks his chops. I shift closer to Enlil, closer to the hammering deep within me.

21

DEVEN

The sap of the thorn tree sticks to my tunic, stinking of rot. Everything in the under realm reeks of decay. Plugging my nose does nothing. I have learned to tolerate the stench.

The early morning hour is quiet. The creatures of the Void have slunk back into their holes for the day. I settle my head against the tree trunk. My own sleep pattern has become nocturnal. I rest when the under realm does.

Thuds vibrate up through the ground. I hold still and wait for the disruption to pass. More quaking comes, accompanied by a rapid drumming. I sit forward and peer out of the thicket into the grayish haze. The noises hail from the city.

Dropping to my belly, I slide forward toward the road. The vibrations strengthen, pulsing into my gut. Creatures march through the city gates. Rabisus of all shapes and sizes travel toward Kur's cave. They pass by the First-Ever Dragon's lair and continue toward the Road of Bone. Toward me.

I have never seen hundreds of rabisus together, let alone congregated during daylight hours. Demons command the group, riding astride ugallus. Triple the size of an adult bear, with the head and body of a lion and wings of an eagle, the tawny ugallus are functional steeds for both ground and air battle. The hideous beasts close in, and I recognize their riders. Edimmu, a crocodile-snake demon; her brother Asag, the rock demon; and their sister Lilu, whom Kali nicknamed Fish Face.

The drummers approach first, bears walking on their hind legs. The mangy army behind them is a crew of demented bears, tigers, wolves, and other predators found in the mortal realm. None of the rabisus display pennants or banners. They wear no uniforms and are not organized into units. They travel like a stampede, crushing everything in their path.

I scoot back from the road, deeper into the cover of the thicket. Down in the muck, the foulness of the Void should mask my mortal scent. I stay low, regulating my movements to half breaths.

The demon commanders ride past on their ugallus. Their lion-eagle mounts are massive, large as an elephant but with the jaws of a monster. They start down the Road of Bone, and the rabisus prowl past next. A wolfish one pants hard as it pads by. The beast and its kind are emaciated to bones and matted fur.

At the rear of the troops, rabisus loiter, sniffing and scavenging for scraps. The army stops at the far end of the Road of Bone. Asag calls orders near the front, his rumbly voice unforgettable. Rabisus set to work, pushing up the ground into big dirt piles. The mounds block the entrance to the road, filling the expanse. The paths to the mortal realm are on the other side of their blockade.

They have locked me in . . . or are they keeping something out?

I stay down, dagger close, and observe the camp. The troops quit moving about and all goes quiet again. Exhaustion threatens to grind me down. The army seems to have settled in for the day, so I return to my tree to rest.

As I drift off, a wolf rabisu howls. Their lonely calls are only common at night. I sit up and spot movement down the road. Rarely do the creatures of the Void stir during the daylight hours.

I crawl through the thicket, and my chest hitches. An army of rabisus set up a blockade at the other end of the Road of Bone. New paw and hoof tracks mark the roadway that runs past my location. They must have marched by me. How did I sleep through their patrol?

I inspect the undergrowth for the answer. Fresh dents are on the ground in my usual lookout spot, as recent as the last hour. Panic skitters through me. *I didn't sleep through their march. I've forgotten it.*

Sometimes, when I am very fatigued, I lose gaps in my memory. The gaps are getting wider and closer in frequency.

I return to my thorn tree and tear off a spiky needle. Turning over the handle of my janbiya, I press the sharp end of the needle into the ivory and start to chisel a *K* into the top.

K. A. L. I.

Over and over, I recite the spelling of her name. I cannot forget her or my friends and family. I must remember there is more to my life than the dark.

22

Ashwin

I can barely breathe. A wool blanket was laid over me, and what feels like sacks of grain pin my back and legs.

"Better than a magic carpet," I grumble.

Gemi nudges me with her heel. "Shush. We're almost to the main gate. Girls? If the prince speaks again, you have my permission to use your elbows."

The temple wards giggle. They sit atop me while I lie on the carriage floor. I proposed that I could hang on to the underside of the carriage, but Gemi insisted this is safer.

She leads the wards in a round of song, a hymn about Anu's great mercy that I have not sung since I was a boy. We roll to a stop at the gate.

"Afternoon, Viraji," says the guard. "Destination?"

Gemi replies over the girls' singing. "The Sisterhood temple. The priestess invited the wards and me for a tour."

"General Yatin said you aren't allowed to leave the premises."

"The general was misinformed," Gemi replies, haughtier than usual. The princess was more imperialistic in her homeland. It pleases me to hear her take a position of power over the palace guards, as this will soon be her domain. She sweeps the conversation along. "Prince Ashwin approved of my visit. You can fetch him if you'd like while we wait in this stuffy carriage. But best hurry. I don't want one of the girls to faint in the heat, and *you* don't want to find yourself on the wrong side of Priestess Mita's temper."

The young choir sings the chorus. *"He is true. He is just. He is one we can trust. We are safe under the eye of his sky . . ."*

"Go ahead," grumbles the guard. "Stay in the wagon until you arrive."

We set off into the crowd. Fists thump against the exterior of the carriage. Gemi sings louder to drown them out. The pounding reverberates through the walls, and the wards' voices wobble on the chorus. In seconds, the bangs stop. The carriage sways faster, and the wards sing without fear again. I had doubts about this outing, but Gemi's assumption that the mob would not risk angering the gods by harassing a group of wards proved ingenious.

We trek unhindered downhill onto less busy roads. In the middle of the girls' third number, we halt and they pile out of the carriage. I strip off the blanket. Gemi is dressed in a blue sari, the attire for temple wards. So long as she avoids eye contact, people will assume she is one of them.

She ruffles my disheveled hair. "I told you it would work."

"Yes, but you didn't tell me I'd be serenaded."

She laughs lightly as we step into the courtyard. I fix my hair, and Gemi stops to greet a myna hopping around the ground. She carefully approaches the bird with the yellow beak and underbelly. I tried to catch mynas when I was young. They always flew away before I could get close.

Gemi creeps right up to the bird. Thinking I can too, I sneak up behind her. My nearness spooks the myna, and it takes off into the sky. Gemi beams as it flies over the rooftops. I should not be surprised by her stealth. The first time we met, she had snuck onto a balcony to eavesdrop.

"Do you have mynas in Lestari?" I ask.

"No. Aren't they lovely?" Her delight is infectious, and I must admit they are interesting birds. "I heard one singing this morning. Do you have any books about them that I may borrow?"

"I, ah, will check the library. You haven't by chance borrowed a book?"

Gemi cocks her head. "I wasn't aware I was allowed."

My face heats. She leaves me with that thought and starts up the outer steps of the temple. Engraved above the main entrance are the five godly virtues—obedience, service, sisterhood, humility, and tolerance. Every threshold in the Southern Isles is adorned with them. We go inside and Gemi surveys the artistry in the entryway.

"Kalinda had the shells brought from the coast to replicate the chandeliers in the Pearl Palace," I explain.

"They remind me of home," Gemi replies wistfully. "Father will be envious. Once he sees this, he may remodel our temple."

The datu is a collector of rare and precious things. "I'm certain Kalinda would share the layout."

"That won't be necessary," Gemi says, striding quickly ahead.

I trail her into the chapel. Minimal progress has been made on the murals since I was last here, but the completed sections are spectacular.

The wards run around, playing sleeping princess on the burned sacrifices altar. In a finished chapel, they would be reprimanded for irreverence. The temple has not been formally blessed by the brethren and dedicated to the gods, so I let them run and play. Gemi and I meander to the mural of the land-goddess Ki and her warrior daughters.

"Magnificent, isn't it?" I ask. "The artist was inspired."

"By Kalinda?" Gemi's flat tone unbalances me.

"The painter had creative freedom."

"Hmm." Gemi stares at the sister warrior on Ki's right-hand side. It may be her comment, or perhaps I miss Kalinda, but the warrior does marginally resemble my cousin.

"Prince Ashwin!" Priestess Mita's voice bounces off the high ceiling as she rants from the doorway. "Why are these girls here? You should have left them at the palace. I asked to see you, not them."

"I'll take them outside," says Gemi. The priestess eyes my viraji suspiciously. Gemi averts her gaze and leaves, the wards scurrying after her.

"Your Majesty, we have a concern with the design. I need your decision immediately." Priestess Mita leads me down a flight of stairs to an open area and posts that will eventually be a door. "The builders want to turn this section into another classroom, but this should be the Claiming chamber. We cannot have a temple of the Sisterhood without it."

None of the temples in operation are currently utilizing their chambers. The priestesses have been commanded by me to postpone the rite. Kalinda and I planned to meet with them and establish a new order after this city temple is dedicated.

I toil to eliminate exasperation from my reply. "The ritual room is no longer relevant, as the wards will choose their own husband and vocations. The additional classrooms are necessary. A proper education will be essential for them to make these decisions."

"I strongly urge you to reconsider, Your Majesty. The Claiming is a sacred rite. Doing away with it will antagonize the gods. The girls should still be inspected and shown to benefactors, but they can accept or refuse who claims them. This compromise will appease our supporters and maintain our teachings of the five godly virtues. Obedience and humility are paramount to a healthy spiritual journey. How will fate direct our wards if they don't submit to the gods' will?"

"It's not the gods' will we oppose."

"Your Majesty," Priestess Mita presses, "our people look to you for guidance."

Perhaps they should look at their own actions. Lives were stolen, rearranged, and imprisoned for this ritual. And not just Kalinda's. My mother and her sister, Yasmin, Kalinda's mother, were claimed as well. Would they still be alive if not for the hold Tarek had on their lives? Who would my mother have become had she been free?

This current institution, upheld and exploited by my father, has no place in my empire.

"Priestess, within these walls, the daughters of the temple will discover their own path. Proceed with the classroom construction."

"But Your Majesty . . . !" She brings her palms together in prayer.

I turn on my heel and find Gemi playing with the girls in the courtyard. I make no sense of their game, except they are hopping about and giggling.

"Are you all right?" Gemi asks.

"Yes . . . no." I rake at my hair. "The priestess disagrees in changes Kalinda and I are making." I imagine the girls who are running about the courtyard older, forced to stand nude and blindfolded before a strange man for the Claiming. My gut curls into a fist. "This is right for the Sisterhood, especially the wards."

"Kalinda is very important to you." Gemi's tone hints at disappointment.

"She's my cousin," I reply. "When it comes to establishing peace in the empire, Kalinda was the impetus. I am the means by which progress will be achieved."

Gemi pauses midnod and her eyes broaden. "We need to return to the palace."

I detect them then, the vibrations surging up from the ground. Every girl in the courtyard stills. Outside the wall, people abandon their work and run for home. The last time our city experienced quakes, we were infiltrated by bhutas.

"Let's go!" I say, motioning to our driver.

Gemi rounds up the wards, and we pile into the carriage. Two girls sit in my lap, one on each knee. Both are in tears. We pull into the road. Families dart about in search of shelter. Mothers huddle under eaves with their children, crying. A loud rumble carries from behind us. I lean out the window and see huge dust plumes rising from the southeast.

Lords of all. Let it have been in the district closed off for reconstruction.

Gemi points ahead. The protestors are still outside the palace gates, crowded near the wall. We must go through them.

The quaking strengthens, detectable over the jostles of the wagon. We ride up to the gates, and people push in around us. Soldiers strong-arm them back and we pass through.

Before the carriage has come to a full stop, Gemi throws open the door and leaps out. The guards shut the gates, and our driver assists the girls from the carriage. I hurry after Gemi to the palace entry. A group encircles a section of the pebble courtyard at the landing of the outer steps. Basma, the older Burner girl, is wedged in the ground. Tears roll down her face. Her arms are free, her nails raking at the dirt. A Trembler boy; her sister, Giza; and several nursemaids hover over her.

Someone opened a hole in the dirt and closed it around Basma, crushing her inside.

The nursemaids quarrel about how to pull her free. One yanks on her upper body. Basma howls. She is jammed in tight.

Gemi kneels beside Basma and grabs her wrists. "I'll hold on to you."

My viraji gradually opens the fissure with her powers. Basma slips some, but Gemi holds her level. When the gap is wide enough, I grasp Basma by the waist and haul her up. Her legs sprawl out, limp and broken in several places.

Brac runs out of the palace and down the front steps. He must have returned to the palace while we were in the city. Basma cries for him until pain overcomes the girl. Her eyes flicker back into her head.

"I'll take her to the healers." Brac scoops Basma up and carries her inside.

"Send for Virtue Guard Indah," I order the nearest nursemaid. "Tell her to meet them at the infirmary." She obeys my command, and Gemi embraces the weeping Trembler boy.

"Tell us what happened," she says.

"Giza burned my favorite toy tiger," he cries.

My gaze flashes to Basma's little sister. Giza's eyes are swollen from sobbing.

The Trembler boy sniffles and points to a pile of ash that must have been his toy. "I didn't mean to hurt anyone. I only wanted Giza to apologize. Then Basma pushed me."

Giza hangs her head. "She was defending me."

"You were all wrong." I regret my anger—they are only children—but the harm they are capable of inflicting warrants sternness. "It's a mercy no one else was injured."

Another nursemaid wrings her skirt. "We're sorry, Your Majesty. The trainees were playing in the garden when we felt the quakes. These few must have slipped past us. By the time we arrived, Basma was stuck. We didn't know what to do."

Other than watching the trainees more closely, they could have done little else. I wipe my sweaty brow. "Take the children inside. Their outside play is suspended until further notice."

The nursemaids corral the last of the children up the palace steps.

"You cannot lock them away forever," says Gemi. "In Lestari, we teach bhuta children to respect their powers. They aren't raised separately or hidden away like they should be ashamed of their abilities. They're brought up like any other child."

"To my people, these are not just children. They're former enemies." I am outraged for the trainees, for my people, for us. Which group is more important? Which group comes first?

Gemi gestures at the ruptured ground. "This was an accident."

"Is that what I tell the people who ran and hid? What do I say to Basma when she wakes? What if she never walks again?"

Gemi flails for an answer, trying to pluck one from the sky. "Bhutas may be half-gods, but we aren't perfect. We'll disappoint you. You cannot pen us up like animals when we make mistakes."

She has transitioned from discussing the trainees to speaking about herself. "I don't expect perfection, Gemi. I expect restraint. Every power must have a limit."

My viraji crouches down and touches the gravel. "We're more fragile than we seem."

She pushes the ground back together. Basma's legs will not be so easily healed.

Commander Lokesh's voice carries in from the road. This entire debacle was visible from the front gate. "Look what those atrocities do even to each other! Imagine what they will be capable of when they're fully grown. Prince Ashwin knows they're dangerous. He trains them to raise an army against us!"

What in the name of Anu's sky is he going on about? I brought the trainees here to protect them and the people from possible mishaps.

Lokesh's shouts grow louder. I spot him on his horse wearing his regular headscarf. His eyes, his only facial feature visible, burn hatred. "Generation after generation we allow these creatures to live among us. They have unimaginable powers, yet they roam free. Just days ago, I saw children wielding the power of fire. That right and responsibility should not belong to a child. Other bhutas can whittle a man's bones to dust."

Gemi grimaces. As a Trembler, she can grind bones, though she would never corrupt her god-given gift with such an act of sacrilege.

"Each bhuta has a shocking ability to harm us: winnowing, leeching, grinding, parching," Lokesh yells. "Our own former kindred parched her enemies, stealing others' soul-fire to wield as weapons." He shakes his head. "Our prince wishes for us to live in harmony. He claims he wants peace. But where is our peace of mind with these monsters living among us?"

"I'll show him a monster," Gemi says.

I hold her back. "He wants us to respond so he can warp our words."

Gemi clenches her jaw askew. "Why must I remind you that this man's actions led to the brutal beating and death of one of your guards?" Before I can inquire how she knows, she adds, "Brac told me."

"I haven't forgotten," I assure her. "See their weapons? Lokesh's men and many of the protesters are armed. He could stir the mob into a frenzy."

"*I* could stop them."

"You would only be proving Lokesh right. We cannot respond with bhuta force."

"Then say something. Don't let his opinion go uncontested. He's *wrong*." She nudges me toward the waiting people.

I walk out into the open. The crowd hushes to murmurs. General Yatin appears on the ramparts, and my soldiers still to listen.

As I near the gate, a man runs up to the commander and speaks into his ear. Lokesh straightens in his saddle and pulls aside his scarf, uncovering his face.

"An abandoned building has collapsed in the southeast district! We're fortunate that neither we nor our loved ones were inside. But it matters not! What guarantee do we have that it won't happen again? What if *our* homes topple next?" From high on his horse, Lokesh opens his arms wide. "What say you, Prince Ashwin? Is this your plan for the new Tarachand? Are you building an army against your own people?"

"No."

"Will you protect us from these destroyers of peace?"

The audience goes utterly silent. How do I convince them they are wrong after this, after what they saw of the trainees' power? How do I tell them bhutas should not be feared or branded?

I try to find the right words, but these people do not want my assurances. Lokesh's rhetoric is incendiary. They want retribution.

"Disperse," I say. "In ten minutes, my general will dispatch my soldiers and arrest every last protestor who defies my command."

"That's your response? To threaten your people?" Lokesh seeks the crowd's support of his insolence. They stand with him, prepared to do as he asks. "We won't quit until you stop harboring bhutas."

"You have nine minutes." I tug down my cuffs and return to Gemi. My viraji looks at me with such raw hurt it rocks me off my heels. "Gemi—"

She runs up the steps and disappears inside.

General Yatin organizes the soldiers to exit the gates, shouting and telling them to ready their khandas. Lokesh's defiant glower slices at me from across the divide. He turns his horse and rides away. His fellow mercenaries, distinguishable all in black, disassemble as well. Many more of my people prepare to confront the soldiers, drawing their daggers and hoisting their clubs. Again, the protestors chant for tradition to prevail.

Tarek's voice slinks into my mind. *Your people must fear you. You must make them obey.*

As I leave my men to execute their orders, I realize that I have, in part, given my people what they wanted.

23

KALINDA

Enlil and I overlook the Valley of Mirrors from a rocky rise. He secured our passage from the bear-size rabisu by feeding it a mango. In turn, the rabisu told us to take the path through the valley, forthright instructions if not for the giant crystal brambles covering the lowland.

The razor barbs fan out, pointing every which way, and infringe upon the narrow path. Nothing reflects off the crystal thorns. They are lusterless, dull and rough like unpolished quartz.

Enlil extends his spear toward the field of serrated crystals and breaks a tip. The thorn shatters, and from the opening, oil oozes. He rubs his finger over the jagged end, collecting a cloudy drop. He sniffs the colorless substance and wipes it off on his sarong.

"The briars weep venom. Do not touch them." He ties my cloak tighter at my throat and lays the hood over my head.

My state of head-to-toe dress feels gutless next to his bare arms, chest, and legs. I contemplate asking what will happen should I be cut, but the danger of venom is evident.

Enlil goes first, his spear pouring out light. We thread through the crystal thorns, some taller than our heads. Our path shrinks, narrowing to an impassable width. Enlil swings his spear and knocks down the infringing spikes. They splinter and the trail widens.

During his next swipe, he sustains a scrape across his elbow. I tug at him to stop and inspect his wound. He does not bleed. The small opening shimmers and heals before my eyes. He goes on without a word. He has spoken little since I scolded him for showing me that . . . that . . . vision. I almost regret my harshness, but this trek does not require friendliness, so I leave him be.

Before too long, the path tapers to a rabbit trail. Breaking through the brambles could take hours.

"I could open a bigger footpath with a heatwave," I say.

"No, you should conserve your powers."

"You mean because of this?" I raise my prosthesis. "My blasts *are* half as strong as they were."

Enlil touches my wooden fingers, clasping them as he would flesh and bone. "I am sorry. I cannot repair your limb, but you have always been powerful, Kalinda. You will always be powerful, no matter your physical form. Strength dwells in the soul." He lets me go and pats his back. "Climb on. I will carry you."

I chew my bottom lip. His suggestion comes from necessity. I cannot go forward without snagging my clothes. Yet an indescribable familiarity falls over me. This is not the first time he has praised my inner strength or borne up my burdens without complaint.

"Kalinda, I apologize for upsetting you. If it eases your mind, Jaya and you were not always master and servant. In other lives, you were sisters." Though he has misinterpreted my hesitation, his mention of Jaya enthralls me. "When Anu crafted mortals from the stars, you and Jaya were born of the same constellation. Your souls find each other in every life. Many of your loved ones reappeared life after life as your friends or family. The forces of nature, the very essence of the sky in your lungs, land beneath your feet, fire in your soul, and water in your blood, call to one another."

My heart falls to my knees. I press my fist over my chest, willing the pain to recede. "Please don't."

"You need not fear me. I would never harm you, Kali."

I *am* afraid of him. Terrified, actually, of what I might learn about myself through his eyes.

But I am also curious. So curious, especially about Jaya . . .

This is not why I summoned him. Dwelling on past lives will only distract me from my purpose in this one. Beyond this perilous valley is another gate, then another, and another, and eventually—Deven. I will get to him, either on my own two feet or upon the back of my guide.

"All right. You can carry me, but no more speaking about what I did before this life."

"No more memories," he vows.

Before he turns around, I do not miss his satisfied half smirk. I climb onto his back, hanging from his neck. My lips hover by his ear. I take his lightning spear, which hums in my grasp.

He turns his cheek into mine, and his voice dips to a husky purr. "Secure?"

This was a bad idea.

He starts off. I lower my chin to his neck and use his spear to smash the crystal fangs that loom too close. Venom spurts and drips from the decapitated prongs. A saw-toothed end cuts Enlil's forearm. He grimaces and his walk turns rigid.

"Are you hurting?"

"I am immortal, not infallible. Pain and agony existed long before mortals."

He sustains more scratches across his bronze skin, yet his step does not falter. I thwack at a particularly large crystal near our heads, and venom showers down. I duck from the patter of poison. Enlil stops.

"Kalinda," he says, muscles tense. "Were you struck?"

"My hood and cloak protected me."

"Hold on." He increases his gait. "Do not concern yourself with the thorns. Our path opens ahead."

His sudden speed bars me from clearing our trail. I settle against his shoulder and watch the crystals stream by. Their gloomy surfaces blur together to a solid wash of clouds. Fog has rolled into the valley. Our path widens, but Enlil slows to navigate the soupy haze.

Lethargy heavies my bones. I blink slowly at the endless stream of gray. An image of a woman peers out at me. Despite my wooziness, I rouse enough to inspect the mist. Another person appears. She has a slim, solemn face, lustrous midnight hair, and penetrating eyes.

"Someone else is out here." I push at Enlil. "Put me down."

"No, Kalinda."

Necessity pumps through me. I must find her. We cannot leave her here.

"Let me go!" I drop the spear.

Enlil bends over to fetch it, and I wriggle out of his grasp. My knees wobble as I side-wind into the fog bank. The deadly spikes have vanished, and in their place the crystals have flattened to a reflective wall. I pad up to the row of mirror glasses. Figures inside the mirrors gaze out. Right in front of me is the woman I first saw. She is no stranger.

An entire spectrum of Kalindas stand before me. At least a dozen versions of myself, all dressed in varying attire and hairstyles, stare out of the mirror. Most are young, my age or close to it. Some are in their middle years, while others must be in their last decade of life.

The first and nearest reflection wields an urumi. Its flexible silver blades snake around her legs. She dons old-fashioned armor that is heavy and clunky, and she is speckled in blood, not her own, judging by her lack of injury.

I tread up to the mirror glass, and her reflection takes over my own. I no longer see myself, only her. She holds herself with self-assurance that I do not exhibit. Her indomitable poise is like a tigress's—exquisite, terrifying. Besides their physical likeness, all the Kalindas are outwardly confident. I envy one more attribute. Every one of them has both their hands.

Something from the deepest trenches of my soul thrashes against the inner trapdoor. The Kalinda before me flings her urumi back and lashes the whiplike blades at me.

A pressure explodes in my chest. The trapdoor flings open, and something—someone—pours into my head. The back of my neck cramps.

Kalinda.

Her voice sounds like mine in tenor, but she is surer, more aware of what is happening. Shakiness jogs up my legs. I rest against the cold, flat mirror glass, my skull aching.

"Who are you?"

Again, her voice engulfs my thoughts.

I am Cala.

Her reflection grins hard. She rests her hand on the mirror glass against my prosthesis.

A shadow stirs behind me. The fire-god's reflection manifests in the mirror. Cala's attention leaps to him. Yearning beams from her eyes. *Enlil.*

"Kalinda, what has come over you?" He twists me around so fast I sway on my feet. "I have been calling your name. We need—child of Kur."

I slump against him, my insides plummeting long after he catches me.

Cala beats her fist against the glass. Enlil touches my face. I have wet spots on my cheek that I did not notice. He scrubs them off. Cala pounds harder. *Enlil! Enlil!*

"You must remain awake." Enlil sweeps me up. The ground and sky spin.

Cala's reflection runs after us. She jumps from crystal to crystal, her voice transferring to my head. Her calls for Enlil are soundless. He hears not one.

The giant crystal thorns thin around us. Cala runs to the last mirror and whips her urumi at the unbreakable glass. We travel farther from the brambles, and she sinks to her knees. I watch over Enlil's shoulder until I lose sight of her. Though her form is trapped in the Valley of Mirrors, her soft weeping rattles inside my mind.

Enlil climbs out of the valley and lays me on the ground. He presses down on my breastbone. "This will be painful."

Searing agony lances into my bones. I shriek and buck, but he presses me down and pushes soul-fire inside every hidden pocket of my veins. His powers scorch out the venom, leaving no part of me untouched. At last, when I have no voice left, the cleansing inferno dissipates.

I wilt into a heap. Sweat dampens my brow and chest from his residual heat. My skin glows with tiny trails of lightning. I feel around inside my head for Cala. She has gone quiet. I wheeze in the fragile silence. Gradually, my radiance dims and my temperature cools.

Enlil rests my head in his lap. "Kalinda?"

"I'm here."

His shoulders slump over his chest. "Had the thorn punctured your skin, the venom would have killed you. Can you stand?"

"Not yet." My teeth and tongue taste of cinders. My bones and muscles have splintered to tinder. "The mirrors showed me versions of myself. The reflections were of me, but not me."

Enlil gazes off at the valley. "They were you before, in your other lives."

"But I'm not like them. They were warriors."

"As are you." The fire-god's gaze sears into mine. "We are always more than we think we are."

I inhale his spring water scent, and longing floods up from a well of secrets that I cannot see or grab hold of. I search for the source inside me, but I am trying to read an expression on a face that is turned away. "Who is Cala?"

Enlil stills, frozen as a statue. "You told me you did not wish for me to interfere with your memories."

I still do not, but I feel her lurking. She is out now, and I do not know how to put her back. Perhaps if I understand who she is, I can force her from my mind.

"How did you meet?"

Enlil picks up my left hand and laces our fingers. "That was a long time ago." He kisses my knuckles in sequence. Memories bubble up from a well of secrets and cascade over my mind. The surge sweeps me from my bearings and drags me further into myself.

I kneel in the garden near the rhododendron forest, my charcoal stick in hand. Father will be irritated with me for sketching on his terrace tiles. The whole of the world is my sketchbook, and the sunshine is friendliest this hour of day.

A shadow falls over the sketch of my mother, blocking the midday sun. I gaze up into startling, fiery eyes. I open my mouth to call for Mother, but Fire Eyes speaks.

"Did you draw this?"

I glance nervously at the open double doors to my home.

He sits near my pile of charcoals. "You are gifted." He brushes my hair behind my shoulder, his touch natural as an afterthought. "How old are you?"

"Eighteen."

"And your name?"

His soothing scent, like spring rain, relaxes me. He must be a friend of Father's for the guards to have allowed him through our front gate. "I'm Cala."

"Would you draw for me, Cala?"

He asks tentatively, as though expecting me to refuse. His shyness does not suit his striking appearance. He must be lonely, like me. "Yes, I will draw for you."

And I do.

The vision swirls around, and a torrent of new memories arrests me. Cala and Enlil stand at an altar in Ekur, Enlil wearing a fitted white-and-gold tunic and Cala a silk gold-and-red sari. She vows to love him until the end of time, and he promises her his heart forevermore.

Enlil kisses the last of my knuckles and lets me go. The loss of his touch reels me back to the present. I gape at him, my head still in his lap. Cala was his wife. Her love for him pushes me to bury my burdens in his embrace.

Kiss him. My emotions twist and tangle with Cala's. *He's our fate.*

Enlil's nearness is intoxicating. Any closer and I will be fully drunk on him. I roll onto the ground. "Get out of my head."

He crouches over me. "Cala? Cala, are you there?"

Enlil! I'm here!

Get out of my head!

I dig my fingers into the dirt and shove Cala back down into my chest. Her presence finds lodging beside my drumming heart.

I blink myself into awareness. Cala's cries for Enlil drift to muffled pleas. I am not alone, but I am in charge. I stagger to my feet.

"My name is *Kalinda*, and you are my guide. We have come to find Deven Naik. He's the entire reason we're in this awful place, so let's move."

Enlil peers into my eyes. I stare icily in return, willing any trace of Cala from my expression.

The fire-god picks up his spear and treads on.

I glimpse a single shadow loitering at the border of the crystals in the valley below. I stomp after Enlil and let Cala's reflection die in my vision.

24

DEVEN

The long-needled thorn slips off the hilt of my janbiya hilt and punctures my thumb. I shake my hand to ease the stinging and slip my bleeding finger into my mouth.

Mistake. I spit out the grimy taste of my skin and throw away the dull thorn. I break another needle off the tree in front of me and return to my project. My progress engraving Kali's name into the hilt of my dagger has been painstaking. I only just completed the first letter.

As I work on the next one, my eyesight blurs. I still have not slept. The rabisus and demons still camp at the blockade down the road. They have been quiet for some time. By nightfall, every one of them will be awake and alert. If I do not sleep now, I will be awake all night again. I drag the needle through the dirt, writing *KALI* so I remember to finish the engraving, and lie on my side.

Knocks come from the Road of Bone. The bones are solid but resonate with a scant tapping when walked upon. I come awake and lie on my front at the base of the tree.

Something travels in my direction from the blockade. Big shapes that begin as shadows soon sharpen. Two demons astride ugallus pause every so often to canvass the thicket. Edimmu and Asag are on patrol.

I roll onto my sides and then my back, smothering myself in dirt. Demons have a powerful sense of smell. After my first few days on the run, the putridness of the Void camouflaged me. I coat myself in grime for extra protection.

On my stomach again, hot breaths blow off some of the filth caking my lips. The demons stalk closer. I stretch out low with my dagger.

Close enough that I can count her scales, Edimmu halts her ugallu and licks the air with her forked tongue. The ugallu's silver feline gaze stays on the trees. I breathe only when necessary and swallow even less.

"The road is clear," Asag rumbles.

"I smell flesh," his sister hisses.

She can only mean me. Her sense of smell must be stronger than Asag's.

Edimmu jumps off her mount, her tongue flicking the air. She follows the taste of my smell closer to the spiny trees. The grove is thick with brambles and undergrowth. To get in, I had to slide on my belly to the middle. Getting out in a hurry, and without them seeing me, is impossible.

Skies above, why isn't my dagger a sword?

Asag rides up to his sister, his ugallu growling and snapping at hers. "The road is clear. We can return to camp."

Edimmu samples the air again. Her crocodile snout bears brown stained teeth. "Whatever it is will soon be carrion."

She mounts her ugallu and they ride up the road. Their ugallus steal away, tails twitching. My pulse hammers at every pressure point. I could seek out another hideout, but I would have to sneak past Kur's lair. The roadblock prevents me from going out to the obstructions, and I will not go into the city. The wanderers live there and so does *she*.

I lessen my grasp on my janbiya. A pattern is impressed into the handle, a *K* and a slash?

The dirt beside me has markings—letters. Near them is a pile of dull thorns. I must have rubbed away some of the letters when I rolled around. All that remains is an *L* and an *I*.

The letters swirl around my mind in a jumble. I inspect the dirt closer. The missing letter is barely visible, an *A*.

Kali. Memories of her flood my thoughts, some hazier than others. The flimsy recollections may float away in an instant.

How could I forget Kalinda? The gap in my mind is expanding like a sinkhole. Any wider and who I am right now, who I was when I was first brought here, will fall in.

My hand shakes as I pry off another thorny needle from a tree. I resume carving her name, faster and more fervently. My remembrances of her turn around and around in my mind as I work. Her solemn expression and thick, silken hair. The way she touches her mother's daggers at her side when she is deep in contemplation. How she juts out her chin anytime someone suggests she do something she does not like.

Thoughts of her bring my awareness back into my grasp.

When Kali's memory is alive, so am I.

25

KALINDA

We arrive at the third gate. The rabisu stands from behind the low stone wall and stretches until its shoulders are nearly in line with Enlil's. The guardian's furry physique is mannish; it even has hands with fingernails. Saliva runs down its chin, dripping from fangs. It watches me and licks its chops. Enlil tosses a hunk of stinky meat at the beast.

The rabisu catches his payment. "Cross the River of Ordeal. The gate is on the other side." It rips into the meat with its teeth.

The bone-chilling noise of its feeding follows us up a steep gradient. When the sounds finally quit, I glance back. Gate and guardian have disappeared.

"Why is the landscape always changing?" I ask. "Where does it disappear to?"

"Nowhere. The Void is empty unless it is not."

I cannot puzzle out the fire-god's meaning. Omnipotent nonsense, I suppose.

Enlil ascends the slope. I drag behind, my legs twinging and my side aching. The long stretches of sleeplessness have dwindled my stamina. Enlil notices my sluggishness and pauses. I almost overtake him, and he climbs on. He does this again and again without a word of encouragement. Cala is still, but I sense her near, like a person breathing in my ear.

He scales to the top and waits. The din of gushing water increases as I crest the rise. I bend over, wheezing. A wooden rope bridge spans a sheer divide and, far below, a river. Rapids tear at its surface, sending up an almighty roar. The flimsy bridge has no handrails. The planks have rotted-out holes, and the gaps between them are irregular, some wider than our feet.

Enlil passes me a mango. "Eat and recover your strength."

I gobble the fruit in record time. My fatigue goes away, as does the pinch in my side.

Enlil sidesteps down the gravel slope to the flat grade where the rope bridge connects to the cliff by double posts. His footing unlooses stones that roll off the edge and plummet into the choppy river.

He motions to me. I clamp his fingers and descend to him. I survey the cliff for another crossing. This rickety bridge is our only path to the other side.

"We must cross one at a time," he says. "I will go first."

Holding his spear across his chest for balance, Enlil ventures onto the first plank. The bridge swings from his weight and the ropes tauten. He hazards another narrow plank and glances back at me.

"Face forward!" I yell.

He grins and straddles another gap.

Gods, what a pest.

Enlil navigates the planks in succession, evading the rotten sections. At the center of the bridge, a portion of the plank creaks. He readjusts his footing. As he waves to let me know he is well, the wood beneath him snaps and he drops.

"Enlil!" I fall to my knees at the ledge.

He hits the river and goes under. His spear surfaces, then him. The rapids sweep him along.

"Oh, gods, gods, gods, gods." I stumble along the cliff, surveying for a trail down to the river.

Enlil floats downstream. Soon he will be out of sight. I will be alone, lost without a guide, and with no means of freeing Deven.

I still cannot find a trail. There is only one way down.

"Please. Please. Please." Gazing up, as if I can somehow see Anu in the Beyond, I leap.

A scream wrenches out of me as I fall. My feet collide with the icy water first. I submerge and resurface into rapids. Gasping and kicking, I spin and bob downriver. On the next surge, I grab sight of land and lose it again. Another swell drags me under. I am heaved up and pushed into a boulder. The strap of my prosthesis loosens, and my wooden hand is swept in one direction, me another. It is swiftly lost in the torrent of waves. I gulp down water, only it is thicker and heavier than what I know.

Enlil's words return about Irkalla casting a plague on the under realm and turning the water to blood.

I gag up the dampness. More wetness splashes up my nose and into my mouth. I am going to drown, choking on blood in this godless river.

A beam of light glows in front of me. The current throws me directly into the radiance. I hug the end of Enlil's spear. He tows me to a shallow bank, and I flop on a bed of pebbles. Blood smears our skin and clothes. A slash on my side bleeds from where I struck the boulder, mingling with the rest. My stomach buckles. I retch on the hard-packed shore and flop onto my back.

Enlil glowers down at me. "You stupid, stupid woman. How many times must I watch you bleed?"

"How. Many. Times . . . ?" I trail off.

Cala shoves into my thoughts. *Remember.*

I flinch at the power of her hold. If she were physically present, her demand would bruise.

Remember what?

Remember who we are!

Her mandate smashes into my consciousness. A murky splotch charges across my vision and hauls me into the chasm of her being.

—————————

Thunderous cheers echo throughout the amphitheater. I hurl my urumi blades. My nearest opponent yields, gashes seeping across her chest. I reel around and slash. The whiplike blades strike another competitor, cutting her down. She howls wildly. I hardly hear her over my inner gong ringing, pushing me to end this match.

One final time, I slice at my rival. My blades slit her throat and put her suffering to rest. She falls onto the stacks of bodies around me. They are blood-spattered messes of ripped limbs, gushing wounds, and silent mouths. No other opponents rush me. She was the last woman, last competitor, standing.

No. *I* am.

The spectators packing the rows of the amphitheater pound their feet and pump their fists. "Hundred, hundred, hundred," they chant.

I thrust my blood-streaked urumi above my head. "Father Anu and Mother Ki—it is finished."

From overhead, descending from a divide in the rolling white clouds, a burning chariot pulled by horses of flame blazes a trail of fire. As the chariot appears, the audience hushes. I drop my urumi. Blood speckles my heavy armor. My lower body is bathed in it, and my own blood flows from a cut near my hip. I tuck my elbow against the wound to slow the bleeding.

The fiery chariot circles the oval arena. I squint into the glory of the horses and their rider. The fire-god radiates vivacity, outshining that of his mounts. His magnificence comes into focus. Flowing hair, wavy yet tamed. Bare chest sculpted from marble. Acres of bronze skin.

Hypnotizing cinder eyes. A full mouth drawn out like a bow and a clean-shaven jawline.

He lands his chariot across the length of the arena. A sarong covers his upper thighs and groin, leaving toned legs wound by strappy leather sandals. He does not carry his lightning spear but a necklace. The hushed spectators bow as he steps off the chariot and strides to me. My gaze holds his, trapped in the aliveness of its color. Swirling golds and reds and oranges, a peek into the living flame within him. He stops and lifts the medallion.

"My champion!" He slips the necklace over my head. The weight lies against my collarbone; the surface is engraved with the gods' quad emblem.

I start to bow, but he halts me.

"You do not bow to me. My heart, my champion." The fire-god lowers to one knee and presents a crown, a delicate arrangement of gold-plated lotus flowers. "You shall be my hundredth queen."

I remove my helmet and drop it in the dirt. The dead surround us, so many I question the sanctity of my soul. But these women tried to separate us. They died so that we might be one.

I place the crown and fall into him.

He cradles the back of my head. "Will you forgive me this trial?"

"You need never ask for forgiveness. I did this for us, and I would do it again."

His eyes flash at the implication of another tournament, another trial standing between our love. "Nothing will separate us. You and I will be united forevermore."

The fire-god lowers his nose to mine, tipping our foreheads together. As our lips skim, Cala releases me from her clutches.

Now you remember.

My eardrums pulsate against my skull. I can still feel Enlil's kiss and smell the misty clouds on his skin. As I reorient myself, he wipes the bloody river water from my cheeks.

Tarek cannot have been right. During my rank tournament, he told our people I was the reincarnated soul of a legend, the greatest tournament champion of all time, who gained the favor of a god. This warrior battled Enlil's wives and courtesans to secure her place as his one hundredth wife, and, in doing so, brought down an army of women.

She had no name, no fate of her own, except the destiny that bound her to the fire-god. She is simply known as Enlil's hundredth rani.

She was me, says the voice in my head. *And you know my name.*

I roll onto my side, away from Enlil. This cannot be. The woman who dominated the first-ever rank tournament was cold-blooded. But Cala's memory is undeniable. She recalled Enlil in detail. She knows him in ways I do not that nonetheless fit my experiences so far.

It's true, Kali. You have my medallion.

My satchel was ripped off while I was in the river, but I pat the outline of the necklace in my pocket. I do not need to look upon it again—it is the same medallion Enlil awarded his hundredth rani.

I bury my eyes in the crook of my elbow. "It cannot be."

"Kalinda, I am sorry I was cross. I could never let misfortune befall you."

"I . . . I was Cala," I say, shuddering.

"You *are* Cala. The soul lives on after death." Enlil rolls me so my upper body rests against his. "Souls who love each other will remember when united again and again."

I recall the other women in the Valley of Mirrors. "You and I met in more lives?"

"Cala's life was the first."

Her championship spurred a romance that lasted lifetimes, so many I am afraid to ask how often I have suffered through this moment, recalling sentiments lost behind my mortal veil.

"Why didn't I remember my past lives before now?"

"Do you recall your Razing?" he asks. I could never forget. The ritual, wherein my back was cut systematically to prevent my body from overheating, was excruciating. "During that ritual, your inner stars consolidated to one. Those stars represented your prior lives. To fully come into your Burner abilities, you had to set aside those connections and accept your inheritance as a half-god."

My truest connection to the gods and my past lives were taken away, cut by cut.

While my waterlogged muscles recover, the sky deepens from heather to sable. Enlil cradles me, still shaken from my near drowning.

"Why did you do that, Kali? This river cannot harm me, but you could have died."

"I don't know."

But I do know. I *had* to leap after him. Our fates are tied together, his and mine. Our bond transcends eras and our union is irrefutable.

He falls and I fall.

He rises and I rise.

Enlil has laid claim to Cala, and, subsequently, to me. I cannot pursue my path without acknowledging his role in my past, my present, and, gods only know, my future. Cala has lived countless lifetimes at his side. What sort of claim does that leave me to my own heart?

I cannot say what has been determined about my fate, but Cala and Enlil's history does not alter the present. The fire-god will not lay claim to my soul or exploit my love for Deven to regain a closeness to Cala. My will and heart belong to me, and my purpose has not changed.

I came for Deven Naik, and even if it means defying the gods and resisting fate, I will free him.

26

DEVEN

Nightfall rests upon the under realm, darkness so thick it stings. Dagger in hand, I slide out from under the low branches of the thorn trees.

The Road of Bone has transformed into an active highway. Rabisus guide the latest influx of souls into the city in oxen-pulled wagons. The oxen's horns curl around their hairy faces and glistening snouts. Souls reach out the rear doors of the wagons, begging for release. A rabisu on foot snaps a whip at them, and the wagons plods onward.

Every night new souls arrive, fresh from their mortal death. They greet the evernight fully aware, remembering who they are and what choices led them to this prison. Before long they forget their pain and wander about mindlessly. The under realm is full of these wanderers, shadows of their former selves. This will not be my fate.

I join the wanderers leaving the city and mimic their expressions. Eyes flat, mouth turned down in a perpetual grimace, and a sluggish gait. Ahead, demons guard the blockade, admitting wanderers out and in. Putting my head down, I tuck my janbiya in the waist of my trousers and cover the hilt with my tunic. I finished engraving Kali's name on it just before nightfall. I will not forget her again.

I come up to the group of wanderers waiting to cross the blockade. Asag is on guard. I have a better chance of getting past him than Edimmu. Asag rakes his stony gaze over a wanderer and grunts, sending him along.

Shoulders sagged and head lolled to the side, I shuffle up to the barrier and bump into Asag. He grabs the front of my dirty tunic. Before I left, I rolled in the dirt again. I will myself not to shudder as I stare at his thick legs. He snorts and shoves me forward. I stride off, so slowly I may explode.

The blockade falls behind me, and pathways lead up into the sky. I follow the instructions on the back side of my janbiya. *1st right. 6th left.*

A shadow stirs behind me. I continue but train my senses on the slinking presence. It could be the same thing that has been following me up to the gate.

Up ahead, the path splits at an overhang. *Right at fork.*

Instead of selecting right, I duck down the opposite way. My pursuer comes up to the divide. I capture his neck and lift my blade, locking him against me.

"Who are you?" I ask. "Why are you following me?"

"Deven," replies a choked voice. "It's me."

"Brac?" I look askance at my brother's honey eyes and coppery hair. I start to lower my blade. "How did you get here?"

"I stepped through the gate after you."

Impossible. Kali tried that without success. "Who are you really?"

He elbows me in the side. I bend over, and he throws me toward the end of the path. My heels teeter over the drop-off. I secure my balance and stumble from the ledge.

Whatever this thing is, he is not Brac.

He stalks up to me and throws a punch. His knuckles smash into my cheek. I wheel around with my dagger, and he kicks me in the side. I fold in on myself. He fists a handful of my hair, wrenches my head up, and knees me in the jaw. One of my lower teeth wiggles.

"What are you?" I garble out.

"I am whatever my queen requires. Presently, she requires you." He robs me of my weapon and tosses it over the ledge.

"No!" I scramble after it, but my dagger has fallen into the night.

My pursuer grabs the back of my head and slams it against the road. I lie in a daze, engulfed by a deluge of pain. When I drift back into myself, the demon, still assuming Brac's appearance, is dragging me down the path.

This monster, this demon, can wear a disguise. If he followed me out of the under realm, through the gate, and assumed the appearance of Brac, the bhuta ambassador . . .

I seek out Kali's soul-fire high up in the nothing. Still, she is not visible. My dagger with my directions is lost, and my memory is dodgy, but I have to get home. Irkalla's sudden interest in me must be related to the demon impersonating my brother. I have to return to the mortal realm and warn Ashwin.

I twist my tunic from the demon's grasp. He stops and cuffs me across the jaw. Braced on my side, blood spills from my split lip. I spit two busted lower teeth onto the ground.

The demon reels back for another swing. I swipe my leg under his ankles, unbalancing him, and shove him over the ledge. He falls out of sight.

I rub at my sore jaw. Skies alive, his fists are like mallets. I stagger to my feet, and the demon climbs back up. He wears Brac's irksome smirk.

"Son of a scorpion," I breathe.

He grabs for me. I rotate from his clutch and totter toward the edge. My inclination is to stop myself from falling, but I let the sky have me.

I plummet through the pathways and lunge for one. My weight drags me over again. Another few seconds, and I land on a lower roadway of shadow. I pant and wait out the aching. Most paths return to the city. I get up and jog down the sloping road.

Please lead me beyond the blockade. My steps weave, my vision watery. *I have to get home. I have to warn the others.*

The path lets me out near the city gate. I am farther from the obstructions than where I began the night. I will have to pass Kur's lair, take the Road of Bone, and sneak through the demon's blockade again.

My legs threaten to rebel. I may not have time to get through the blockade before daytime. Then the wanderers will go to rest, and they are my cover.

I sway on my feet, exhaustion replacing my alertness. Tiny specks explode in my vision. The white streamers consolidate to one distant star. Kali's soul-fire.

She's here? That must be her. No one else shines that brightly. Her light is a dot far out in the obstructions.

I cannot fathom how she got into the under realm. I would be angry, but knowing she is here provides clarity. The demon's attack on me could be related to her. Kur summoning his commanders. The blockade. The demon patrols. The army of the evernight would not go to such lengths for a lowly, half-dead mortal. They must want something from Kali. I have to warn her, then I can alert Ashwin about the possibility of an imposter demon in the palace.

I scrub the blood off my chin and wipe it on my trousers. The dead do not bleed. By the time I revisit the blockade, my wounds should clot or else the demons will smell me and I will never pass as a wanderer.

Joining the meandering throng, I tread by Kur's lair. Nothing moves or makes a sound from within. I am not tempted to linger and wait for a sign of his attentiveness. On the Road of Bone, I set a more decisive pace. I cannot lose this connection to Kali.

A gong rings in the distance, hailing from the city.

No. Not now.

All captives of the under realm halt, no matter their direction. Compelled to blend in, I stop too. Without an uttered word, the wanderers turn around and return to the city to heed their queen. I peer at

Kali's far-off gleam. I will never get through the blockade now. I must behave like a wanderer, and no wanderer ignores Irkalla's summons.

I turn around. As I pass Kur's lair again, a big golden eye peers out. I direct my attention ahead to the daggered spires of the Umbra Palace. No other structure compares to the lair of the queen of the dead. She shares it with no one, not even her king.

Rabisu sentinels guard the city gate. I heavy my step to imitate the wanderers. The blood on my trousers and lip has dried, and the lumbering crowd is thick. The rabisus look right past me. I enter the rows of crumbling huts, roofs caving in and walls rotting. The scent of hopelessness strengthens. Last time I entered the city, it took me weeks to sweat the stench from my pores.

Once out of the sentinels' sight, I stoop behind a wall. Wanderers plod past, heading for the palace. Kali's soul-fire is less visible here. The darkness is a squirming, sludgy wetness that dampens my skin. I can outlast this short detour and return to finding Kali. For the first time since I have been trapped, the stillness and loneliness are not crushing.

Pairs of rabisus prowl the streets for idlers. I slip back into the crowd. My chest constricts on every step I take closer to the palace. I have another rule of survival that I must break. Avoid the queen of the dead.

27

KALINDA

We cannot see more than a few feet in front of us, yet the fourth gate makes it easy to locate. The rabisu appears up the riverbank, near a copse of dead trees. My damp clothes flake drying blood and smell a fright. I must look as though I am wearing a gutted beast.

Enlil's great strides eat up the land. I scramble to keep pace with him. His anger over my trip downriver feels disproportionate, so I speak up.

"I don't understand why you're still mad. I was trying to find you."

Enlil whirls on me. "You leaped in after me for that mortal man. You only need me as your guide—to find *him*. Your lack of concern for your own soul is reckless. Mortals who die in the Void suffer an eternal death. You would have been permanently cut off from the Beyond. No other life justifies that risk."

I clutch the collar of my tunic. I could have perished forever.

Enlil strides ahead to bargain with the rabisu. The guardian has the girth and stature of a bear standing on its hind paws. His shaggy coat of fur is putrid. Enlil pays him with a larger slab of meat than the last and receives our instructions. The rabisu growls at me, bear claws out, but lets us by.

We cut through the spooky grove of trees. I dodge the thorns protruding from the spindly branches. Despite his anger, Enlil remains by my side. I dislike being the cause of his troubled expression.

"Enlil, I'm sorry. I'll be more cautious."

He tugs me against him. "I could not live knowing you were trapped here."

His sentiment puts my own emotions for Deven into order, but my heart has made room for another. Cala has elbowed her way into my core and lit a fire for Enlil. His eyes occupy my sight, their swirling flames mesmerizing.

He halts and cranes his neck like a bird of prey.

"Be still," he orders.

His spear stops shining and he shuts his eyes, locking in his living flame. A blackout eclipses the grove. Then flapping. Something is flying overhead. The beating wings circle over us. Enlil quits breathing. Like food, perhaps gods do not need air.

The flapping noises diminish, moving farther out. Enlil uncurls his body from mine. He taps his spear, and the illuminance goes on. I squint from the abrupt brilliance. He grabs my wrist and pulls me through the trees.

"What was that?" I ask, stumbling after him.

"Demons. They know we are here. One of the rabisus must have reported us. Demons are very territorial, especially about their realm."

"They can live elsewhere?"

"Before the First Bhutas were given powers, and the gods made a pact not to interfere with mortals, demons could go anywhere."

When I was a girl, the sisters told the wards tales of demons dwelling in the caves of the mountains near our temple. I thought their stories were to frighten us into better behavior. Long ago they may have been true.

We exit the last of the trees and reach a wasteland. The desert lacks the warm ginger sand dunes of those in the mortal realm. Twisting cracks snake across the dried-up ground, hardened and flat. No vegetation or boulders are in sight. Should the demon patrol circle back, we will have nowhere to hide.

"What is this place?"

"The Desert of Anguish."

The accuracy of the obstructions' names so far adds to my wariness. A path slices through the center of the desert, set apart by skulls on either side of the trail. Enlil leads me down the outcropping and we start across. Every skull marker along the path stares at me, prying at my nerves.

"Where are my parents?" I ask, requiring a distraction.

"Kishan and Yasmin are waiting for you in the Beyond."

"My mother too? I thought mortals had to live as a bhuta first."

"Your mother sacrificed her life to bring you into this world. She did not need to serve as a bhuta to earn Anu's blessing. You will meet them again in your next existence."

His explanation is mostly a comfort. My father was executed by Rajah Tarek for falling in love with my mother, and she passed on soon after my birth. My parents are dwelling together in the greatest place of peace afforded to any soul, a fine reward for their tragic demise. Yet I still must bide my time to join them as a family.

"Why couldn't I have had parents who raised me?"

"They met their fate, as did you. Anu gave you as a daughter to Kishan to inherit his Burner abilities. That was your soul's innate predisposition. Bhuta powers are physically determined by lineage, but more so by the soul." Enlil smiles sideways. "You were meant to wield fire."

After what I saw of Cala in the arena, I understand his assessment. Her voice invades my thoughts.

Ask him about our meetings.

I am curious too. "How many times have we met?"

"I have been present in most of your lives."

"But you didn't find me in this one."

Cala's voice grows stronger. *Ask him why not.*

"Why didn't you come before now?"

Enlil sighs. "I could not."

My annoyance laces with Cala's. Had Enlil come before my Claiming, he could have stopped Tarek from separating Jaya and me. My best friend would still be alive. "You forgot about me?"

Enlil tugs me to a halt. "I have not lived a moment without you that I did not wish you were at my side."

"Then where were you?" I whisper, my voice mingling with Cala's.

"You are a bhuta. Your responsibilities set you on a different path." His spear brightens one side of his face. "Kali, this mortal man you seek is not your fate."

"You don't get to decide that."

Or does he? As a god, Enlil does not see time. His life has no beginning or end. Fate is a spectrum, not a destination.

A pressure builds at the base of my neck, my worries compounding into a headache. I block it before I am off-balance. "I told you from the start, I've come for Deven Naik."

"As you desire," Enlil replies reasonably. I await a bigger reaction, yet he is the very picture of acceptance.

"All right," I say, stretching out my reply. We set off, and I look at him askance. "You never told me what my payment will be for our bargain."

He makes a noncommittal "Hmm."

"Well?" I ask archly.

"As I clarified before, I will require compensation when the mortal man has been freed."

"His name is Deven Naik."

"Of course. Forgive me."

Enlil resumes our hasty pace. I let silence reign, ignoring his insincere apology. Our discussions help to distract me from this grim landscape, but I will not debate with him about Deven's importance.

We progress through the dusty wasteland, my mouth and throat parched from the scorched air, like inhaling stale smoke. When the desert rules every direction, I hear a groan. Off the trail lies a person.

"Water," he rasps, clawing at the barren ground.

I come to a halt. "Who is that?"

"A wanderer," Enlil replies. "Let him be. The Desert of Anguish is a mercy."

"Dying of thirst is a mercy?"

"It is in the Void." Enlil ushers me along.

More wanderers appear off the trail. Some lie on the cracked ground, while others crawl. Fewer stumble about blindly. All of them beg for a drink, but do not cross onto the road. The pleas of the suffering torture my ears.

"Can we not spare them food or water? You could give them mangoes like you did me."

"Nothing can quench their thirst," Enlil replies. "The living pray for them; thus, Irkalla cannot confine them to her city. Trust me. Wandering the desert is a more compassionate sentence."

The City of the Dead is worse than this? Deven said he hides near there.

"Kalinda," a voice calls from within the open wasteland.

A woman drags herself toward us over the rough ground.

Kindred Lakia.

The last time I saw Ashwin's mother, we were in the amphitheater arena locked in a duel, an impulsive conclusion to my rank tournament that led to her death. Though she still wears her training sari and sandals, her attractiveness has lessened from a sharp blade to a dull spoon.

"Please, Kalinda. Water."

Someone in the mortal realm has been praying over her soul, and I would wager it is her son. My memories of Lakia are not the fondest, but if Ashwin were here and this were my mother, I would expect him to show her compassion.

"Don't leave the trail," Enlil warns.

"It's all right. I know her." Stepping over a skull, I go to Lakia. She appears even more miserable up close. Her once-glowing complexion has a lusterless hue. Patches of her hair are missing, the rest knotted in stringy clumps.

"Kalinda," she cries, guttural, tearless gasps. "I left him out in the desert. He's gone and I could not stop it."

I kneel on the sandy desert floor, which is softer and finer than it seems. "Who's gone?"

"My little boy." She sobs into the crook of her elbow. "Tarek sat in my chamber and waited with me. I heard his cries as the carriage pulled away. My husband wanted me to cry or run. He wanted to punish me for my weakness." She lifts her bloodshot gaze to me. "I didn't cry. I held it in until I was alone. But my boy . . . my boy was gone."

"Ashwin is home, Lakia," I promise, her heartbreak pressing upon me. "He's living in Vanhi again, in the palace. He's home."

Lakia rubs her forehead in the dirt, further matting her hair. She lifts her head again, her gaze wild. "Water. Please, water."

I wave for Enlil to come over so I can ask for one of his mangoes. He sends me a stern glare to return to the path and does not budge. "I don't have any water for you. I'm sorry."

Lakia pushes up and cups my cheek, her fingers icy. "You're my husband's kindred . . . ?"

"Not anymore."

The fact of this strikes me deep. I never wanted to be Tarek's kindred. Then I was his kindred, and I was good at my role. Gods curse him for that. Without the title that I earned, I no longer know what to do with myself.

"Much has happened since you . . . left," I continue. "Prince Ashwin rules Tarachand now. He reigns with fairness and mercy."

Lakia grabs my chin hard. "I know not who you speak of. I have no son." Her other hand grasps the back of my head, securing me in a vise. I immediately realize my legs are stuck. I have been sinking into the sand. "No water? Just as well. I'll drink the water from your blood."

She lowers her mouth to bite me. I push her off and yank at my knees. I have sunk farther into the ashy ground. Lakia lunges and her teeth snap at my nose. I hold her back, her flesh frozen and lifeless. I cannot parch her to render her unconscious. She has no soul-fire to draw out.

Enlil enters my side vision and aims his spear at her. A lightning bolt shoots from the end, striking Lakia in the side. She flies back, smoke rising off her still form. Our squabble attracts more wanderers across the open area. They amble toward us.

"Hold still." Enlil aims his spear at the sand around my feet and shoots. It solidifies to glass. He smashes it and heaves me up. "Next time use your dagger."

"I didn't want to hurt her."

"Kalinda, *everything* wants to harm you here. Even the ground would devour you."

Back on the trail, I brush myself off. The dustiness persists. "What is this sand?"

"Bone ash." Enlil drags me onward while I knock the dust off faster. "We must not tarry. The wanderers cannot enter the path, but we best not tempt them."

I skip along, stunned from my encounter. "Did Lakia truly forget her own son? She was weeping over him one minute, and the next she said he didn't know him. How could she forget him? She had her faults—*many* faults—but she loved Ashwin."

"She was not the woman you knew. The Void boiled her down to her worst attributes and pains."

"I took her life," I whisper. Lakia will recover. After all, she is already dead. But leaving her to suffer . . . "I sent her here."

"You took her life to preserve your own. You did *not* condemn her. Her actions did."

I wait for Cala to add her opinion of murder to the matter. I saw what she did in the arena. She killed all those women to secure her place as Enlil's wife. She remains quiet.

The souls in the desert beseech us for water. I cannot do anything for them, so I focus on escaping this morbid wasteland. "Will you be punished for breaking your pact not to interfere with mortal affairs?"

"No," Enlil replies shortly. "My unusual paternity formed lower expectations of my behavior."

"How many times have you saved me?"

Enlil slows to a more official gait. "My dear queen, it is you who saved me. Before our first meeting, I was floundering. My sister Enki was the epitome of obedience. I was . . . less so. My true parentage had been revealed, and I felt I did not belong with the gods. I hid my pain in the joys and passions of the mortal realm. Then I met Cala. She loved me as I was." He adds tenderly, "Every time you are reborn, I rediscover the wonder of watching the sunrise."

Is he speaking to Cala . . . or to me? The separation between us has blurred.

I rummage around inside my head for her commanding voice. *Cala?*

Her memories are hazy yet accessible. I resist traveling through them. We can coexist and still have our privacy.

After several more minutes, the wanderers dwindle. We pause and I catch my breath.

"This fell from your pocket." Enlil slips the medallion over my head so the gold disc rests against my breastbone. He kisses my cheek.

I wait for Cala to melt, yet she watches as a bystander. Her presence has swiftly become familiar, her thoughts and feelings second nature. Dread needles at my heart. Is she disappearing into me, or am I disappearing into her?

We are one and the same, Cala answers. *Enlil is our forever love.*

Enlil waits for me to announce I am ready to go on. Only he knows the path I am to follow, even if coming here was my choice. As we set off, I wonder how much of a choice Cala had. Was she happier following Enlil's path instead of finding her own? Maybe she never learned the difference. She may have trusted the gods would not lead her astray. She may have sought Enlil's companionship above all else. Or maybe she did not have to sacrifice for his love. Perhaps she had it all along and he was always her only fate.

28

DEVEN

I amble up to the Umbra Palace with the crowd of wanderers. The last time Irkalla summoned her subjects, she publicly disciplined the demon Udug for failing to aid Kur in conquering the mortal realm. His screams stayed with me for days after. Udug has not been seen since.

The palace casts a shadow across the courtyard. The few intact walls have gaping holes that resemble eye sockets. Night and day, shrieks carry from the high windows. I once saw the rabisus unload wagon-loads of new souls and lead them inside. Not long after, the screams began. Those same wagons are parked out front. The new souls have been cleared out, but the oxen are still yoked, their harnesses nailed into their bloody backs.

The wanderers shuffle me along in the throng funneling up the stairs. Fish Face Lilu examines the entrants with her huge, glassy eyes. She lets me pass without her gills flapping.

We congregate in the massive throne room. The grandness of its pillars and high arches resembles the finest imperial chamber in the world, the difference being everything here is sooty and tarnished, corrupted by the evernight. Similar perversions can be seen across the under realm.

In this immortal stronghold, where power should rule just and fair, the mockery of authority is loathsome.

Rabisus guard every exit, and a pair of ugallus oversee our entry from the dais. Sitting on their haunches, the lion-eagles' wings tuck around their sleek bodies, their wingtips dagger sharp. Also on the dais, souls are chained to the far wall, unmoving and silent. Draperies span from ceiling to floor. Once we are all inside, a female voice slithers out from behind the curtain.

"Welcome, slaves. You must wonder for what purpose I have summoned you."

Every wanderer wears the same vacant expression. None have wondered anything in a long while.

Irkalla extends a big black claw into view and slices the chains off an imprisoned soul. She curls her talon around the wanderer and snatches him behind the drapery. His screeching is replaced by bone-chilling crunches. My ears burn and my teeth grind until the feeding stops.

"We have a visitor," Irkalla explains, smacking her chops. "A mortal man has trespassed into my realm, my city, my *palace*."

I lock my joints. This summons was for me?

"General Naik, step forward and announce yourself."

The silence from the dead is suffocating.

"De-ven," Irkalla singsongs. "Mortal blood reeks of starlight, and yours is especially potent. Forgive our late introduction. Kur believed you would perish shortly after your arrival. Unlike me, he does not value the mettle of mortals."

My stillness itches.

"I grow impatient, General." Her breaths billow the curtain. "If not for propriety's sake, perhaps you will step forward for her."

Lilu leads out a chained woman with long midnight hair. She wears a blue sari, identical to the one she wore the first time we met in the lower story of the Samiya Temple.

"Deven?" Kali scans the audience. "Please come out."

"Yes, please do," Irkalla intones.

This woman is a fair replica of my love, but the real Kalinda shines like the midday sun. Her soul-fire is unmistakable, and this woman has no notable radiance. I recheck the doorways for a clear exit. Rabisus still guard them.

A large red eye peers out of a hole halfway up the curtain. Irkalla must be massive, as big as Kur or larger. Her gaze sweeps to me. "There you are. Did you think you could hide from me under all that filth? Son of man, your soul-fire is blinding."

I backtrack a step.

"Uh-uh," she tsks. "You must not flee or I will kill your beloved and eat her soul."

Lilu presses a sharp fin against Kali's throat. I grimace despite it not being her.

"Go ahead," I bellow. "That isn't Kali."

Irkalla expels a laugh-hiss. "Clever little mouse."

Lilu lowers her razor fin. Kali bears her teeth, and before my eyes, she transforms into me. I hardly recognize myself. My jaw is bruised and my body gaunt. I touch my bottom gums, swollen and sore. When did I lose two teeth?

"Marduk is a gifted chameleon demon," Irkalla says. "Mortals are so easily fooled by him. Hopes and dreams distract them from basic truths."

"I would settle for the truth. Why was your chameleon demon following me?"

"He does as I command," Irkalla answers grandly. "We have not had a mortal visitor in centuries. You must be weary of hiding. Come to me and I will see that you have food and drink, a warm bed and a soft pillow."

Her offer is a barefaced lie. The under realm offers no such comforts. Irkalla wants me for some awful purpose. Since she dangled a false version of Kali before me as an enticement, I suspect that I am bait.

Irkalla huffs. "Your indecision is tiresome. Guards, bring me the mortal."

The twin ugallus stalk down the steps. I push through the wanderers. The ugallus knock them down and chase me to an exit. The fox rabisu in the doorway lunges. I throw it off and dash out of the palace, down the steps to the wagon and yoked oxen.

An ugallu leaps over me and lands, blocking my path. The second prowls up to my back. I slip between the oxen, and the ugallus roar.

The oxen stomp their hooves and snort in defense at the lion-eagles. I jump into the driver's bench and snap the reins. The oxen and wagon take off into the city. Once I leave its walls, I will lead my pursuers in the opposite direction from Kali. Her soul-fire shines in the distance, alerting me to which way not to go. Irkalla will not get us both.

I lose track of her light and push the oxen faster. The city gates lie wide open. For the briefest moment, I glance down at the reins and my mind empties.

What am I doing? Where am I?

Out of the corner of my eye, a monster leaps from an alleyway. I bend back, but its claws smack me off the driver's bench. I tumble to the road, and the wagon bounds out of sight.

Two big creatures prowl to me. They have wings like a bird of prey and sleek, feline bodies. I have never seen anything more horrendous. I roll off my side. Blood spreads down my hip from a slash. I cannot recall what got me into this predicament, but stubbornness drives me to my feet. Whatever these monsters want, my instinct is to defy them.

I take three strides before the nearest beast bats at me. I sail into a wall and slump to the ground. Hunks of brick shower down. My mental faculties scramble to latch on to something tangible, something hopeful.

I am already adrift.

29

ASHWIN

Brac and Indah come out of the infirmary to meet me. I push up from the floor of the corridor, my back stiff from sitting against the wall all night.

"How is Basma?" I ask.

Brac rolls down his sleeves. "She'll walk again."

"The breaks were clean," Indah explains, carrying an empty pitcher. Asha assisted her, coming back and forth from the infirmary to refill it with healing waters six times over the course of the night. "I was able to knit her bones. She shouldn't stand for a while, but she'll recover. You should try to sleep."

I nod and nod, grappling with my regrets over yesterday. Catching up on sleep is the furthest concern from my mind.

Indah uses her quiet voice that she usually reserves for patients. "Ashwin, the infirmary is out of sleeping tonic, but you can follow me to my chamber and I can give you some of ours. Jala is still being fussy. A tiny drop in her water helps us all."

"No need," I say. "You go on and rest."

"Both of you take care." Indah pats Brac's cheek affectionately and goes.

My ambassador slumps against the wall. "That accident never should have happened. I should have been with the girls."

"I'm not sure you could have prevented this." I lean my shoulder by the door. "Please tell me you uncovered who Commander Lokesh is working for."

Brac pushes his lips side to side. "He was held in the military refugee camp for a while. Then he rallied with the demon rajah and marched on Vanhi. His mother fell ill, and she died as he was bringing her back."

Bhuta guards oversaw the military refugee camp. "Perhaps that's where the commander's dislike for bhutas comes from."

"Many of our soldiers were in that camp and stayed on," Brac answers shortly, irritated with our lack of progress. "Lokesh does his business in the early morning. The night before last, he met with someone. I got close enough to listen, but they were writing notes back and forth to each other to avoid Galers eavesdropping."

"Was it his employer?"

"They did not exchange payment. When I tried to follow his associate, he vanished." Frustration rebounds in Brac's tone. "One second he was there, the next he was gone."

"What did he look like?"

"You aren't going to believe me." He rubs at his mouth.

"I'll try."

"He looked like my brother."

I stare into Brac's red-rimmed eyes. Why would Deven meet with Lokesh? *How* did he meet with him? "That's not possible. Night before last, Deven visited me. I saw him enter and leave Kali's chamber."

Brac pinches the bridge of his nose to fight off a headache. "I know what I saw, but I . . . I don't know what I saw."

His confusion about Lokesh spreads to me. Deven would never conspire with Lokesh, but I also trust Brac. He believes he saw his brother.

Yatin jogs down the corridor. He has also been up all night. "Sir, someone snuck out of the palace grounds." My neck stretches in alarm. "We've been monitoring the gates. The one by the elephant stables was opened. The footprints were smudged, but we think it was a soldier."

Brac slams his fist against the wall. The bang is extra loud in the morning quiet. "Lokesh has an ally inside the palace."

I rake at my hair, which already stands on end from repeated tousling. We still know too little about the renegade commander. Every day the possibilities become more dangerous.

"Sir, perhaps you should delay your wedding," Yatin suggests. A day's worth of stubble covers his jaw. I do not comment on his uncomely appearance. Brac and I are not pictures of respectability either. "We can postpone your nuptials and post an announcement to appease the people."

"No." I will not be bullied into risking our ties with the Southern Isles. "Datu Bulan will arrive in two days. My wedding celebrations begin in three days. We must bring Vanhi under rule. Increase the soldiers in the city. Assign a man to every corner."

"Ashwin," Brac says tiredly, "the commander won't be pressured."

"We're past coercion. Yatin, summon Commander Lokesh. I'll see him at noon without you, Brac." I clasp the Burner's shoulder. "I have to establish that I can lead without bhuta allies."

"Lokesh wishes to separate you from your allies. Be careful that you don't give him what he wants." Brac yanks from my grasp and stalks away.

Yatin's gaze hops from my ambassador to me. He wants to follow his friend, so I excuse him. He rushes after Brac, leaving me alone in the empty corridor. Lords, I wish Kalinda and Deven were here.

By the time I return to my chambers to wash up, I am wide awake. Someone in the palace could be aiding Lokesh. A new soldier or guard doubling as his informant? A defector he planted in our ranks?

While I comb my hair, the thought of a spy sneaking about nags at me. I could confer with Gemi. She knows just what to say to focus my thoughts, but after yesterday, I doubt she wants much to do with me.

I open my dressing cabinet and groan. Natesa has been here again. She added more tailored tunic jackets and fitted trousers to my wardrobe and snatched the last pair of loose pants that I had stashed at the back.

Gemi stomps into my chamber and draws up short. Her face flames at the sight of my bare chest. I look over the wardrobe door at her.

"You could knock," I say.

"I'm too angry."

Her accent is stronger when she is upset. I turn around to pick out an ivory tunic, and she crosses to me.

"Who did this?" she asks, touching a scar on my back.

"Tarek whipped me for disobeying him."

Gemi traces the raised white marks. "Do they hurt?"

"Not anymore."

"I cannot imagine a father doing this to his child." Gemi's gaze loiters around the room. She halts on a portrait of Rajah Tarek and Kindred Lakia, the only one left of my parents. "Everyone says you look like him, but I think you look more like your mother." She runs her palm over my shoulder. The sensation untenses my muscles.

"I thought you were angry."

She slides her satiny touch down and toys with my fingers. "Brac said you summoned Commander Lokesh and you don't want bhutas present."

"This isn't a matter of not wanting you there. The people believe I rely too heavily on my bhuta guards. I must set a precedent that I can stand on my own."

Gemi slings her arms over my shoulders. Her short silk blouse presses against my chest, her warm skin radiating through the thin cloth. "You can rely on me."

I drop my tunic to the floor and hold her. She smells of lavender and rose hips. The rash along her elbows has nearly healed. "Trust me to manage Lokesh."

"I do, but that doesn't mean you have to confront anyone alone." Her gaze lowers to my mouth and lingers there. My viraji makes me feel seen, not as a prince but as a person. "Eshana and Shyla are fascinated by your 'fancy hair and plum lips.' They talk about you incessantly. I'm tired of listening to them go on about your splendid features."

"You don't think they're splendid?"

"They are. Maddeningly so. Shouldn't you have one flaw?"

"You've seen my back."

Her touch slides over my scars, leaving a wake of gooseflesh. "It's perfect too."

She tucks in closer, sealing the gap between us. I mold my palms to her hips. Hunger collects in my mouth, building . . . building. She dips her nose near mine, a breath away from a kiss.

"Are you in love with Kalinda?" she whispers.

"What? No. That's long over." I squeeze my viraji against me, locking her pounding heart against my chest. "She's the one who suggested you and I wed."

Gemi angles back. "This was her idea?"

I continue to embrace her, certain she will understand. "At first. I wrote you weeks later after I determined this would be advantageous for the empire." Gemi pushes from my grasp. "I . . . I said that wrong."

"I think you said it right. You just don't like how it makes you sound." Her fingers curl into fists. A vibration carries up through the floor and a vase trembles on the bedside table. "Did I secure my throne by default?"

My mouth falls open. One could say Gemi was my second choice, but my feelings for Kalinda had gone by the time I proposed our alliance.

"Ashwin, I'm not Kalinda. I don't have scars like the sister warriors, and despite my willingness to learn your people's customs, I don't want to train with weapons for the rest of my days. I'm a teacher, and I want the man I marry to care about me." Her voice trembles, her accent heavy. "I'm willing to contend against Kalinda or any other woman for your affections, but I cannot vie against your throne."

"You don't have to compete against anyone or anything. You're my viraji."

"I wish that meant as much to you as it does to me." Gemi revolves and dashes out.

I slam the door of the wardrobe closet shut. It bangs closed, then swings open again. A shelf's worth of clothes slides out and falls at my feet.

How can Gemi be upset? I was honest about our betrothal. Neither of us signed the alliance out of love for each other but for our nations. She understands the demands of ruling. She knows what this alliance means for Tarachand's growth and her people. The Southern Isles stands to benefit from better trade and agriculture. Romance would be a convenient outcome, yet our duties come first.

Pons appears at the door to escort me through my daily schedule. I pluck a tunic off the floor. I will think on how to make amends with Gemi later. Right now, I have a busy morning ahead and a meeting with Lokesh for which to prepare.

Pons and I step out of a council about the wedding festivities—a meeting Gemi did not attend—and come upon a small group of ranis in the corridor. The ranis see me and swiftly walk the other way. My betrothal is still unsupported by the bulk of the women of court.

A sudden strong need to see Gemi cinches down on me like a vise. "Pons, where's my viraji?"

He leads me to a balcony overlooking a lower courtyard. Gemi sits at a fountain, encircled by Trembler trainees. Their nursemaids and some ranis watch off to the side. Gemi holds a large coral seashell to each child's ear so they may listen to the musical rush of the sea. The ranis and nursemaids wait their turn. Their eagerness draws them nearer to Gemi, and soon the group is talking and smiling.

"Your Majesty," says Pons, "everyone is waiting for you in the throne room."

My presence above draws Gemi's eye. In one glance, I read her expression. Despite our disagreement, she is glad to see me. That is all I need to know. "Thank you, Pons. I'll find my way."

I enter the throne room through an antechamber. General Yatin waits by the main door. Rows of soldiers stand in formation between us, dressed in their impeccable uniforms. Boots shined. Turbans wrapped tight. Khandas slung at their side. Tunics buttoned to the top of their stand-up collars. Their presence pulls my own shoulders back and lifts my chin.

At the front of the room, close to the dais, Eshana, Parisa, Shyla, and Natesa speak in low voices. They followed Yatin's instruction to dress in their finest and wear gold-embroidered tangerine saris, smudged kohl around their eyes, and rouged lips. I have no question Natesa led the effort to coordinate their apparel, and, for once, I am grateful for her overbearing directives. These women could never be mistaken for former competitors. Together they look like friends, or at the very least, a female guard.

In addition to their eye-catching attire, each carries a weapon of her choice. Natesa selected a khanda, Eshana a haladie, Parisa a pair of silver daggers, and Shyla a machete. The cold steel blades are for show, but the weaponry adds a reminder that these women are more than their stunning looks. I asked Yatin to invite them and the soldiers to establish that I have an array of defenders.

"Thank you for coming," I say. The women take turns kissing my cheek in greeting. First is Parisa. "I'm especially glad you agreed to my invitation. I know circumstances have been stressful as of late. Your support is appreciated."

"As is yours," Parisa returns. "I hope I don't stink. I came straight from the elephant stables to dress."

"You smell like a flower garden," I assure her.

Eshana kisses my cheek next. Her fingers find a ticklish spot at my side, and I subtly extract myself. Next, I come to Shyla.

"You look so handsome, Your Majesty." Shyla's lashes flutter down to her cheeks. I resist teasing her about my "plum lips" and move on to Natesa.

"No viraji?" she asks archly. "What are you up to, Ashwin?"

"You'll find out soon. Thank you for organizing the women. You all look magnificent." I swoop in and kiss Natesa on the cheek. "Yatin cannot stop staring at you. Marry the man already, would you?"

She bats my shoulder, then winks across the entry hall at her intended.

My nerves rattle as I climb the steps to my dais and sit on my throne. Never have I thanked the gods that I take after my father in appearance. Today, I am relying on just that.

I wave at Yatin. "Let him in."

My general opens the double doors. Lokesh enters, flanked by two more mercenaries. Yatin unarms them, and then the renegade leaves his cohorts near the door and comes to the dais.

Lokesh bows low. "Your Majesty."

"You disregarded my orders, Commander."

"Your bhuta trainees gave me no choice. How is the girl?"

His contrived sympathy mocks me. "She will make a full recovery."

"Then you'll have one more Burner in your personal guard. That makes a total of four. Considering Burners are the rarest bhuta, you certainly have a lot of them under your command."

"I'm not raising a bhuta army, Lokesh. I warned you not to spread lies."

He looks up with a partial grin. "I would be glad to stop my speeches, but you must make a concession, Your Majesty. By tomorrow, the people will be calling for you to send away the bhuta children. This is your opportunity to prove you're listening. You brought bhutas into your palace, opposed bhutas wearing a mark to identify themselves, and selected a foreigner as your viraji. You must concede on at least one account."

"I have." I rise, towering above him. "You're done here. General Yatin will escort you out of Vanhi."

"You're banishing me?" Lokesh sputters out a laugh.

I drain all mercy from my expression, drawing upon memories of my father. "Be grateful I'm not ordering you hanged."

"*I'm* not your adversary," he rejoins. "You've invited your enemy into your bed and asked us to accept her as our kindred."

The last of my self-control snaps. "Look around. These people are the future of the empire, and you are no longer welcome."

He glances at the sister warriors and their blades. "You cannot force peace."

"Of course I can. Removing you will be the start." I signal at Yatin to fetch him.

The general arrives at the dais and grabs Lokesh's shoulder. He wrenches free and snarls, "My men will rebel against you."

"I'll apprehend anyone who interferes with my wedding, and I'll root out any informant in my midst. From this moment forward, Vanhi is under occupation. The unit of soldiers I relocated to the palace will maintain order on my behalf. A group of them will escort you out into the desert and return your swords. Leave, Lokesh, and do not come back."

His lips twist arrogantly, then he strides through the lines of soldiers and departs, his lackeys after him.

213

Natesa lowers her khanda. "You didn't have to banish him. I would have happily done him in."

I sink down onto my throne. "I have no stomach for bloodshed."

"You fooled me," she says. "I almost mistook you for Tarek."

Eshana murmurs a sober agreement. Parisa's attention has not left the door since Lokesh walked out.

"Nicely done, Your Majesty," Shyla says.

"I should have shut him up sooner."

Lokesh's lies are less valuable than pig slop, but one of his warnings holds merit. In three days, Gemi will become my first wife and I will ascend to the throne as rajah. Nothing and no one will stop our union.

30

KALINDA

The sky grays as we come up to a body of water. The wind picks up, tugging at my hair like little hooks. Something strikes me as familiar. The bloody waves and deserted shoreline . . .

"Is this the Sea of Desolation?" I ask.

"It is."

I whirl on Enlil. "But we were already here."

"This is the way to the last obstruction."

I kick at a bone mixed in with the rocks. "The under realm makes no sense!"

Our gate appears near the water. I am tempted to throw a stone at the low wall. How could the rabisu lead us in a circle? We have trekked for hours. I have no idea how long, since the sky of the under realm has no celestial powers. We have wasted so much time!

The bloody waves lap against the short wall. Bubbles dot the liquid near the gate, growing in number. Enlil walks down to the shoreline. A sea monster slowly surfaces and stares at us with egg-size eyes. This rabisu, partially submerged, must be the largest yet. Bonelike ridges run down its twisting back and disappear underwater, the bloody sea dripping down its sleek scales.

Enlil takes a massive chunk of meat from his satchel. "We seek passage across the next obstruction."

The rabisu answers in a gruff timbre, flashing its pointy teeth. "The Mount of Ruin awaits your arrival."

Enlil throws the rabisu his payment. It catches the hunk of meat in its jaws and dives under. Waves ripple out from its descent. I rub at my chilled forearms, wondering what other horrors lurk in the sea.

The fire-god returns to me. "Are you prepared to climb?"

"Climb what? There's no—"

He pivots me into the wind. In place of the desert we left stands a mountain. The misshapen landform is nothing like the Alpanas. Instead of a sharp apex, the peak is rounded like the end of a boot. Its ridges are not pinnacles of strength but slopes of rocky sluices. As with all else in the Void, the Mount of Ruin is a poor replica of its cousins in the mortal realm.

I glance back at Enlil to find that the sea has vanished. We are stranded on an overhang on the mount, which is no longer far off in the distance but under our feet. My belly spirals from the sudden shift. The only constancy is the badgering wind. Gusts chisel at the slopes, sending lone pebbles down to our precipice. The rocks bounce past us and sail off the edge.

Enlil clutches my elbow, steadying me. "Our path is ahead. Do not stray."

After my incident in the desert, he does not need to warn me again. Enlil locates the path, though I cannot tell how he distinguishes it from the rest of the gravelly channels. I gaze up the vertical incline. "Must we hike to the top?"

"And down the other side."

"A flat path would be boring in this hole of misery," I grouse and trudge upward.

We have been living on the verge of injury every godsforsaken second. My exhausted nerves misfire, and I deviate slightly from Enlil's course. The rock crumbles beneath me. I fall onto my front and skid down to the end of the overhang.

My hand grasps the firm lip and stops my fall. My shoulder spasms from holding my weight. Enlil pulls me up. I lie on my back, my pulse bellowing at me for my clumsiness.

Enlil helps me stand. His nearness has become a second skin. Cala wants him closer. She desires to cozy up to him and—

I retreat from her aspirations.

"Kalinda, are you well? Did you harm yourself?" Enlil checks me over, his frown positively dashing. Cala wishes to touch his hair. I stop her—myself—before we do.

"Let's keep going." I wave him along.

Enlil's expression transforms from worried to charmingly perplexed. He begins up the trail once more. My muscles relax once he is out of reach. Cala, however, grinds my teeth. I direct her strength of mind into climbing this mountain. In a short time, we are single-minded in our objective.

Do not trip.

Do not fall.

Keep moving.

The atmosphere thickens the higher we hike, the air an amalgamation of foul gas. I dare not dwell on its content. We crest the final rise, my thighs quaking. Cala and I are in agreement. We are tired of traveling.

Enlil halts just shy of the summit.

"What is it?"

"Shh." He swaps his grip on his spear from walking stick to weapon.

I hear flapping. Two ugallus soar over the peak. I learned about the vicious lion-eagles in the book I studied about the Void. Edimmu and Asag, demon siblings, ride on the ugallus' backs.

Enlil shifts in front of me, my god shield, and addresses the demons. "We have honored the directives of the under realm and secured passage over the Mount of Ruin. We do not wish to contend with you."

"Relinquish the Burner and depart," Edimmu says, her crocodile jaws snapping.

"I will not," Enlil rejoins. "Kalinda and I have an agreement."

Asag aims his poleax at him. "You are not welcome in our realm, son of Ki."

Enlil speaks to me from the corner of his mouth. "Remember when I advised you to reserve your powers? Now you must call upon them."

He shoots a lightning bolt from his spear at the demons. The ugallus veer apart and out of the line of fire. Edimmu flicks her tongue, hurling a dusty spiral in retaliation. We duck low to the ground, and the howling wind tunnels over us. The rocks beneath us rumble, the path buckling. Asag is turning the mountain against us.

Enlil dispatches more lightning and wallops Asag's ugallu in the flank. The lion-eagle bellows as it plummets into the peak. Big rocks loosen and vault past us, bouncing down the mountainside.

Edimmu dives at Enlil, her ugallu's claws outstretched. We stoop low, and the creature misses. I summon my powers and throw a heatwave. The ugallu's tail lights. The lion-eagle lets loose a feline screech and lunges. Its claws tear into Enlil's shoulder. He drops his spear as he is lifted into the air.

I hurl a fire blast at them. It falls short and dies off midair.

Enlil calls from above. "You limit yourself with your mind, Kalinda! Never hide who you are for who you think you are!"

Am I hiding? Or at the very least doubting myself? I tested the use of my powers with my right arm once and gave up.

Enlil swings his feet up and kicks the ugallu in the ribs. Edimmu whips her tongue at his back. He bellows, an agonized noise that rattles the stones beneath my feet.

She hurt Enlil, Cala seethes.

I do not think. I lift my arms, channel my powers through them both, and lob a heatwave at Edimmu. A huge blast explodes from my left hand and right wrist. I stumble back as the discharge curves off and fizzles out. I gape at the glowing base of my wrist.

I have total access to my soul-fire?

You have complete access to your powers, Cala answers.

I repeat the realization aloud for Enlil. "I have my full powers!"

Edimmu whips her tongue at him. Enlil swings out of reach, and she strikes her own mount. The ugallu shrieks and dives sideways into its injured flank.

Lifting my arms once more, I cast three consecutive flames at the demon. They pelt her ugallu's wings, and the screeching monster drops Enlil. He lands uphill on the gravelly slope. The stones beneath me rumble and start to slide.

Edimmu and her injured mount plummet down the other side of the mountain. I scoop up Enlil's spear and fight the drag of the rock-slide, running uphill to meet him. We grab for each other. Our hands clasp, and the avalanche sweeps us away.

Our momentum escalates as we summersault down into a pile, half-buried by rock. Enlil lies beneath me, jaw slack and eyes shut. Coughing on the ashy dirt that covers us both, I set aside his spear and unbury us. Asag and Edimmu are nowhere in sight.

Enlil does not stir, yet his cuts are healing. Cala is not consoled by his recovery. Her panic compels me to tap his cheek and shout, "Wake up," in his ear. He gradually rouses.

"Thank the gods," I breathe. "You scared Cala."

"Just Cala?" He drags me to lie on top of him. Before I connect what is happening, he covers my lips with his own.

I go starkly still. Cala's need for him debilitates me, paralyzing my impulse to stop this. Her joy brims over, her spirit centered upon Enlil. Through me, she has found her love.

How I envy her. I have felt lost since I stepped down from my throne. My place in the empire, in the palace, in the Sisterhood has changed. Nothing has turned out as I wished, yet Cala is positive that where we belong is with Enlil.

Cala touches his chin, then the nape of his neck. She tucks my curves against his hard planes. I am losing myself to him, to her.

Enlil's lips grow needier. His body heat flows into me, fusing Cala's emotions to my own. Her longing for Enlil aches from every pore. Nothing in all the realms matters more to her than him.

No, I tell her.

She delves further. *I am Enlil's hundredth rani. I never concede.*

Enlil's grasp slides up my waist and over my back. He whispers her name over and over. Cala shoves me far inside myself and slams the trapdoor.

Let me out!

I sense Enlil and her kissing. My body experiences the touches, but I cannot stop them. I want to shove him off. Wash my skin. Rinse my mouth. I continue to wail at Cala, my inner voice screaming. She disregards me and becomes more lost in Enlil. My revulsion gags me. There must be a way to escape.

Cala's memories splay before me, laid out for the picking. I delve through them for something that will compel her to listen. The memory of her tournament is still foremost, closest from our last connection. *No, not that one.* But my mere acknowledgment of the recollection wrests me to it.

The past rushes in, pushing me off-balance. I stagger into the middle of the dusty arena. The crowd cheers Cala's name. I am separate from her, a bystander. She wields her urumi against her competitors. One of them runs past me, khanda raised, and attacks Cala. They battle, oblivious to my company. I am an unseen onlooker like in the first flashback Enlil showed me.

Cala dispatches her last two challengers, slashing through them without remorse. Countless women have fallen and bleed out on the arena floor. I turn away from Cala's barbarity, repulsed, and catch sight of one of the fallen.

Jaya.

My lungs twist on a gasp. I stumble to my friend, passing by more slain women. They stare up lifelessly. In the present, they are very much alive. Indah. Tinley. Natesa. Each one pulverizes my soul. I identify Eshana and Parisa next. *No more.* Additional blank gazes bore holes through me. Shyla . . . and Asha too?

I collapse to the blood-speckled ground. *My sisters, my friends.* I crawl to Jaya and bury my sobs against her.

"I'm sorry. I'm so sorry." My apology is for breaking my promise to protect her from the Claiming. She swallows loudly. I meet her open brown eyes. "Jaya? Jaya, it's me. Do you remember me?"

"Kali." Her hand finds mine and squeezes. I sputter out a coarse laugh. The squeeze is our secret way of saying *I love you.*

"I've missed you terribly," I say, returning her clutch. "I didn't do this to you. I would never."

"Cala isn't you," she says. "You're Kalinda, and Kalinda doesn't serve herself. She serves others."

I press her hand to my tearstained cheek. "Please don't leave. I cannot lose you again."

"You haven't lost me. I'm waiting for you in Vanhi." Her assertive gaze confirms what I supposed about Jala. "Free Deven and promise you'll return."

Fresh tears race down my face. "Last time I made you a promise, everything went awry."

"You're a rani now. A Burner. A sister warrior. You were always those things, only now everyone sees you as I do. Tarachand needs you. You have more to give."

"Jaya," I cry, grabbing her close. She understands me better than anyone. I will fight for any opportunity to return her to my life, to have a life of my choosing with the people I love. "I'll come for you. I swear."

She kisses my palm and slips away.

Crying harder, I shift onto my knees and bow. Memory or not, I will not leave here without a prayer for the fallen. "Gods, bless these women's souls to find the gate that leads to peace and everlasting light."

After a moment of silence, I rise. The crowd in the amphitheater disappears, as do Cala and her slain opponents. Even the arena begins to vanish. The memory is fading. I will not return to confinement. Leaning back, I harness my resolve and shout at the sky.

"Cala! No more!"

My fury shatters the door she locked me behind. The amphitheater disintegrates to sand in a cyclone. I ride the whirlwind up, up, up. I am myself again, my awareness acute and senses heightened. Cala and Enlil are flagrant in their affections. The violation fuels my anger against Cala.

How could you harm Jaya? You slaughtered my friends!

They were my challengers. They tried to come between Enlil and me. I couldn't let them.

I will never forget my friends' horrible wounds, injuries inflicted upon them by my former self. Cala's callousness and disregard for my will appall me.

I am not this. I am not you. I heave every ounce of injustice storming through me at her, casting it as I would a heatwave. *Get out of my head!*

Control slides back into me.

"Stop." My protest garbles against Enlil's lips. I leverage more disgust. "Stop!"

His lips withdraw, his arms still around me. "Cala?"

"Stop calling me that!"

"She is within you. You are the same."

"I will never be her." I wriggle against him. "I saw her tournament. She slew my *friends*."

"They were your enemies," he says, sensible and aggravating. "They were my wives. They challenged your throne. You won and became my hundredth rani."

I shove against him harder. I might as well be wrenching against bricks. "I am not yours!"

"You deny our kinship after what you witnessed?" He tries to nuzzle me. I twist my head to the side. "Your previous lives exist inside your soul, layers and layers of devoted warriors. They were all mine."

I growl in frustration. Must I belong to a man, any man, even a god, to fulfill my measure? Is my purpose to serve as a shadow to another? The daughter, the sister, the wife . . . When am I myself without owing my life—my fate—to a man?

I ram a finger into his chest. "You knew Deven was trapped before I came to you. All my prayers, all my pleading . . . You heard me and knew I would come for help. You left him to suffer so I would climb into your web."

"You came to me of your own choosing. I am not a man, Kalinda. With me, your happiness will know no bounds. As my companion, you will be free to do as you wish."

"I will live to suit your needs," I retort. Cala takes offense, but I still dominate our voices.

"Deven can make you a wife. I can crown you a goddess. He can give you a life. I can bless you with an eternal home. Pick me and you will thrive in Ekur. You will be above the anguish and misery of the world. Mortals will worship you and hail your name. I offer more than a future. I offer everlasting peace." Enlil relaxes his iron embrace. "Is contentment not your heart's wish?"

"My heart's wish doesn't include murder."

His displeasure turns icy. "Would you not battle for a life with Deven?"

"He would never ask me to." I take off Cala's championship medallion and thrust it at him. "I don't like who I was with you. What Cala did for you."

"You spoiled child." The fire-god's eyes go molten. "After all I have done for you."

Cala cowers. I lean into the deity, weathering his feverish temper. "Will you keep your bargain?"

"You question my honor?" he bellows.

"I question your motives for guiding me here. Your honor is your own concern."

Enlil's intense glow stings, yet I do not flinch. He replies, his tone incredulous. "Is the worth of one soul so high?"

"His soul is invaluable." I jangle the medal, urging him to take it.

Enlil ignores the outstretched ornament. I pocket it and rise from the dust. Cala has not reemerged from hiding. For someone so aggressive, she is easily undone by Enlil's temper. He can throw a fit without me.

I set out from the base of the mountain. Whether I truly saw Jaya or her visit was born from my imagination, I made a promise. She believes I can prevail, so I will.

31

Ashwin

Preparations for the wedding are everywhere. I sidestep servants carting linen baskets and flower bouquets. Rich aromas of coriander and turmeric permeate every corner. The kitchens will be bustling from now until the matrimonial feast.

The main outdoor terrace has reached full-blown chaos. Servants hang lanterns and erect tents, while others clean and set out furniture. In the Southern Isles, weddings are held at sundown and followed by a banquet under a new moon. Guests feast until all the food is devoured. According to Datu Bulan, the celebration can go on for days. Although most Lestarians do not consume meat, we will serve an array of dishes. As Gemi did not attend the meeting this morning, I hope she does not take offense to my decision to include plates of roasted lamb. Now is not the time to try her patience. I already owe her an apology for our earlier disagreement.

General Yatin and several guards patrol the gates. The soldiers' camp is deserted; the men are on task in the city. Lokesh was escorted out quietly in a prison wagon. As of now, all is calm. By the time the people learn he was banished, the datu and navy will have arrived. I am less concerned about the mercenaries disrupting my nuptials than of those living under my roof.

Basma sits upright in her cot, her legs set in splints. Her younger sister keeps vigil at her side, drawing a picture. They go silent when I enter the infirmary.

Healer Baka wipes her hands off on her apron. "Prince Ashwin, I'm making tea. Do you care for a cup?"

"Not presently." My belly could not withstand a drop. "I've come to see Basma."

The healer drags a stool to her bedside for me. "Isn't that kind of the prince?" She tucks Basma's hair behind her ear and then resumes preparing the tea.

"You're looking better, Basma." I make a point of studying Giza's charcoal sketch. She depicted Brac wielding his axes. "That's very good. Have you shown him yet?" Her eyes grow and she blushes. Oh, she fancies him. "Don't worry. I won't tell him."

She adds more shading to his hair.

I rub my knees, gathering my nerves. "Girls, I have news. I've found you another home."

"We're leaving?" Basma says. "But we like it here."

"The Sisterhood temple in Hiraani is in a green valley near the sea. Have you ever seen the open water?"

Giza sets down her charcoal stick. "I've drawn it."

"The Sea of Souls is big and blue. The fine sand is powder beneath your feet, and the waves sound better up close than listening to their echo in a seashell." I am overemphasizing the appeal of the seashore; however, viewing the extent of Basma's injuries has confirmed my conclusion. "All the bhuta trainees are moving to a Sisterhood or Brotherhood temple. The boys will stay here in Vanhi, and you will go to Hiraani."

"Why can we not stay?" Giza asks, pouting.

Healer Baka grinds herbs with her stone mortar and pestle while she listens. I speak over her. "In Hiraani, you will have lots of room to run and play. It'll be a better life for you."

My words drill into me. Is this how my mother rationalized sending me away? Did she truly think I would be better off without her?

Giza concentrates on her sketch. "Will Master Brac come?"

"We haven't discussed it. I will send my bravest guards with you." After I left the throne room, I messaged a brother at the temple. I still need to send word to the Hiraani priestess.

"Am I allowed to travel?" Basma asks.

We all seek Healer Baka for her recommendation.

"You can, but a healer must accompany you." Her flat tone implies that I should not be moving anyone. I never intended for the bhuta trainees to stay. Their visit was proposed as a temporary solution. Moving them out before the wedding will free up room for our guests and verify to the people that I do not value bhuta children above their own. More important, this will give the trainees a true home.

"We could have a bonfire on the beach," Basma says to her sister.

"I *would* like to swim in the sea," replies Giza.

"Good," I say, my gladness forged. "You'll leave tomorrow."

Healer Baka crushes the herbs faster, every click of the pestle against the mortar a mark of her disapproval. I add to the girls' excitement with additional stories about the beaches and then take my leave.

Priestess Mita kneels at the altar in the palace's small chapel. Thick trails of sandalwood incense hang in the air, and a significant pile of ash from burned sacrifices spatters the altar. Natesa must have come earlier for her daily offerings.

The priestess lowers her head to pray. I step backward to go, and she quickly stands.

"Your Majesty."

"Pardon the interruption." I shift on my feet, fingers twitching to swipe at my hair.

"I was just finishing. You may have the chapel to yourself." Her tart tone speaks to her opinion of me and my need for prayers.

I wave at a floor cushion. "May I have a word before you go?"

Priestess Mita kneels again and clasps her hands in her lap. I join her on the floor, my knees bent to my chest. She scowls at my casual position.

"I'd like you to write to the Hiraani priestess. I'm sending the female bhuta trainees to her for lodging."

"You wish to send those *girls* to a temple of the gods?"

"I won't debate their value, Priestess. The Hiraani Temple is isolated in a southern valley near the sea. They'll be under less scrutiny there."

Her censure deepens. I hold myself taut to keep from fidgeting.

"And what of their training?" she asks.

"Suspended until I employ live-in bhuta instructors. In the interim, they will attend the temple courses with the other wards. A spiritual upbringing would do them well. I can think of no better teachers than the sisters."

Priestess Mita snubs my flattery. "The Hiraani priestess will honor your request. But if I may, I must express a concern. Now that our temple wards will not be claimed by a benefactor, what will they do? Will the public accept them as more than servants, courtesans, and wives? What will become of them when they are no longer under your or my care?"

The ramifications of no longer relying on benefactors to take in the wards are a mighty adjustment. Without the Claiming, no man will be held responsible for their welfare. I had thought of this, which is why my plan for the ranis also includes the wards. Their participation is integral. "If you will grant me your patience a little longer, I'll present a solution that will satisfy your worries."

Her dubious look hints otherwise. "I'll write the Hiraani priestess forthwith."

I thank her and listen as she exits the chapel. I hunch over my knees and shake out my hands. During the whole of our meeting, not once did I touch my hair.

Before I go, I light incense, one stick each for Kali, Deven, and my mother. I am not in the habit of lengthy prayers, so I offer a short plea for their safety and get on my way.

Rosy sunshine warms the tiles in the corridor. The day has vanished, and I have not yet visited the nursery. Rehan must wonder what has become of me.

Nursemaid Sunsee and Rehan play on the rug in the main area. My sister raises her arms to me. I lift her and she bops my chin.

"Ashin."

"Did you hear that?" I ask Sunsee. "She said my name."

"So she did." The old nursemaid's eyes crinkle.

I bounce Rehan and she giggles. "Say Ashwin. Ash-win."

Gemi throws open the door and stomps up to us. "What did you do?" she asks.

I pass Rehan back to the nursemaid, then lead Gemi to my childhood chamber for privacy. "I intended to speak to you," I explain. "I understand your people don't eat meat, but—"

"Ashwin, this is about another matter." Gemi sets the empty lotion jar before me. "I stopped by the infirmary to get more of this and saw Basma and her sister in tears. You're sending them away?"

"The girls were in good spirits when I left," I reply, my voice constricted. "They were excited to swim in the sea and have a bonfire at the beach."

"What could they say? You're their ruler."

"Which is precisely why I must think of their care." I attempt to control my exasperation, but my fidgety hands get the best of me and rake my hair. "I'm *trying*. I'm considering the welfare of all our people. It's a bigger, more complex task than I was prepared for."

"I know you're doing all you can," Gemi answers softer. "What did Lokesh say to you?"

"Nothing," I snap, unable to help my gruffness. Speaking of the renegade commander always triggers my temper. "Shyla said I managed him well."

"Shyla was at your meeting?"

I wince at my error. "I invited a few sister warriors to attend as my supporters."

Gemi twists her earring. "Of course. They aren't bhutas."

"I'm sorry I excluded you. I meant no offense. Lokesh is gone, and more soldiers are stationed in the city, but none of that will matter as long as the trainees are terrifying the people." I step closer to my viraji, her floral scent familiar now. "Our wedding mustn't be compromised."

Gemi tames my rumpled hair, her fingers pacifying. "When I first arrived, I thought you might care for Kalinda or someone else."

"I assure you I do not."

"Falling in love isn't an imposition, Ashwin."

"It isn't necessary either. Love starts with good intentions but rarely meets the fullness of its measure."

Gemi tucks her lower lip between her teeth and releases it. "Before we met, my life on my island was small. I knew everyone in Lestari and had studied all the plants and animals I could find. Then your proposal came. The alliance between our people promised I would see more of the world—and you. I admired your courage during the war. You see the best in people and believe we can accomplish great things. I wanted to be part of the changes here, but my father discouraged me."

"He did?" The datu never indicated he was against our alliance.

"Father hoped I would wed for love. I told him I would arrive early and visit with you. I did come to train with the sister warriors. Mainly I wanted to find out if you could come to care for me." My pulse slows to deep thuds, and Gemi's voice thickens. "Neither of us anticipated this unrest. Your people may not forgive you for taking a bhuta for your wife. It would be better for you to wed one of the ranis and start your reign as rajah with their approval."

My chest falls in on itself. "You wish to suspend our nuptials? Everyone is coming. The preparations have begun."

"The preparations can be postponed until you select another kindred." She cups my cheek, and her focus turns inward. "My father taught me that rulers don't have paths, we have places. We must choose our place and never falter. You've always known your place is here, Ashwin. I thought mine could be here as well. I need to know I can win your heart, or I'll worry that someday you could find my powers an inconvenience and send me away too."

"I wouldn't," I promise. "I want you here."

"So long as I *am* here, I'll be to blame for this unrest." Gemi takes my face in her grasp. "Wed someone your people respect. Someone who can be content as your friend."

I have come to care for Gemi, but dividing my dedication between the empire and her will weaken my commitment to both. This marriage was to align our homelands, our citizens, our thrones. I cannot guarantee her a partnership upheld by love.

"It's all right, Ashwin." She lays her lips against my cheek. This is our only point of contact, yet her sadness pierces me. "I'll speak to my father about taking the trainees home with us. They'll never be misunderstood or mistreated by our people. They will be cherished."

Gemi scans the dusty bedchamber and, lastly, me. Before I can put my regret into words, she leaves.

32

KALINDA

The Road of Bone starts as a stripe on the horizon. As night falls, the ivory takes on a grim, grayish hue. At last, I stride up to the lane.

"Kalinda, halt." Enlil's first words since we departed from the Mount of Ruin do not affect me. "Kalinda, *please*."

I stop and revolve. Must he always tell me what to do?

He crouches to inspect hoof and paw prints in the dirt. The numerous tracks are concentrated around the base of the road.

"Rabisus were here." Enlil lifts his spear to illuminate the roadway.

No gate and guardian appear to admit our passage.

Enlil meanders to a hole in the ground off the side of the dirt road and drops a dead chicken by the opening. He returns to me.

"Something spooked the guardian. It will not come out. Be vigilant."

He takes the lead into the sixth obstruction. I halt before the Road of Bone and thicket lining the thoroughfare. Everything within our sight is deserted. After enduring endless horrors, I did not think a roadway would alarm me, but this visual of death reignites my fears.

What would startle a rabisu into hiding? Glancing back, I notice the chicken in front of the burrow is missing. I set a resolute pace down the road. Travelers and wagon wheels have worn down ruts and paths in the bones. Despite these signs of use, the thoroughfare remains empty. I scurry along until we put the grisly road behind us and tread down a dirt lane. The woods open to hills and a cavern in a knoll.

"That wasn't difficult," I say.

"We are not through." Enlil dims his spear. "Stay behind me."

He treads sideways, his front turned to the cave. A golden eye stares out of the shadows. I know that eye. I plant my feet.

"Kur! Where is Deven Naik?"

Enlil gapes from the First-Ever Dragon to me, shocked by my audacity.

Kur answers with an intelligible growl and dips his head out of the cavern. Ugly, swollen scars mar his blue-black snout. His whiskers are singed down to varying lengths. His closed eye has been sealed shut by severe burns. I tuck my right arm close. The same venomous fire that blemished his leathery hide took my hand.

Enlil lifts his spear. "We seek no quarrel with you, Kur."

"You accost me with your luminance." Kur lowers his head closer; our reflections shine in his gold eye. "Have you come to dwell with your father, my son?"

"We are visiting," Enlil says crisply. "Kalinda and I will be on our way."

"No, wait!" I grab the fire-god's spear and shine it in Kur's eye. The demon dragon flinches. "I'm not leaving until you tell me where to find Deven."

"You request *my* aid?" Kur asks. "I lost an eye by your treachery, Burner."

"Spare me your self-pity. Where are you holding Deven captive?"

"*I* am not holding him anywhere." Kur's nostrils flare, his exhale stinking of sulfur. "Inquire of the queen."

He blows a scalding breath over me and lumbers back into his lair. Enlil wrenches his spear from my grasp and speeds off, his long legs putting mine to shame.

"I don't understand," I say, skipping after him. "Kur brought Deven here. Why doesn't he have him?"

"Irkalla rules the under realm. Kur is her consort."

Once Kur's lair is well behind us, Enlil returns to a cautious tread. I cannot rub the gooseflesh from my skin. Kur is the most frightening monster I have ever beheld, yet he bends to his queen.

"Where is Irkalla?" I ask.

"Where else does a queen reside?" Enlil sweeps his spear low and points at the onyx sky. My eyesight adjusts to the dimness and etches out a city skyscape. "The Umbra Palace."

We set a direct course for the City of the Dead. The imperial stronghold is a skeleton of civilization, a mockery of what life represents. Treading toward it feels akin to approaching a scorpion's burrow. Though all is still, malice crouches within and waits to strike.

At the city wall, Enlil directs me to stop and detours to a ramshackle guardhouse. He drops a handful of chicken legs by the open door. A foxlike rabisu with a bushy tail darts its head out, snatches one, and returns inside to feed. Its crunching noises follow us through the gate.

Every building is in poor condition, as if bhutas blasted them with their powers and abandoned them to ruin. The real culprit is the unceasing march of time. Negligence eroded the city to shambles.

Enlil skillfully navigates the nameless roadways. He has been here before, inhaled the foul air and tasted the rot of death, yet he returned and has not uttered a single complaint. I am still furious that he took advantage of my desperation to save Deven, but I would not wish to confront this trial with any other god.

We round a corner to an unobstructed view of the Umbra Palace. The roofline is a crooked arrangement of spiny towers, thin and serrated as splintered bones. Every broken window is replete with gloom.

On the lower floors, several walls are missing. The gaps line up so the palace itself appears to leer at its entrants. Enlil's glow reveals an empty courtyard and intrudes upon the footing of the open main door—an arch so lofty Kur could pass through.

"It's . . . big," I squeak.

"Once we crest the threshold, you cannot turn back."

Cala quivers. Her vote is to abandon this trek and retreat with Enlil, but she does not ask this of me. Not when I am almost to Deven.

I cross the courtyard first and we ascend the steps. Statues of ugallus are stationed before the door, roaring with their tongues out. The glint of Enlil's spear breaches the throne room. Within, the evernight thickens, tangible as oil. A haunting melody resounds off the cathedral beams, ruining any chance of pinpointing the source of the song. Though no rabisus or demons are within sight, I sense watchers in the evernight. Chains dangle from the far stone wall, and more are piled on the floor.

On the far side, past chipped pillars, a drapery hangs from ceiling to floor. The cloth ripples periodically, coinciding with breaks in the melody. I learned the tune about Anu's greatness in the temple when I was little. This off-key rendition is eerie.

Enlil bows to the dais. "Hello, Irkalla."

The humming stops.

"Only one being would dare trespass in my domain," says a female voice. I heard her in my nightmare, right before claws dug into my thighs and dragged me into the abyss.

"We have come for the mortal man," Enlil explains.

Irkalla's curtain stirs, then a single talon draws the covering back a little, revealing Deven chained to the wall.

Enlil blocks me with his spear to prevent me from running to him. Deven's arms are clamped about his head, and more iron secures his ankles. His chin rests against his chest, which rises and falls. In the short time we have been apart, he has withered to frailty. Blood, wet and dry, stains his side, seeping from a wound.

"What did you do?" I demand.

"I was cordial." Irkalla's tone takes on an amused lilt. "What will you trade for his freedom?"

"What will you accept?" I counter.

"I could be convinced to give him up—for your soul."

Enlil's spear flares. "You go too far, Irkalla."

"This is her beloved," she says, feigning concern. "Let her decide."

Deven's soul-fire is faint and fading, a dying ember. Of the two of us, I am more likely to escape here. "Return him to the Turquoise Palace alive, and we have a bargain."

"No, Kalinda." Enlil grows bigger in dissent.

"At the palace, Indah can heal him," I explain. Demons cannot leave the Void without someone else opening a gate, so I address Irkalla. "How will you get him there?"

"I am the queen of the dead," Irkalla replies, her vague declaration sweeping across the hall. Apparently arrogance is not confined to the gods.

Enlil steps between me and the drapery. "You cannot play her game."

"You think this is a game?" Irkalla's voice pitches higher. "You broke your word, Enlil. You swore never to return, yet here you are, aiding a mortal man you want gone."

"What does she mean?" I ask.

"Ravings of a demon," the fire-god replies.

Irkalla cackles. "You did not tell her. She thinks this is the first time she has come here. The first time she has come for *him*." She levels a talon at Deven. "Kalinda, you have entered the Void before, only then you went by another name."

"Cease these lies." Enlil sends sparks off his spear. They hit the stone floor and burn out. Any closer and the drapery would ignite. "Deliver the man and we will take our leave."

"Then what will become of them? You will not have your precious queen again. Can you not see she yearns for another?" Halfway up the curtain, Irkalla's bloodred eye appears. "Tell her or I shall."

Enlil pinches his lips closed.

"Sssssso be it," Irkalla says, and then addresses me. "Generations ago, when your soul-fire was more star than fire, you fell in love. You and your beloved had lived and loved many generations. Repulses me, frankly, but one god had another reaction—jealousy. You can imagine his surprise when you came to him for aid, desperate for a god's mercy. A chameleon demon had assumed your form and lured your intended into the Void, the night before your wedding, no less. The jealous god led you here, stood on this very dais, and demanded I return your beloved."

"But that's not possible," I whisper.

Irkalla singsongs her rebuttal. "Before you were Kalinda, you were Cala. Before you were Cala, you were . . ."

I feel flung off a ledge. Tumbling, tumbling, tumbling . . .

"Inanna," Enlil says, his expression stony. "Before Cala, you were Inanna."

I hit the end of my disbelief, and everything goes watery. I claw through the heaviness, fighting for a solid hold. "Why didn't you tell me?"

Enlil reverts to sullenness.

I seek out Cala. *Did you know?*

No, she answers weakly.

Our voices combine, strengthening as one. "Explain."

"I told you a portion of the truth," Enlil replies, hushed yet unsparing. "After Inanna was reborn as Cala, I visited her. I thought I was unworthy of her love, but she did not treat me so. Our affections were genuine."

I do love him, Cala confirms.

"Show me my time as Inanna," I demand.

Enlil touches me, and time peels away. We are still in the throne room, but Deven is tied up and gagged on the floor. Enlil frees Deven, and we run from the Umbra Palace. The scenery blurs and changes to a humble hut on a green hillside. Deven and I are together again, tending to a garden and a small herd of sheep. The picturesque vision is so vivid, the sunshine warms my hair.

The fire-god releases me, and the brief vision disappears.

"How did you know that's my heart's wish?" I ask, clinging to the same lovely dream I saw in the Beyond.

"I was unaware," Enlil says bleakly. My ideal afterlife is devoid of him. "Those were Inanna's memories."

He showed me recollections of actual events. My discussions with Deven about building a peaceful life together were not dreams or wishes—we were remembering our past. Our first meeting in the Samiya Temple must have been fated.

Irkalla said we met and loved many lifetimes in a row . . . until Enlil visited Cala. Then her love for him usurped ours.

I didn't know about Deven when I met Enlil, says Cala.

You do now. You and Enlil had your time together. This is my *life.*

I swing toward the ominous red eye. "Irkalla, we have an agreement."

"Ssssplendid," Irkalla hisses.

Enlil's expression sags in disappointment. I have behaved predictably. I cannot determine what Irkalla wants, but it is evident that she was not after Deven.

I sprint to him and unhinge his bindings. He tips against me. My knees give out under his weight, and we slump to the floor. He does not move, his clammy skin ashen. I find his pulse and push small bursts of my soul-fire into him. His body temperature warms, his color returning.

Deven wakes and looks around the throne room. I cradle his bearded jawline and rest my forehead against his.

I did it, Jaya. I found him.

"Who—who are you?" Deven hears his lisp and touches his lower gums. Two of his front teeth are missing.

"I'm Kali," I say, relieved to hear his deep voice.

"What is this place?" He sits up and wraps his arms around his shivering torso.

"You're still cold. Let me warm you." I lift my shining fingers to touch him. His eyes pop open, and he backtracks across the floor, cradling his bleeding side.

"You're a . . . a Burner." Deven spots Enlil with his lightning spear. "I won't reveal the rajah's location. Tell the warlord Hastin I'll die before I betray the empire."

Hastin? The rebel bhuta warlord is long dead. Deven saw him die.

"Deven, I'm Kalinda," I repeat, withdrawing my powers. "What's the last thing you remember?"

He appraises the daggers at my waist. "I was preparing my men to escort the rajah on a tour of the Sisterhood temples. Rajah Tarek intends to claim his hundredth rani."

A growing panic bangs around inside me.

"We met during that tour," I say. "Your party came to the Samiya Temple. You caught me listening outside the rajah's door and shooed me away before Tarek discovered me. He claimed me, and we left for Vanhi. I was his viraji, and he promoted you to captain of the guard." Deven stares at me blankly. I go on, each word more frantic than the last. "You were my personal guard during my rank tournament. Tarek's ranis tried to sabotage me. I lost my best friend, but you were there. We . . . we fell in love."

"You and I are in love," he says, a straightforward sentiment. I wait for recognition to dawn in his gaze. He slowly angles toward me for a closer view in the dimness. "Kalinda?"

"You call me Kali," I say, leaning into him.

He reaches for my face. At the last second, he lowers his aim to my waist, steals my dagger, and positions the blade under my chin. "Take me to Hastin."

Enlil shoots a lightning bolt over our heads. It strikes the wall behind us and explodes a hole. Deven scoots away from me, taking my dagger.

"Kalinda," the fire-god says, his tone authoritative. "He doesn't remember you."

Irkalla cackles, a deep, resonating sound. "Mortal minds are so easily shattered."

Deven searches the throne room for the source of her voice. He looks at me with the same wariness, without warmth or fondness.

I fight back tears. "Enlil, remind him who I am."

"His mind and soul-fire must be intact or I could cause further damage."

"You won't even try," I rejoin. Enlil wishes to keep us apart, but Deven's memories must be inside him.

I advance on my beloved cautiously, holding my hand up in peace. "You're a good soldier, Deven. You know you cannot fight your way past the man with the spear. You're not in danger from us. We're trying to help you, but you have to trust me. Some part of you must know I'm not an enemy, even if it's simply your warrior instinct." He starts to lower the dagger. "Give me the weapon, and I promise no one will—"

He lunges with the blade and slices my palm. I gawk at my bleeding cut. He hurt me. Deven has never hurt me.

"I tire of this," Irkalla says from her hideaway. "Marduk, return the man to the mortal realm."

A squat demon with smashed, grotesque features emerges from behind the curtain and clubs Deven over the head. He buckles to the floor, and Marduk drags him away. The swiftness of the demon's cruelty leaves me aghast.

"Wait!" I kneel beside Deven and crush my lips against his. "You'll be safe soon."

Marduk lugs him down the outdoor steps. A bear rabisu heaves him into a wagon, then the demon climbs onto the driver's bench and the oxen plod off.

A rattling returns my attention to the dais. The high drapery parts from the center, revealing a monstrous dragon. Irkalla is substantially larger and thicker around the middle than Kur. Spiny prongs line the ridges of her back. Horns protrude from her giant skull, and whiskers cover her long snout. Her onyx scales form diamond patterns down her girth and serpentine tail. A minor bulge rings her head and drops between her eyes into a stately point.

Irkalla rules from a throne of tall, sharp rocks that fan behind her like a wall of spikes. She curls her upper lip and fangs large as battle poles glisten at us. An army of rabisus charge in. At the lead are Edimmu, Lilu, and Asag astride ugallus.

"Surrender your weapon, Enlil," orders the queen of the dead.

He hesitates and then casts aside his spear.

In a blur of speed, Irkalla breaks a spike off her throne and impales it through the fire-god's middle. She slams the barb into the wall, pinning him. Asag shifts stones to encase Enlil's hands and feet. He tenses, fighting against the agony, and fades from consciousness.

Irkalla sharpens her sneer on me. "Chain the bhuta."

Edimmu dismounts. "Against the wall, slag."

I hardly hear the demon over my internal thrashing. My devastation is deafening. *Deven forgot me. I was too late.*

Edimmu locks on cuffs, securing the one on my right arm above my elbow. "Melt your confines, and I will pluck your eyeball out and force you to watch me devour it."

The demon licks her chops to reinforce her threat. I do not recoil. I have glared into the maw of the evernight, and it did not break me.

"What happened to Udug?" I ask. "Was he punished for failing to overthrow the mortal realm?"

"Silence," Edimmu snarls.

I should not provoke her, but any hurt I can lob back at these monsters will be a victory.

"Was Udug tortured?" I press. Edimmu slams her elbow into my temple. My consciousness tips on the brink of numbness. "He must have wept. Did you hear him crying—?"

Edimmu whams me square in the forehead with her own. Pain pours down my body, and then I am afloat.

33

ASHWIN

I read the list of names for the dozenth time.

The throne room is hushed and the hour late. Two lanterns glow behind me, casting a muted glow across the empty hall. Upon leaving the nursery, I asked Pons to halt the wedding preparations and then sought fresh air on the roof. Half an hour later, he delivered Gemi's letter. I brought it here.

My throne's shadow stains the floor. Gemi is free to find "her place," but sending me a list of ranis that I should consider as my kindred an hour after she canceled our wedding struck me like a crossbow bolt.

Shyla's name is at the top of the list, followed by Parisa, Eshana, and Sarita. Gemi finished with a brief comment—*These women care for you. Perhaps you could care for one of them?*—followed by her signature.

I sniff the paper. It smells like lavender.

"What in the skies did you do?" Natesa stomps into the throne room and up to the dais. "The wedding is delayed?"

"Gemi advised me to take a non-bhuta Tarachandian as my wife."

Brac marches in and slides right into our conversation. "Did Gemi change her mind before or after you decided to exile my trainees?"

My gut bunches. "I didn't exile them. They would have been well cared for by the sisters. Gemi insists on taking them to Lestari."

Brac halts before me, his stare daggered. "Your solution to the protests is to send bhutas away? Who will you dispose of next? Me?"

Natesa wags a finger at him to settle down and refocuses on me. "Ashwin, did you ask Gemi to stay?"

"For what purpose?" I rest my chin on my fist. "She's made up her mind."

Natesa takes off her chunky bracelet and throws it at me. It strikes my knee and lands on the ground. "Stop feeling sorry for yourself. This is your fault."

"My fault?" I rub my sore knee; it will undoubtedly bruise. "Gemi gave me this list of alternatives. *She's* finished with *me*."

Brac groans. "You're so unobservant! The entire time I spent with Gemi in Lestari, she prattled on about you. She was so eager to see you again she told the datu she would accept your proposal whether he negotiated the alliance or not."

I manage a hard swallow. "Why would she do that?"

"She cares for you! While you were busy moping for Kalinda, Gemi was watching you with moon eyes. You really didn't see it?"

Natesa waves Brac back, and he paces away.

"Ashwin," Natesa says in an *I am trying not to throw another bracelet at you* tone, "when it comes to matters of the heart, you are a dolt. Gemi came here for you. That makes her the right kindred for you *and* the empire."

I lean my back into my throne. "Then why is she leaving?"

"Did you give her a reason to stay?" Natesa questions, turning her lotus engagement ring on her finger.

Brac paces back to her. She holds him off.

"We're going to a farewell gathering for Gemi in the Tigress Pavilion," she says. "Parisa organized it. She feels bad about how she's behaved and wants to make amends. You should come and talk to the princess."

"Thank you, but we said our farewells." The princess should enjoy her final hours here without me hovering.

"There, then," Brac grumbles to Natesa. "We can go."

Natesa treads backward after him. "You should come, Ashwin. Not many women would leave their home to move to a far-off desert for marriage. You could have found other ways to pay for the empire's regrowth than an alliance and picked any woman on that list. Maybe it's time you consider why you chose Gemi."

As Natesa's footsteps recede, my attention drifts to the kindred's floor cushion. I barely knew Gemi when I proposed, but I had observed enough. She had stood up to the datu, something I never did against my own father, to defend my homeland. Since her arrival, she has pointed out treasures in my world that I had not noticed. She honored her duties to teach the Tremblers and trained with the sister warriors, yet still made time to study her surroundings. Gemi is untainted by Lakia and Tarek's oppressive reign. In her company, I feel less tainted by them too.

I do not know what that means, except that I do not want to lose this feeling.

I dart into an antechamber and take a servants' passageway to the upper floor. I climb the stairs two at a time and arrive at the entry to the wives' wing short of breath. Throwing open the silk curtain, I enter the dining patio right behind Brac and Natesa.

All conversation at the candlelit tables ends. Gemi dines on cardamom rice with Eshana. Indah and Pons eat across from them. The couple must have left their daughter with a nursemaid. Parisa serves wine to her small assembly of guests. She pales upon my entrance.

"I'd like a word with my viraji," I announce, then stroll off to the side and wait. Gemi drinks half her wine and then rises and brings her chalice with her. Her long sarong is tied low on her hips, her blouse cut high above her stomach. Her hair flows around her slim shoulders, loose and wavy.

Lords, she's a sight.

"Why are you here?" she asks, glancing at our audience. All ears are on us.

"Please stay."

Gemi drops her gaze. "I don't think—"

"Just listen." I pull out the list she gave me. "I don't picture any of these women as my kindred. This isn't about an alliance, it's about a better future. My parents had a terrible marriage. I don't want that for myself. I don't know where this is leading between us, but you must admit it *is* leading somewhere. We'll never find out if you go."

Gemi sets her chalice on a table. "But marriage?"

"We can postpone the wedding and spend time together, just us. Whatever you decide, please know that I care about you. I wouldn't have proposed otherwise." I rear back on my desperation and level out my voice. "Of course, you may stay regardless. The palace will always be open to you. You're welcome to research our plants and animals and use my library for as long as you like."

"You'll let me into your library?" she asks, her golden eyes wide.

"Only when I'm present." I qualify my answer with a teasing wink.

Gemi sways forward as she laughs. I grab her against me to catch her from falling. She blinks up in confusion, her legs weakening. "Ashwin?" she slurs, then turns limp in my arms and blacks out.

I shake her a little. "Gemi?"

Crashes come from the table.

"Son of a scorpion," Brac says. He crawls off his floor cushion and slumps over.

Indah and Pons are passed out against each other, the contents of their wineglasses spilled down their fronts and Pons's blowgun untouched at his waist.

"Guards!" Natesa calls. She confiscates Eshana's chalice and sets it aside with her own. "Don't drink that."

"Your drinks are fine," Parisa drawls, drawing a haladie. "I only altered the bhutas' wine. Put down your weapons." She disarms Pons of his blowgun and Indah of her dagger. She holds out her palm to Natesa and Eshana. They lay their concealed blades on the table.

"Parisa!" Eshana says. "Did you kill them?"

"I slipped sleeping tonic into their drinks. They'll recover." Parisa crushes Pons's blowgun under her foot, her expression sour. "The prince wouldn't listen, so we had to act."

Gemi's deadweight slides down my front. I lay her on the floor and frown up at Parisa. "You said *we*."

"A bhuta foreigner cannot become our first rani. Our kindred should be a sister warrior proven in the arena. Not this, this . . . *princess*."

"But Gemi called off the wedding," Natesa counters. "Why do this if she's leaving?"

"What will prevent the prince from selecting another unsuitable viraji over those of us who earned our place here?" Parisa takes her argument to Eshana. "Gemi never went through the Claiming, and she's not a tournament champion. She knows nothing of our sisterhood."

"Those trials didn't make us sisters," Eshana replies, her eyes watery. "Standing together did."

"I'm doing this for *us*." Color splotches Parisa's complexion, her pitch rising. "After everything we gave the empire, we were passed over for a foreigner. She and the prince will decide whether we can stay in the palace or must go."

"That choice is yours," I break in. "I'm organizing a council for women. I hoped to present my proposal to the court at my wedding feast. We're establishing a palace guard of sister warriors, and alternately we'll offer occupational training for those who would rather lay down their weapons and join the workforce."

"An all-female guard?" Parisa asks, her blade still.

"Women deserve independence." I gaze down at Gemi and my voice chokes. "The idea came to me after visiting the Southern Isles. Their women don't marry out of necessity . . . but for love."

A man speaks from the entry. "More reform and changes. Your Majesty, when will you learn to leave our beliefs alone?" Commander Lokesh and his men file in. Clothed in all black and armed, they are an unsettling lot. Lokesh wears a headscarf over his nose and mouth. I nonetheless sense his smile. "Next time you banish someone, send guards that cannot be bribed."

I edge in front of Gemi. "How did you get in?"

Lokesh steps over Brac without sparing him a glance and strolls to me. He pulls aside his scarf; his smirk is broader than I imagined. "*You* let me in."

A replica of me enters the patio. The man does not resemble me in the way that I do my father. He and I are identical from our tight trousers to our mussed hair. Eshana gawks at my twin. Even Parisa appears confounded.

"What trick is this?" Natesa demands.

"No trick," replies Lokesh. "Prince Ashwin has come to his senses. He withdrew the troops from the city and sent them home on leave for their service. He then notified the palace guards that he hired my troops for security. The guards were amiable, except for the general."

Natesa tries to grab at Lokesh. The mercenaries block her. "What did you do to him?"

Lokesh signals at his lackeys, and they haul in Yatin. The general's head hangs and his feet drag behind him. They dump him on the ground. Natesa rushes to his side. Yatin's eyes are unfocused and his nose bloody.

"Commander," Parisa says breathily, "you said you wouldn't hurt the guards."

My look-alike snorts at her gullibility.

"Parisa," Eshana asks, "how do you know Lokesh?"

"We met after one of his visits to the palace." Parisa kneels before Eshana and grasps her knees. "He's going to preserve the empire, Eshana. We won't ever have to leave our home."

"No one planned to turn you out," I say, tossing the list at her. "Not me or the princess. Those are Gemi's recommendations for who would make a good kindred. Your name is second from the top."

Parisa blanches. Eshana peers over her shoulder and reads the list for herself. Parisa murmurs excuses, but Shyla turns her back to her friend.

"Don't give that any credence, Parisa," says Lokesh. "The prince and his viraji will dismantle our beliefs. They don't share our vision." He rounds up his men with the spin of his finger. "Bind the prisoners and lock them in the dungeons. Leave the prince."

The palace dungeons are reinforced with neutralizer herbs that suppress bhuta powers. Once the sleeping tonic wears off, the bhutas will be trapped like any other prisoner.

Eshana does not resist capture, but Natesa grapples with three men trying to pin her down. Lokesh lowers the blade of his pata to Yatin's head.

"Concede or I'll use this blade."

Natesa quits struggling, her glare vowing retribution. The mercenaries restrain her, then prod her and Eshana out, dragging Yatin after them. The rest of the invaders tie up Gemi. One of them throws her over his shoulder. Her hair swings down his back. They cart her off, leaving me with my look-alike, Parisa, Lokesh, and a handful of his men.

"What will you do with them?" I ask.

Lokesh claps me on the back, overplaying our closeness. "Tomorrow, my Prince Ashwin will order the viraji hanged. Everyone far and wide will be reminded that bhutas are not welcome in Tarachand."

249

My look-alike leers. Gemi will hang, and my people will believe I gave the order. "Who is this imposter?" I ask. "How long has he been imitating me?

Before I get a response, one of Lokesh's men rushes in. "Commander, the children are gone. A healer helped them get away."

My head flinches back. What children? My siblings in the nursery?

"Gone?" Lokesh yells, then reels on Parisa. "You said you would put them to sleep!"

She elevates her chin. "I was afraid of giving them too much sedative. I borrowed books from the library and read about the effects. One of them said an abundance of sedative could kill them."

Parisa must have taken more than one book from my library besides the childhood-studies title. I did not think to search for other missing texts.

"Find them," Lokesh orders his men. "I need those children tonight."

"She will be vexed," warns my look-alike, his voice ratty.

"We'll get them," Lokesh replies. He draws his second pata sword and aims both at Parisa. "You have fulfilled your usefulness."

He cuts her down in consecutive slashes. She crumples, her haladie useless in her fist. I lower to her side and cup her injured ear and scar. My gut heaves at the sight of her fatal wounds.

"Tell Eshana I'm sorry," she rasps.

Before I can pledge that I will, life bleeds out of her.

Mercenaries bind me and push me out of the pavilion after Lokesh. My look-alike stays behind, contemptuous in his farewell smirk.

Guards are stationed in every corridor, all aligned with Lokesh. More wait in the front courtyard with a trio of camels. A fine indoor rug is spread over the stone tiles. Lokesh shoves me down so I land on top of the rug. I fall on my stomach and flip onto my back.

"Who are the children you're after?" I ask. Lokesh murmurs to his men, disregarding me. "Who are you working for?"

Lokesh bends over me, eyes narrowed. "I have no employer. My payment will be the palace, city, and your coffers. I'm taking back my throne." At my prolonged befuddlement, he says, "You still don't know who I am."

My first introduction to Lokesh was the day he deserted the army. I comb my memory for an association I may have missed.

"My mother was a palace servant. Rajah Tarek took a shine to her long before he wed Kindred Lakia. When it was discovered that my mother was with child, we were cast out. She raised me on the streets, begging and stealing to survive. You were a year old the first time I saw you riding through Vanhi with Lakia. I remember thinking—*he stole my life.*"

Lokesh is my *brother*?

Reason swiftly replaces my shock. It is possible. Tarek was a serial philanderer, and a servant would never be permitted to live in the palace with the rajah's bastard son.

Family resemblances float to the forefront of my awareness. Lokesh has the same thick shoulders and long arms as Tarek. I may have recognized the resemblance sooner if not for the man's customary headscarf.

"The Turquoise Palace is my rightful home," Lokesh says, flinging one side of the rug over me. "I swore on Mother's deathbed that I would set the empire back on course."

His men roll me up in the rug. I wrench at my bindings, but the thick cloth confines me. Someone picks me up and throws me over the back of a kneeling camel. I hear the beast grunt and then Lokesh's voice.

"You'll suffer a death befitting your betrayal of Father. Good-bye, young Prince."

My world joggles as the camel rises and plods off. I wriggle to expose a foot to passersby, but the effort is pointless.

Everything I have worked for has been swept out from underneath me.

34

KALINDA

Cackling wakes me from my stupor. I must not have been unconscious long. Enlil is still pinned to the stone wall by the spike Irkalla drove through his belly. His spear is propped against the wall on my opposite side, far from reach.

Rabisus have congregated around the fire-god, jeering and jumping. One spits in Enlil's face, and they all screech in hilarity. Cala's fury mounts at his mistreatment. I am too hurt by his omissions about Deven's and my past to defend him.

Irkalla lounges on her throne and softly hums the hymn about Anu. After witnessing how the Void corrupted Deven's memory, I have no tolerance for her irreverence.

"Why are you singing about the sky-god?" I ask. "Aren't you rivals?"

She opens one red eye and closes it again. "Before Anu usurped the saltwater-goddess Tiamat and banished Kur and me, we sang Tiamat's praises. After Anu's conquest, he rewrote the lyrics about himself and taught it to his mortal slaves. Unlike him, I will never forget my origins." She picks up where she left off humming.

A wolf rabisu sprays saliva at Enlil's lower half. The spit dampens his sarong and drips down his legs. Enlil comes alert. From my angle,

I notice cracks in the spike restraining him to the wall. He scours the throne room until he locates me. Cala relaxes some, happy he is awake. I can hardly meet his gaze.

Another rabisu spits on his arm and snickers. Enlil glares at his tormentors and sends a small burst of luminance at them. They scatter, hissing and whimpering.

Asag and Lilu march through the main entry followed by four visitors, one of whom carries a torch. Irkalla lifts her head to greet them. I assume her demons have brought prisoners, but Commander Lokesh holds the torch. Two of his mercenaries escort him and—

"Ashwin!" I wrench against my chains.

His face melts away to reveal Marduk, the repulsive demon that returned Deven to the mortal realm. *What in the gods' names . . . ?*

Marduk must be a chameleon demon. Reasons why he would impersonate Ashwin swim through my mind. Harassment, extortion, assassination. Each one plunges worry further into my gut. Marduk leans casually against a pillar while the remainder of the party addresses Irkalla.

"My queen," Lokesh says, bowing.

"Where are they, Commander?"

"We had an incident." Lokesh's voice vibrates with fear. "They hid from us. We searched the palace most of the night, but they haven't been found."

I listen so closely my head aches. *Who couldn't he find? Ashwin? Gods, please let it be the prince.* Lokesh could only have searched the palace if his men had gained control, which would only happen if Ashwin was dethroned.

"Our bargain is contingent upon their delivery." Though Irkalla speaks matter-of-factly, she could turn vicious in half a second.

"I'll find them during the day and return with them tomorrow night," Lokesh swears.

"Do not break your word," Irkalla says, "or he will remain mine."

None of this makes sense. Even though I can hear their every word, I am missing huge sections of meaning.

"My queen," Lokesh stutters, "may I see him?"

"You failed to deliver what you promised, yet you request a favor?" Irkalla's tone has a callous edge. Lokesh drops his head. She narrows her eyes and flicks her tail. "Oh, all right."

Chains rattle above us. A stairway, large enough for the queen of the dead to pass through, winds from the upper floor to her dais. The jangling closes in. Edimmu and rabisus lead a prisoner down the staircase. Irkalla's underlings drag a soul with a shaggy beard and hair.

Gods alive. It's him.

Tarek's shoulders have sunken over his rib cage, and his tunic pulls against the knobs of his spine. He passes me without a hint of recognition. Nor does he react to Enlil's mighty luminance or physicality. He is a husk of the man he was.

I find no joy in his affliction. My only solace would be to never see him again. I thought I had earned that reward. Tarek is like a house cricket, silent all day long and then, when one lies down for the night, a strident invader of peace.

Edimmu leaves him between Irkalla and Lokesh.

"Your Majesty," Commander Lokesh says, bowing, "it's my honor."

A trace of Tarek's identity returns to his expression. "You serve me?"

Lokesh perks up. "I'm your commander. You have my undying allegiance, Your Majesty. Prince Ashwin is a traitor to your great authority."

More of Tarek's demeanor returns. I see the moment when he remembers himself in his clenching fists. I leave my powers on standby in case this summit of evildoers goes awry.

"Commander," Tarek says, "I order you to free me and return me to my empire."

Irkalla clenches her claw, drawing in her talons. "Remind him who rules here."

Edimmu pushes against Tarek's shoulders to force him to kneel. He pushes back. Beside me, Enlil wiggles against the spike impaling him. Slowly, nearly imperceptibly, the weapon is withdrawing from his abdomen. His wound is healing and extracting the stone spike.

Edimmu tires of Tarek's defiance and strikes his back with a flick of her forked tongue. Tarek sags forward, and the rabisu guard finishes compelling him to his knees.

"I warned you, Tarek," Irkalla says. "This is my domain. Do you recall what happens when you disobey me in my realm?"

Tarek quivers from rage. "I am rajah."

"You are vermin." Smoke whirs from Irkalla's nostrils. Tarek shuts his bloodshot eyes and coughs as it streams over him. "How many piles of refuse must you shovel before you accept your fate?"

"Temporary fate," Lokesh inserts. "I'll return tonight and we'll make our exchange."

Irkalla arches her head to better glare at him. "Tarek remains my servant until you deliver the bhuta children."

Enlil's glow lessens, his godly version of paling. What does he know? I glance at Marduk reclining against the pillar, all smug and disinterested. His reasons for arriving under the guise of Ashwin's appearance must mean that Lokesh and his men *do* have control of the palace. To find the bhuta children . . . ?

Merciful gods. Irkalla wants the trainees. Lokesh will bring them to her, and in exchange, she will give him Tarek. The commander could not mean to replace Ashwin with Tarek, could he? Is that even possible? According to Enlil's expression, it may be.

"I'll leave one of my men to reopen the gate," says Lokesh.

"Then you do not need the other one." Irkalla jabs her talon through the nearest soldier's chest and yanks it out.

He drops, and the rabisus pounce on him. Lokesh and the other soldier skirt away from the feeding frenzy. I quell my gagging and look away.

"Take our visitor upstairs with Tarek," Irkalla tells Edimmu. "They can muck out my chamber. Marduk, escort the commander out. Hurry, or he will be trapped here all day." She cackles at the idea; she is the only one.

Marduk saunters off with Lokesh as ordered. Edimmu grabs Tarek's chain and drags him across the floor. He shutters his eyes to Enlil's natural glow and reopens them. Our gazes connect. A range of emotions play across Tarek's countenance. Surprise, disbelief—and rage.

"Kalinda!" He wrenches at his bindings. I grab for my soul-fire. I doubt I could aim well enough to land a hit, but I could certainly scare him. "You disobedient wretch. You did this to me. I will find you! You will wish you'd never defied me!"

I stare him down while Tarek shouts more threats about claiming me and how I am his wife. None of his rancor cleaves through my armor of disregard. As soon as he disappears up the stairwell, I bank my fire and shudder.

"Do not fear, Kalinda," Enlil says. "Tarek is never leaving here."

The spike has been freed from the fire-god's chest another finger length. Irkalla licks the mercenary's blood from her talon.

"How did Lokesh find you?" Enlil calls to her.

"*I* found *him*," Irkalla replies. "He was present the night Kur took Kalinda's beloved below. Kur sensed hatred in the commander for those challenging our rule. We knew he could be motivated. Marduk said Lokesh did not need much persuasion. He recognized his true queen."

Screams come from the upper floor, followed by the unmistakable crack of a whip. I study my bindings, wanting them off even more than before. The screams stop first. The whip goes on several more strikes.

Enlil speaks, his voice colored by revulsion. "Tarek can never return to the mortal realm as the man he was. His mind is wrecked. Does the commander know?"

"Who's to say what that mortal understands? Our bargain is binding."

"As is mine with Kalinda," says Enlil. "Let us go. You will never see either of us again."

Irkalla glances indirectly at him. "Your living flame irritates me. You may go. The Burner stays."

"I'm not one of your followers," I say. "I'll never serve you."

Irkalla swings her head so close her whiskers nearly jab me. "Do you know what becomes of bhutas who die in my realm?"

I grit out my response. "They suffer an eternal death."

"Ah, but that is a mortal's fate. What will become of *you*?"

Enlil's jawline bulges from clenching his teeth.

"He did not tell you?" Irkalla's insidious mocking frays my nerves. She indicates Edimmu returning from upstairs. "Edimmu was once a Galer, Asag a Trembler, Lilu an Aquifier, and your old friend Udug? He was a Burner."

I must have misheard her. These demons—these monsters—were bhutas?

"Young soul-fire is more malleable. Once I have the bhuta children, I will raise them up as my fledglings and integrate them into the evernight. My army will be unstoppable." Irkalla's big red eyes reflect my horror. "You are more skilled than Udug was. You will be my greatest general yet."

Enlil's radiance stings my vision. "You will not pervert her."

"I will *improve* her." Irkalla lowers her head even more, her horns forward like a bull's. Her foul breath is hotter than the desert sun. "My army is coming, and they will need a leader."

Enlil blasts apart the weakened stone spike and rock confines with an internal heatwave. Irkalla rears back and roars. Edimmu shrieks and runs off, her scales smothered in flames. Irkalla lands, her thunderous impact quaking the palace.

The fire-god scoops up his spear and leaps in front of me. "You may not have Kalinda. I staked a claim on her soul."

Cala and I balk. He claimed me?

"You lie," Irkalla says shrilly.

"I swear on the sun, moon, and stars, Kalinda is mine. Thus, you cannot claim her without declaring war on the gods."

"You deceive me. She loves the mortal man."

"Kalinda," Enlil says, "tell her you wish to spend eternity at my side."

"You must not lie or I will know," responds Irkalla.

Enlil is trapping me. Even if I lie successfully, I will be trading one set of shackles for another.

"Tell her," he presses.

Let me speak, says Cala.

This better work.

I listen for Cala's prompting and then repeat her truth. "My heart's wish is to dwell with Enlil forevermore."

The queen of the dead canvasses me for weakness. Cala cringes and pushes as far from the present as she can without disappearing. I stay close to my love for Deven and hold firm.

"Truth resides within her," Irkalla says, declaring her judgement, "but Kalinda herself tells a falsehood. Her soul is more Inanna than Cala, and Inanna loves the mortal man. Thus, she belongs to no god."

I don't belong to Enlil. My life and heart are mine, regardless of Cala's affections.

Irkalla sweeps the fire-god to the side with her claw. Asag and Lilu spring at him. Enlil launches lightning bolts at the pair. Lilu leaps behind a pillar, and Asag blocks the assault with boulders.

I melt the cuff at my wrist first and reach for the binding high on my right arm. Irkalla wedges my neck between her talons.

"I will make you perfect," she hisses.

She stabs her longest talon through my center. My soul-fire flashes and dies out. Lagging heartbeats strum into my bones. Enlil bellows like a thunder crash and shoots lightning at the queen of the dead. I do not see if it connects. The evernight ambushes my soul and snuffs out my star.

Sunshine eases me from my slumber. My parents come into focus. I am nestled between Yasmin and Kishan, hugging my mother and grasping my father's hand. I close my eyes again and soak in the serenity.

"Kalinda, you must wake," my father says.

Mother strokes my back until I stir. The sky is aquamarine, soft-hued yet effulgent. We are seated on a downy lounge in a rhododendron garden. Yellow butterflies explore round clusters of white blooms. This must be the Beyond. It is even more spectacular than Ekur.

"Kalinda," Mother says, "you cannot linger."

I run my fingers through her hair, marveling at the silkiness. "You don't want me here?"

"We've never been more content, but your path is not finished."

Father ducks his head near mine, his eyes mirrors of my own. "For too long you have questioned your potential. Do not waste another moment agonizing. You are a warrior. You were born to shine. Embrace how powerful you truly are and carve your destiny from the sun."

A distant urgency plucks at me. My soul has come to the Beyond, but a tether ties me to my physical form in the under realm. I cling to my mother. "I don't want to leave."

"Your father and I will be close. The rest of your family and your friends need you."

"You have all you need to defend them," Father says.

I lean into him. "What if I fail?"

"No matter how bleak the world may seem, or how mighty the night, dawn always comes."

I grip him harder. "I love you both."

Mother caresses my hair, my own fingers tangled in hers. "Whenever you need us, look for your inner star." She touches my forehead between my brows, forewarning me to seek her and my father within. "We're with you."

The far-off tugs intensify to sharp yanks. Enlil calls to me. *It's time.* *One more minute.*

My father presses his lips to my forehead, and my mother holds me closer. I indulge in their presence and sketch this memory on my heart. The pull of mortality strengthens. My parents' warmth changes into tearing-hot pain.

Something heavy hammers at my chest. Air inflates my lungs.

I gasp as my head jerks up. I hang from my bindings, faint and woozy. Enlil melts the final chain with his spear. My legs falter, and he throws me over his shoulder.

The hole in my middle is healed. *I'm alive.*

Cala still lodges inside my head. *Enlil saved us.*

The fire-god races for the main entry of the throne room. We pass Asag and Lilu on the ground. Burn marks riddle their bodies.

Irkalla blows venomous fire at our backs. Enlil outruns the blaze and throws a single white flame at her. It lands on the ground and instantly grows. Irkalla and the rabisus recoil from the glare. As the blaze expands, the color deepens to a rich blue, and its shape transforms into a dragon.

The cobalt dragon is solid and real, not built of fire like Siva. Her scales have a pearly sheen, and her eyes are just as vibrant. Although the living flame dragon is shorter and less stout than Irkalla, Enlil's creation springs at her. They lock jaws and tumble across the throne room, smashing through two pillars. Rubble rains from the ceiling. I hang on as Enlil dashes outside and down the palace steps.

Rabisus and two ugallus block our route. Our dragon bellows and then breathes white flames at Irkalla's snout. The queen of the dead lurches back, her whiskers on fire. Her rabisu troops hasten to her aid. The ugallus prowl in front of the exit to the city.

Enlil sets me down. "Wait here."

I totter but stay upright.

The ugallus crouch to pounce. Enlil swings his spear and slices at the nearest one's maned neck. It goes down yelping. The second swipes its claws at his side. Enlil rolls closer and drives his spear up through the ugallu's chest.

He returns and helps me limp to an alley outside the grounds. Irkalla's roars tremble the pebbles on the road. I lean against a wall and look back. Inside the palace, rabisus dangle from our dragon's neck by their jaws. More besiege her flank and snap at her hind legs.

Enlil checks my middle, front and back. No signs remain of my attack.

"How did you . . . ?"

He pulls me into a hug. "It is as I told Irkalla. I laid claim to your soul."

Some part of me must care for Enlil. Whether that fragment belongs to Cala or dwells within my heart, his loyalty restored me. For that, I can overlook his omissions. Enlil hoped I was just like Cala, yet even Irkalla discerned that I am not. I cannot forge my love for him or be the woman he wishes.

A bellow pulls us apart. Irkalla accosts our dragon with a steady stream of fiery breath. The cobalt creation staggers sideways and topples. Irkalla stomps her talons down on our dragon's head, standing on her, and locks her jaws around her neck. The dragon stills and vanishes.

"Bring them to me!" Irkalla screeches.

Her rabisus bound down the palace steps.

"We'll never get out," I say.

"We will." Enlil whistles and sprints. I barely keep up as he darts past buildings and down roadways. Howling rabisus pursue us. Enlil stops at one of the taller structures. "Go inside and climb to the top."

The first room inside the building is packed with wanderers. They stare mindlessly at the walls, floor, each other—me. I slip between them and inadvertently bump into one. My contact sets off a ripple of activity. They revolve toward me and grasp at my clothes and hair. I rip free and push them off, searching for a stairway. Enlil bursts inside. A rabisu leaps through the open door, and he fells it with his spear.

"This way!" He beckons me up the stairs.

Above the city, we see the rabisus filling the roads and surrounding our building. Enlil and I stand back-to-back, mindful of our footing. The rooftop is riddled with holes to the main floor far below.

Rabisus scale the outer walls and climb over the edges. Enlil bangs his spear into the floor, and a tidal wave of heat explodes, leveling the rabble. I cough in the aftermath of smoke and char. Sections of the unstable roof smolder.

Enlil points his spear at a blazing arch speeding toward us.

His chariot and horse.

"Kalinda, go to the ledge!"

I run into the cleared section. Rabisus swarm up from the stairwell. Several fall through the floor gaps, while others block my route. Smoke stings my eyes. It is too hazy to battle with my daggers, and I am too weak to summon my powers. Enlil hews down a fair number of rabisus behind me, but they continue to multiply.

Siva, I need you.

Tendrils separate from the scattered flames left from Enlil's heat-wave. They combine into a whirling blaze larger than a cicada or lynx kitten. Siva grows into a scrappy dragon the size of a full-grown tiger.

My fire dragon plants herself in front of me. I climb on her back and pat her neck, resting against her. Her nature-fire warms me and loosens my muscles. Reenergized, I draw my dagger. Siva awaits my command. She is too small to heft my weight in flight, but she can run.

Get them.

She bounds into the fray. We pummel through the teeming monsters, dagger and talons slicing. At the ledge, I kick a rabisu and it plummets over. The chariot flies alongside the roof. I leap off Siva onto it, and Enlil barrels after me. Rabisus jump on and hang from the wheels. Enlil jabs them loose and snatches the reins.

"Siva!" I wave for her to join us.

"You have to leave her!"

Siva snaps her fangs at the mangy rabisu. She jumps off the ground, trying to reach me, and dozens more pile onto her.

"Go!" Enlil commands his horses.

Chaser and his team take off. I watch for Siva's escape. The rabisus mob her, smothering her flame. But my fire dragon is born of nature-fire. She will rise again.

I settle next to Enlil at the helm. "I thought you said we would be expulsed for cheating."

He sets his lips in a grim line.

Oh gods, Cala and I exclaim as one. Enraging the Void is risky, but any course that leads to the mortal realm merits an attempt.

The chariot flies above the palace spires. Irkalla roars below, and storm clouds gather. Shards of night appear in the gray sky like demented bolts of lightning. The jagged spears take shape into rows, resembling serrated teeth in a vicious maw.

"Prepare to be expulsed!" Enlil says, steering for the open muzzle.

I clutch him as we fly directly into the razor jaws of the evernight.

35

ASHWIN

Arching my head toward the opening of the rolled-up rug, I work twice as hard to breathe. Every mouthful is a battle. I am entombed by my bindings and confines, stifled and beaten by the heat.

Thoughts of asphyxiation loom, so I focus on the cadence of the camel's stride. The rocking goes on and on. My captors have yet to stop.

As I am taken farther from the palace, it is hard to forget the day I spent leaning out the window of the carriage, watching the horizon for my mother. At least then I had hope that she might come. Few know that I am gone, much less my destination.

Sand works its way into the rug, dusting my hair and ears. Lokesh gave me almost the same punishment I gave him. I have no confusion about the difference. Mine was a banishment, his, an execution order.

The rocking stops. A camel grunts, and my world drops. All goes motionless, then I am hauled up and thrown to the ground. I roll to a stop, shedding my rug. A wind sprays hot sand over me. I spit out the granules and squint through the blazing sunshine at the outlines of two guards. One of them cuts my bindings.

I push onto my knees, my wrists chaffed and raw. "Don't do this. Don't let Lokesh hang the princess. She's innocent."

The closest guard's headscarf hangs open, his expression pitiless. "She's demon spawn. Her very existence is a sin."

"Please." My father would whip me half to death for begging, but I must get to Gemi. "I'll reward you and your families. I'll give you anything you want."

"My father was crushed by a Trembler and left to rot. Anu willing, you'll die slowly."

His foot reels back to kick me. I turn my head, and his boot connects with my ear. I cradle my splitting skull, my vision flashing in and out. Eyes covered, I wait for the pounding inside my head to dull. Moments later, with ears still ringing, I heft myself up.

The mercenaries and all three camels are gone.

I stagger into the wind after their tracks, shielding my eyes from the dust cyclones. The winds sweep away the trails. The men and their mounts have vanished between the dunes. I keep after them, guessing their course. Every direction appears the same, but if I put the sun to my back in the morning and walk toward it in the afternoon, the heavens will lead me west.

I trudge up a dune, into the sun. Several times my feet sink up to my ankles. Sand slips inside my boots and rubs against my heels. Before long, sunshine seeps through my tunic and heats my shoulders. I have no cloth to spare to protect my head.

At the crest of the next dune, I pause. The desert rises and dips endlessly. I start down the other side and climb another rise. Then another. Each time I reach the top, more dunes fill my path. Sweat pours into my eyes, changing the sand to sticky grit.

As I flounder up another dune, the steep slope gives way and pitches me downward. I tumble to the bottom in a heap of dust. A gust spatters more sand over me. I shut my gritty eyes and let my tears wash them clean.

I should have never given Lokesh a chance. Lords alive, did Tarek know he's my older brother? I am still his kindred's firstborn and rightful heir, but Lokesh embodies the warped values of our father, the customs so many of our people love.

Lokesh is who I would be had I stayed.

The realization comes at me sideways. My mother made the hard decision to send me far away. She gave me a gift—the opportunity not to become like my father.

Lokesh never had that chance. Tarek tarnished him and everyone else he subjugated under his rule in Vanhi.

Why should I fight for my city? My people will never change. I could abandon Vanhi and let the desert have me. The probability that I will return to the palace on foot is negligible, yet pretty pale-gold eyes consume my thoughts. Gemi could be the kindred of my heart. I brought her here to Vanhi. I idealized this political transition, not fully considering her feelings or my people's reaction. Everything that happens to her is my fault.

"Gods," I pant, "whichever of you is listening, you know I'm not much for praying. But don't you let Gemi die. This is my fault, not hers. Do you hear me?"

A gust blows more sand in my face. Coincidence? Or condemnation for making demands? I get up and trudge onward into the sun.

The horizon is a sepia blur, barren of anything or anyone. I slog up another hill, ignoring my blisters and parched tongue. My prayer may not have been heard, but uttering my motivation for surviving has given me a boost of strength. I cannot lose Gemi.

At the top of the dune, I glance back to judge my progress and spot two mahati falcons off to the east. I rub at my eyes, questioning my sight. When I look again, they are still there, sailing nearer. The one in the lead is . . . Chare?

She circles overhead, confirming my identification. Tinley waves from her saddle as they land. I wave back and fold over to catch my breath.

Tinley jumps down and bounds over to me. "I heard you nearby and couldn't believe it."

Heard me . . . ? She must have overheard me threatening the gods. "What are you doing here?" I ask.

Chief Naresh and another young woman land behind us on the second falcon. The chief tosses me a water flask. I chug the warm, clean drink while he responds. "We were on our way to your wedding when the wind carried a warning to us that the palace has been occupied."

"A former army commander has taken control." I wipe at my wet mouth. "He opposes my choice of viraji and means to hang Gemi."

Naresh sharpens his ear to the wind. "The execution is set for sunset. We must go now or we won't make it."

I climb onto Chare after Tinley and ask, "Who's the woman with your father?"

"My sister, Maida." Tinley scrunches her nose at my sorry state. I smell of foot rot. "You have a lot to tell us."

I was thinking the same about her. Last I saw, she was flying off with Kalinda. "Help me stop Gemi's execution, and I'll tell you anything you want."

The mahatis take off across the desert. Chare outraces the chief's falcon by several wingspans. I attach my gaze to the horizon, overanxious to see the golden domes of my home.

36

KALINDA

Enlil holds the reins steady as Chaser charges through the abyss. After we went through the monstrous mouth in the sky, it retched us out here. I thought I had seen every horror of the Void, but nothing compares to this lonely dreariness. A sea at night has breaks in the waves. A desert has dips and rises that add variety. This chasm continues without end.

"How do we get out?" I ask.

"We must find Deven's gate!" Enlil replies. Sound does not travel far. Communicating feels like shouting into a box. "Occupants of the under realm cannot leave without a mortal opening a gate for them. Once the gate is open, it will reopen for the same mortal until destroyed."

Deven inadvertently released Marduk. Returning to me night after night gave Irkalla access to our realm. We did not know, but our ignorance is little consolation now.

Enlil and I fly onward for what could be minutes or hours; my senses cannot discern up from down, let alone the passage of time. Enlil does not admit it, but we are lost. The Void has swept us up and locked us in an unbeatable oblivion.

The horses tire. Strips of their flanks tear off and vanish in our wake. Enlil sends his living flames at the steeds to repair their breakages. The glowing tendrils roll off them and wither to smoke.

I speak directly into Enlil's ear. "What's wrong?"

"The evernight is too strong! It is choking their fire!"

One of the horses shatters to embers. By the time we fly through them, the ashes are cold. Two more horses split apart, as does the back end of the chariot. Chaser, the only horse remaining, pushes on.

Enlil and I clutch each other. Cala would usually take advantage of his closeness, but she hid when we left the City of the Dead. Perhaps she knows the evernight will eventually snuff out my soul-fire and she will disappear too. Enlil risks another fate. As he cannot perish, he would plunge through obscurity forever.

My strained eyes pick up on a disparity to our right. The Void, with no variance in color, has a spectrum of textures.

"Look there!" I indicate at the patch. "See how the darkness there is coarser like gravel, whereas the parts around it are soft like muslin?"

Enlil concentrates so hard his eye twitches. "I do not see it."

Chaser loses a piece of his hind leg. Our weight wears on him.

Without another option, Enlil passes me the reins, and I redirect for the gravelly path. The closer we get, the firmer the roadway appears. Chaser's hooves touch down, and the chariot wheels spin. Enlil emits a grunt of surprise.

The reins start to turn brittle in my grasp. I strain my eyes, searching for the doorway out.

A sudden pitch and angled slope of the chariot nearly throws us off. We lost a wheel. I hold on as the bottom of the chariot drags against the path, sending off sparks.

A section of the floor flies off and disappears. Enlil coaches Chaser to keep going. I peer down the road. The texture ahead evolves into a grainy wall.

The end of the trail.

I snap the reins and Chaser gallops faster. Flames shoot off from his mane and tail.

"Hurry along, old friend," Enlil calls. "Give us all your might!"

The fire horse stays on course. Enlil and I brace each other as Chaser disappears into the wall of shadow first. Our momentum throws us through the gate into daylight. I tumble across the floor into a wall. Enlil rolls into the bed frame. Pieces of the smashed carriage smolder on the furniture and floor around us.

Chaser did not make it through.

I crawl toward the open doors of the sunlit balcony and inhale the flowery air. I missed sunshine. And my chamber. And my bed. I will never complain about the desert sun again.

Enlil pulls himself up and stomps out a small flame. He reviews my sketches of Deven on the table. The prospect of seeing him again both delights and terrifies me. *What if he still doesn't remember who I am?* My heart is too tender from our last meeting to consider how badly that would hurt.

I grab a handful of dried fruit from a dish and shove it in my mouth. "Let's find those children."

"I must not meddle with Lokesh and Irkalla's agreement," Enlil replies. I stop midchew. "They have a binding contract that I cannot interfere with. Furthermore, it would be unwise to leave the gate unsecured."

"Then tell me where the trainees are hiding."

"I do not know."

So much for omniscient knowledge. "Can you at least close the gate?"

"Yes," Enlil replies. "However, Marduk would be trapped in your realm." I imagine the chaos the chameleon demon could cause and decide against stranding Marduk here. "I will guard it."

"How magnanimous of you," I say. Enlil nods and then rightfully interprets my statement as mockery. I pause at the door. He may infuriate me, but leaving without him feels wrong.

"Proceed ahead with caution, Kalinda," Enlil says, his tone wrought with worry. "I will ensure no one enters or exits the gate."

How can you stay angry at him? Cala asks.

If those children are captured, it'll be easy.

I steal down the empty corridors. The quiet is unnerving. Movement outside the door to the wives' wing halts me. I press my back to a wall. Mercenaries lead the ranis and children down the stairs by knifepoint. The ranis and nursemaids guide the older children by hand, and Shyla carries her daughter.

Once they have passed, I creep to the corner and peek around it into the entry hall. The women and children are going outside. I slip down the corridor to a balcony that overlooks the front of the palace. People in the city congregate at the gates, all looking up. I follow their gaze to Lokesh high on the roof. I do not see Ashwin—or Marduk impersonating Ashwin.

Lokesh's break from locating the bhuta trainees sets me on edge. What could keep him from honoring his promise to Irkalla?

Unless he has the children and is waiting for nightfall.

I think of the trainees, especially my own students, Giza and Basma. They must be petrified. But they *are* bhutas. Lokesh's men would not be a match should the children fight back. He would be clever to imprison them where their powers would not work . . .

The possibility will not let me alone. As I have no other ideas, I tiptoe to the stairwell that leads to the dungeons and start down the circular stairway. At the bottom, a pair of guards protect the entry. One of them is a mercenary. The other man is clean-shaven and wears a black uniform. His fat lip and bruises have healed. He is still scarily thin, but I love that face in any condition.

I round the corner and throw a heatwave at the mercenary. He hits the stone wall and falls, knocked out.

Deven draws his khanda. "The rajah said the rebels would come."

Letting my powers fade, I hold up my hand for peace. Deven has confused Ashwin with his father, a mistake I made myself when I first met the prince. For simplicity's sake, I leave his assumption uncorrected. "I'm not a rebel. I'm a warrior. The children the rajah captured are innocent."

"They're rebel children."

I pace closer, wary of Deven's fast striking abilities and considerable arm length, both traits I appreciate when they are on my side. "They're trainees. We cannot let the rajah have them or they'll die. I know you would never hurt a child."

He retreats a step, his blade outstretched. "I'll give you a chance to surrender before I call for more guards."

"Those aren't palace guards. I understand it's your instinct to obey your ruler and defend the palace, but sometimes it takes more courage to step back than forward. You said those words once when we were standing up to a tyrant. I've never forgotten them."

Deven wavers long enough that I feel encouraged to move closer. He centers his blade on me and shutters his warm brown eyes. "Don't come closer."

I match his stare despite my thrashed heart. "I'm sorry about this."

I throw a minor heatwave at him. As he cringes from the scalding slap, I slide up to him and touch his freshly shaved cheek. Skin to skin, I parch his soul-fire and he faints.

His stand-up collar is loose from his weight loss. I rebutton the top hole and graze my nose against his. "I love you, you loyal dolt."

I pilfer his keys to unlock the dungeon door and drag Deven inside.

He's not a god, Cala notes, *but I understand your fascination with him.*

As I haul in the second guard, she rummages through my memories of Deven.

Cala, those are private!

So were my kisses with Enlil.

I shut us in the dungeons, and the neutralizer toxins that are built into the walls douse my abilities. Without my powers differentiating us, the divide between me and Cala closes even more.

"Kali?"

I follow Brac's voice down the low-ceilinged tunnel to a cell and let him out. Indah and Pons are asleep on the sandy floor. "Are they sick?"

"They'll wake soon. We were sedated." Brac identifies his brother's inert body by the exit. "Why is Deven—"

"He isn't himself." My stomach balls into a fist. "But he's home."

Banging sounds farther inside the dungeons. "Down here!"

Five cells down, Eshana calls to us. I unlock her door, and she embraces me. Natesa sits on the floor near a sleeping Yatin. Neither woman asks where I have been, nor do I spare the time to explain. "Where's Ashwin?"

Eshana's voice hollows. "I don't know."

"Lokesh came for Gemi a little while ago," Natesa says. "He means to execute her."

The people must be assembling for the execution. "Where are the bhuta trainees?"

"They aren't here," Brac answers from behind me.

"Are you certain?" I ask, and he reaffirms his account.

Then where . . . ?

This must have been a distraction, Cala replies.

I groan at myself. Deven is not strong enough to battle a Burner, yet Marduk stationed him at the dungeons. He anticipated I would come here. Nightfall must be minutes away, and the roadways of shadow leading to the City of the Dead will be ready for moving the children.

I toss Brac the keys. "Wake the others and go to the roof. I think Lokesh means to execute Gemi up there. Oh, and Deven may be surprised you're alive since he doesn't remember much of the past year, but I doubt he'll harm you. Watch your back as a precaution, and if you could tell him something nice about me, I'd be grateful."

Brac blinks as he digests that feast of catastrophes. I pat his shoulder and dash out.

37

ASHWIN

I sit forward to better see the sun descending into the city skyline. The sight of the Turquoise Palace fills me with readiness. I made it home.

Tinley tilts her head to the wind and impels Chare faster. She and the chief bank their falcons south, out of the direct line of the palace.

"Why are you changing course?" I shout in her ear.

Tinley's voice carries to me on a gale. "The execution is on the rooftop. We'll approach from the rear."

The falcons race the failing sun. Chare pulls ahead from the chief, and he and her sister section off to wait out of sight. Tinley spares them no glance. Despite their lack of communication, their decisive, controlled movements are a comfort.

We sail over the elephant stables to the rear of the palace. Chare hovers near the lower roofline. I slide my legs together and jump down.

"This is as far as I can take you." Tinley tosses me her crossbow.

I sling the strap over my shoulder. I am not up to par with the sister warriors' training, but Tarek made certain that my weaponry skills are sufficient.

"Send a bolt into the sky, and the chief and I will fly in," Tinley says, then cocks her ear to the wind. "Hurry."

I run across the rooftop and leap up the wall. My fingers hook the molding. I pull myself onto the next level. Tinley gazes up at me in astonishment. She assumed I would go through the palace. This will be faster. I ascend several levels, relying on the balconies and archways for handholds. My arms and back ache and the fascia scrapes my palms. Tinley's warning propels me upward.

Hurry. Hurry.

Barking voices carry from outside the aviary. I climb onto the next rise and crouch low. Mercenaries swarm the rooftop. Several of them are archers, bows slung over their shoulders and quivers full. I slide the crossbow to my front and squeeze the fore grip. Lokesh directs his men from his position by the ledge. He wears his headscarf open, while the rest of the men don turbans to continue the charade that they have been hired as imperial guards.

I search for the thief that has stolen my appearance. My look-alike is not in attendance.

Mercenaries walk Gemi out. Her naturally straight posture has bowed. She sways as a pendant in the wind while the executioner slips a noose over her neck. Dry blood stains her wrists. I clamp down on the crossbow, ready to inflict pain on her captors. They cut her. They let her blood to weaken her powers.

My people crowd up to the main gate below and line their rooftops. Tarek fed their hunger for bloodshed with the tournaments and public stonings. Here they are again, eager for violence. I withhold my rising disgust. Their participation as spectators in Gemi's mistreatment shames the empire.

More mercenaries hold the ranis and children by sword point in the courtyard. Lokesh is forcing them to watch, but it is he who should be punished. I take aim at him with the crossbow. Gemi is between us, so I hold my fire.

The final sliver of sun melts into the western horizon.

Lokesh lifts a cone amplifier to his mouth. "Citizens of Vanhi, welcome!" On the ground, the crowd stills to listen. "Today we witness the restoration of Tarachand! Prince Ashwin has returned to the teachings of his father. He asks that you please pardon his absence. He felt burdened to remain on his knees in prayer, pleading for forgiveness that he might no longer lead us astray." The commander lying about me—yet again—goes on his long list of offenses. I balance the crossbow and wait for a clear shot. "Upon the death of his viraji, the empire will be cleansed and undergo a rebirth. We will have a new life without demons, without fear!"

"You know nothing of fear," says Gemi. Her head is hung, her hair in her eyes. "My admiral will bleed every drop of blood from your body, and my father will feed it to the sea."

"Be quiet, filth." Lokesh backhands her, and she folds in half. "Put her on the partition!"

The guards heft Gemi onto the rim of the roof. I have walked that ledge many times and never felt this sick. My finger strains on the trigger. Lokesh is out in the open, but he could fall back against Gemi and knock her over the drop-off.

A little left and I can fire.

"Hang the demon!" Lokesh proclaims.

His men reach up to push Gemi. I switch my aim to the aviary window and pull. The bolt zips through the window. A quarter of a second later, the doves flood out. Lokesh and his men shield their heads from the flurry of birds.

Gemi remains balanced amid the onslaught of flapping wings. As the doves fly away, thunder crashes overhead. Gray clouds brew up a storm. The moody thunderheads usher in cold, sweeping winds.

Lokesh traces the angle of the bolt back to me. "Shoot him!"

Archers prepare their arrows. Gemi raises her gaze to mine. Adoration warms her countenance. I was a fool not to see it before.

Arrows whiz past me. I slide down to the other side of the roof in plain sight of Lokesh. He grabs Gemi and shoves.

"Tinley, wind!" I cry and jump from the ledge.

I dive headfirst past Lokesh. Nothing lies between me and the ground. Gemi swings down, the rope almost fully stretched. A frigid gale heaves her up at the same time one pushes me.

In our momentary suspension, I reach out and pull her in.

Another well-timed gust redirects us. We swing to a higher ledge and land against the palace on a narrow recess. My body secures Gemi's against the wall. We pant in tandem, our heartbeats pounding.

Tinley and Chief Naresh circle above in the storm, their falcons drawing the archers' attack. The temperature plummets to wintry conditions. My cold fingers fumble to untie Gemi's wrists. She removes the noose and embraces me. Although her wrists no longer bleed, she will have scars.

"Down there!" Lokesh's men call.

The archers take aim and unleash their assault. We have no safe cover or path down.

Chief Naresh drives winds between us and redirects the arrows back at the bowmen. Then a curious phenomenon occurs—snow falls in the desert. Big, fluffy snowflakes pinwheel down and nest in Gemi's hair. I pluck one off, and we watch, mesmerized as it melts.

Tinley flies up on her falcon. "Jump!"

Arrows stream at her and Chare. The mahati retreats, and another string of arrows stops them from returning.

High above, Chief Naresh and Tinley's sister dart about on their falcon. Maida elevates her arms to the clouds. The snow falls heavier and faster. Frigid winds wail. The blizzard is so thick, I cannot see the ground. The archers shoot at us blindly.

"This is our cover!" Gemi shouts.

Tinley lowers again on her falcon. Gemi leaps first. The recess is slick, but I lunge, and Gemi grasps me. I sit behind her and Tinley. The falcon soars up the exterior of the palace and levels off above the archers. Most of the mercenaries are retreating inside from the whiteout, many of them injured by their own arrows. Lokesh and a small band of men withstand the gusts from Chare's flapping wings and heavy snowfall.

Gemi slides off the falcon and lands in a crouch on the roof. As I reload the crossbow with my second-to-last bolt, she heaves the clay tiles underfoot and fells the nearest mercenary. Another one slashes his khanda at her, cutting her arm. She kicks him in the jaw and disarms him. Taking up his blade, she swings at the next man.

Lokesh runs at Gemi, his pata swords out. I jump off Chare, landing between them, and take aim.

"It's over, Lokesh."

"You have much to learn, young Prince." He swings his double patas. I fall back onto my rear and release the bolt. It zips at him and embeds in his thigh. He bends and clutches his leg.

"I may be young, but I'll bring peace to the empire." A gale amplifies my voice, carrying it far and wide, Tinley's doing. Maida lessens the snowfall. Onlookers below stare up from their huddle, my confrontation with Lokesh visible. "Bhutas are welcome in Tarachand. Anyone who opposes their freedom will pay."

"The people won't listen," Lokesh says, straightening. "They love *me*."

Gemi boosts the clay roof tiles beneath him and trips him onto his back. His headscarf falls off into the snow. She wrenches sections of the brick ledge away and drops them on his patas, warping the metal blades.

"They fear you," she corrects, her arm bloody.

"You belong in the Void with the rest of the demons," he snarls. "I'm Rajah Tarek's firstborn. The throne is *my* birthright."

He grabs Gemi's ankle to pull her down. I slam my foot onto his forearm.

"Don't touch her."

Lokesh drags himself back to sit against the ruined ledge. "You think I did this for myself? I can bring Tarek back from the dead."

I step back, gripped by shakiness. I do not care how he plans to resurrect our father, but he will fail. "Tarek had his reign. The empire is my responsibility now."

"You abuse your power!" Lokesh screws up his mouth and rises, favoring his injured leg. "I'll never follow you. I'll dismantle your supporters one by one until you're alone."

He will never stand down. I have seen what men like him do. They have no limits. So long as he lives, everyone and everything I care about is in peril.

Lifting the crossbow to my shoulder, I take aim with the last bolt. "I tried to reason with you, Lokesh. I could have forgiven the lies, manipulations, and even you stranding me in the desert. But you shouldn't have hurt my viraji."

"I'll gut your demon viraji and any other bhuta ally."

"No, you won't."

I release the final bolt into his chest. The impetus throws him backward over the drop-off.

I cast aside the crossbow and stagger a step. The wind lifts Lokesh's scarf and spins it off into the sky. The entire palace is dusted in snow.

Gemi and I peer over the edge. Lokesh lies below, encircled by people. Many more watch us from the city. I have no words left for a speech, but they will hear from me soon.

I wrap Gemi in my arms, embracing her for all to see. Her cut has stopped bleeding. The wound is shallow, but she will have another scar. I would not be surprised if she leaves Tarachand and never returns.

Snowflakes rest on her eyelashes and ring her head in a crown. I slide my hand up her cheek. "I hope you can forgive me for this."

"I already do." Gemi sweeps her fingers across the nape of my neck and cozies against me. "This wasn't you, Ashwin. I won't let them chase me away. I stand with you."

I tip my forehead against hers, those pale-gold eyes filling my world. Vanhi and the palace and the empire are my place. At Gemi's side, I am more convinced that my home could become her place too.

38

KALINDA

Go to the Tigress Pavilion, Cala says, tapping into my memory. *Enlil will hold off Marduk. You need a better weapon than those daggers.*

I am the weapon, I reply.

We pass the pavilion en route to my chamber, and Cala nudges me again. I go in, straight to the racks, and select a haladie.

No, not that one. This one. Cala directs me toward the urumi.

I'm not trained for that.

Let me use my training.

Fine. I hope you're left-handed. I clasp the handle of her favorite weapon, and Cala grins—at least that is how her glee feels. Wary of the spray of blades, I extend the urumi out in front of me. The multiblade weapon is surprisingly light. My left hand can wield it without my right, which is still a bare wrist without my prosthesis.

Carry it off to your side.

I do as Cala says and drag the steel blades to my chamber. Enlil lies on my bed with his ankles crossed, his spear beside him. Cala's mind turns to lustful memories.

Stop that, Cala.

Sorry. She redirects her thoughts.

"The children weren't in the dungeons," I say. "Where's Marduk?"

"Not here." Enlil props his arms behind his head.

Clouds blot out the sun, and frigid wind stirs in from the balcony, ruffling the draperies and tossing my sketches of Deven across the chamber. They float to the floor and draw my eye.

A tremor shoots up my spine.

In the Void, Deven's front bottom teeth had been knocked out. When I saw him in the dungeons, he had all his teeth again.

A shadow fills the doorway. I reel around, and Deven flashes a full smile.

"Marduk," I say by way of greeting. Enlil bolts out of the bed and scoops up his spear. "Where are Deven and my friends?"

"Your friends are locked in the dungeons. For a moment, I thought you had sensed it was me instead of your beloved." Marduk sneers, his beady gaze alight. "Your words to him were touching."

"Marduk," Enlil barks, "where are the children?"

"I was getting to that," the demon says. Edimmu enters behind him. The reptilian horror is dappled with burns from Enlil's earlier attack. She leads in the bhuta trainees, and they crowd together against the far wall. Basma hobbles against Giza, her legs in splints. "I discovered them in a servants' passageway."

A boy steps out of line to ogle Enlil, and Edimmu flicks her tongue at him. The child recoils with a stinging mark. Enlil levels his spear at the demon. She drags Giza in front of her as a shield.

"Let us pass," she says.

"I would heed her." Marduk is so calm, so ordinary in his harshness.

Nightfall filters into the room, the murkiness made drearier by the storm. Cala readies the urumi, letting the blades slide around me. We function in unison, her thoughts my actions.

The gate of shadows to the under realm shifts and opens. An ugallu's front paws come forth. The back half of the lion-eagle fills the gate, its wings tucked in. Asag rides atop the beast. My Deven—the *real* Deven—is draped over the ugallu's back. At first sight, he is unconscious.

"Is . . . is he . . . ?" I trail off.

"Alive," Asag grumbles crossly, as though he is willing to fix that.

Enlil re-aims his spear at Marduk. "Irkalla promised his safe return."

"I *did* return him." Marduk tips his head to the side, weighing his reply. "Then I sent him back. We have a tumultuous history, he and I."

"Liar," I spit out. "Deven has never wronged you."

Strangely, snowflakes fall outside. The flurries dance into my chamber on the chilly wind. I would dwell on the astonishing sight if not for Deven still slung over the back of that beast.

"You both wronged me." Marduk transforms into a tall young woman with a grave expression and delicate features. I have never seen her before. "I wore this appearance when I visited your beloved Deven the night before your wedding. He was quick to follow when I told him I had a surprise at your marriage property."

Marduk's claims are illogical, as Deven and I are not intended to wed. The demon's story, however, is all too familiar for another couple. The woman he is imitating must be Inanna. Cala and I arrive at the same conclusion at the same time.

Marduk is the chameleon demon from the tale.

"The hillside you built your hut upon was my hunting ground. You greedy mortals stole it."

I doubt we knew our haven in the mountains was favored by a demon. "You've gotten your revenge twice. Leave Deven be."

"You may have him after you let us go," Edimmu says, her claws around Giza's throat. "Irkalla is waiting."

Enlil shoots a lightning bolt in front of them, blackening the floor. "The children stay."

"We would sooner kill them," Marduk says, resuming his hideous form.

This has escalated past negotiations. I fear the children and Deven will be caught in the cross fire. We need an army to stop three demons and close the gate . . .

Oh, Cala says. *Good idea, Kali.*

I hope so.

"Trainees," I say. Their expectant gazes fasten onto me. "Always be ready."

I let my call to arms drill in, then channel Cala's expertise and whip the urumi at the ugallu. The lion-eagle rears back. Asag hangs on as Deven slides to the floor between the beast's legs.

Giza burns Edimmu and gets away. As the demon shrieks, the six Galers summon winds that slide her into the wall, pinning her and her sadistic tongue. The five Aquifiers call upon the melted snowflakes and pelt her in the snout with water. Though the demon is restrained, the Galers and Aquifiers do not let up, and the four Tremblers buckle the floor in a line around the trainees, creating a barrier.

Enlil grabs the ugallu's mane and shoves the beast and its demon rider backward into the gate. The ugallu digs in its claws and presses back. As they push against each other, I drag Deven to the opposite wall. Thank the gods, the fall did not seem to harm him.

Marduk looms over us in his squat, ugly physique. Cala reacts fast, and together we strike. The demon leaps away to the balcony, stepping in fresh snow.

My turn, I tell Cala, dropping the urumi.

Using both arms, I fire a heatwave. The tremendous blast opens a huge hole in the wall and throws Marduk outside. Enlil and the ugallu are still in a shoving match, and the trainees are keeping Edimmu pinned. I leave Deven to ensure that Marduk is good and gone, passing through the blazing draperies into the smoke.

Charred stone smolders and steams in whiteout conditions. Marduk is not here. The blast must have hurled him over the edge.

As I revolve to return inside, Marduk swings down from the level above and slams into me, flinging me backward. I slide across the balcony and grasp the ledge.

As I dangle from my left arm, Marduk stomps on my wrist and two of my fingers slip. He lifts his foot to do it again. A heatwave hits him from behind. He staggers away, his back on fire.

I swing a leg to the balcony, and Giza helps me up. Inside, Basma stands vigil over Deven.

"I did well?" Giza asks.

"You both did."

We start for Basma and Deven. Enlil succeeds in shoving the ugallu and Asag through the gate, but a bearish rabisu leaps out. Enlil smacks it back into the Void with his spear. More rabisus jump into the chamber, snarling. The fire-god fights them off with his spear. Three get past him and prowl for the children.

I redirect from Deven to their aid. Marduk blocks me, the fire on him extinguished, and pushes me hard. I fly into the wall and drop, short of breath.

Basma throws fire at him. He dodges and swipes her and Giza aside. They fall in a pile. The rabisus are nearly to the children. Marduk grabs Deven's legs to drag him off. I attack from my sitting position on the floor.

"Enough!"

Grabbing my inner star, I raise my arms and shove my soul-fire at Marduk. Vivid white flames slam his torso. He howls and soars back against the wall beside the gate. Enlil retreats from the line of fire. The trainees and rabisus flinch from the luminosity. My flames persevere. Rising to my feet, I reach further inside myself.

I am more than I think I am.

I was born to shine.

I can carve my destiny from the sun.

Enlil's and my parents' counsel feeds the continuous blast, heat humming off my skin. Cala stands with me, helping me maintain my concentration the same way I held the urumi hilt for her.

We are Inanna, she says. *We are Cala and Kalinda. We are one and the same.*

Together, we draw from that single glorious star at our core and focus the massive, unbroken flux on Marduk. He changes forms so he looks like Giza. His attempt to weaken us merely adds to our ire. I step sideways, flush with the gate.

"Tell Irkalla this is my domain! You and your kind stay out!"

Siphoning Cala's fiery temperament into mine, we hurl a greater blast at Marduk. The mighty volley throws the chameleon demon to the gate, and he falls through.

My powers immediately cut off. I bend over, gasping and perspiring.

"Kali!" Enlil shouts.

My heatwave struck the gate and compromised its structure. The doorway to the under realm is caving in.

"Push them through!" Enlil instructs the trainees.

A coordinated gust from the Galers sweeps a rabisu out. The Tremblers lift the floor in a wave, carrying the last of them to the hole. The rabisus slip on a puddle of water that the Aquifiers rushed to their feet. A blast from Giza knocks them into the shadows. Edimmu tries to run. Enlil strikes the demon with his spear, and she flies into the shrinking hole.

The gate becomes smaller. Enlil lifts his spear and jams it into the shriveled gap, collapsing the portal more, and discharges a lightning bolt.

A blinding flash explodes from the spear, shattering the weapon to a shower of sparkling dust and propelling Enlil back. The last of the gate turns to ash and rains to the floor. The unmarked wall appears as if the portal was never there.

I stagger to sit beside Deven. Ashwin and Gemi run into the room. They stay near the door, as astonished by the destruction as they are at the presence of a god. Outside, the wind and snow have ceased. Cala has gone quiet, her presence shrunken.

Are you hurt, Cala?

I'm just resting, she whispers. *See to Deven.*

He has not woken, his inner light a faint flicker. I pulse my own soul-fire into Deven. After battle, I am often depleted. Cala's partnership gave me access to a deeper well than I usually possess. I send several more pulses into him. His condition does not improve, nor does he wake.

"Enlil?" I ask, my alarm spreading.

"I am sorry, Kalinda."

"Why?" I say, not understanding. "I trekked through the under realm for him. He's home and safe. He just needs a healer and some rest. He'll be back to himself soon."

"No healer can repair the damage the Void has done to his mind and soul."

I touch Deven's cool skin, still not comprehending. Someone must have the power to help him. Indah is a gifted healer. Enlil just does not know what she is capable of.

Gemi and Ashwin usher the children out. I call after them.

"Indah is in the dungeons. Tell her to come quickly!"

Enlil strolls over to us and lowers to one knee. "Kalinda, nothing can be done. I am not being cruel."

"But we haven't tried—"

"Deven is dying." My lungs contract sharply. Enlil grasps my shoulder. "You spared Deven Naik from an eternal death. He will be reborn again. In time, you will reunite in the Beyond."

"I wish to be with him in *this* life!" I point at Enlil. "Heal him. I know you can. Death is temporary. Delay it and let him stay."

"He is past revival. I can only restore him into another form."

"Then do it." My words transform into unbidden pleas. "Please don't let him die. I cannot . . . I cannot bear it."

"He will not be as he is now."

"So long as he is still Deven, I don't care." The fire-god hesitates, his expression pensive. Deven's soul-fire continues to diminish, the glow weak as a cinder. "Enlil, if you love me, you will fix him however you can."

Enlil's gaze roams around my chamber, taking in the shattered mirror glass and broken furniture. "I will do this to make amends. I apologize that I was not forthright with you."

"I understand that you did what you felt you must for Cala," I say, my voice tiny. "Just please, hurry."

Enlil lifts Deven and carries him to the bed. The fire-god lays him down and tears open his ragged tunic. Deven is so thin. *So thin.* Enlil ignites a living flame above his palm. All my hopes pour into that pure blaze. He tips his hand, and it falls onto Deven's chest. The flame soaks into his skin like a raindrop dissolving into soil and vanishes.

I hug myself, offering my own comfort. Cala watches avidly and waits with me. She feels stronger and closer, close enough to hold my hand.

Seconds stretch into eternity. Enlil's inactivity almost brings me to tears. I hardly allow myself to blink, worried I will miss a change.

A pure light fans out across Deven's chest and travels down his limbs. He gleams, resplendent as a new day, building to a sustained, concentrated radiance. In a flash, the incandescence flares and extinguishes.

Color returns to Deven's complexion, and his bruises and cuts heal without scarring. His gaunt frame fills out, returning to his healthy weight and structure. With his lips slightly parted, his teeth grow back as I watch. These miraculous changes occur in seconds, a revival unlike any I could have imagined. I sense his inner light, a lambent, golden intensity that I long to touch.

His chest expands, drawing in a long pull of air. I place my shaking palm over his heart. A reckless laugh pushes out of me. His soul-fire feels like him, solid and splendid.

"He will wake soon," Enlil says wearily. "As he was not formally reborn through a bloodline, his soul's innate predisposition will determine his powers."

My chin snaps up. "He has *powers*?"

"His next reincarnated state was a bhuta. As his current life was finished, I had no choice but to progress him to his next physical form. He may be disoriented for a few days. Let him rest. His powers will reveal themselves soon."

I gape down at Deven. He looks and feels the same, but he is not. "Will he . . . will he remember me?"

"I cannot speak to his state of mind; however, he is the same soul he was." Enlil withdraws from the bedside, his movements slow and heavy. "I must return to the Beyond and report my happenings to Anu. He will have questions."

"Are you in trouble?"

Enlil smirks. "No more than usual. Do not fret, Kalinda. You are regaining your independence. No longer must you rely on me as your guide."

"You're leaving right now?" I ask, Cala's sadness mingling with my own. "Cala hoped you would stay."

The fire-god wipes ash from my cheek. "We had beautiful lives together, Cala. More happy moments than there are shells on the seashore."

I love you, Cala whispers.

"She says she loves you."

"And I love her." Enlil grasps my chin and his voice softens. "You will always be my sunrise."

"I'll miss you," I reply, in sync with Cala.

"You will live on in my heart. We had our time, and it was unforgettable." He kisses my mouth, his lips soft as petals. I allow his nearness one last time for Cala. "I will cherish you forevermore, my dearest. My champion, my queen."

He separates from me and steps over a piece of broken mirror glass. I consider my reflection. Somewhere in my mind, Cala is staring out at me.

Thank you for allowing me more time with him, Kali.

I couldn't have done this without you. Where will you go?

Back into your memories. Be content.

She sounds wistful. We cannot touch, so I send thoughts of hugging her. She passes them back.

Farewell, Kali.

Good-bye, Cala.

She relinquishes the control she has on my faculties, untying her memories, thoughts, and will from my own. The second she is detached, she sinks inside me. The domain in my mind expands wider as she drops deeper, diluting into my soul-fire until we burn as one.

A knot in my neck unravels. My reflection appears the same as when Cala was with me, yet I will never look at myself again without thinking of her.

I revolve toward Enlil. "She's gone."

"You were very kind to her. Not everyone would have managed these circumstances with your compassion." Enlil extends his hand, and a new lightning spear materializes. "I should be going. I cannot change your mind?"

He refers to his invitation to dwell with him in Ekur. "My decision isn't in my mind, it's in my heart. And hearts are difficult to change."

"That they are." Enlil traces my knuckles. "You gave me a gift I will never forget. More time with Cala was a mercy. You owe me nothing, Kalinda. Consider your debt paid."

A horse whinnies. Seen through the hole in the wall leading to the balcony, Enlil's chariot suspends in the sky, waiting for its rider. I go to the horse team and pet Chaser's nose. He nickers and nudges his head against my shoulder.

Enlil wanders over to us. People in the city gather to gawk at the deity. Perhaps now they will give up their foolish ideas about bhutas.

"How did you bring Chaser back?" I ask. "Never mind. You're a god."

One side of Enlil's mouth ticks upward and then swiftly drops. Neither of us can bring ourself to part ways.

I take Cala's medallion from my pocket and slip it over his head. "To remember our journey by."

He grasps the medallion and presses it to his chest. "I will think of you fondly, my dearest Kalinda." His great arms enfold me, and he kisses the spot he cleaned on my cheek. He embraces me until my skin glimmers to mirror his. When he lets go, the luster fades.

"Will you be all right?" I ask.

"Of course. I am Enlil, Keeper of the Living Flame."

I let loose a dry chuckle and pat Chaser farewell.

Enlil steps onto his chariot. He snaps the reins, and his horses charge upward over the city. Citizens all over Vanhi stop to witness the ascension of the fire-god's chariot shrinking into the desert night.

A groan sounds behind me. I dash back to my bed. Deven is just as I left him, only he has managed to wedge one of my many silk bed pillows under one of his knees. I pull it away and adjust the covers. His warm brown eyes home in on me and he frowns.

Enlil, let him remember me.

He contemplates my wrecked chamber, his bewilderment deepening. His attention returns to me. "Kali? I had the strangest dream about your parents."

A laugh-sob bursts from my lips. I lie down and lean my head against his shoulder, resting my hand over his healthy, beating heart. I have so much to tell him that I cannot decide where to begin.

He drifts off again, so I snuggle into him and let him rest. He said everything I need to know.

39

Kalinda

I clench the passenger's bar and smile despite the precarious side-to-side cadence of the howdah carriage. The box carriage with a red silk canopy is tied to the back of an elephant. Children run alongside us, keeping pace with the gentle beast's patient lumber.

General Yatin patrols ahead on horseback, clearing stragglers from the roadway. The onlookers cooperate, moving aside for the army general in his dress uniform. As I near, they cry, "Burner Rani," in praise.

Gods, what a difference time makes.

The imperial procession winds through the packed roads, my view swinging with my ride. A canopy shields me from the midday sun, and a dry breeze whisks away my perspiration. The rest of the procession leaves the palace after me and snakes through the packed roads.

On their own elephant behind mine, Ashwin and Gemi wave from their howdah, both dressed in finery. The people's cheers grow to a roar for their prince and his viraji. They have gone from despised intendeds to celebrated rulers in three moons.

Ashwin has doubled his efforts to rebuild Vanhi. The southeast district is nearly complete, which eased tensions somewhat. Mostly we have Enlil to thank. The chapel altar is littered with burned sacrifices day and night for the fire-god. He must feel so smug. One appearance to our citizens, and suddenly the Brotherhood temple is full of worshippers.

The fire-god also contributed to the empire-wide reacceptance of me as a champion rani. Our public embrace before he flew off on his chariot revived the rumor that I am Enlil's hundredth rani reincarnated. I have advised my friends and family not to dissuade the gossip. Wherever Cala is, she, too, is smiling.

We round a corner. The howdah tips, then rights itself. I leave my grip on the bar and wave at a child below. I rarely wear my prosthesis anymore, but Indah added carvings and jewels to this one. Today is my first time showing it off.

We pass Little Lotus Inn. Natesa bends out the top-floor window, brandishing a headscarf and blowing kisses to Yatin. Two moons ago, they wed and moved here. Natesa complains regularly about how busy they are. She is very happy.

Soldiers open the gates to the Sisterhood temple. Yatin stops outside them, monitoring the crowd for suspicious rabble. The last of Lokesh's mercenaries have gone underground. As the public becomes more accepting of bhutas, the likelihood of an insurgence of dissenters lessens.

My elephant enters the courtyard and halts. I climb down onto a temporary stairway, and a handler leads the elephant off. The sisters and wards are lined up outside the temple, hair brushed to a shine and skin scrubbed clean. Priestess Mita stands by the steps, Healer Baka beside her. A couple of my art students wave. I return their quiet hello, earning a glower from the priestess.

Gemi and Ashwin enter the courtyard, the people's adulations ushering in after them. A servant assists them from their howdah. Halfway down the staircase, Gemi kisses Ashwin full on the mouth. The crowd hollers with enthusiasm.

Ashwin tugs at his high collar, embarrassed. The princess leads him to me.

"Viraji," I say, bowing. "You've stolen the empire's heart."

"Hopefully we can maintain this approval after our wedding," Gemi says, twisting her shell earring nervously. She draped her sari so her scarred arm is visible. No one would guess she was not a sister warrior.

The whole city is abuzz about their wedding. When the datu arrived for the original date, he was perturbed the ceremony was postponed. His daughter explained that she and Ashwin wanted more time together. Thus, she remained while her father returned to the Southern Isles. The datu will come back for the real wedding, the evening of the next new moon.

More attendees arrive, the rest by horse, camel, or foot. The ranis and children come in as a big group. Shyla and Rehan are mixed in with the rest of Ashwin's siblings. The ranis have been nattering non-stop about the wedding gifts they are making Gemi. As the prince and princess welcome each of them by name, I nearly miss Indah and Pons's entrance.

Jala is tied to Indah's front with a cloth binding. I shake her little fist and smooth down her hair. She grins, her top two teeth sticking down like a bunny's.

Oh, do I love that sweet face.

Tinley leads in the bhuta trainees. No one in the crowd at the gate spits or boos. They cheer just as loudly for them as they did for me.

And well they should. Those who saw Enlil also witnessed the bhuta children battling demons, which raised questions about why they would do so if they were, in fact, demons themselves. Those who lived in the empire before Tarek rewrote our history flocked to the Brotherhood temple to learn about bhutas as half-gods. Since this collective epiphany, the number of palace guards is up, and the general phobia of bhutas is diminishing.

The people's fickleness sets my veins on fire. Ashwin often reminds me this is the change we wanted. Acceptance of bhutas is the true return to tradition.

Giza and Basma run ahead of Tinley. The Galer is visiting from Paljor, her current primary residence. Maida asked Tinley to come home and help her lead. Ashwin calls the sisters the frozen fist of the north. Instead of arguing with each other, they advocate for their tribe. The prince always emerges from their trade meetings wholly drained.

My Burner students run to stand by me. They straighten as the last of the procession comes in, the all-female guard. Eshana rides a camel at the front of her unit. Ashwin assigned her as captain of two dozen women who alternate shifts with the other palace guards. Eshana's service helps to distract her from grieving for Parisa. I was saddened when Ashwin told me of her demise. Little will heal the knowledge of her death other than time.

At last, Deven and Brac approach on horseback, the conclusion of the procession. Deven's broad chest fills out the navy-and-silver tunic. He rides at ease, his sword slung at his side. I have yet to adjust to him not wearing a uniform. Deven did not feel right about displacing Yatin as general, so he accepted an advisor position, acting as a liaison between the army and the prince.

Deven dismounts and kisses me in welcome. His trim beard brushes my skin, his sandalwood scent mild. The Burner girls giggle and make room for him at my side.

Separate from the procession, Mathura and Chitt arrive. They have stopped traveling to spend time in Vanhi with us. Deven thinks they will reside here now. Natesa and Yatin come in last and find standing room at the back of the audience. People on the streets fill the temple gate to listen. I pause to absorb the view of my friends and family.

We are all here.

Ashwin strides up the temple steps. The priestess passes him a cone amplifier.

"Citizens of Vanhi," he begins, "we're honored to gather today at the completion of the first Sisterhood temple in the City of Gems. Before the priestess dedicates this sacred home, I would like to say a brief word about forgiveness. As the brethren of the Parijana faith taught me, our godly purpose is to learn and grow into the greatest versions of ourselves. Along our way, we inadvertently and, at times, intentionally hurt or offend those in our path." Ashwin speaks out to those in the roads and on the rooftops. His voice embeds within me. I am touched by the care and delivery of his words. "All of us have someone to forgive. Perhaps it is someone we love or someone we hoped would do better. I promise you, as we seek the finest versions of ourselves, the gods will give us strength and hope to believe in goodness. I will lead you in this journey as I aspire to become the rajah the empire rightfully deserves. Gods be with us."

Ashwin passes the cone amplifier to the priestess. We applaud, Gemi beaming at him, and he swiftly rejoins her side. Priestess Mita and the head priest of the Brotherhood temple proceed with the ceremony.

I eye the temple wards dressed in their blue robes. Before when I used to see them, I could only think of the purpose behind all my teachings—preparation for the Claiming.

None of these girls will experience that humiliation.

The temple priestesses across Tarachand unanimously agreed to do away with the ritual. Even Priestess Mita acquiesced after she heard about Ashwin's educational advancements. Gemi has been instrumental in the formation of these policies, using what she learned in the Southern Isles as a foundation. A new curriculum is in development for the wards. When they come of age, they may work in education, science, history, arithmetic, and the arts. Looking at them, tears brim in my eyes. They may choose who they become as they rise in strength together. The sisters will continue to teach them the godly virtues and train them in the sparring ring. Some wards may elect to join the all-female guard or the Sisterhood. They have so many paths to choose from, I can scarcely imagine how they will decide.

I am sorry I will not be here to view all their achievements, to see what the city becomes with their talents nourishing its future. Vanhi may finally suit its name as the City of Gems and deserve the reputation as the stronghold of the Tarachand Empire.

Deven's fingers seek out mine. "Kali, it's done."

I join the closing applause. Healer Baka offers the benediction, and then the temple is open for touring. Children dart about the courtyard, playing. Deven and I seek out the refreshments for a chunk of ice to cool ourselves. Tinley rushes over.

"We're playing toss the coin." She grabs Deven by the arm. "You're on my team."

She drags him off. He looks back, shrugging. I saunter over to the sparring circle and stand around the perimeter with Ashwin. Within the ring, Deven and Tinley contend against Gemi and Brac in a children's game.

"Your speech was moving, Your Majesty," I say. Ashwin ducks his head modestly. "Have you settled on your honeymoon?"

He cheers for Gemi, then answers, "Out of the nine places we picked, we whittled it down to . . . nine." He tousles his hair, bemused. "Gemi wants to visit them all. I haven't the heart to tell her no. Can you and Deven stay until we return? I would feel more comfortable knowing Brac and Natesa are not left unattended. Lords know what I would return to."

"We can stay," I agree at once. Deven and I have organized a trip to Paljor before we survey the lower Alpanas for a piece of land to settle on. My mahati hatchling, which I named Chaser, is old enough to live with us. Tinley said she will grow happier and healthier in my company. I am certain I can write to Maida and ask her to bring Chaser along during her next visit.

"I'll speak with Deven as well," Ashwin says. "I know he's looking forward to leaving the city."

I wear a tight smile, but his attention has already returned to the game.

Gemi and Brac have collectively flipped the coin the highest. Tinley finishes her turn, accomplishing an impressive height. Deven must achieve a coin toss half as tall as hers for his team to win.

He steps into the middle of the ring and kneels beside the coin. Hands on each side, he slaps the ground. A pillar shoots up, lifting the coin above his head.

The crowd cheers. Deven pats Brac on the back, beaming. He out-tossed his brother.

Gemi removes the coin from the pillar and shows the bhuta trainees. "See what Deven did? This is why you should practice."

The first day back on his feet, Deven joined Gemi and the Trembler trainees for lessons. We had discovered almost immediately which bhuta powers he had acquired. While bedridden, he had dropped his spoon over the side of the cot. Before I could collect it, the floor had shot up and delivered it for him.

Brac calls for a rematch. He will play until he wins.

This could be a while.

"I'm going inside," I tell Ashwin.

He sneaks in a quick kiss on my cheek, then sends me off.

I navigate the crowd inside the quieter, cooler temple. I bypass the chapel and go to the back stairway. The area is closed and dim. I pluck flames from the line of wall lamps. They spin together and form a lynx kitten.

Siva gazes up at me from the floor. I set her on my shoulder, and we sneak down the stairway. The lower corridors of the temple are half-done. I enter the biggest classroom, the art room. Pails of tiles and mortar are set around for a project I designed. I want a tile mural of the

Alpana Mountains. The execution is taking longer than anticipated, but the result so far is spectacular. I shut the door to the classroom.

Siva jumps off my shoulder and sits in front of it. She sniffs around and finds a broken piece of tile to chew on.

"You shouldn't be down here."

I reel on Deven. "Are you going to tell the priestess?"

He strides up, his hands tucked in his trouser pockets. "Consider this your second offense of sneaking around the lower level of a temple."

"Well, then." I pretend to slip past him, and he snags me. "I like your new uniform. It makes you look taller."

"Does it?" After he realizes I am teasing, he asks, "Why are you down here?"

"I was hoping the prince's advisor would follow me so I could be alone with him."

"Does he know about this scheme?"

"He's about to." I arch my chin, our lips close. My lighthearted mood evaporates. I cannot kiss him without first expressing my thoughts. "I like it here, Deven. I enjoy teaching the wards and trainees. My students are so talented at their drawings, and Basma is starting to get fevers. Brac wants to plan for her Razing before it affects her health. And Jala is still little. I want to be here when she says her first word. I miss the mountains. I do. But I want to stay in Vanhi."

Deven strokes my hair. "Why didn't you tell me?"

"I didn't want to disappoint you."

"When I was in the Void, do you know what kept me from giving up? Thinking of you." Deven hugs me close, clutching the small of my back. "I don't care where we are, Kali. Only that we're together."

His immediate agreement leaves me hesitant to accept. This is his dream too. I do not want to take it from him. "You won't be upset if we don't move to the mountains?"

"The lower Alpanas would be peaceful, maybe too peaceful. I'd miss my mother and Chitt, Natesa and Yatin. I'd even miss Brac . . . some days. If we stay, I could continue to train with Gemi. I doubt Ashwin would leave me as an advisor. I think he may promote me to serve as his Trembler Virtue Guard." A bit of excitement resides in Deven's tone. "In this role, I could really do some good. I could work with the Brotherhood and Sisterhood to teach the truth about bhutas." Deven leans his head against mine. "We can visit the mountains on occasion for quiet, but this is home."

He sounds a tad disappointed that our long-held dream is going away.

"Why don't we have both? Within the year, Chaser will be large enough to fly. It's only a day's flight from here to the lower Alpanas. When Chaser is older, we can travel back and forth."

"Spend fall in the mountains and the other seasons here."

"Or summer north," I say. "It would be nice to escape the heat."

Deven squeezes me against him. "Would you leave Jala?"

"Once we build a hut, we can have visitors. Pons and Indah would like the lower mountains. The sky is so clear."

Deven chuckles. "You cannot invite them before Natesa and Yatin. Natesa would banish you from the inn for life."

"We can invite all our friends and family." I rest my head against his shoulder, the dream in my mind expanding to include more than I thought possible. Siva winds through my legs, rubbing against me, her fire crackling contentedly. "Did we just dream up a new heart's wish?"

"I don't think so." Deven's voice resonates through me, rich and full. "I think we finally found the real one."

CHARACTER GLOSSARY

Kalinda: orphan turned first queen, Burner
Deven: general of the imperial army
Prince Ashwin: heir to the Tarachand Empire
Natesa: former imperial courtesan
Yatin: captain of the guard
Indah: Aquifier Virtue Guard
Pons: Galer Virtue Guard
Jala: Indah and Pons's daughter
Priestess Mita: leader of the Samiya Temple
Jaya: Kalinda's deceased best friend
Healer Baka: palace healer
Brac: bhuta ambassador, Burner
Mathura: Deven and Brac's mother, former imperial courtesan
Rajah Tarek: deceased ruler to the Tarachand Empire
Udug: demon unleashed from the Void, the Voider
Kur: demon, First-Ever Dragon
Irkalla: queen of the dead
Edimmu, Lilu, and Asag: demon commanders and siblings
Commander Lokesh: defected imperial soldier
Marduk: demon
Basma and Giza: sister trainees, Burners
Shyla, Parisa, and Eshana: former ranis

Asha: palace servant
Princess Gemi: heir to the Southern Isles, Trembler
Datu Bulan: ruler of the Southern Isles
Tinley: daughter of Chief Naresh, Galer
Chief Naresh: ruler of Paljor, Galer
Chieftess Sosi: wife to Chief Naresh, northern Aquifier
Maida: Tinley's younger sister, northern Aquifier
Hastin: deceased bhuta warlord
Yasmin: Kalinda's deceased mother, former kindred
Kishan: Kalinda's deceased father, Burner

ACKNOWLEDGMENTS

What an honor it is to write a series. With each new book, my gratitude for my team has grown. A hand over my heart and bowed head to:

Marlene Stringer, a passionate fighter for my stories. I will forever appreciate your championing Kalinda and me.

Jason Kirk, if only I had the patience to listen as you do. I needed your compassion and empathy many times during this series. You really do bring out the best in your authors. Without your support and enthusiasm, this fourth book might not have been. Cheers to more stories in our future.

Clarence Haynes, your intuitive emails and love of comics have made you my friend. But your generosity of time, pacifying words, and piercing insights have put me forever in your debt. My warmest thanks.

Lauren Ezzo, thank you for channeling your inner warrior princess and narrating Kalinda. And the rest of the incredible crew at Skyscape, especially Kristin King and Brittany Russell, thank you. Also, not enough credit is given to those toiling behind the scenes. Michelle Hope Anderson and Katherine Richards, you made sense of my nonsense and polished my manuscripts to a shine. I'm forever in your debt. Sister warriors rule!

My badass all-female guard, including Jessica Farr, Kate Coursey, Kathryn Purdie, Kate Watson, Natalie Barnum, Shaila Patel, Breeana

Shields, Katie Nelson, Caitlin Sangster, Charlie N. Holmberg, and Tricia Levenseller, you bring my "fabulous" level up a notch.

Thank you to my army of trusted early readers: Leah Garroitt, Jessica Clark, Jessica Guernsey, Brekke Felt, Lauri Schoenfeld, Tammy Thierualt, and Teralyn Mitchell, and also to my early reviewers: Beth Edwards, Benjamin Alderson, Cassie James, Wendy Jessen, and Teralyn Mitchell. I'd also like to thank my local book club, the YA and Wine Gals: Krysti, Sarah, Amanda, Rach, Katherine, Shelley, Jenessa, and Mckelle George. And, of course, the Storymakers Tribe.

My favorite book club in Texas, Daughters of the Black Madonna, Sharon, Versil, Novlette, LaVorne, MiMi, Stacy, Meisha, Chanelle, Lisa, and Jenia, thanks for bringing me into your fabulous sisterhood.

For coordinating my incredible bookstagram tours, thanks to the incomparably talented Bridget @darkfaerietales_ and Kristen @ myfriendsarefiction.

I would be remiss not to attribute much of my productivity to Diet Coke, as well as to reruns of *The Good Wife* and *Justified*, which kept me company while everyone was asleep.

Mom and Dad, thanks for stepping in when I needed you . . . which was more often than any of us thought. My high school sweetheart, John, we've come a long way since band class. Your smile still makes my day. Joseph, Julian, Danielle, and Ryan, the brightest, funniest, most amazing children, I'm glad you think having an author as a mom is cool.

My fiercely loyal readers, I appreciate every kind email, comment, and shout-out. Thanks for coming along this journey with me. May you find your own place of peace.

Finally, my father in heaven. None of this would have been possible without you.

ABOUT THE AUTHOR

Photo © 2015 Erin Summerill

Emily R. King is a writer of fantasy and the author of The Hundredth Queen Series. Born in Canada and raised in the United States, she is a shark advocate, a consumer of gummy bears, and an islander at heart, but her greatest interests are her four children. Emily is a member of the Society of Children's Book Writers and Illustrators and an active participant in her local writers' community. She lives in Northern Utah with her family and their cantankerous cat. Visit her at www.emilyrking.com.